The Secret of the Gullah Treasure

The

SECRET

of the

GULLAH

TREASURE

A Novel by

CARL E. LINKE

ℱ

Philip-Forrest Publishing

Ƿ Philip-Forrest Publishing

Published in the United States by Philip-Forrest Publishing
Visit at: www.carllinke.com

Book Design by Carl E. Linke
Author photograph by Tina Lee

ISBN-13: 978-0-9827421-0-5
Library of Congress Control Number: 2017948152

PRINTED IN THE UNITED STATES OF AMERICA
First Edition: (August 2017)
1 2 3 4 20 19 18 17

This book is dedicated to the Nine.

PREFACE

Fiction remains the enduring autonomous vehicle of our time, a magic carpet riding waves of imagination between daydreams and nightmares. This book is, was and always will be a work of fiction. The characters and events in this story never existed until they appeared on these pages. I have taken liberty to use Beaufort, my hometown, as a backdrop for scenic and historic purposes only. I have dropped a few names, historic figures who have no active role in the story. If you take the time to scan the QR codes throughout the book you will find vintage photos and background information for scenes or events in the story. And, if you must ask, yes, there truly was (or is) a Gullah treasure; it remains for you to find.

The characters I heard while writing were not simply in my head. Several were voices—whispers as well as shouts—to whom I owe so much. Barney Forsythe, Phil Bardsley, and Alex Dunlap, who, as first readers, wrestled with my petulance and misguided efforts, draft after draft; John Warley who deserves endless thanks for his review and comments on the story; Grace Cordial who assisted in researching the time period around our town; Rowland Washington who shared his insight as the first to integrate our schools; Ailyn Griffin who shared a letter from Poe. To my editors Nicole Ayers and Robin Samuels for their guidance and deep cleansing; and to select others who wished to remain anonymous.

To family and friends who trumpeted my travails through the darkest of times. To my understanding wife Penny who brings beauty into my life every single day; my daughter Carrie and husband Ryan Jackson, my son

Jay and his wife Casey Linke, my sister-in-law Wendy Wilson; also Janelle Proctor, Jane Forsythe, Kathryn Cullinan, Eleanor Thacker, Forrest Sharrock, Ken Schneider, Katie Dooling Votaw, Susan and Steve Greene, and my divine inspiration, TZiPi Radonsky.

To the dozens of folks in Beaufort—you know who you are—who willingly shared your memories and comments as background; I apologize for twisting your words and thoughts to create an existence far from what you might have shared.

PROLOGUE

Case 3:10-RSG-91029
Filed 02/24/93
Document 1   **Page 7 of 32**

Special Agent = SA

Interview: J.R. Eddings reference background
                   investigation pertaining to ██████████

TRANSCRIPT (cont'd):

JRE: Just so you know, first off, it's not a lie if you're the only one that knows the truth. That's how I see things.

67. SA: Details? Can you provide details?
JRE: Just not fair. (Pause) Mary Alice, Miss Forten that is, she doesn't deserve this. I mean, it was her first year in the Lowcountry. And Robin Gundy. Not right to talk about that now either. A lot has happened since then. All that was so many years ago; most of those people in Beaufort have changed. People left and others, those Yankees, moved in. They were "snowbirds" then; now we call them residents. Full-time, tax-payin', law-makin', aggravatin' residents…citizens, mind you. Most of them aren't in the city, neither. Nope. They are on the islands. They bought our land, Gullah land, and built on the Sea Islands. If you'da ask Grandpa Gabe, he would have told you that all started back in the sixties, down on Hilton Head. Kinda funny it was just about the same time flapper-jawed Swanson became famous in town.

1

68. SA: Surely the details go much deeper. Either way, there's no need to lie.

[Pause]

JRE: Then you can bet a secret isn't a secret if only one person knows.

[Chuckle]

Otherwise, it's just one of those unknown facts, sorta like how tides were before Galileo—or was it Newton?—figured them all out. They were always there, not really a secret, just an unknown. My mamma would say, "Let well alone." And she was right. Some things just need to remain secrets, at least private knowledge. Better than a lie.

69. SA: Sometimes it's good to let loose some of those pearls and let others judge them for themselves.

[Pause]

JRE: Okay, let's assume I have some of those secrets. And maybe some of them still haunt me, keep me awake at night. Some might even hurt me or possibly surprise me or, even worse, humiliate me, make me angry. (Pause) Of course, some of them might be funny things that come back, funny now because they weren't so funny then. Painful things. Some I haven't ever shared with anybody. (Pause) Some as vivid as if they were yesterday…but that yesterday was October, 1964. I'll tell you how it was.

CHAPTER 1

Hey, boys and girls. What time is it?" The outburst came from a gangly teen, an undeclared poster child for the "before" photo on a Clearasil ad. His scraggy blond hair looked like a haystack and his bulk more like uncooked angel hair pasta than fettuccine. "Why, it's Ricky Retardo time!" he continued, interrupting the guest speaker in the front of the eighth-grade classroom. A student one row over and three desks up had been painstakingly stacking his books on the top of his desk when a slight fumble caused an avalanche of texts and the spontaneous ridicule of Skeet Gundy. "Wanna play pick-up-texts, Ricky, baby?"

"Excuse me, Mr. Swanson. I am so sorry," the teacher said, addressing one of two guest speakers she had invited to her classroom that day. She turned toward the class with her stern face—a look that was a facial mix of sucking a sour pickle and licking a lollipop. "Robin Gundy, that will be quite enough. We don't say things like that in this classroom and we most definitely do not interrupt. You stand up right this minute and apologize."

The accused boy slouched lower, his eyes at periscope depth above the flat of his desk.

"Young man, I am not going to repeat myself. Now stand up and apologize." Her voice was rose petal soft and slathered in an accent different from the others in

3

the room. Unfortunately for her, it did not project her disgust.

The child's response was nothing short of that expected from a student now set to repeat the eighth grade for a third time. Skeet slid deeper in his seat, his head resting on the back of the chair and his legs outstretched in the aisle as he belted out his sing-song apology, "I'm so sorry, little Ricky. I'm so sorry if I caused you any pain. I hope I didn't hurt your poor wittle feel-wings."

The ink on her college diploma barely had time to dry before Mary Alice Forten welcomed her first class at Beaufort Junior High School less than a month earlier. She was a big-city girl who grew up outside of Washington, DC in Falls Church, where she earned an in-state scholarship to the University of Virginia and graduated in three years. Nothing in her student teaching assignments had prepared her for this.

As the frazzled rookie teacher made her way between the desks down the aisle toward Skeet Gundy, students turned in their seats and their snickers faded like crickets at dawn. Behind her back a boy smirked as he pointed his index finger toward Skeet and stroked it with the same finger on his other hand, to acknowledge the naughty behavior.

"Young man, our guests have been kind enough to donate their time to talk to us. I expect that you would be a gentleman kind enough to listen and not interrupt. And it is most rude to make fun of your classmate."

She turned to look back toward the front where Ricky Clemonds sobbed; his hands covered his head on his desk. "Ricky, it's okay. It was an accident. Just pick up your books, please, and leave them on your desk." She worried her words were too harsh for her student, one of the challenges Principal Sydney Langhorn mentioned when he hired her. He shared that the parents of the boy seemed overly concerned about their son starting in a new school, in a higher grade, and commented that their son suffered from "a syndrome."

"Stand up, Robin." She paused. "Stand up and politely apologize to both Mr. Swanson and Ricky." She folded her arms and glowered at the boy. "Now!"

Robin "Skeet" Gundy tossed his head to whip hair out of his eyes. He grabbed a pencil and tapped it on the desk a few times before he stood up in front of the teacher. At fifteen, Skeet's height and wiry physique were attributes that had developed much more quickly than his brain. He looked down on the petite Miss Forten, then jammed his hands into his pockets, turned toward the sea-going treasure hunter—sort of a Moby Dick-type himself—and said, "Uh, Mr. Swanson, I am sorry I interrupted you."

Swanson squinted and offered a slight, almost unnoticeable nod. His eyebrows pulled together.

"And, Ricky, I am so sorry that book just jumped off your desk," Skeet said with an emerging smirk. "If you need help, you can always count on me." From the back of the room someone coughed out a masked message that sounded like "bullsha," which prompted another round of chuckles. With his hands raised Skeet plopped back into his chair.

Mary Alice took a deep breath, swallowed hard, and looked back toward her guest.

"Mr. Swanson, again I apologize, sir. Do you have anything more to add?" the teacher asked as she moved to the side of the classroom.

"Nah, let me wrap it all up this way. I want all you little buccaneers to remember, there's buried treasure around here in Beaufort. I have old treasure maps, letters, and charts. The whole nine yards. Better come out and find that treasure before I do!"

"Does anyone have a question for Mr. Swanson?" she asked as she looked out over the class. No hands raised, but the buzz among the students gave her the indication they were interested. Or was it just that it was almost time for the final bell?

"Thank you, Mr. Swanson. What an exciting story. Your profession is certainly full of surprises. I trust your experiences will trigger a great deal of interest and surprising research by our students. Am I right, class?"

No response.

As Geordie Swanson returned to his folding chair, the second guest speaker strolled front and center with a notepad and a thick book in hand.

"Class, I would like to introduce our next speaker, Mr. Gene Skyles. Mr. Skyles and I attended college together," she said with a smile in his direction. "He's here today to talk a little bit about mysterious things. The kinds of things you might watch on *Perry Mason*, not *Twilight Zone*. Real things. Real mysteries. Actually, he's researching the 'Father of Modern Mystery.' Who can tell me who that is?"

Silence. She looked around the room but prompted no response.

"Last week we talked about this person in class? He wrote poems. Who remembers the author of the poem we discussed that starts with, 'Once upon a midnight dreary'? I read it last week during English period."

Again silence. The teacher rolled her eyes.

"The same author also wrote 'The Gold Bug.' " Immediately several shouted out answers.

"Raise your hands, please." She saw a half dozen hands, some taller than the others, all of them girls. "Linda."

A ponytailed girl sprang up and with no hesitation at all said, "Miss Forten, the author was Ethan Allan Poe," then quickly took her seat.

Miss Forten smiled and offered a silent applause. "Close. I believe it is Edgar Allan Poe, not Ethan. But very good. Thank you, Linda. So Mr. Skyles is going to tell us more about Edgar Allan Poe and his connection to South Carolina. I'll let him explain." She swung both arms like she was tossing a hot potato to a spot center stage in front of the class.

Skyles noted the collective groan from the class and remembered those days, the teenage years. He was not all that far removed. Working on his doctorate degree on a 2-S student deferment from the draft, Gene Skyles accepted the fact that boys the age of his audience had far less interest in poems than they did in centerfolds from *Playboy* magazine. And the girls? They all seemed to be staring at him, rather entranced.

"Thank you, Miss Forten. I promise to make this as painless as possible," he said, drawing out each word just a little bit longer than normal. He smiled. "In fact, I'll mention a number of things I'll bet you never knew about Beaufort." He walked down one aisle and doubled back on the next aisle over. "I guess you've been discussing Poe. Have you read the poem 'Annabel Lee'?"

No hands went up.

"How many have ever heard of that poem?"

A group of hands—again all girls—shot up.

"Well, did you know that the girl in that poem, the girl Poe wrote about, was from Beaufort? And…she was probably only four years older than some of you?"

Nothing but silence. Boys with plastic soda straws popped up and down like prairie dogs to take spitball-potshots at unsuspecting victims.

"And when she died during the plague of dengue fever that swept through the Lowcountry, the girl's father covered up her death and her burial to hide it from Poe. Anybody ever heard that?"

The silence in the classroom continued. Skyles looked at the teacher standing in the back of the room. She shrugged her shoulders. The look on her face said, *I told you so*. Skyles quickly took a different approach.

"All right, well then, how many of you have heard of 'The Gold Bug'? It's another of Poe's great works, probably his best-known story." Still nothing. "So I guess that means none of you had heard it was written about Charleston or that Poe talked about buried treasure? See, I believe he was writing about Beaufort." Skyles looked over his shoulder toward the first speaker, whose eyes popped open wide as he nodded. The class began to stir in their desks at the mention of "treasure" and "Beaufort" in the same sentence, especially after hearing Geordie Swanson minutes earlier. Slouched backs straightened. The boys deescalated their straw wars but the girls continued to primp and swoon.

"In my research, Edgar Allan Poe led me to Beaufort. And part of that research is exciting because I think the treasure Poe spoke about in 'The Gold Bug' is actually here, somewhere in or around Beaufort."

Ears continued to open.

"In 'The Gold Bug' there is a character, an old colored man named Jupiter, and Jupiter turns out to be sorta the hero in the story. Jupiter was a freeman, not a slave, who worked for a fella named Legrand. And it was the colored man, Jupiter, who puts many of the pieces of the puzzle together to find the treasure."

"He could read?" a shout came from the sun-drenched side of the room, the aisle closest to the windows.

"Well, not exactly, at least we don't think so. Actually, it turns out some of his mistakes were keys to the treasure," Skyles said as he walked down the row to the desk of Jackie Robinson Eddings, the first and only Negro student to attend Beaufort Junior High School.

"See, without Jupiter helping Legrand—climbing a tall tree, placing a human skull in a certain spot, dropping a line—Legrand would never have found the treasure." He tapped his fingertips on Jackie's desk and walked on down the aisle. "The real excitement was in a coded message."

Cuddled in a cocoon of teenage interest, Skyles talked while he strolled back toward the front of the classroom. He turned his head toward Jackie and continued in a normal voice, "Poe liked codes. The code in this poem, Poe's first, was like other codes he used in letters to friends and other people all the time. Here's what I think from what I have discovered. In this code—in 'The Gold Bug'—Poe mentioned the 'bishop's hostel.' Well, it just so happens that here in Beaufort in those years, around 1827, the pastor of the Saint Helena Episcopal Church was a man named Joseph Rogers Walker. He had been pastor for about fifty years and the people called him 'bishop.' I believe, in the poem when Poe mentions 'bishop's hostel,' he was talking about Joseph Walker." His audience didn't really understand the logic or the history, but they accepted what they heard, no questions asked. "And the poem also talks about an azimuth, a direction, from where the 'bishop' sits to the treasure. I took a compass and I started at the Saint Helena Church.

The highest ledge is wide as a seat just below the roofline. Sitting there I used that azimuth, that direction in 'The Gold Bug,' and it pointed to the house people in Beaufort call the Castle."

"That's so stupid," Skeet shouted. "That house probably ain't that old."

Skyles raised his hands. Once he squelched the buzz in the room, he headed toward the doubting Skeet. "Nobody said it was. Pirates don't live in houses, do they? They use maps and landmarks like hills or bends in rivers. Things like that."

"So why bury anything there?" Skeet questioned.

"Guess you should do some research, Mr. Gundy," Skyles said with a smile and looked toward Mary Alice. "Research is the key. Read the poem if you're that interested. Or find a map somewhere."

Skeet shook his head and looked away.

Mary Alice noticed the large brown plastic clock showed only six minutes left in class, then walked to join her guest. "Thank you, Mr. Skyles."

"Wow, pirate treasure in Beaufort." She passed by her desk, stuffed a clipboard under her arm, then turned toward her speakers one last time.

"I apologize. I wish we had time for questions. I still need to give the class their research assignments, so class, let's thank our guests." She began to applaud. "If you will excuse us." With clapping hands, clipboard under her arm, she led the guests toward the door.

The two men smiled and returned the applause as they walked. Geordie Swanson slapped the littler Gene Skyles on the back and made a comment that brought out a laugh between the two of them as they exited the room together.

"Okay, quickly. I want each of you to do some research, but I will assign the projects to groups so you can research together. I will read off the names of the group members and assign the project topics—the hurricane and floods of 1893, the fire that destroyed Bay Street in 1907, and the Great Skedaddle of 1861."

In groups of three, as the clock ticked closer toward dismissal, she read names and assigned topics amid groans, cheers, and an undercurrent of crowd noise that made it difficult for the last group to hear.

"The last project team will be Robin Gundy, Ricky Clemonds, and Jackie Eddings. And your project topic is the Gul—"

"You smokin' dope?" Skeet Gundy flipped his books off his desk and stood defiantly in the aisle.

"The Gullah treasure," she continued, looking up.

"I ain't doin' no project with that retard nor that cotton-pickin' coon."

"Robin! Hush! Stop that! Stop right there, young man."

"I don't have to do nothing with that black boy. My daddy told me and I ain't doin' nothin' with him."

For that moment, Jackie was thankful for skin dark enough to hide any signs of embarrassment, fear, or anger. He stared at his desk and felt the eyes of all thirty of his white classmates poking at his skin.

Miss Forten slapped her clipboard onto her desk and stomped a beeline toward Skeet for the second time in the hour. As she neared him, the bell rang and students scrambled to avoid the confrontation. With the aisle blocked in front of him, Skeet grabbed his books off the floor, vaulted over his desk, pushed aside two Chatty-Cathy girls and disappeared.

"Robin Gundy, come back here!" Forten yelled. She knew full well the boy would not return that day and wondering if—maybe hoping—he might not return the next. Never did any of her college role-play scenarios approach what she had just witnessed: the Raging Recalcitrant. She had no idea what to do. How would she ever begin to restore discipline? How could she encourage the teamwork she hoped to build in her class? Principal Langhorn told her when he interviewed her that the first year would be a challenge, but he failed to mention he was doubling down on the challenge by integrating her class, making it the first integrated junior high class in the entire county.

As the last of the students filed out of the room—sneaking looks and sharing whispers—the headache of all headaches began a march through her head. She clamped her hands against the sides of her skull to keep it from exploding. When she opened her eyes, she saw two Negro boys moving off to her right. When she blinked, she realized she was seeing double. The last person to leave the classroom was Jackie Eddings. She started to call his name but decided otherwise.

Outside by the Hamar Street entrance to the school, Ricky Clemonds met his mother. In a new grade, in a new school, in a new town, Cybil Clemonds made it a daily practice to pick up her son in the family's used Buick station wagon at the end of each school day. For most anyone other than Cybil Clemonds, interrupting afternoon activities every day would have been an unbearable annoyance, but for her it was simply motherly love. For Ricky the twelve-block walk home would have been a death march of stumbles and falls, provided he could even remember his way. The ride took less than three minutes with no traffic lights and only one stop sign, at Carteret Street. It was the one time during the day when Ricky would blabber on and on about all that happened at school. His recap of that day ended at the point when his books fell off the desk. No mention of the guest speakers or the research teammates or Skeet's comment; he just broke down into tears.

On the Bay Street sidewalk, Josh Dulane and Mike Lassiter—both on a repeat of the eighth grade—razzed Skeet about his research buddies. Defenseless with words, Skeet pushed and shoved in response until he noticed Jackie Eddings headed away from the school down Bay Street in the opposite direction.

"Hey, Geechee boy," Skeet hollered. He jogged up behind Jackie, grabbed him by the shoulder, and spun him around. "Listen up, Buckwheat. Meet me next to Western Auto at eight o'clock Friday night. Got that? We're goin' to do some research, goin' treasure hunting." He showed his teeth and checked to make sure nobody except his two pals saw him talking to a Negro. "And leave that Ricky Retard at home. Just us. Got it, boy?" he stressed with a grunt.

Jackie stood firm with one hand full of books and the other hand curled into a fist. His eyes slipped to a squint and his brow dipped toward his nose, but he held his tongue.

"Don't be late or you'll be having a come-to-Jesus meetin'. Catch my drift?" Cocksure and confident there would be no rebuttal from his colored classmate, Skeet wheeled around and jogged back toward his pals. Jackie watched as Skeet and the other two white boys pushed and shoved their way down the sidewalk. Once they moved out of sight, Jackie turned and walked in the opposite direction down Bay Street. *Why am I in dis white school? I wants to be wid my friends at de colored school,* he said to himself. He looked back in the direction where he last saw Skeet with his two buddies and wished he had his friends alongside for the walk home.

CHAPTER 2

At that end of the street he lingered to enjoy the fresh green and seasonal brown thickets of marsh grasses and take in the acrid but calming smell of the pluff mud in and around the Beaufort River. At the Bluff—a scenic overlook carpeted with grass sprinkled with dandelions in powder-puff white—he leaned against the historic and gargantuan oak that once provided shade for Union soldiers' tents.

During his walk home, his head was down, but when he occasionally looked up, he noticed every person on the street was white. He hastened his pace, turned at Charles Street, walked a block to Port Republic, and found comfort and assumed safety in front of the Piggly Wiggly. He saw Edreca Witsell, mother of one of his friends, as she entered the grocery. Three other colored shoppers hoisted brown paper grocery bags into the bed of a rundown pickup, then climbed onto bench seats along opposite sides in the bed of the truck. Once everybody was seated, a large lady near the front knocked on the roof of the cab to let the driver know he could head back out to the Sea Islands where most of the Negroes lived.

Once again he was alone avoiding the paths of the white shoppers with their bags in hand, as they walked three abreast, engrossed in conversation without any interest in sharing the sidewalk. He stepped off the curb, crossed back over the street, continued to West Street, and stopped at Tom's Shoe Repair. Didymus Sandiford, known to most as Tom, was the only black shop owner and operator in all of downtown. He was well known for that fact but better known for being the best cobbler and shoe repairman in the Lowcountry. He was so good, the drill instructors from the nearby Marine Corps Recruit Depot at Parris Island would parade in, dressed in their prized, broad-brimmed "Smokey" (the Bear) campaign hats, to drop off old spit-shined oxfords for "Old Tom" to restore with new heels, thicker soles, and a promise of a "gig-proof military shine."

The small brass shopkeeper's bell mounted above the entrance rang when the boy pushed open the door and stepped into a long, narrow space choked with the noxious fumes of shoe glues and polish.

"Evenin', Jackie. How's it be goin'?" the shop owner said, looking up from behind a cluttered workbench. He dropped his stitching awl next to a shoe last with a small saddle oxford mounted on top. "How'd it go today?" he asked as he wiped his brow with a kerchief he pulled from his leather apron. His dye-stained hands looked more leathery than the cowhide-apron he wore.

Jackie managed a polite smile that raised the corner of his mouth ever so slightly. "It was all right. It's not ever going to be good. Dem white kids don't wants me there. I don't wants to be there, neither. I wants to be wid my friends over at Smalls."

Tom Sandiford sat down on the short bench just inside the door and motioned for Jackie to join him.

"Boy, you is makin' history over there. You de first colored boy to get into de white school. Ef you do good, dey might jus' let more colored kids go there next year."

"I knows da'..." Jackie said with his head bowed before he looked up toward the old man, "but dey hates me there."

Old Tom noticed a peculiar tone in the boy's voice. "You afraid, ain't you, boy? I can sees it. Ain't no reason to be afraid." His eyes wandered around the shop, then back to Jackie.

"But today, de teacher assigned projects and I have to works wid Skeet Gundy."

"Oh Lordy! A Gundy? Oo-ee." Old Tom walked away, his hand massaging the back of his neck. "Gundy, eh? Da' family jus' not friendly," he said. Sandiford recalled an incident years back where Skeet's father, Waymon Gundy, was involved with the Klan. Waymon Gundy had been married twice. First time to Ida Mae Gundy, who ran off to parts unknown to avoid her husband's constant bruising abuse. Provoked by her audacity, Waymon quickly remarried the true love of his life, a bottle of Jack Daniels. He continued the physical abuse with his next wife, though Jack Daniels got the best of him. He had not been seen around Beaufort in a good while. "Da' boy now livin' wid dem Newcomb folks, Hank and Mailyn Newcomb." Once again Tom pulled the kerchief from his apron, this time to wipe his brow, and may have caught a tear or two. "So, what's your project, boy?"

"De Gullah treasure. I ain't never heard nothin' about da'," Jackie said. He bent forward, rested his elbows on his knees, and shook his head; his concentration drifted to last year's calendar on the wall by the counter. The faded image was a black-and-white photo of the "Secession House"—the Milton Maxcy House—where the "first meeting of secession" was held and one of Beaufort's largest most recognized antebellum homes.

"Huh…Gullah treasure," Tom chuckled. "Yes indeed, boy. True, but ain't nobody never proved none of da' be true and ain't nobody found nothin' neither. I sure believes it here somewheres"—he went back toward his workbench—"but never have seen nothin' of it. You goes out dey and finds it. You be real famous then. And dem white peoples, dey sure be impressed."

"But who knows anything about da'? Jus' stories is all."

"Aks your Grandpa Gabe. Gabe know somethin' about dem stories. He heard dem all, for sure, probably more den any of us."

"Yeah, guessin' he'd have somethin'. He know about everythin' ever happened around Beaufort since he's been here longer than anybody. He gots lots of stories, jus' not sure ef he remembers too good. Thanks, Uncle Thomas. I gotta get on home."

"You welcome, boy."

The tinny brass bell rang when he opened the door and a second time when the door closed behind him.

Elsewhere, in another part of town, a different conversation began.

"Operator 24."

"Switch, patch me through to the Director."

"Sir, authenticate alpha blue twenty-four sierra."

Silent delay.

CHAPTER 3

True to his name, Didymus made a believer out of Jackie. If there was anyone in the Lowcountry that knew about the Gullah treasure, it was Grandpa Gabe.

From the first day in his new school, Jackie had adopted a safe, comfortable path home. Same streets, same turns, and same stops every day, all to avoid the scrutiny of judgmental white eyes. Plastered against the outside of the shoe shop door, he heard only the wind in the trees and the whine of a mosquito that circled his ear. He stretched his neck to look left then right before he stepped onto the sidewalk headed north on West Street. Beyond the shoe repair, his next stop was the Rudowitz Bargin Shop. There he allowed himself the simple pleasure of eyeballing the window display. Like most stores in town, the Bargin Shop had a tiny storefront window with a collection of "whatever floats your boat." For window shoppers heaps of fabric in a rainbow of colors covered a table on the other side of the glass; patterns on onion skin paper and sewing materials scattered across the floor. None of that interested Jackie. Above the bolts of material and baskets of cloth patches stood bald but curvy pale-white mannequins dressed in tight black knit blouses with pink poodle skirts or flowered dresses puffed up by crinolines. None of those

19

interested him, either. It was always the magic of an iconic World War II Eisenhower jacket adorned with worn ribbons and tarnished brass displayed on a headless torso tucked in the corner on a squat three-legged stool that captivated him. The jacket was a symbol of pride—of hope—in a world his classroom never touched.

News of a new war rumbled halfway around the globe but had no effect on Jackie. He was too young and his father was too old to be drafted. Besides, Irvin Eddings had done his time. He served three years in combat, notably in Italy as a member of the Ninety-Second Infantry Division—"Buffalo Division"—a segregated, all-Negro unit in the Second World War. The memories his father shared were always about how the chaos of war brought him closer to the other soldiers without the mention of killing. Jackie admired his father for that, for all he had done, but he admired him even more for what he made of himself since. He had worked his way up as a leader in business to become the foreman of the local crab cannery. For Jackie the "Ike" jacket was emblematic of victory and success that brought peace; that's exactly what Jackie wanted—peace. With winter coming he knew his mother could resew the missing buttons on his old coat, but the sleeves had inched their way back and now stopped well short of his wrist. The "Ike" jacket would be a better fit and say something about him as well. For now, it all remained only a dream.

He cut his daydream short when, out of the corner of his eye, he spotted two white ladies in their feathered hats and print dresses, purses slung over their forearms, cross the street and point in his direction. Though their gesture was likely directed at the window display, Jackie wanted to avoid another encounter with a white person. He pivoted, gave the pair of walkers a wide berth, and continued down West Street behind the bobbleheads of pigeons that waddled ahead of him.

At a distance he could hear the rhythmic *tap*, *tap*, *slide* of the tappers in the Beaufort Dance School. A rusted box fan rattled against the pavement as it pulled air through the wide-open studio door. The cacophony of cleats against the hardwood floor was an audible elixir that soothed Jackie's spirits. Different wood surfaces allow different sounds, Sharmane Johnson once told him. Her family couldn't afford lessons at the dance school; she learned by listening to the radio, then choreographed her rhythm by watching the first Negro regular, Arthur Duncan, on the *Lawrence Welk Show*. She was the only Negro girl he knew that had worn tap shoes and danced in a variety show at the colored elementary school the previous year.

He was amazed feet could move so fast, then, a split second later, so slow. At times it sounded like the old-fashioned telegraph on *The Lone Ranger*. At other times it was even faster, like popcorn in a kettle. Faster still it sounded, like the *hiss* and *buzz* of a rattlesnake tail. Then it would slow to stomps and slides, like the chug of a freight train up a steep hill. The varied cadences helped him take his mind off all that had happened at school. Inside the *tap*, *tap*, heel-toe-heel-toe rhythm, there was a quiet that tranquilized him for a short while, but soon enough it was time to move his feet. He had to see Grandpa Gabe.

Jackie lived on the Point, a neighborhood of checkerboard streets shrouded by a canopy of trees planted well before the Emancipation Proclamation. Considered the historic district, where concrete sidewalks, buckled by roots, connected dilapidated slave quarters to meaty antebellum mansions, the Point was—

with the exception of four houses deeded during the Reconstruction period—home for whites only. Jackie Eddings's house was one exception; Grandpa Gabe's was another.

Gabriel Sampson Pritchard, known simply as Grandpa Gabe to most everyone—even his great-great-grandson Jackie—was born on Saint Helena Island to former-slave parents. The cotton fields of the Pritchard Place Plantation wrested more than the mandatory blood, sweat, and tears from a young Gabe, and after ninety-six trips around the sun, he had given back most of the physical attributes of his youth that had earned him the nickname "Driver," a title he carried into his senior years off the plantation. An untreated thyroid swelled his tongue and jumbled his speech, which was nothing more than a whisper, a side effect of his struggles with emphysema. Amid the wheezes, coughs, and groans, Jackie found it difficult to understand his feeble great-great-grandfather. He was the oldest Negro—man or woman—in the state of South Carolina, possibly in all of the fifty states. That honor earned him no special privilege in the Lowcountry, but for coloreds and whites alike, he was a symbol of the past—respected by most, tolerated by many, and still despised by a few. He lived alone, a short block from Jackie and his parents. For that the boy was grateful and spent a good bit of time with his Grandpa Gabe.

"Jackie, how you been, boy?" Obadiah Whytsom said as he pushed open the screen door, coming out of Gabe's house, followed by a well-dressed black man who looked straight ahead and left without as much as a nod. Jackie did not recognize the man in the suit, but he definitely knew the other. Obadiah was a man of the marsh. Every day, regardless of weather—except hurricanes—he wrapped his lunch in the same wax paper, threw it in an overused brown paper sack, and shoved off in a paint-starved bateau made from wood that could have come off the Mayflower. Nonetheless, he claimed it as his own. He never told anybody where he went. *Da' for me to know an' for you to finds out,* he always said. Top-secret spots for shrimping, fishing, and plucking oysters from the mud, all in their appropriate seasons. When he was younger—he was fifty-eight now—he had crab pots scattered throughout the creeks. He rowed or poled from pot to pot, collecting crabs to sell to local seafood vendors. Word off the street said Obadiah was the best waterman on the marshes, a title which made him proud, but poor. He wore a pair of khaki pants that once passed inspection but were now cinched like a potato sack at the waist clutched by old USMC surplus canvas belt with a buckle that had retained its shine since his days in the Corps. On a stained white shirt, buttoned navel to neck, he always wore his faded Purple Heart medal earned on Saipan in 1944.

"Doin' jus' fine, Uncle Obadiah," Jackie said.

"Stopped by here to drop off swimps for your grandpa. Ef you be good, he might share wid you, boy." Obadiah gave the wiry kink on Jackie's head a good rub; to Jackie it felt like someone dropped a deflated basketball on his noggin. "How be school? People's been talkin' 'bouts you a lot down by de Piggly Wiggly."

"It's jus' school. Ain't nothin' good about it at all, is all I can say." He looked up at the slender visitor who, at times, walked with such a stoop his medal dangled. He thought about the "Ike" jacket, then said, "Would rather be back over wid my friends at Smalls." The schoolboy pushed the screen door open wider to try to squeeze inside while Obadiah walked through.

"You gots to do what right over there, boy," Obadiah said. "Jus' do what be right." He passed by the boy and wobbled down three warped steps off the porch. Before Jackie went inside, he watched the man disappear around the corner onto Hancock Street.

"Well hello, Jackie. Didn't expect to see you here," said the familiar face with a stethoscope pinching his ears.

"Good afternoon, Dr. Palmer," Jackie replied.

"Just here for Grandpa Gabe's weekly checkup is all. I'll be done shortly," Joseph Palmer said. Voices chattered in the background. Jackie looked up; it was the radio. Dr. Palmer paid a routine visit to Old Man Pritchard's house every week, always gratis. As the only Negro medical doctor in Beaufort, he made it a point to visit Gabe, his senior patient.

"Everything sounds good," he added, pulling the diaphragm chest piece off his patient and wrapping the eartips around the back of his neck. "Strong as an ox and stubborn as a mule, this old fella is going to outlive us all. I've half a mind to send him off for research to learn what keeps an old field hand like Gabe kicking," he said with a smile as bright as a piano keyboard. When Palmer noticed Gabe fumbling with his shirt, he gently eased his fingers on top of Gabe's arthritic hands, slipped a button through the hole, and wrapped the quilt back over his bony shoulders. The quilt—a frayed shoofly patchwork—was Gabe's prized possession; his mother made it for him on the plantation when he was a child. With his eyes closed, Gabe snuggled his ear into the quilt and melted into a smile; the doctor smiled as well.

Joseph Palmer was a first-rate medical doctor, the only card-carrying Negro doctor in the Lowcountry with a sheepskin to prove it. Though he grew up with and respected the hoodoo of the noted root doctors on the islands, Palmer practiced traditional medicine. He left the Lowcountry long enough to receive his medical degree from the Howard University College of Medicine, then returned immediately to give back to the Negro community he loved. He had grown up on Saint Helena Island under the care of his grandmother, one of eleven children orphaned when both parents perished in an unfortunate church fire, a case local authorities never could seem to solve. Palmer's worn medical bag, a graduation gift from the congregation of that church, was testimony to the thousands of times he had passed through the haint blue doorframes on the Sea Islands.

"You have all of those white kids in that school of yours under control yet, Jackie?" he asked with a chuckle as he gathered his equipment.

"No, sir, not yet." Jackie pulled an ottoman alongside Gabe. Stuffing poked through the seams on the tapestry cushion top, and the bottom had only three short wooden legs, but it was the perfect height for Jackie to lean close to hear his grandpa.

"Dr. Palmer, you ever heard of de Gullah treasure?" Jackie asked.

Palmer smiled. "If you haven't heard of the Gullah treasure, you probably not lived around here," he said with a nod. "That story is as old as they come. It ranks right up there with all those other stories. You know, the ghost story of the Lands End Light or the Castle ghost, all of them. I'm sure Gabe here will tell you." He nodded toward Gabe. "I know he knows those stories and probably dozens more." He closed his bag, tapped Gabe on his knee. "I've got to run out to Saint Helena. Few more folks to see today. You take care, Grandpa Gabe," he said in a big voice loud enough for Gabe to hear, then quieter, "You too, Jackie. Keep doing good work at that school of yours. There are a lot of people counting on you."

"Yes, sir, I will," Jackie answered, reluctant to agree.

After the doctor left, Jackie pushed Gabe's walker out of the way and nudged a little closer. When Gabe spoke, which was not often—more to Jackie than anyone else— his voice was hushed like fog through the spartina at sunrise. The chatter from the radio was simply white noise for Gabe but made it difficult for the boy to hear the old man's muffled voice. Jackie pretended to be old and used the walker to hobble to the other room to turn down the volume of a news report about a trip Malcolm X made to Mecca six months earlier and how it changed the notorious Muslim minister's preaching from separatism to integration.

"School be hard?" Gabe strained in a whisper as Jackie settled back on the ottoman. Reared with only a plantation education, Gabe was never comfortable with English, and as he aged, his grasp of the language weakened even more. What few words he spoke were most always in the language of his childhood—Gullah.

"Yeah, Grandpa Gabe, and I hate it."

"Why you hate school?" The old man's words dribbled from lips that barely moved.

"Because it ain't right. I ain't right. I be de onliest colored boy in de school an' dey jus' stare at me. Dey pay me no mind. Times I wish I be invisible. People dey don't talk to me. I can't talk to nobody. Dey keep sayin' 'what you doin' in my school?' Dey jus' don't like me. And some want to make trouble. I tries to step back and avoid it but it gettin' worse." He spoke up so Gabe could hear.

Gabe shared an audible breath before he responded. "Whites be dangerous." He rolled his head away from Jackie, gasped, and coughed. "You get through dis." He coughed again. "I scared to death of you there." He paused, blinked his eyes, and sputtered, "God know ain't right."

"De teacher assigned us school work, a project for teams, and I have to work wid a white boy who hates me. He don't like no colored peoples. Remember when de KKK was goin' to protest in Beaufort, but some dem high school boys stopped dem?" Gabe's eyes widened. He leaned back in his chair and stared at a point where the wall met the ceiling. "One dem KKK was Waymon Gundy, dis boy daddy." A vein ticked in Gabe's temple; beads of sweat began to form above his brow. He closed his eyes.

"And now I gots to work wid him." Jackie paused and studied the old man's puckered face. He quickly changed the subject.

"Grandpa Gabe, what do you know about de Gullah treasure? It be for true?"

Thoughts and sentences were time-consuming for Gabe, each equally taxing. While Jackie waited, the stillness made the voices from the radio grow louder, words he did not understand amplified, like "Pan-Africanism" and an "African Union." His world was different. He was alone, one Negro boy in an all-white school. Gabe was quiet; his expressions seemed to slip and changed as he listened to the voices, though Jackie knew Gabe couldn't really hear them. When the theme music started, he opened his eyes and looked down at the boy.

"I been heared dem stories from a time"—he wheezed—"when I be younger than you be." He breathed deeply. "I not seen no treasure...and I ain't know nobody ever looked for da' treasure." He rolled his head away, closed his eyes.

"I don't needs to find it, Grandpa. I jus' needs to report on it," Jackie said, louder than normal. "And da' Gundy boy, he ain't goin' to help. I know he ain't."

With the mention of the name Gundy, Gabe stiffened. A muscle in his jaw began to twitch.

"And da' other boy, Ricky Clemonds, he gots something wrong wid him. I ain't sure he be much help neither."

Gabe dabbed his lips with his tongue several times, then swallowed hard. "I tells you"—he eked out in a short breath—"what's I heared." He closed his eyes and began again. "My mamma told me..." He labored but slowly told his story; with each passing breath his words became more garbled. His eyes closed and his chin drooped until it settled on his bony sternum.

Jackie waited, unalarmed. For years it had been much the same. Gabe would fall asleep midsentence. Like a babe he would wrap in his quilt and nap, constantly. It didn't take much to exhaust him. The body of the Negro man who, on the plantation, ran all the field hands in 1888 was not the same as the still frame in the chair by Jackie's knees. His body was in compact dimensions now. The freedman of five foot ten and one hundred and fifty-nine pounds had shriveled some eight inches and sixty-five pounds. The endless energy that kept him in the fields for fifteen hours in his youth, now lasted fourteen minutes in a chair before his eyes closed and he slipped into a never-questioned slumber.

Jackie leaned forward, hand cupped behind his ear, when Gabe lifted his chin and began to mumble. Only every third word seemed audible; less than half did Jackie understand. He concentrated on every syllable, but his efforts ended when Gabe returned to his sleep, leaving Jackie to wonder if Gabe really woke up at all.

Five minutes passed. Then ten. Then Gabe started talking again. This time without lifting his head. Jackie pieced together words, none of which formed sentences. "Hawk." "Jesus." "Silver." "Slave." "Killed." "Indians." And then more silence. The next time Gabe uttered a sound, he lifted his head like nothing had happened, except in his eyes Jackie saw fear.

"De Gullah treasure be here," Gabe said. He breathed rapidly like he had run a hard race.

"Here? In dis house?" Jackie asked.

"Here. It be in de Lowcountry. For sure," he said with a hollowed-out stare.

"I don't understand, Grandpa Gabe."

"It be here." Gabe closed his eyes and began to sob, then snore.

When he awoke, Jackie wasted no time.

"Grandpa Gabe...here? You said de Gullah treasure was still here. Tell me more. What do you know?" He gently shook Gabe's knee. "Can you tell me more?"

Gabe cleared his throat with a cough; he appeared to be awake. His head flopped toward Jackie, then he began to speak, slowly, with an exaggerated breath between every third or fourth word. "In de Great Skedaddle...when de buckruh whites left...de slaves took...all de silver...from de plantations...and de town. Dey hid most it...only a few knowed...where it was hid... Then some dem peoples...was murdered...terrible ugly....dey says...dem plat-eyes guard da' treasure...and nobody allowed at it...'cept one person...and he mind dem haints." Gabe closed his eyes and cherished scant life-giving air, which came in rapid gulps.

"You say it be here, but nobody knowed where?" Jackie asked, noticing how Gabe struggled more.

"One person knowed...but nobody knowed...who da' person be. Da' mean...it could be anywheres....You jus' tell abouts de story?"

"Yes," Jackie replied, "but then maybe I can finds it, Grandpa Gabe."

Jackie noticed the old man shiver under the quilt. He snorted as he twisted toward the boy and said louder than before, "No. Leave da' alone."

The white noise seemed louder after Gabe spoke. A loud bird outside the window caused Jackie to jump. Startled and confused, he wasn't sure what to say or what to do. "Grandpa Gabe, I needs to get home. You going to be all right here?" he said, his only retreat.

"I be fine, boy." Pause. "Get home to your mamma." He rolled his head away and stared at his favorite spot on the ceiling.

When Jackie stood to pull the quilt back over Gabe's shoulder, he heard Gabe's whisper above the jabber in the background, "I always dream dis"—he inhaled—"da' you be schooled...like dem white boys. Now you has de chance." He cheated a drowsy peek at Jackie. "Makes it work. For me...makes it work."

Jackie looked at the tired old man in the chair. He saw scars of a lifetime braided in the wrinkles that groaned across Gabe's cheeks. He managed a sympathetic smile and nod, then walked away.

"Careful dem white kids. Dey has ways," Gabe mumbled.

"Okay, Grandpa Gabe, I'll see you tomorrow."

"Da' be good," Gabe said as the screen door slapped shut. "Be like da' Br'er Rabbit. Da' be good."

CHAPTER 4

O perator 24."

"Switch, patch me through to the Director."

"One moment." [Pause.] "Authenticate alpha blue twenty-four sierra."

[Pause]

"Foxtrot green thirty-seven tango."

"Stand by, please."

A brief dial tone preceded the connection.

"I've been waiting," an angered voice announced, followed by another silence, which spawned a further rebuke by the Director. "You're late. I expected your call over an hour ago." The voice was slightly high pitched. It didn't bear any accent. Could have been Midwest or somewhere in the mid-Atlantic along the coast. "Tired of excuses. What's the latest?"

"It's definite. Zorro is headed to my location."

"When? What do we know?"

"Two weeks, maybe less."

"Not good enough, Coyote. We need exact dates."

"Will do. I have someone working that already."

"Besides Zorro, who else?"

"Expect the normal entourage. Eight advisors, the inner circle group, and bag holders. On top of that, sounds like we can expect quite a few more, maybe as many as fifty."

"Fifty? From where? Who are they?"

"All over. Representatives. Zorro plans to drive spurs into them, to get them organized for their next round."

"What are those Communists up to? What do we know?"

"Nothing nailed down. Rumors are all we have, but…"

"I've told you time and time again we are a fact-gathering organization only." The phone filtered the spittle of exasperation. "You're not there to get rumors. We need facts. We can't act on rumors."

"If the Director will hear me out." A pause brought no reply. "We've heard rough topics. Some of the leaders have chimed in. Nothing firm or final with the agenda. Zorro holds the cards close to the chest. Not much to go on just yet."

"Dig! I don't care what you have to do. Get your moles energized or you get in there and dig up the dirt yourself. I want to know their plans, next steps, changes to their strategy, next activities—where and when. We need to stay ahead of these characters."

"Piecing together other conversations, locals. Talk. Something about a guy, a Poro guy."

"Damnit. Call me. The minute you identify something, anything. Concrete stuff, not rumors. Subject or time or place. We need to know what they're up to."

"Yes, sir. Will do."

"Get on it." With a click, the line went dead.

CHAPTER 5

But soft, what light through yonder window breaks? It is the east, and Juliet is the sun. Arise, fair sun, and kill the envious moon…' " Mary Alice Forten recited as she emerged from the cave-like darkness of the school building into blinding matinee sunlight, unsure of whether she should take a knee with head and eyes tilted backward, arms outstretched toward the heavens, or simply twirl endlessly like a fanciful Cinderella; she allowed for neither and squeezed at the pain that lingered in her head. "Oh my god."

"Bravo, bravo," Gene Skyles said, striding toward her across the scorched lawn. He stopped short, dropped his hard-shell briefcase, and offered a dramatic metered applause.

Forten curtsied. "*Romeo and Juliet*, act two, scene two," she said in her truest Shakespearean accent, capped with an authentic hee-haw laugh. "Those kids are going to be the death of me," she moaned, brushing her red hair from her eyes.

"I guess professional life is not like college?" Skyles said. He picked up his briefcase and started to walk with her.

"Lord, I take back all those terrible things I said about college. Tell me why I rushed to finish early. Just send me back there. Please!" She snickered with more than a smidgeon of pain in her response.

"Think about it. A year ago right now we were probably planning for another weekend of football and endless frat parties," Skyles said.

"After that last class...I feel like a tackling dummy. I just need a punching bag or something," Mary Alice added. She fanned herself with her free hand, though her effort did little against the relentless wall of humid air.

"Whoa. I was just about ready to invite you out for dinner, but..." Skyles said as he playfully nudged his shoulder into hers.

She rolled her eyes. "Grrr...those kids. And, this school... Oh, this town. Somehow I get the feeling I've already been hung out to dry"—she hesitated—"or just plain hung."

"And why did you want to come here?" Skyles asked.

"Silly me. Big-city girl longing for a quiet little town to make her mark in teaching. Spreading knowledge to the less fortunate. Et cetera, et cetera. Seemed a few steps up from going to Appalachia, though now I wonder."

As they stepped onto Hamar Street, the appearance of a colored man brought a smile to Mary Alice's face, which eased the pain that continued to rumble through her head. "Hey, Uncle Freddie," she said with a sigh and an exuberant howdy-do wave.

"Hey, Miss Mary Alice. How you be today?"

"Can't complain, Freddie," she said, careful not to let her face expose her fib. "Uncle Freddie, I want you to meet a friend of mine, Mr. Gene...I mean Mr. Eugene Skyles. Mr. Eugene is here doing research for college. Gene, this is Freddie Lembath, the Lowcountry's most beloved singing farmer," she said with a broad smile.

"Pleasure to meets you, Mr. Eugene," Freddie said, flashing one large snaggletooth on the top jaw against a bottom desperately short of six teeth in the front.

Freddie Lembath made toothpicks look chubby. He had narrow shoulders, sinewy licorice-black arms, and tiny hands, which held a rope to control his big-eared, temperamental John mule, Jupiter, pulling a cart full of squash, pumpkins, collards, and yams. The two of them had matching straw hats, though Jupiter's had two holes in his for his ears. Jupiter, like his owner, was scrawny and underpowered. The rope in Freddie's hand was needed less for steering and more for pulling, and Freddie always had his cane pole with a carrot tied to the end as essential equine incentive.

"Nice to meet you, too, Uncle Freddie," Skyles said in return. He started to extend his hand, but caught himself. "Lembath is your last name?" Skyles asked with a squint.

"Yessir, dems a lot of peoples named Lembath 'round here. Sees, dey was a plantation owned by a massah wid da' name way back. Lotsa folks out on Saint Helena where I be from. Me an' old Jupiter here comes in to sell produce from de cart. Needs anything, Miss Mary Alice? Gots some real nice yams here today."

"Oh no, not today. We're headed to dinner. Maybe next time. Thanks."

The two left the vendor behind and reminisced as they continued down Hamar Street. They had not walked far before they heard Freddie. They stopped to look back.

"Dang you, Jupiter. Sometimes I thinks you de laziest mule ever born."

The couple turned to see the harness rope over the old man's shoulder. Freddie—nose forward—leaned at a forty-five degree angle as he tugged to move his four-legged business partner down their regular route. After several unsuccessful tries, Freddie stood up, turned toward the mule, and launched into song. Oddly enough, in a magical transformation à la Gomer Pyle, the bedraggled vendor sounded remarkably like Ray Charles belting out "Georgia on My Mind," made all the more difficult with so few teeth. Jupiter, apparently, liked what he heard and followed Freddie while he sang. They shuffled off in a different direction, up Hamar and into the Northwest Quadrant.

"That Freddie's quite a character," Skyles said as they picked up their walk again.

"Oh, we have all kinds here in Beaufort. The place is full of history and a lot of it still walks the streets," she said.

House by house, Mary Alice gave her friend a personal tour of the sites through the heart of Beaufort. Headache gone, she chattered like a cartoon duck the entire length of Bay Street with a brief pause at each of the city's oldest and finest homes, where she waxed eloquent on the trivia of each. "And that is Tabby Manse... And that one is the Robert Means House... And this is the Cuthbert House... And that's 'The Anchorage.' " She droned on and on. What she didn't know was that, as a PhD candidate, Skyles had done more research on the history of Beaufort than his female teacher friend would ever attempt. He was considerate enough to not correct her as she talked, but briefly interrupted her rapid-fire monologue to ask, "Where would you like to eat?"

"Oh, uh. I know. Let's eat at Harry's Restaurant. They have great food and the specials are the best."

"Lead the way," he said.

For three blocks, his tour guide passed most of the small shops with only minimal commentary, though she did hint at her "need" for a stop at Ray's Liquors or Luther's Pharmacy—"the best soda shop in town." She stopped talking long enough to drag her escort into Bitty's Disc Den where she bought the latest chart topping single, Roy Orbison's "Oh, Pretty Woman." She clutched the 45-rpm vinyl as if it were a Stradivarius. "This is my new favorite sound. I could listen to this for hours."

Gene Skyles shook his head and grinned until she kicked him in the shin with ladylike gentility.

Harry's Restaurant was hopping. A mouthwatering serenade of seafood filled the air. It was late afternoon and the evening crowds were deep into the Friday Early Bird special, Harry's signature crab cakes with roasted red pepper aioli. Guided by their noses, they settled into a cluttered table for two just outside the kitchen door.

"So tell me about these projects you gave your kids today after the presentations," Skyles said while the waitress cleared plates and empty glasses.

"I don't even want to think about school tonight." Unconsciously, she lined up the condiments according to their height off to the side of the table. "You talk. Tell me again how you arrived at this notion about Poe and Beaufort and your dissertation topic. Poe? In Beaufort?" she questioned in disbelief.

"Yeah, Poe. One of my favorites. Always has been. You know the macabre," he replied, wiggling his fingers in front of her eyes. "Over the past year he's definitely become my favorite by virtue of all the time I've spent with the guy." He pushed his glasses farther up the bridge of his nose, then waved his hand over his head for the waitress.

"Really? Poe?"

"He's cool. I mean…he is considered the 'Father of the Modern Mystery,' " he emphasized. "Still a lot of mystery and unanswered questions about him and his writing."

"So, your thesis? You narrowed it down to 'Annabel Lee'?"

"Yeah. Sweet, sweet Annabel Lee."

"Why? I could think of so many other poems or stories or just topics around Poe to research or write about. Why 'Annabel Lee'?"

The waitress, an older woman in a flowered dress and a bouffant hairdo, approached. "Are you ready to order, sugar?" she said with a come-on smile toward Skyles. The way she said it made him think she had something more than dinner in mind. Mary Alice rolled her eyes.

Skyles nodded and winked toward his dinner partner.

"Sure, I'll have the crab cakes please."

"You want french fries with that, honey?"

"Yes, please."

"And you, sugar? What can I get you?" she said, her breath as toxic as an ashtray.

"I'll try the Mussels Saint Charles, with french fries, too, please. And a Coke."

"Oh, and may I have a glass of sweet tea, please?" Mary Alice added, sheepishly.

The waitress jotted down the final request, slipped her pencil back into her puffy hair, and marched off toward the kitchen with an exaggerated wiggle in her behind and a look back over her shoulder, a finger on her lips. Mary Alice rolled her eyes.

"Okay, so why 'Annabel Lee'?"

"It's one of those poems that's had researchers, I mean scholars and fanatical literature buffs, all scrambling for answers for over a hundred years."

"So?" she questioned.

"So I think I have proof to definitively identify who the real Annabel Lee was to Poe."

"Proof?"

"Yeah, proof."

"Well, if you have proof, why do research in Beaufort?" she asked.

"It's a long story, but my proof rests in letters that connect Poe to a man whose daughter was Annabel. I'm sure of it."

She stared at him with raised eyebrows.

"Oh, and that character we met on the way over here…"

"Uncle Freddie?"

"He said his last name was Lembath, right?"

"Yeah, why?"

"Because the last name of the girl who was Poe's Annabel Lee was also Lembath."

"Why not Lee?" she asked after a short sip of water. "And how did you come to that conclusion?"

"I've been through tons of boxes of records in Baltimore, Richmond, and at the campus library back at school. Even went to the West Point library. It's crazy Poe ever went to West Point. I've taken pictures of old letters and notes. Actual handwritten scribbles from Poe. They have the name of Anna Belcher Lembath. There was an Anna Belcher Lembath who died in Charleston about the time Poe was serving in the army at Fort Moultrie."

The waitress arrived with their food, then lingered until Skyles picked up his fork and nudged a few fries around on his plate. When he gave her a patronizing glance, she left and he continued. "There's a church in Charleston— the Circular Congregational Church—that has the oldest cemetery in the city. In those cemetery records, there are several possible burials listed, people without headstones and where pastors failed to properly record the information. I found a record for Anna Belcher Lembath there, at that church, though the burial was purposely hidden so Poe couldn't find her."

"How do you know that?" Mary Alice asked as she shooed a pair of determined flies away from her food with the back of her hand. "Flies are Satan's little spies, you know," she said waving her fork toward Skyles.

"Have you ever heard of Lizzie Doten?" Skyles asked.

She shook her head and shoveled a bite of crab cake into her mouth.

"Lizzie Doten was a psychic and a poet in the mid-eighteen hundreds. She claimed Poe's spirit continued to write poetry through her. In her personal notes, I saw her comments, more than once, where she wrote that Poe raised the name Anna Belcher Lembath. Though the poem was not even released until after his death, most people think it was written while he was at Fort Moultrie."

"And the name?"

"Poe was clever. He loved mystery and detective work, like the code he used in 'The Gold Bug.' He disguised her name, combining two and abbreviating her last name," he said. Using a two-handed technique, Skyles surgically removed a mussel from its shell, dipped it into a small bowl of melted butter, chewed twice, and swallowed.

Forten was totally confused. She rested her hands on the table's edge, opened her mouth, shut it, and opened it again. "Okay, I am not sure I followed all of that, but again, why are you in Beaufort?"

"Lembath. The key is finding out more about a guy who I believe was that girl's father. Lembath was a big merchant. He had shops in Savannah and Charleston. He vacationed in Beaufort. Owned a house here. I need to dig up more on his background. Maybe I can find the final link to close the chain, prove my theory, and, *voila*, thesis defended," he said. He pushed back from the table, leaned his head against the wall, and smiled, smug and satisfied hands raised in capitulation.

"Well, good luck with that one. When you're done, how about bailing me out at school?" she said, shaking her head and waving her last french fry in his face.

"Why? What do ya need? Hopefully today wasn't an ordinary day in the classroom."

"Well, not ordinary, but close." She inhaled deeply, hissed it out, and took another deep breath.

"I'm not sure I can control some of those kids, like that boy Skeet Gundy." She growled. "I wish I could wring his neck sometimes." As she shoved the last fry in her mouth, she dropped her eyes and studied the rim of her glass of tea. "But thanks for coming by class today. I really do appreciate it."

"Hey, it was fun. Interesting group of kids."

"Interesting? You call that interesting?" She rocked back in her seat and allowed her head to flop backward, her mouth and eyes open wide, prepared to take a big bite out of the ceiling. "You missed it. After you left I gave them their research projects. Gundy went berserk." She lowered her head and tapped the table lightly with her forehead.

Skyles chuckled. "Why? What set him off this time? That boy Ricky again?"

"No, well not exactly. I put him on a team with Ricky and the colored boy, Jackie Eddings. He jumped up, said he wasn't working with no coon, pardon my French. And—"

"Why did you do that?" Skyles asked, alarmed.

"I figured if I put those three in one group, I was grouping my three biggest challenges into one team rather than wrestling with them on three separate teams."

"I get your point, but…wow, that team will be a challenge." He paused and smiled. Before she could say another word, he waved her off. "Hey, let me have another crack at them. Now that you've assigned topics, I think I can play with that a bit to give them all a few pointers on things from time to time. You know, like how to research. May even be able to teach them a little something about respect," he added with a smirk.

"Behave, Gene. Come on. They're kids…" she said, then laughed. "But, sure, if you can spare the time. I can always use the assistance."

"Okay if I intimidate your little loudmouth buddy, Skeet? I mean, at some point, that boy needs to learn that being a smart-ass is a lot less about being smart than it is about being an ass."

"Gene!" she chided, then added with a smile, "Sure. Be my guest."

CHAPTER 6

Though programs at the big three in South Carolina—USC, Clemson, and the Citadel—had struggled for years, Friday nights in the fall were all about football in the Lowcountry. Beaufort reveled in their small-town, big-time-football image. The band in the stands. Parents hawking hotdogs. Girls in short skirts climbing bleachers. Roughneck boys with Brylcreem fenders and ducktails. Others—the hipper ones—with mopheads, looking more a part of the British Invasion than the southern gentlemen their parents reared on fried okra and grits. Sidelines of rabid football fanatics roared support for their champions of the gridiron who knocked heads and exchanged blows in defense of hometown pride at the scholastic level. This night was no different, at least not at the field.

Skeet Gundy and his sidekick for the night, Hoss Lassiter, dressed in faded green Beaufort High T-shirts, never intended to mingle with the crowd. They weren't in position to hear the half-time performance of the Sea Island Sound Marching Band with their tribute to Elvis. Instead the two boys moved steadily up Scott Street where gusts in advance of a front nudged them toward Western Auto. It was five past eight and there was no sign of Jackie Eddings.

"That chicken-livered nigrah," Skeet said. His head swiveled in all directions. "That little pecker better get here pronto if he knows what's good for him."

"He ain't goin' to show. You're goin' to have to teach him a lesson on how things work around our school," Hoss added as they neared the building. Hoss Lassiter was an awkward, chubby teen—a victim of too many Twinkies. Another gust spun between the buildings and plastered the them with sand. When they cleared their eyes, Jackie Eddings stood directly in front of them.

"Where you been, boy?" Skeet demanded.

"I was here...here before eight," Jackie stammered, words jamming up in his mouth.

"Well, we ain't seen ya till now," Skeet replied.

"I was standing over there...on de other side of de building...out de wind."

Skeet considered the comment a bit too uppity and stepped toward Jackie. "Watch your tone, boy. We got work to do. Who knows you're out here? What you tell your folks?"

"Dey visit wid my grandpa on Friday," Jackie said, a bit more timidly than his last comment.

"We goin' to make you an outlaw tonight, boy," Hoss Lassiter said. He turned to Skeet and laughed.

Jackie shoved his oversized hands into his pockets and waited with locked knees.

Skeet motioned for the others to follow him to the far side of the building, out of the wind.

"Here's our plan, Geechee boy," Skeet said with a toad face. "Remember that guy that came to class, the guy with the boat who looked for treasure?"

"Swanson. Mr. Swanson. The guy that had that gap in his front teeth," Hoss added. "Come on, you jackass.

Remember, he was there and that other guy who talked about Poe."

Jackie nodded.

"Remember he said he had treasure maps? And then that other guy, the Poe guy said there might be treasure here? Well, we goin' to go swipe us some maps, honey child. And you is goin' to help us."

"I can't do da'. Da' ain't right. What ef we get caught?" Jackie said. He took a step backward and raised his hands like Skeet had a gun in his chest.

"Listen. We ain't goin' to get caught. We got a plan. We figured this out already," Skeet said. He grabbed Jackie's wrist. Jackie struggled to pull away, but Skeet latched on tighter. "Let's go."

He pulled Jackie back into the wind, away from the shelter of the Western Auto. All three of them jumped when two cats darted out from under the bush near the building; their spray followed them in the wind as the group headed down Port Republic Street for a block, then turned toward Bay Street and the waterfront.

Skeet sent Hoss out ahead. "You get on the other side of the street, Geechee boy, and stay about fifteen feet behind Hoss. Don't try to run off or do anything stupid because we got you trapped. I'll be right behind you, boy."

Jackie took a few steps and stopped to look back. Skeet stared but said nothing; his expression was dark. Jackie continued down West Street with Skeet a few steps to his rear.

At Bay, Hoss crossed. Seconds later, Jackie crossed, not paying much attention to his surroundings. His focus was on Skeet and the crime they were about to commit.

"Holds on up dey, boy," hollered a male voice, deep enough to be Lou Rawls. It was Obadiah Whytsom,

Grandpa Gabe's shrimper friend. He struggled with a rusted bucket in one hand, a cane pole in the other. A wet shrimp net across his shoulders left his white shirt nearly transparent, save for the mud and the ribbon of his Purple Heart medal stuck to his chest. "Where you be headed dis time a night?"

Jackie froze with a stiff glance back across the street. Skeet had dropped to a knee and was retying his shoe with an eye on Jackie.

"Just goin' down by dis here dock, Uncle Obadiah," Jackie said, unsure of whether this accidental encounter would save him from or complicate Skeet's plan.

"Nothin' down dey for you, boy. Just finished clean out da' boat of de captain's. Why ain't you at de game?"

"I missed my ride. Just wanted to walk is all." The lie left a foul taste in his mouth as it slipped off his tongue.

"Weather be too nasty to be just out walkin' in dis, boy. You get you butt home. What you parents up to?" Obadiah asked.

"Dey wid Grandpa Gabe."

Skeet eyed every second of the exchange between Jackie and Obadiah. He had finished one shoe and quickly did a double genuflection to tie the other.

"Then you best be gettin' on home an' not be walkin' 'round downtown. Gives me some help here. Takes dis here bucket down to Beaufort Seafood down dey at de end uh de block down dey."

"But, I need to…" Jackie felt like he was going to throw up; he swallowed hard. He dared another look back. Skeet ran his index finger across his throat like a knife, then motioned a two-handed shove. "I need to—"

"Not good for you to be out alone dis time uh evenin', not down here," Obadiah said. "Now gives me a hand."

For a brief moment Jackie considered an out: just run away, escape the crime scene before it happened. His thought quickly rolled back on itself. He realized even if he could outrun Skeet tonight, tomorrow or Monday Skeet would find him. He spotted Hoss Lassiter near a lamppost farther down the alleyway. Over his shoulder he saw Skeet headed in his direction. Jackie grabbed the bucket from Old Man Whytsom and took off running. Under the weight of the wet gear, Obadiah shuffled after him in a pair of cracked black shrimper boots that were two sizes too big. When the door to the seafood company closed behind him, someone flipped the cardboard sign to "CLOSED."

Skeet pinged across Bay Street and met Hoss on the side nearest the water. At the end of the alley, tied to a piling of the rickety city dock, they saw the treasure hunter's boat.

The *Wile E. Coyote* was a tin can held together by a spider's web of rusted welds that stained the blistered white paint well beyond the surface of the water. The wheelhouse was barely the size of a phone booth and not much more. A simple shelter for the captain in bad weather while the crew, aka "paying customers," enjoyed the finer parts of life at sea, au naturel. Rigged with cables, hoists, and chains large enough to secure Godzilla, the battered wreck was legendary up and down coastal Carolina, but its captain, Geordie Swanson, had yet to haul any real treasure on board.

The alleyway funneled the breeze off the water into a tropospheric jet stream that howled. At the dock Skeet and Hoss tucked in tight under the porch overhang of the Beaufort Yacht Club. Choked by the smells of cigarettes, beer, and overflowing trash barrels, they put their heads together on the plan, startled when Jackie whipped around the corner to join them.

"You dumb jigaboo," Skeet said. He grabbed Jackie by his shirt and pulled him in close. "What were you thinking? What'd you go and do that for?" he chided before he let Jackie loose.

Jackie put his hands on his knees and struggled to catch his breath.

"You just about signed up for a meeting with the Lord, Geechee boy. You run off from us again and you is dead." Skeet paused. "You tell that colored man anything? Anything 'bout us?"

Jackie shook his head side to side, still short of breath.

"Okay. Here's the plan. You and me is going to climb aboard that boat. You check them hatches on the deck and see if there are steps to rooms below. I'll check up there where the wheel is. Don't waste no time, boy. We ain't got no time. Hoss, you stand over there, up by Bay Street and watch. If you see anybody, give one of them *Lassie* calls, you know, *kee-ah-kee*," Skeet said softly. "Then distract them. Try to get them to give you a ride home or something."

Both boys nodded. The white boys looked hard at Jackie. He nodded a second time with one hard and long jerk of his head. All three snuck into action like they had been professionals in crime for some time. Jackie crept across the deck. He lifted three hatch covers one at a time. Each time he looked into deep empty storage bins below. Skeet rummaged through piles of papers on clipboards tied up along the wheelhouse walls. Hoss stood, hands in pockets, looking back and forth, up and down the street. They had all the bases covered until Jeffrey Oatley, one of the cigar-chewing short order cooks at the Beaufort Yacht Club, opened the second-story window just off the stern of the *Wile E. Coyote* and poured a bucket of slop into the water below. It was usual practice to dump the garbage into the river—so usual he failed to see if anybody was watching (or if anyone was below). He knew all the boats, their owners, and crew. He rarely saw any of them or anyone else on the water at that time of day. The slurry of shells, scales, bones, and veggies hit the water with a splash and startled Jackie. He fell backward over a rustled pulley on the deck. The movement caught Oatley's eye. He focused in on a petrified Jackie, and then he saw Skeet's head when it popped out from inside the wheelhouse.

"Hey, what are you clowns doing down there?" Oatley yelled. Even in the dim light he saw Jackie's black face. In a panic, Skeet jumped out of the wheelhouse and darted down the deck. Oatley pulled the bucket back inside the window and ran to the stairwell headed outside to catch him.

"Get movin', boy. We gotta get out of here, pronto," Skeet said as he passed Jackie, locked in fright. Seconds later both boys were off the boat and in the alley. As soon as he heard Oatley yell, Hoss dropped his reconnaissance and consequently never saw Obadiah Whytsom come out of the Beaufort Seafood Company door headed toward him. The old colored man moved slowly, but when he turned down the alley right in front of Hoss, the scared guard changed direction and took off running up Bay Street away from the scene.

Skeet and Jackie hit the ground and immediately ran into Obadiah. He didn't think anything of it at first.

"Hold up dey, boy. I wants to give you dis here nickel for helping me wid da' bucket." Obadiah grabbed Jackie's wrist as he ran by, and when he did, the boy's momentum pulled both of them to the ground.

Skeet looked over his shoulder but continued on across Bay Street. He ducked under the steps to the Verdier House to watch Jackie.

"I gotta go, Uncle Obadiah," Jackie said, helping the man back to his feet. "You told me to head on home. Da' what I fixing to do."

Jackie took off and plunged nose-to-belly into Geordie Swanson, who fiddled with a toothpick in his mouth as he stepped out of the Rebel Grill on the corner.

"You watch where you're going there, boy," Geordie said with a scowl.

Jackie looked up but didn't say a word. He did a quick shuffle with his feet and dashed across Bay Street, where he met Skeet. The two of them ran up West Street while Geordie Swanson looked on.

"Hey! Stop those kids," Jeff Oatley hollered as he came through the ground-floor door of the yacht club. He scrambled up the alley toward Swanson. "Hey, Geordie, them boys was on your boat," Oatley said, bent over to catch his breath. He wiped his face with his cook's apron, which left green slime with splotches of red and brown goo on his forehead.

Swanson took another, harder look at the boys. He recognized the Negro boy; it was the kid from the junior high class, but from that distance, he couldn't get a good look at the second kid.

Obadiah Whytsom stood at the other end of the alley by the door to the Beaufort Yacht Club. He never knew a Negro boy to turn down money. And for sure, he never saw a colored boy running scared along with a white kid. With Swanson and Oatley blocking his path to the street, Whytsom walked undeterred along the waterfront back toward the bridge, unnoticed, scratching his head.

The boys raced on for two blocks. When they reached Craven Street, Skeet turned right and headed toward the historic but dilapidated arsenal. He skidded to a stop to make sure Jackie turned to follow; he did. At the Beaufort Arsenal, they stopped to catch their breath.

"What did that guy say to you? What did you tell him?" Skeet said, still winded.

"He wanted to give me money. I just ran off. I told him I had to get home," Jackie replied in three short breathless bursts.

"Did you take anything from the boat? See anything?"

"No."

"Me neither." Skeet waved Jackie to follow him and kept talking as they walked toward the back side of the library across from the arsenal.

"Okay, we gotta find a map or something. We need to check the other guy's room at the motel."

"What other guy?"

"The Poe guy. He said he had stuff from Poe or about Poe or codes or maps or something, just like that story he talked about."

"What's he goin' to give us?"

"He ain't goin' to give us nothing, stupid. We're going to take stuff."

"Steal it?"

"You got it, Buckwheat."

Jackie cringed.

"Come on," Skeet groaned as he picked up the pace. "I heard Miss Forten say they were going to the game tonight, so I know he ain't there. And I know where his room is 'cause I staked this out already."

The Lord Carteret Motel was definitely the marquee low-end lodging in downtown Beaufort. Short term or long term, there was no better place to stay, for twelve dollars a night, than 301 Carteret Street. Billed as: *Red Carpet Service, Downtown, opposite the post office. In sight of Parris Island. Wall-to-wall carpeting, full tile baths with tub and shower, private dressing rooms, TV, FM radio, room phones. Fine restaurants nearby.* The Lord Carteret Motel was perfect for a starving college student, the home away from home for Gene Skyles.

The target was a room far from the office, bottom floor, where the two wings of the L-shaped motor lodge met. The parking lot was nearly empty. One upscale '57 Chevy Delray sat front and center by the office, a treasure under constant watch by the night clerk. A radio in a nearby house filled chilly gusts with loud music. The boys snuck between the bushes that grew behind the motel then crept up the outdoor passageway and passed the ice machine that sounded like it was crashing through the Arctic Circle. Fortunately, the corner room was outside the dim ring of light cast by a sidewalk post lamp that had surrendered its plumb. There were no individual lights by the room doors and the light socket at the end of the walk had no bulb.

Gusts, stronger than earlier, tumbled discarded newspapers and trash across the rutted parking lot outlined with weeds. Skeet snuck out from behind the ice machine in the service area to open the window to the room. The skinny teen was fairly strong, but no match for the locked window. He quickly opted for a second approach. Convinced he could open the door like "The Man from U.N.C.L.E.," Skeet snagged a Dixie cup the wind had plastered against the wall beside the door. He flattened it to wedge between the door and the jamb. When he went to grab the knob, the door drifted open. Skeet stepped back and pancaked against the window.

Nobody appeared. Nobody came out. Nothing happened. Skeet waved for Jackie to join him.

Skeet elbowed the door open farther, wide enough for the two to look inside. There was enough light from the lamp post across the lot for them to see the room was empty, but what they saw otherwise shocked both of them.

"Holy smokes," Skeet exclaimed and pulled Jackie inside. "Look at that. Somebody else must be after the map or whatever."

"Or to get Mr. Skyles," Jackie added with a worried look on his face.

Adrenaline that choked Jackie earlier had solidified in his belly. "Do you think Mr. Skyles was here?" he whispered. "Think dey was a fight? Think dey took him somewheres?"

Skeet scanned the parking lot one last time before he closed the door and sent the room into darkness. He stepped to the window and slid the curtain back just enough to be able to survey the damage. A nightstand lamp on the floor. Suitcase emptied on the bed, where the sheets had been ripped off and tossed aside. Papers everywhere.

"Shoot, I don't know and don't care about him neither. It's the maps. Look for maps."

Jackie stood by the door. His palms grew sweaty. His heart whammed so loudly in his ears, he couldn't hear the fight-or-flight voices in his head. He watched while Skeet rummaged through the piles around the room.

"We can't stay here. De police could be here any minute ef somebody heard all of dis happening," Jackie said. He eyed the papers by his feet and picked up a glossy brochure of the Point. He noticed the Castle was circled in pen. Next to the circle were four handwritten letters, "NEbN."

"What's that?" Skeet questioned when he noticed Jackie had something in his hand.

"It's not a map. It's a brochure with some marks on it."

Skeet grabbed it. "Let's go."

Their stay was less than three minutes, but in that short time Mother Nature cranked up her winds. The post lamp—tottering before—broke free from its rusted anchors and rocked like a drunk on stilts; its light flickered intermittently with the motion. A block away, the rigging of shrimp trawlers banged against raised outriggers in a cacophony of metallic clanks and dampened clunks.

From the far side of the parking lot, Robert Caplin, the most respected and overworked Negro attorney in all of Beaufort County, was about to open the door to his Chevy Delray when he spied the boys leaving the room. Dressed in a dark gray suit and charcoal fedora with a red feather, he was merely a silhouette, if that. Though the boys didn't notice him, he watched them sneak behind the motel, then race down the street back toward the arsenal, this time with Jackie in the lead.

"In here," Skeet shouted from behind and ducked into the entrance to the public library, out of sight. Jackie joined him.

Skeet took a minute to look at the marks on the brochure. "See here, the Poe guy circled the Castle. He must think the treasure is there, just like he said in class," Skeet concluded. Jackie was less sure of the assumption.

"I say we get ahead of him on this one. We need to get there tonight."

"What? Tonight?" Jackie questioned as the wind howled passed them. "And do what?"

"We knock on the door and ask them to show us the treasure," Skeet scoffed. "No, idiot, we break in like we did at the last two places."

"People. Dey people da' live there. And it's late."

"The Dansons ain't there. While I was scouting out Skyles' motel room, I saw them get on that bus going to the Clemson football game at Duke," Skeet answered. "But Hoss is gone. We need another person." He paused. "Hey, your buddy Ricky Retardo lives right over there. That's on the way to the Castle ain't it? Go get him."

Headlights appeared on the street in front of the alcove where the boys hid. They pulled back farther into the corner of the space. The car was the same Chevy Delray they saw parked in front of the motel. They didn't recognize the driver and felt sure the driver didn't notice them as he drove very slowly past.

"He can't come out wid us. He don't even walk fast, Skeet."

"He can be the lookout. We need a lookout."

Jackie stared at the ground and shook his head, well aware this would only put him deeper and deeper in the quicksand of crime.

"Come on. Let's go to his house. You just walk in front of me and don't try nothing funny, Buckwheat, or when I get done with you, your Aunt Jemima won't even recognize you. You understand?"

Jackie understood he had no good alternatives. Screaming for help was no option. If he ran Skeet would catch him. He could punch Skeet and maybe win a fight, but one fight against Skeet meant another fight against Skeet and all his pals. Jackie couldn't afford that, nor did he want to round up his Negro friends and start a race riot. Everybody—his family and colored friends—had told him over and over how much they were counting on him to break the barrier into the white schools. And he knew, if there was a fight, the white kid would always win, one way or another. His grandpa had warned him. He knew he had to get smarter in dealing with Skeet and the others, but for now his options were limited.

"Yeah, I understand," Jackie said.

"Okay, you lead. I'll be right behind you."

The weather was their strongest ally, conditions worse now than they were earlier down on the boat. Since he was in the lead, Jackie took a chance and stayed on the main street where there was a chance somebody might recognize him and offer a ride or at least stop to talk. There was also the chance somebody would be out for a lynching. It was not likely in Beaufort, and maybe it was the weather, but Jackie had a feeling inside. Separated by only a few yards, the boys passed the Carteret Street United Methodist Church where Elliott Clemonds— Ricky Clemonds's father—had assumed duties as pastor only four months earlier.

The minister and his family had never developed a tie to the brutality of football, in part because of Ricky's physical handicaps. On Friday nights while others in town headed for the Friday night lights, Elliott Clemonds invited the older members of the congregation for a potluck dinner, followed by a social hour at the church hall. Ricky was never expected to attend. In their previous town, the Clemonds had a special assistant, not a babysitter, who came over to spend time with Ricky, more as an adult companion than a nurse. However, in Beaufort, Cybil Clemonds had not yet found that special someone Ricky would approve of; she had several recommendations and had interviewed a number of them, but she had not selected the right person to sit with her son. Since the church was a few short blocks away, Ricky stayed home...alone.

Jackie climbed the steps to the Clemonds' house seconds ahead of Skeet. He was unsure of how he would convince Ricky to join them.

"Go on. Knock on the door," Skeet urged. "His parents ain't home. We know that."

"What am I supposed to tell him?"

"Tell him, just tell him...tell him we are going hunting for treasure, like the pirates. You know. He thinks like a four-year-old. He'll probably pee his pants he'll be so excited."

Jackie stepped up to the door. Close to the house he was out of the wind, a good calming feeling. He knocked. While he waited he looked back at Skeet. Finally, he heard footsteps on the other side of the door.

"Who—who—who is it knocking on my door? That's my door." The nervous inflection in Ricky's voice faded and dropped with the last word.

"Ricky, it's me, Jackie Robinson Eddings."

"Jackie Robinson. Brooklyn Dodgers. 1947 to 1956. Lifetime batting average, three hundred and eleven," Ricky replied in an involuntary recitation of the baseball hall of famer's statistics.

"No. From school. Jackie. Jackie Eddings."

"Rookie of the Year 1947. National League MVP 1949. Brother Mack, silver medal, 1936 Olympics. Berlin. Hitler. Bad. Real bad. Bad man. Go away, bad man." The top half of the door was glass, covered on the inside with white lace curtains, handiwork of an old-world artisan. In the corner of the glass, Jackie noticed the curtain slid away from the frame and one of Ricky's eyeballs appeared. When he saw it was Jackie, he opened the door, but only a crack.

"Hi, Ricky," Jackie said, too soft for Skeet to hear.

Ricky was a confused child. His appearance was cartoon-like, an Elmer Fudd type. He had an oversized head on a potbellied body with a bulbous nose and a crew cut that made him look bald. Small in stature, another complication of his disorder, he stood just over five feet tall. Some suggested he was just a late bloomer since many boys in his class were pushing a foot taller. But the Clemonds knew that Ricky would never be big; he would probably never be any taller than he was now.

"You were knocking on my door. You knocked on my door. This is my door. Hi, Jackie. This is my door," Ricky replied with his nose through the slight opening. "Why did you knock on my door?"

Jackie's heart rate hit the accelerator and raced his breathing. He looked back at Skeet a second time. Skeet cringed, nodded with his head, and waved him to go ahead. "Ricky…we're going on a treasure hunt, me and Skeet Gundy and we, uh, want you to come wid us."

"Treasure. Pirate treasure. Captain Kidd. Long John Silver. *Treasure Island.* Robert Louis Stevenson," Ricky rambled in a stream of consciousness lost on Jackie.

"Yeah, pirate treasure," Jackie repeated.

As Skeet predicted, Ricky's eye widened and he stepped through the door. "Sure. Yo-ho-ho, and a bottle of rum! Yippee. Treasure."

"But it's with Skeet. You know, Skeet Gundy," Jackie whispered.

"Pieces of eight! Pieces of eight!" Ricky continued until Skeet pushed Jackie aside and grabbed Ricky's wrist.

"Hey, you two Looney Tunes, quit talkin'. Let's go."

Ricky locked his knees as Skeet pulled him along. "Why are you with him?"

"Well"—Jackie walked alongside Ricky and tried to explain—"because we have de assignment at school for de Gullah treasure an' Skeet is sure he knows where it is."

"But…" Ricky started but stumbled forward behind Skeet's tug.

"You retard," Skeet growled. Concerned someone might spot them, he let loose of Ricky's arm and stomped across the street to the opposite sidewalk, where he followed catty-corner a few steps behind Jackie and Ricky. For a Friday night to see three boys walking up North Street on The Point was not a common sight, especially when one was a colored boy and the other two were white—one with his right leg shorter than the left and the other Skeet Gundy.

On the corner where East Street crosses the dead end at Craven stood the historic Joseph Johnson House; to the locals it was the Castle. Built in the 1850s, it remained one of the few houses owned and occupied by family members of the original owner. It was a solid stone structure with seventy-nine windows, some of them massive, French palatial walls of glass that overlooked a saltwater inlet off a majestic bend in the Beaufort River and the Intracoastal Waterway.

With the huge house in sight, Skeet prodded the others to pick up the pace. They approached from the rear, concealed by massive camellias and azaleas that bordered the lot. Clumps of bamboo in the adjacent yard rising six feet into the air made an easy cover for entry through the iron gate in the back. They moved with only token regard to stealth, silenced by the gusts, understanding nobody was home. Skeet grabbed the other two, one at a time, and planted them in specific spots inside the arch of the basement floor, out of sight while he moved from window to door to window hoping to find one open. The rear of the house was secure; from what he could tell those openings had been nailed shut. He motioned for the others to follow him around to windows on the side of the house hidden from view by the two-story porch balcony supported by six columns the size of redwood trees.

"Look. See that window there," Skeet said, pointing to a window left open a hair at the bottom. It was at least six feet tall and an equal distance off the ground. "Geechee boy, come here and kneel down like a dog so I can stand on your back to open it." Even in the dark Skeet could see the shiny white of the Negro's eyes—like peeled hard-boiled eggs—as they moved from Skeet to the window and back to Skeet, straddling a crease of doubt that ran down the colored boy's face.

"Get on down, boy," Skeet pressed in a hushed voice. He grabbed Jackie by the back of his neck and shoved him to the ground. Jackie landed with his nose in the turf. He pushed up onto all fours under the window. Confused, Ricky stood nearby and rocked side to side, lifting each foot an inch off the ground while his fingers busily picked at his nose. "Yo-ho-ho and a bottle of rum!" he repeated to himself, like a mantra or contemplations with prayer beads.

"Shut up, you retard," Skeet barked as he hopped on Jackie's back and noticed a century's worth of layered paint across the bottom of the window. Using his thumbs, Skeet popped the window from its sill and pushed it up until his arms were fully extended. The opening was barely enough to squeeze through. He had to hop to get his waist onto the frame, then pulled himself inside. He instructed Ricky to kneel down as the step for Jackie. It took a little extra coaching but Ricky finally understood. Skeet hoisted Jackie up and in from Ricky's back. When he landed Jackie heard a dog bark outside.

"Ricky, stay there and keep your eyes open. If you see anybody coming, holler," Skeet instructed with his head out the window.

"My mamma told me not to holler."

"Well, do you see your mamma here? She ain't so do as I says, Ricky."

"Mamma says no hollering. Hollering is bad."

"Okay, okay. Then just yell 'Pieces of eight! Pieces of eight!' like a pirate parrot, tardo."

"What? What?" Ricky shouted back as he rocked, preoccupied with ten restless fingers that fidgeted in front of his belly.

"Shoot, just yell 'Who goes there?' or 'Yo-ho-ho' or something. Whatever you want," Skeet said before he ducked back inside.

"Okay. Yell not holler. Pieces of eight! Pieces of eight!" Ricky replied. A smug grin blossomed on his face, caught up in a pirate's life and a full-fledged member of the break-in in progress.

Glad to be out of the wind, Skeet and Jackie felt their way down a main hall of shadows cast from a dim light at the far end. Jackie was awed by what he saw. Magnificent wooden mantels, gold-framed portraits of creepy subjects, small bright *objet d'art* made of plaster, porcelain, clay and milk glass, plates of china and crystal, tea sets of silver, ceilings that were twelve feet high, and a double stairway wider than his house. When they reached the end of the hall, he saw the small but colorful Tiffany lamp that provided their only light.

"What are we looking for?" Jackie asked. He whispered though it appeared only Skeet was there to hear.

Exasperated that this Negro companion should even question him, Skeet replied, "I don't know, you idiot. The Poe guy said treasure. I don't know, maybe a map or something?" With no moonlight to breach the windows, when they entered a parlor or sitting room or something off the hall, Skeet considered turning on the lights. He rubbed the wall inside the arched doorway until his hand hit something made of wood and a flashlight fell on the floor. He flicked it on.

"Ha. We're good now," he said and moved quickly through the large arched passage to an adjacent room. The deep silence was broken only by a low creaking sound somewhere deep inside the walls and the whistle of the wind through cracks in the window frames. He scanned the room. The beam from the flashlight splashed a far wall covered floor to ceiling with shelves of books behind old leather chairs with high backs. Tucked behind the leg of one chair, the light reflected off two red eyes and one nasty set of canine teeth married to a low growl that wasn't meant as a warning.

The Castle had no moat and didn't need one. The Dansons, owners of the Castle, had their baby—a black Rottweiler named Hitchcock. "Hitch," a healthy specimen of guard dog, easily weighed over a hundred pounds. The boys could see only his head, which appeared to be the size of a bushel basket. Black with a touch of tan under his muzzle, he was all eyes and teeth.

Jackie was the first to move. He grabbed an antique floor lamp and swung it like a baseball bat toward the dog. The shade flew off and hit the dog just behind its ear. Then he flung the pole beyond the dog. With the distraction, Skeet pushed Jackie aside and ran through a double pocket door opening opposite where they entered. When Jackie cleared the doorway, Skeet banged the doors shut. Hearts beating in an unrehearsed duet, they backpedaled until they ran into a large desk of carved walnut covered with papers, a telephone, and a small tape recorder. Skeet kept the flashlight pointed toward the pocket doors. They listened as the dog growled, pawed, and scratched like he might come right through the wood at any minute. Suddenly the flashlight died. Skeet shook it, which changed nothing with the light but the dog stopped its whine. The pawing stopped as well. The boys remained still. Wind packed with the tang of old wood, dirty leather, and Cuban cigars whistled a high-pitched C-note through an opening somewhere. A minute passed, maybe two. They heard nothing. When Skeet smacked the flashlight against the palm of his hand, the beam reappeared. It jittered across the floor to the door where they last heard the dog. The muffled growl returned. Jackie grabbed the flashlight from Skeet's hand and spun quickly to the side wall. Another huge bookcase stuffed with old volumes covered the entire wall except for a narrow door where Hitch had reappeared.

Skeet grabbed the light from Jackie, slammed the pocket doors open, and dashed down the hall, back to the window he had opened minutes earlier. Jackie followed. He had the presence of mind to close the pocket door behind him as he made his way to the same open window.

Skeet hit the ground with a three-point thud—one leg bent under the other, butt cheek, and then head. Under normal conditions a jump from eight feet was not a big deal, but diving through an open window with a bear-sized pooch on his heels was less than normal. Jackie saw Skeet crawl out from under the window and made a more graceful exit. With his arms fully extended, Jackie hung eighteen inches off the grass. Before he released he looked back inside. There was no sign of the dog, but on the window glass he saw a small strange red handprint, one definitely too small to be Skeet's.

In the end the biggest difference in the boys' landings wasn't the distance to the ground but the dog that had exited the house somewhere, somehow, and now had the three boys cornered. Hitch stood back about twenty feet from the boys, far enough away that he could not smell the wet spots beneath Skeet's zipper and down his pants legs. The only weapon they had was the flashlight rendered unlit and semi-worthless when it hit the ground during Skeet's flying exit.

Skeet cranked his arm back, shouted "Run," then winged the metal flashlight at the dog, hitting him in the side right behind his front leg. As soon as he released the flashlight, Skeet set course for the front of the house; Jackie made a similar motion toward the rear of the house. When he heard Hitch yelp, he took a look back and saw Ricky plastered against the house. Hitch took a few choppy steps toward Skeet, then changed direction, pointed toward Ricky, and hunkered down. Crouched like a sphinx with an angry dog head, Hitch only had eyes for the mentally confused boy. Too scared to move, Ricky no longer rocked. He lifted his knees higher and higher, running in place, too terrified to do anything else. "Pieces of eight! Pieces of eight!" he cried, pulling at his hair, his ears, and his crotch.

Without a second thought and without a second to spare, Jackie pulled off his shirt and twirled it propeller-like in front of him—bravado shown only between a lion tamer with a big cat—as he tiptoed toward his frantic friend. The dog shifted his attention away from Ricky and tracked Jackie. Every move the colored teen made caused the dog to growl until Jackie slid in alongside Ricky and Hitch attacked. Jackie reached forward, his shirt wrapped around his forearm, which offered the margin of protection Jackie needed to pull his arm from the dog's jaws. He was bleeding but he still had his hand. And the Rottweiler had the boys trapped between the cold stone walls.

The gusts that whistled fair warning inside the house had blown themselves out, replaced by a calm that surrounded the two regretful and unsuccessful vandals suckered into their impossible predicament. Ricky hiccupped and gagged like he might retch. Jackie's ability to think dimmed like the flashlight. Sweat ran between his shoulder blades and down the centerline of his back as fear augered deeper inside of him. He shivered when a chill filled the air. It didn't come as a blast or in a breeze, but a temperature inversion that sucked the humidity and sound with it. Hitch shifted his posture from the vigilant crouch to an attentive, stiff-legged alert. Ears tall. Eyes wide. The hair on his back spiked in porcupine mode. The dog whimpered, yawned, and whimpered again with his head cocked back toward the tidal inlet alongside the house. In the stillness, a mist drifted toward the boys. The cloud roiled as it rolled; the closer it came, the colder they got. Then, as if moved by forces of nature, the mist molded a smallish figure of a man. But he (or it) was not really a person. At least he did not appear to be a person, a real person, because he (or it) was translucent. Even the clothes he (or it) wore, strange as they were, did not block sight of the shrubs behind him. Hitch reacted first.

He tucked his tail, yelped, and charged off in the same direction Skeet had gone.

"Come on, Ricky. Let's go," Jackie said as he inched away from the see-through figure in the fog. Ricky didn't budge. Jackie was already on the move, but when Ricky did not follow, he turned back toward his confused classmate. He reached for Ricky's wrist. "Come on," Jackie insisted. He yanked on Ricky's arm hard enough to pull him off balance. Ricky jerked his wrist from Jackie's grip.

Ricky had stopped crying. His hands now down at his side, he began a slow, hypnotic walk toward the figure stalled on the grass a short distance to his front. He showed no signs of nervousness. He walked without his usual limp. Jackie stood and wondered. The tension in his body melted away, but his stomach whammed and echoed the pounding inside his chest. His eyes popped wide, fixed straight ahead on Ricky. His jaw dropped when he tried to scream, but all that came out was a wordless moan. His throat was too dry to utter even a whisper of the words he knew he should say. Ricky moved farther and farther away, baby steps that seemed never to touch the ground; he floated on air, cold air. The short man, shorter than Ricky at five feet tall, raised his arms in an embrace. Again, the fog from the inlet crawled up the bank and along the grass until it reached the spot where the figure stood. As Ricky reached out to grip the outstretched hands, the fog formed a cloud around both of them.

"Ricky," Jackie screamed, breaking his icy silence. "Ricky." Nothing. Jackie looked around. He grabbed the flashlight that had ended up near an azalea by the house. He smacked it against his palm several times with no luck, never taking his eyes off the cloud. The chill was more constant now. The marsh-side noises of the night were strangely nonexistent. Jackie heard nothing except his blood as it pulsed through his ears and a soft voice deeper inside his head that challenged him. *Do something.*

With long strides on weak knees, Jackie crossed the lawn to the edge of the cloud. In his right hand, he held the flashlight, now nothing more than a blunt object. He reared back and cocked his arm like he would to throw a long strike from center field. He twisted toward the cloud and with his left hand he reached into it. He felt an extreme cold, much colder than where he was standing, but no Ricky. He pulled his arm out and called for Ricky. No response. The voice in his head spoke louder. *Do something.*

Jackie stepped into the cloud. The cold was a deep, frigid, burning sensation he had never felt before, even colder than his holiday visits to his Uncle Art's in Poughkeepsie, New York. Then it all melted away. He was standing there, one minute alone in the cloud, and the next, standing with Ricky on the lawn. The boys stared at each other. Ricky with a glowing pink face and Jackie as pale as his black skin would allow. The cloud was gone and with it the chill.

"Come on. Let's get out of here."

Ricky simply replied, "I know."

CHAPTER 7

From the outside the building looked like many others. Nondescript stucco front layered with a flaking façade set back off Bay Street close to the river. For weeks the large sign from the front had been in the shop for a fresh coat of paint. The inside could use the same; actually, it could use a few gallons of disinfectant and bleach, anything to kill the mold or mask the peculiar odor—a mix of flatulence and old-man halitosis. Jackie had never seen the inside of the Beaufort Police Department. His stomach was filled with a nervous gas that swelled from his navel to his tonsils. Nothing about him offered encouragement to be still. He stood between his parents, Hestelle and Irvin Eddings, concentrating on the mousetrap wedged in the corner behind a messy gray metal desk and listening to the moan of the ceiling fan furred with dust.

On the wall behind the desk, a lineup of beady-eyed black-and-white portraits in thin wooden frames stared back at him. On the left was the President of the United States, Lyndon Johnson, then the not-so-familiar faces of Governor Russell and Mayor Scheper, and, on the far right, was Otis T. Heimer, who had been the Chief of Police for twenty of the past thirty-two years he had been a member of the force.

By Monday after a weekend of super-sleuth detective work that would have made Perry Mason proud, the chief had rounded up a roomful of people to explain a few things. The first in a series of reported incidents came from Geordie Swanson, who bumped into his friend Otis on Saturday morning at Anderson's Barber Shop. His words, *those kids were up to no good.* Heimer said he would look into it.

When the chief swung by the office minutes later to read the log from the night shift, he read the details of another reported break-in at the Lord Carteret Motel. By the time Monday rolled around, he had sketchy details behind the first two incidents, both on Friday night. But, when Ed Danson came in Monday morning with a boy's bloodied, shredded Ban-Lon shirt, the events of a typically quiet football Friday night struck him as odd, and possibly related. Highlighted by other facts Danson provided—the damaged pole lamp in the study and his flashlight on the lawn—the chief had cause to believe these were more than coincidental, random, and separate disturbances.

Seated in a tattered chair with horsehair stuffing bulging from the rip in the cushion, Otis Heimer held court, southern style, with all the parties standing. He waved his hand to close the office door, then dribbled a slug of tobacco juice into a half-full repurposed Coke bottle. In addition to Jackie and his parents, Chief Heimer directed the presence of Geordie Swanson, Gene Skyles, and Ed Danson.

"Now…" He rummaged through the chaos in print that lay on his desk to find a tablet with his notes. "I called y'all in here 'cause I want to make sure we're on the same sheet of music on what's happened around here. Mr. Swanson here says he saw this colored boy running away from his boat on Friday night."

"Well, to be specific, I saw him running up the alley. It was Jeff Oatley at the yacht club who said he saw him on the boat."

"So, what you're sayin' is you just saw this boy runnin', is that right?"

Geordie Swanson looked toward Jackie with an empty face and nodded. "Yeah, up the alley away from my boat."

"Where's Jeff? I told him to be here," Heimer said and waited for a response. When none came, he reached for his Coke bottle and added another juicy brown drool.

"And you told me you knew it was this boy here, Jackie Eddings. Not nobody else?"

Again, Swanson nodded. "Positive. No question about it."

Jackie fidgeted from behind his mother's hip; Irvin Eddings yanked on his son's arm to steady his feet.

"Are you sure, Geordie? You know all them coloreds look alike."

"I saw this boy only a few days ago. I saw him in a classroom over at Beaufort Junior High. He was wearing that shirt or, at least, one that looked exactly like that one." He pointed at the ripped shirt on top of Otis Heimer's desk.

"Ask Skyles, there. He was in that same classroom. He saw the boy in that shirt, too."

Chief Heimer pointed a fat, tobacco-stained forefinger toward Gene Skyles.

"Yes, sir, I saw this boy and he was wearing that kind of shirt, but there are probably many of those around, sir," Skyles said.

Otis Heimer was an old-time police officer. He was one of the "Magnificent Seven," the original city officers. He knew most everybody in Beaufort. Gene Skyles was new to him, and he wasn't sure what to make of the young college kid from Virginia. "Okay, well then, Mr. Skyles, since you're talkin' can you tell me if this boy here had anything to do with what might have happened in your room Friday night?"

"No, sir, I can't. I wasn't there when it happened. When I returned from the high school football game, I found the door partially open. When I looked inside, it was all torn up. I didn't see anybody at all at the motel at that point."

"Had you seen anyone earlier?" Heimer asked.

"I saw a Negro man in a suit park a Chevy Del ray in the lot, and he headed off down the street there by the arsenal. Probably around half past six, just before I left for the game."

The chief nodded. "Had to be that colored lawyer, that Caplin fella. He's the only one with a Delray in town and he parks it at the motel. Some of them colored housekeepers keep an eye on it for him during the day." Heimer shared his disgust with a shake of his head and continued, "Nice car. Not sure how he got the thing, though."

Again, Heimer reached for the Coke bottle. He rolled his eyes up toward his guests, specifically at Ed Danson.

"Where was this shirt, Ed? You ever seen it before?"

"Nah. Never saw the shirt or that boy before," Danson said.

"So no clue how it got there?"

"Your guess is as good as mine. You know Hitch. I mean he's probably the best guard dog in town. Grace and I left on the bus for Durham to watch the Tigers game at Duke on Saturday. Bus left at three thirty or so on Friday. I mean, if this boy was in the house and Hitch caught him, there'd be more than a ripped shirt. There is some blood on the shirt, at least it looks like blood."

Chief Heimer picked up the rag that was, apparently, a shirt at one point. He leaned back in his chair, pushed his glasses farther up his nose, and examined it for all the group to see, stretching the collar, which was held to the shoulder of the shirt by a thread or two. He looked up and saw Jackie in front of his desk. He pulled his glasses back down his nose and said, "Come here, boy."

Jackie hesitated. He looked to his father for approval. Irvin Eddings, hands crossed behind his back, motioned the move forward with a nod.

"What do you say, boy? Is this here your shirt?"

The knot in Jackie's throat swelled. He knew better than to lie. Ants of anticipation crawled up and down his legs. He choked to swallow. "Yes, sir," he answered. His fingers picked at scabs on his forearm. Heimer noticed.

"What did you do to your arm there?" Heimer said, tipping the Coke bottle toward Jackie.

"I cut it, sir."

"Ya know, boy, I kinda figured that. How?"

"Out in de field," Jackie answered with no offer for details.

The chief leaned forward and locked in on Jackie's eyes. "Now don't be lying to me, boy. You tell me, out in the field doing what?"

Before Jackie had a chance to choke out his answer, there was a knock at the door.

"What is it?" the chief growled.

The door opened and Robert Caplin walked through. While the others looked on, he took off his hat and closed the door.

"Sorry I am late, Chief Heimer. I had another appointment that ran a little over," Caplin said.

"And why are you here at all, your honor?" Heimer asked, his voice raised in a sing-song tone, surprised to be interrupted in his cross-examination.

"Mr. Eddings mentioned you had requested to see Jackie and I thought I could offer some assistance for the boy; that's all," the attorney said.

Chief Heimer was unaccustomed to challenges, especially from any coloreds and especially the colored lawyer in town. "Now I'm not sure there is any need for your help, Mr. Caplin. If you will excuse us, I believe we're having a private discussion concerning some incidents that occurred in Beaufort over the weekend." He looked down at his desk, pushed some papers aside, gathered and shuffled others, and most definitely would not acknowledge Caplin's continued presence.

"Chief Heimer, sir, if you don't mind, as an attorney, I would like to remain to assist my clients."

"Well, now then, Mr. Caplin, let me just tell you again…this is a private discussion and your presence is not needed. Actually"—the chief looked up again—"it's not wanted." The chief raised his brow, opened his eyes wide, and pressed his tongue inside his lower lip. Caplin didn't move. Nobody moved until the chief broke the silence.

"So you hurt your arm in the field?" Heimer continued, ignoring Caplin, the boy once again his focus.

"Sir, in my yard," Jackie said, taking the spotlight off Caplin.

"Not in someone else's yard?"

"No, sir," Jackie answered; he remained noncommittal.

"Who else was with you?" Heimer said.

"Nobody."

"Nobody? You were alone and hurt your arm?"

Jackie nodded.

The chief disregarded the answer and fired back, "Who else was with you at the Castle, boy?"

"He never said he were at de Castle," Irvin Eddings said, moving to the boy's side.

The chief looked up. His faced burned red; veins slithered up his temples and knotted on his forehead. He wasn't buying it. He excused the senior Eddings's comments and opted to drag Caplin back on the carpet.

"So, Judge Caplin," he mocked, "you park your car at the Lord Carteret, don't you?"

"Yes, sir, I do."

"Did you happen to see anything or anyone Friday evening, anything at all happening at the motel?"

"I picked up my car and drove off," he lied. "Just like every other night."

"Boy, I'll tell you. Everything I hear says to me you were there, on the boat, and at the Castle, and probably in that room, too. Weren't you, huh? And sounds like you were with somebody else. Who was the white kid running down the street with you, the one on the boat with you? Was he at the Castle, too?" Heimer said, looking down his nose to Jackie.

"Now hold on, Heimer," Robert Caplin said. The police chief contorted his face in total disbelief.

Caplin's presence threatened the chief's standard operating procedure for investigating matters. He had never had a Negro man familiar with the law stand in for a case or a hearing or even a discussion and he had no idea how to get rid of this one.

"Okay, I think I've heard enough for now," Heimer said. He stood behind the desk, but bent down to address Jackie straight on. "Boy, I'm still looking into this. I am going to talk to Jeff Oatley, and I'll have you back in here if I need to, to have him look at you close up. And if he tells me there was a white boy with you on that boat, then you better tell me who that was or you are going to do time for you and him both."

"Time?" Irvin Eddings blurted.

"Chief, best not get ahead of yourself here. This boy has done nothing wrong. You heard him. Until you have evidence that he has committed any crime, the boy is innocent. And he remains innocent until he is proven guilty," Caplin said, his voice soft and his tone mellow, his chest inches from the chief, his nose well above the portly man behind the badge.

"Y'all can leave. This investigation is over...for now," Heimer harrumphed. He gave the colored attorney a sour look and watched, hands on hips, as the room cleared, then reached into his desk drawer for his pouch of Red Man chewing tobacco.

Outside the air was cooler, fresher, lighter, light enough to lift the elephant that had been sitting on Jackie's chest. After a couple deep breaths, a cavalcade of goosebumps marched slowly down his legs and disappeared somewhere on the sidewalk. The knot in his stomach was gone. He felt free again, exhausted but free. And it felt good.

Robert Caplin led the Eddings family to a spot out of hearing distance and away from passersby.

"I'm not sure about Heimer. He believes he's a self-appointed judge and jury with these things. He's way out of bounds here, but we need to step back and let him do whatever he plans to do," the smartly dressed attorney said. "I'll have my eyes and ears open. If anything starts to rumble, I'll let you know, but you need to tell me if you hear anything, too."

"My boy ain't done nothin', Robert. He would never do dem things da' Heimer accused him of doing," Hestelle said.

"Okay. I understand that. I understand how you feel," Caplin said as he looked down toward Jackie. "So tell me, slugger, were you on that boat?"

"No, sir," Jackie said without hesitation. His eyes and chin dropped to the sidewalk, but bounced back up. "I don't know anything about any of da', uh, that stuff, Mr. Caplin, sir," Jackie said with a look toward his mother. He rushed his speech almost to the point of slurring his words. "All da' be wrong. I wouldn't do da'…that."

"And the Castle? Did you go to the Castle?"

"No, sir," Jackie argued. "I wasn't around de Castle."

"Can't you leave de boy alone, Robert?" Irvin Eddings asked. "I think he's been through a lot already, a lot of unnecessary treatment. Jackie wouldn't do dem things. He a good boy."

Jackie looked up and fashioned a slight smile.

"One more? May I ask him one more thing, Irvin?" Caplin said, addressing the boy's father directly.

"Yeah. One more. Da' be okay."

Caplin often offered free counsel throughout the Gullah community, but beyond his pro bono services, he made frequent visits to old Gabe. In almost every visit with Gabe, Caplin ran into Jackie. He knew the boy admired his grandpa; the two were inseparable. Gabe was Jackie's wisdom and an honest check on his conscience.

To ask his question, Caplin took a knee in front of Jackie, his lanky frame reduced to a size or two shorter than the boy.

"So, tell me, Jackie, were you at the motel like Chief Heimer said?" His question was quiet, intentionally quiet so neither parent could hear. Jackie hesitated without ever looking at the lawyer. The pause was enough for Caplin to follow up with, "I need to tell your Grandpa Gabe."

The attorney closed his eyes. He never saw Jackie nod his head yes. He really didn't need the boy's response and coaxing a lie was not his intent. He left it there.

"I need to move along, Irvin. Got other people who have problems, real problems. Problems they generated, not problems others dreamed up," Caplin said when he reached for Irvin Eddings's hand. He put his hat back on and tipped the brim gently toward Hestelle. When he walked off, he looked back. "I'll be seeing you around your grandpa's house, Jackie."

CHAPTER 8

At school, the usual Monday morning buzz about *American Bandstand* gave way to gossip about how the cops were investigating three break-ins over the weekend and that Jackie Eddings had to go see the chief of police. Fueled by his unquestioned false bravado, Skeet Gundy was quick to add substance to the rumors. He knew his boasting was safe; none of his band of prepubescent followers would dare challenge what he said. Skeet fudged the details of the boat search and never mentioned how Hoss tucked his tail and ran off. He quickly brushed over the scene at the motel, but boasted heavily of his stealth and bravery at the Castle—how he outwitted the guard dog, fed the black boy's shirt to him, and walked off after saving their lives.

"Ain't that right, Hoss?" Skeet would say. The response, regardless, was always, "You got it, Skeet."

What Skeet didn't count on was how what he said would come back to bite him when those around him noted that Skeet chose Jackie Eddings, the colored boy, and not any of them to be a part of his exploits. By Tuesday afternoon, on the school lawn after classes, they showed no signs they might forget that fact.

"Hey, Skeet! Where's your pet coon?" one boy asked.

"Yeah, Skeet's a Geechee lover now, for sure," came the reply from another.

Skeet didn't like the tone in their voices.

"Sambo Skeet! How's that sound, fellas?" one said, which earned a good laugh from the crowd and a solid knuckle punch in the sternum from Skeet.

"Yeah, sounds 'bout right to me," was the twangy shout from the other side of the circle around Skeet. With trouble brewing, "watch dog" Hoss Lassiter drifted to the periphery.

"Y'all just shut your traps," Skeet yelled. The group of six teens laughed, confident that as a group there was safety in numbers and they were less subject to Skeet's frequent-flying fists and point-toed shoes.

In the midst of the gibes, one boy shouted out, "Bet your Geechee buddy ratted on you, Skeet. I mean the chief probably had him crying and all. He probably told the whole story about how you and Mike were both in on this."

"Yeah, you make life bad for that tar baby and he ain't going to care about you," suggested a chubby kid with Einstein hair. "Speak of the devil, here comes your pet piccaninny now."

With that comment the boys in the circle quieted their harassment. Skeet turned to watch Jackie walk out of the school, headed in their direction. Jackie noticed the ring of boys about the time he reached the sidewalk, right before Skeet emerged from the crowd. Jackie planted one foot to pivot and change direction. As he turned he heard a voice in his head whisper, *Da sidewalk be for yours too. Be careful dem white boys but dey not own da'. Go 'head. Walk da' way. Dey needs to see you ain't scared.* He looked around to see who else might be watching and realized those who were certainly would not join him. He didn't turn; he kept walking toward the crowd.

"Hey Geechee boy, come over here." Skeet led his posse of ne'er-do-wells down the sidewalk toward Jackie.

Carl E. Linke

Jackie had grown accustomed to the effects of adrenaline on his body, like ice in his veins at the Castle and a heat from a furnace in front of the chief. But this adrenaline was different. The pounding inside his chest grew faster. He grew light-headed. He blinked and wobbled, small steps, closer to the boys. Others—even some of the girls from the class—who heard Skeet's challenge were quick to circle up around the boys.

"So, what did the police chief say to you, boy? Hope you ain't in trouble," Skeet said. He jammed his hands into his pockets and rocked back on his heels, his head cocked to one side.

"No," Jackie volunteered. His eyes were on Skeet, but he was well aware of the mix of eyes, ears, noses, and bangs of the others, none of which posed a threat. He knew Skeet controlled them through fear, but on their own, they could care less about Jackie. Though not friendly, like Ricky Clemonds, the white kids in the group were much like the kids he had lived around his entire life. Skeet was a different story.

"What did he ask you? Did he ask about the boat?"

"Yeah."

"Did you tell him somebody else broke into that motel room, huh? Did you tell him we was there?"

"Yeah, I mean no."

"What? You told him we was there but somebody else got there before us?"

"No, I didn't tell him anything," Jackie said, still eyeing the all-white crowd that had grown larger and closer.

"Well, dang, Buckwheat. You done good. Did he ask about the Castle?"

"Yeah."

"What did you tell him, huh?"

"Nothing."

"You didn't mention my name, did ya, boy?" Skeet quizzed, now a step closer to Jackie.

Jackie said nothing, but on one hand his fingers curled into a fist.

A voice from farther back in the crowd yelled, "Bet that colored boy ratted on you, Skeet."

Embarrassment, more than the words suggested, provoked Skeet. He laid into Jackie with both hands, sending him back about four feet. School books flew in all directions. Jackie staggered and slipped to regain his footing.

"You did give him my name, huh, didn't you, boy? You ratted on me." Skeet moved nose to nose with Jackie.

"I didn't rat on you," Jackie said convincingly, without any suggestion of weakness, though he realized his odds.

"You did, too…you…little…jigaboo," Skeet said with a push after each accusation. The crowd shifted to allow more room for Skeet to push Jackie around. Then Skeet grabbed Jackie by the shoulders. Jackie reached to ward off the attack, but the older boy had the leverage and threw him to the ground. Jackie landed on his backside then scrambled back to his feet before Skeet or anyone else could jump on him. As soon as he stood, Skeet shoved him across the circle. Off balance, Jackie banged into Hoss Lassiter, who shoved Jackie back across the ring into a chubby boy with a flattop who shoved him sideways through the middle of the group. Back and forth Jackie bounced without a word, though the crowd had plenty to say.

"You don't belong here."

"Get out of our school."

"We don't need no cotton-pickers here," a voice said, then chuckled.

"We don't like rats!"

"Go cry to your mamma."

"Yo mamma," he heard once more before he was shoved hard back toward Skeet.

"Don't trust no cotton-pickers, Skeet. He lyin', he dyin'!"

Skeet threw a haymaker that would have leveled Jackie had he not stepped back. When he whiffed, the oomph behind Skeet's punch took him to his knee. Jackie stepped toward him. When he bent over Skeet, two of the bystanders grabbed him long enough for Skeet to get back on his feet and land a sucker punch to the gut that folded Jackie in half, his arms wrapped around his midsection. The pain of the blow was not nearly as powerful as the shock.

"Don't hurt your little coon-buddy," someone hollered. Skeet took his eyes off Jackie and looked around the crowd. Some were smiling, some yelled words of encouragement, and some just stood there, numbed by the scene. The girls in the back, a safe distance away, covered their mouths and eyes. Several began to cry.

"Come on banjo-lips, show us how tough you are. When you're done with that sissy, I'll show you a thing or two," a tall boy in the back yelled. When he saw Skeet take a step in his direction, the long-legged kibitzer hightailed down the street past two young mothers on their way to meet their children after school. The women stared at the boy as he breezed by, then looked the other direction and noticed the crowd. They could hear the taunts and finally saw Skeet reach over and grab Jackie by his shirt with Jackie flailing to fend off the attack. The women were horrified. Petrified. They looked at each other and immediately looked around for help, screaming, "Fight! Fight!" They noticed a man coming toward them, a half block away on North Street. They waved frantically and pointed toward the crowd of teens.

The man looked in their direction. When their alarm registered with him, he spotted the circle of boys. He could tell one of the fighters was a Negro boy, one he knew. Still concerned that his buddy Otis Heimer didn't throw the colored kid in jail for trespassing and vandalizing his boat, Geordie Swanson waited and watched. *Justice comes to those who deserve it*, he thought. Definitely true for this Negro. Unfortunately, the screaming women gave him no chance for an alibi or excuse. Unsure why or if he should stop the fight—after all, boys will be boys—Swanson stomped across the lawn, his efforts at least a temporary relief from the crazed mothers.

His size did not allow him to move too fast, but while he approached the crowd, he noticed, though the fight was one-sided—white against colored—none of the white boys seemed to be overly supportive of the white kid.

"Hey, knock it off!" Geordie yelled as he gently pushed kids out of the way to get to the two boys in the middle. When they heard his voice, kids scattered every which way. With fewer heads to block his view, Swanson recognized the white kid in the fight as the troublemaker from Miss Forten's class the day of his presentation. Things began to make more sense.

With an adult on the scene, more of the boys started to bail; a few girls waited, curious to see how much trouble the boys would be in.

Swanson walked directly between the two fighters and grabbed each with a hand. "What the heck are you two doing? What's the problem?"

Skeet, still charged by his early punches, made futile attempts to work free, but a man the size of Geordie Swanson was no match for the skinny fifteen-year-old.

Swanson tightened his grip on each of their shirts and pulled them a little closer to his chest while he looked over his shoulder at the two young mothers standing on the sidewalk, now wrapped in conversation. Swanson was able to make out only a few words, which included integration, school board, and lynchings.

"Who started this?" Swanson demanded. Neither of the boys responded. Their silence fueled his rage. Veins appeared on his forehead and forearms as he gripped the boys' shirts even tighter. "I said...who started this?" Still nothing.

Since the crowd had now dissolved to nothing, he carefully lifted each of the boys enough to leave only their toes on the ground. "Aren't you two in the same class, Miss Forten's class? I remember you two." He looked at Skeet. "You were the smart aleck wise guy, the guy with the big mouth." Then he turned his head toward Jackie, grunted, and gripped him harder. "And, seems we meet again there, Mr. Eddings. You out for more trouble? Got a chip on your shoulder? Think you're some tough guy now or something?"

Jackie wanted to respond but no words came to mind, none that would convince Swanson and not ire Skeet short of another fight at another time in another place.

Swanson pulled Jackie close until he could put his forehead on the top of the boy's head. "You really can't afford to get yourself into any more trouble right now, boy," he said, slowly emphasizing each word. "The chief has his eyes on you and so do I." He relaxed his grip, stood tall again, and threatened, "What do you say the three of us take a walk? Let's go visit Chief Heimer and have a talk about a few things."

Hearing that, Skeet pried at Swanson's grip and kicked repeatedly at his shins. He realized a visit with the chief might have repercussions that would land him in the reformatory in Florence. As a foster child and ward of the courts, Skeet was living with the Newcombs, Mailyn and Hank. The social worker who placed Skeet with the Newcombs had told him *one more stupid stunt, Robin, and you'll go up the river as they say.* Nothing Skeet did had any effect on his burly captor, but when the flash of a "bubble gum machine" atop a squad car caught his eye, Skeet sensed the grip soften.

A hundred feet away, down the middle of North Street, a South Carolina Highway Patrol cruiser led a motorcade of vehicles. Behind the wheel of the lead vehicle was Corporal Stanley Francis, known locally as "Francis the Talking Mule" because he was considered as stubborn and lazy as one. He poked along at no more than five miles per hour per instructions from his boss. *That uppity loudmouth Negro wants attention, we'll give him attention, nice and slow like. And if he stirs up any trouble we'll make sure he gets all the attention he wants.* Any of the junior high schoolers in the yard could move faster than the Mule and the three black Cadillacs behind him. All three escorted vehicles were like new, 1959 Eldorados with dual taillights halfway up the giant fins on either side in the back.

Something about the string of cars was different. Everyone within eyesight, including Geordie Swanson, strained to identify the passengers. He let loose of the boys and tromped flat-footed toward the street for a closer look. Jackie and Skeet had similar moves, in opposite directions and away from the silent procession.

Despite the slow speed, Swanson was only able to determine that each car was driven by a Negro man and each car had three other occupants. Though he could see figures seated front and rear, Geordie could not identify any of them. He noted all three of the cars had Georgia license plates, a strange fact knowing the escort was one lone South Carolina Highway patrolman.

It wasn't until after the cars passed that Swanson realized his two young fighters were nowhere to be seen; that in itself was a blessing. He had more important business to tend to now.

CHAPTER 9

The screen door creaked, slammed, and rebounded twice before Hestelle Eddings could get words out of her mouth.

"Young man, you knows better than to let da' door close like da'. You better pays more attention to how you come an' go around here."

Jackie gnashed his teeth and looked her in the eye. He kicked out a chair from under the kitchen table and plopped down. His actions, not all that different from any other day, were the typical teenage incommunicado.

"How was school?" she asked, wiping her wet hands on a flowered apron that draped loosely over her neck and around her waist.

"I hates da' school, Mamma," he said with his elbows on the table, his head pressed firmly between his hands.

"That school," she emphasized. "How many times does I needs to remind you? Speak properly." She pulled out a chair and sat across from her son. A stern concern shriveled her face. "Now what, Jackie? What happened dis time?"

"A fight, Mamma. Dey tried to make me fight dem."

She ignored correcting his grammar a second time and angled closer, her brow slipped to a vee as her words lingered. "What you mean fight?"

Jackie turned away and slapped his forearms on the table. "Fight, Mamma. I mean, fight! I left school and a bunch of dem trapped me in a circle. Dey was all watching. Everybody."

"Teachers?"

"No, dey weren't teachers. Just de kids, de white kids. Boys and some girls in de back."

"What'd dey do? Who was it?" she asked calmly, though she found it difficult to appear compassionate when every cell in her being roared with anger.

Jackie wouldn't answer. He bent over the table and stared down, his head nestled in the palms of his hands. He didn't want to drag his parents into this. He didn't need his parents' help. After all, it was his parents who put him in the school. He missed his friends, his colored friends. He had no one to talk to. His days were zoo-like. People staring at him, talking about him. Fear filled every second of his day. He felt some of the fear even when he attended the Negro school, but now it was constant, from the time he left his house until he walked back through door. Even then, he feared what his parents might do if they knew.

"Just a bunch of dem white kids. De boys in my class. Seemed like all dem. I don't know. Dey was a lot." He wouldn't take his eyes off the table. "Just forget it, Mamma. Leave me alone."

But she wouldn't. "Did dey hit you?"

Jackie sighed but did not answer.

"I says...did dem white boys hit you?"

"Two of dem pushed me around, I mean from side to side in de circle."

"Did dey hit you?" she said, her voice louder, but with a worried sympathy only a mother knows.

"No," he lied.

"Did you hit any of dem?"

Jackie raised his head and caught her eyes for a split second. He saw her tears before he looked away. "No."

"Did you run away?"

Jackie whipped his head back toward his mother. "No, Mamma, I ain't goin' to run from dem."

"Jackie, you can't fights a mob. You can't," she said as fear leached through her anger. She had heard the stories of the violence beyond hatred which led the march of racial unrest through the South, from Mississippi to Alabama to Georgia. Brutal torture and lynchings. Bodies found weeks and months after the Negroes disappeared. One—Emmett Till—was just fourteen years old, the same as her son. "You can't stand der, Jackie. You gotta run," she said deliberately. Her heart, lodged in her throat, choked out the only words she could find.

"Mamma, I ain't goin' to run from dem."

Hestelle shut her eyes, then opened them and looked at her hands on the table. They shook and she couldn't stop them. She got up from the table and wiped her nose with her wrist as she walked toward the window so her son would not see her tears. Out the window she saw the two white neighbor boys. Timmy Chambers wore a white ten-gallon hat and a cheap leather holster which hung down past his knee. His younger brother Fred had a headband with one feather sticking up in the back. He was crouched behind a broad live oak, his toy rifle pointed at his brother. Both fired shots endlessly from rolls of red caps that cracked with each pull of the trigger. Harmless play. Free to do whatever they wanted. She wanted the same freedom for her son, but knew life wasn't the same. Not outside this neighborhood. She stared. Every breath brought more pain; every exhale carried pain with it. The tears lingered, but as they slowed she walked back to her son, patted his shoulder, and continued on to the pantry.

"How did you get away from dem?" she asked.

"Some man. Da' man da' was at de police station, de one wid da' boat."

Hestelle turned back with interest.

"He came up de street an' pulled de kids off me."

Hestelle didn't know what to think. She was amazed Geordie Swanson would defend her son, the kid he had just accused of looting his boat.

"And—"

"He pulled us apart, den de Highway Patrol car came up."

"Highway Patrol? Came up to you?" With fear still screaming through her like a tornado, she grew light-headed and used the wall for support.

"No, de car was leading a bunch of cars up Bay Street. I couldn't see much because de guy had hold to me an' my back was to de street. He let go so he could go up to de street for a look. I just ran."

Hestelle couldn't find words. She clutched herself with both arms and paced, out of sight from her son.

"I hate da' school, Mamma. I don't want to be in da' school no more. Dey don't want me der and—"

"Hush up, boy. And it's 'that' school and 'they' don't. You ain't leavin' da' school, you hear me?" She stepped in front of the table. "You look at me, child."

Jackie lifted his eyes and saw his mother standing in front of him, her face hardened with a scowl. He lifted his head when she folded her arms across her chest.

"Dem white kids ain't no better than you. You belongs in da' school. Da' why your father and I puts you dey. You belongs dey just as much as dem white kids. Da' your school, Jackie. You hears me? Da' your school." She looked at her son like she was scolding a puppy. "Does you know how much dis mean to Grandpa Gabe? His whole life he be waiting for de chance to do what dem white men does. A chance to hold his head high and not wait in de shadows. To walk in de front door of all dem buildings. To go where he want. To sit where he want. To speak his mind where he want. He wants da' for you an' you has de chance to be what he always wanted to be. Da' your school, Jackie. Da' ain't changing' an' you ain't leavin'. You understands me?"

"But, Mamma, dey—"

"Don't you 'but mamma' me. I says, does you understands me, child?"

"Yes, Mamma," Jackie said. His jaw tightened.

"Now, get up, go back dey an' do your homework before your daddy get home. We see what he say, too."

"But, Mamma—"

She looked at him, a look that said, "I dare you to say one more word."

"Mamma…we ain't gots to tell daddy about de fight, do we?"

"The fight! An' no…don't has to mention da'," Hestelle said, fearing what her husband might do. She closed her eyes with her hands formed for prayer in front of her lips.

Jackie closed his eyes and sighed. He pushed away from the table and went to his room, which was little more than a single bed with a closet. With books on the floor, bedside, Jackie fell onto the mattress, stared at the ceiling, and thought of Grandpa Gabe while the wheels inside his head began to scheme his survival.

Hours before, curious gawkers craned their necks from sidewalks and storefronts as the motorcade crept toward the swing bridge across the Intracoastal Waterway and onto Lady's Island. Corporal Francis, on orders from higher up, maintained a constant highway speed of ten miles per hour, which caused the traffic on the two lanes of the loosely paved, mostly crumbled tarmac of Highway 21 to back up for miles. Duty-bound Francis didn't care one iota. He had his orders and, more importantly, his cigar.

Across the bridge, landmarks were more natural than not. The only two manmade markers were the Red & White grocery, about the size of a small two-car garage and, farther down the road, the Beaufort County Airport, a one-strip, no-tower landing field known to locals as "Frogmore International." Beyond a narrow causeway through the marsh and across the tidal Cowen Creek, the road connected Lady's Island to Saint Helena Island, a stretch where the sights included a few shacks slapped together with tar paper over weathered planks and a handful of rundown mobile homes in overgrown, grassy fields.

At the one and only stop sign between Beaufort and the Atlantic Ocean, the string of cars turned right and continued for a half mile to the Penn Center. Once crowned with furrowed fields, the site remained a historic remnant of the post-Civil War Port Royal Experiment, hallowed ground where one could sense the presence of shackled spirits.

Over the years Penn Center had morphed from an academic hall for Negroes to a technical trade school for the colored population and finally stood as a community services center, catering to the Gullah community, locally and throughout Beaufort County. When President Kennedy created the Peace Corps, the federal government piggybacked on the community training in a pilot program to prepare volunteers for aid assignments in Africa. The climate, the agricultural setting, the ancestral knowledge base found in the books of Penn Center library were all ideal for preparing volunteers in the ways, customs, and traits of African tribal life. Interestingly enough, it was about the same time that it became a hub where liberal minds and civil rights activists could host retreats for open discussions and planning sessions to advance their cause.

A head or two more than fifty people—regional staffers and executives of the Southern Christian Leadership Conference from twelve southern states—cloistered in the moonlight beneath the oaks around the Center's main building, the Frissell Community House. Mostly coloreds with a few white faces. Mostly men with a few women. And fewer still, recognizable names such as one entertainer, the "barefoot Madonna," who sang of social justice with a voice that could be heard across the grounds. It was one big "kumbayah" experience. Peace Corps workers integrated into dorms with conference attendees—women in Benezet House, men in Arnett House. The Peace Corps group of six had been at Penn Center for over ten months and knew the facilities well enough that they were responsive to every need of the retreat guests. All the retreats and planning sessions had been somewhat unique, but this retreat had an element of secrecy not disclosed to the planners, attendees, staff, or even Penn's Executive Director Ezra Perry.

Among the Peace Corps volunteers Clifton "Cliff" Gilbert had been a quiet, energetic student. Always willing, first to volunteer. He would drop whatever he was doing to help others. A perfect team player. More than any of the others, Cliff was eager to learn everything there was to learn about Penn Center and the African heritage it preserved. His enthusiasm was exhausting, so much so the other trainees talked about him; all found him to be the model student for the Peace Corps pilot program. What others did not know was his enthusiasm was not all natural-born curiosity and camaraderie. His assignment to Penn Center was considered "of key interest to national security" and far more important than tribal cultures of the Dark Continent.

In the summer of 1963, in the months leading up to the rally known as the March on Washington, J. Edgar Hoover directed his Federal Bureau of Investigation to secretly step up their surveillance of civil rights leader Martin Luther King, Jr. His presence in many cities was often known and well-publicized, but not so much his presence at Penn Center, where it was said he drafted the text of his "I Have a Dream" speech. In the winter of that same year, James Michael Endelson—alias Cliff Gilbert—was tasked with an undercover assignment to monitor all meetings, rallies, and retreats involving any civil rights activities at Penn Center. Endelson was a rookie in the FBI, this being his first solo assignment. He was young, straight out of Dartmouth College, idealistic, and heavily moved by his conservative roots though undercover as a volunteer for Peace Corps duties in Africa. He had cut his teeth and showed great value to the Director with his data gathering conducted during the retreat months earlier in March 1964. Between telephone intercepts and Endelson's spot reporting, the FBI generated intelligence that kept them one step ahead of King and the SCLC. Considered radicals under Communist controls, the SCLC was thought to represent an apparent threat—possibly a strong threat—to national security and, regionally, to South Carolina.

Cliff Gilbert was a mole. He reported data to a supervisor he had never met, a talented and experienced field agent who analyzed the field reports to generate information and intelligence relayed directly to the Director. Over the preceding six months, reports allowed the Bureau to monitor the SCLC movement to train Negro citizens via their "Citizenship Education Program," an effort to co-opt rural Negroes to become more active and vocal in the Civil Rights Movement. Though he never realized his contribution, the mole was key in the effort thanks to his nameless, faceless, go-between boss.

Gilbert made it a point to be in the middle of all the first night activities at Penn Center. From the back of the room he served soft drinks and sweet tea during the sessions where representatives listened to tactics to use on marches. With each presentation he recorded that the speaker always emphasized nonviolence. At dinner when he waited tables, he hustled his way to the head table, positioned within earshot, leaving only long enough to slip into the kitchen pantry, where he wrote notes on a tiny pad in his back pocket. His evening closed with the fiery kickoff speech by "Zorro," transcribed almost verbatim from outside a window of Frissell House. As the crowd began to break up and head to their dorms, Gilbert asked one of the motorcade drivers if he could run him up the road to buy supplies for Penn Center. The driver, clueless to who Gilbert was, figured he could use this opportunity to buy a pack of cigarettes and maybe a bottle of beer.

When they reached the Sea Island Parkway, the air was cool and filled with the distinctive aroma of fried liver and bacon grease. The driver opted to follow his nose into the Lowcountry restaurant. Gilbert closed the door to the phone booth in the parking lot and dumped a pocketful of quarters on a tray above a rather torn and useless phonebook. He listened as each coin he deposited rolled down the shoot and plunked into the tinny coin box at the bottom of the phone. The salty, wet air had destroyed the numbers and letters on the phone faceplate. Gilbert carefully selected the hole in the dial before he spun. After the normal verification, the Bureau switchboard directed his call.

"Hello."

"Coyote?" Gilbert questioned, keeping his voice low despite the fact there was nobody in sight.

"*Sí, señor,*" was the response, the only words that would verify Gilbert had contacted the right person.

"I have a message from Atticus," was his trained reply; his only other alternative was to quickly hang up.

"Be brief. Facts. What do you know?"

Gilbert flipped through his tiny notebook. "In addition to Zorro, on the grounds—Young, Williams, Abernathy, Palmer, Lawson, and Lee," he rattled off. "Oh, and Baez is here singing like I reported last time."

"Actions?" the voice grumbled. "What are they up to?"

Mole made his sentences short to summarize events since his last report. Only one raised the ire of the voice on the other end of the receiver.

"What do you mean, special meeting?" the voice probed.

"I wasn't able to get much more than—"

"What do you mean you weren't able to get much?"

Gilbert continued, "It was two guys. Couldn't tell who they were without them seeing me. I thought I should stay hidden and get as much as I could."

"Yeah, well, great. Hidden with no details. What good is that? Can't even track down who it was?"

"I heard them say 'praise house' and 'kidnap' but never connected who," Mole said with a dry, nervous choke.

"For crying out loud, kid, which praise house?"

"I was told a praise house is one of those small buildings where slaves held services—"

"I know that, you idiot."

"Nowadays small groups of Negroes still use them on Saint Helena for meetings. Old-time religion," Gilbert added in an attempt at humor.

"Well, Sherlock, I know all of that. They have their shouts there."

Gilbert flipped another page in his notebook. "Oh, and they said the meeting and grab would be November nineteenth."

"Grab? What do you mean grab? Son, you have until November eighteenth to figure out what this is all about. Who? What? Where? When? How? Got it? You better be a fly on the wall of that praise house or your butt will find all that training you've had in that school of yours there will come in handy when you wake up in some grass hut in Africa. You *capisce*?"

"Yes, sir."

"Please deposit another twenty-five cents," the operator said.

"Goodnight."

Mole held the receiver to his ear for a good ten seconds after the dial tone kicked in before he placed it back in the cradle.

"Go ahead, Coyote. The Director is on the line," the FBI switchboard operator said.

"Sir, the kid says there's a meeting November nineteenth at some local spot. Something about a grab.

Given that group and their activities, I'm assuming something to do with a kidnapping."

"And did he have any details? The meetings?" the Director asked, still calm but warming.

"Usual suspects in attendance there tonight. Nothing new."

"But details about the meeting?" Getting warmer.

"Nothing."

"Well, that kid's a thirteen-karat dimwit. I mean he gets the big picture but we can almost guess that stuff."

"I think this kidnapping thing could go back to what I picked up when I first got here. That Poro guy. He could be as dangerous or critical as Malcolm X. Sir, if I may, I suggest we get some inside taps on this Poro."

"Got any names?" the Director said with obvious sarcasm. "Give me a name, one name. You can't even do that. In all that time you've had the kid on that operation down there and all the times you've mentioned Poro, you still have nothing, no name, no place, no nothing. Give me something to go on."

"Sir, I'll get a name."

"You get the name and you get one tap. Get on it! Call me when you have it."

Click.

CHAPTER 10

In the two weeks that followed, it was difficult to tell who burrowed deeper underground, the mole or young Jackie Eddings. With his mother's voice resonating like a gray wolf through his head, he kept a vigilant eye on Skeet Gundy and his shaky-kneed gang of intimidated stooges. Wherever Skeet and his troupe went, Jackie chose a path of least resistance in a different direction. For as long as he could remember, he had always heard the Lord said, "turn the other cheek" so Jackie decided to do exactly like the Lord said and show both cheeks. He would just go his own way. In class when Miss Forten asked if he had made any breakthroughs with the team in the research, he frowned and answered with a curt *no*. Over the weeks he had made no attempt to collaborate with Skeet or with their silent partner, Ricky Clemonds. He was less concerned with his grade than he was with survival. If there was going to be any research at all, he would do it on his own. But, while Jackie researched, Skeet spent his time on other plans.

An earlier light rain licked the oil off the pavement. Now darker clouds hung ominously low. With or without the showers or the clouds, the new moon made it easy for Skeet to steal his brother's truck. Eddie Newcomb, Skeet's foster brother, was a legitimately ugly, pimple-faced seventeen-year-old high-school dropout who worked as the delivery boy at Western Auto. Eddie wasn't the most reliable kid in town, but Old Man Croft, the owner, trusted him enough to send him out in the company pickup truck to collect monthly payments due on appliances he had sold to the Negroes on Saint Helena Island. Skeet knew that Eddie hid the keys on the inside of the front fender so he could come and go as he pleased, a not-so-clever practice that made it easy for Skeet to do the same.

Skeet and buddy Hoss stole the truck around a quarter past six. Skeet was too young to get a license; besides, he could never pass any kind of test if they gave him one. Hoss was big for his age, but still not old enough to take the driver's test. Skeet sat tall in the driver's seat as he drove down Scott Street, through the heart of downtown Beaufort, then stopped in front of a small one-story house on Duke Street. Nothing about the house was extraordinary. Whitewashed clapboard siding, simple front lawn. No name on a mailbox, only the numerals, five-zero-two.

Through his informal grapevine of eavesdroppers—all ready-to-please but clueless conspirators—he learned that Irvin and Hestelle Eddings took Gabe Pritchard to the Pritchard Praise House every week for the "shout." It was their way of keeping the patriarch of the family in touch with the past. The Pritchard Praise House was located on property formerly a part of the Pritchard Place Plantation. As a young boy Gabe attended weekly "shouts" in the small shack along with his parents who, as slaves, helped build the original building before the Civil War. His memories of those times remained clouded, subject to his imagination. Jackie often tagged along to watch the expression on Grandpa Gabe's face.

It was biblical, in a sense, to see and hear Gabe come alive in the ring shout service, but this week Jackie mentioned to Ricky he was staying home to work on the Gullah treasure project. When Skeet overheard the comment, he knew it would be a perfect night to remind Jackie about their unfinished business from the schoolyard.

"Come on, boy, we is goin' to take us a ride," Skeet said as he swung open the screen door, bolted into the house, flicked off the lights, and lassoed Jackie on the floor in the front room. Before Jackie had a chance to say anything, Skeet shoved a sock in his mouth and pulled a knitted watch cap over his head. With the light from the small black-and-white television flickering through the room, Hoss pinned Jackie with his heft, and Skeet wrapped the smaller boy with a rope—mummy-style—from his shoulders to his knees. Skeet flipped off the television and dropped Jackie's school work on the floor in his bedroom. Jackie struggled to no avail, while the two bigger boys dragged him out the door and planted him in the middle of the bench seat in the Ford pickup.

Raindrops splattered and wormed their way up the windshield on the joyride out of the city, across the bridge to Lady's Island, toward the Sea Islands, where the night was a deeper shade of black. From Whitehall Point to Polowana Road—a distance of five miles as the crow flies—no streetlights, no stoplights, no starlight marked their way.

When Skeet turned onto Lands End Road going thirty miles per hour, he swerved across the centerline into the path of an oncoming car. Skeet jerked the steering wheel and stood on the brakes. The truck snaked across the wet pavement, passed over Skeet's lane, and ran off the road onto the berm. Jackie—still gagged and tied—rolled hard and smashed Hoss against the door.

"Dang, Skeet, slow down." Hoss laughed nervously and pushed Jackie back toward the driver. "What's the big hurry?"

"Shut up. You ain't driving this heap. You get us killed if you were," Skeet said. With the right wheels off the road, the truck bounced down a quarter mile of sandy ruts and pools of water before Skeet managed to get it back on the pavement. He slowed as they passed the Penn Center and again as they passed the Chapel of Ease. A mile or so farther from the road, they could see light near the woods from inside Pritchard Praise House, a handful of cars on the surrounding grass. Skeet knew he had to be close to their destination.

"Goin' treasure hunting, ain't we, Hoss? Goin' to find us some spooks. Ain't that right, Geechee boy?" Skeet laughed. He took his eyes off the road, leaned toward Jackie, and barked "Boo!" in his ear. "We be looking for spooks tonight. Ooooo-oooo! About time for them ghosts to come creeping up this road, don't ya think? Our boy Jackie here, he's goin' to find 'em for us." Skeet broke into a ghoulish laugh and added, "Just gotta find that hanging tree."

From the time he was thrown in the truck, Jackie labored to breathe with the sock in his mouth and squirmed to get free. He noticed the *whop-thump* of the windshield wipers had stopped, and after the high-speed turn which tossed him on Hoss, they returned to a smooth paved road. He had no idea where he was or what was going to happen, but when Skeet mentioned the hanging tree, Jackie recalled his parents had talked about recent lynchings and the story of fourteen-year-old Negro boy from Chicago that whites murdered in

Mississippi. He was unsure about Skeet, but he had no intentions of being any part of history. Again, his mother's voice howled in his head.

Jackie thrust his shoulder into Skeet, then into the steering wheel. He grunted and kicked his feet wildly until he landed a shot on Hoss's shin. When Skeet shoved Jackie back, he used the momentum to slam into Hoss. The bigger teen grabbed Jackie by the neck and sat him upright.

"Hey, boy. Settle down," Skeet yelled.

"Just sit there, boy. You ain't going nowhere," Hoss added when he pressed Jackie's shoulders hard against the seat. Skeet rocked the steering wheel from side to side. The truck responded in a zigzag before it rolled to a stop beneath a mammoth live oak on the right side of the road. Skeet inched it forward a few feet to position the truck bed where he wanted it.

"I think we're there, Hoss." Skeet reached across and ripped the cap off Jackie's head, grabbing some hair with it. "Come on, Buckwheat. Let's get you out of the truck. We got business to tend to."

Jackie didn't want any part of whatever Skeet had in store for him. Locked in his rope cocoon, he butted and kicked, squirmed and rolled until he fell to the floorboards. Hoss slapped Jackie's feet out of the way and dove in head first to grab the rope around Jackie's knees. Skeet pushed Jackie's shoulders until he fell out the door on the passenger side and landed with a hard bounce. The grass around him had a fresh, wet smell; Jackie could feel the water as it soaked through his clothes. He snorted like a bull to breathe; the sock inside his mouth felt attached, like a raw layer of extra skin.

"Now you ain't going nowhere, boy, so stop your fussing. You're only goin' to make things worse for yourself. We's havin' us a little chat, then we is goin' to pray, then we is goin' back home, well some of us is. Right, Hoss?"

"You got that right, Skeet. Right on!" Hoss replied. He lifted Jackie into a bear hug.

"Bring him 'round back. We need to get him up in the bed of the truck," Skeet said as he dropped the tailgate.

Even the pitch of the night couldn't hide the massive tree. One branch in particular scared Jackie, one that arched out over the road like a gallows with a single strand of Spanish moss hanging like a rope down to the bed of the truck.

Hoss had his arms full. Jackie kicked at Hoss's shins as he dragged him from the side to the back of the truck. Skeet reached down from the tailgate and grabbed the rope around Jackie's chest while Hoss lifted from below. When Jackie kicked Hoss in the head, the big white teen bit Jackie on the leg.

"You dang coon," he yelled and heaved him up to where Skeet could haul him in.

"Get up here, Hoss. This boy just ain't cooperating, now is he?"

Hoss clawed his way into the truck bed, avoiding Jackie's legs. When he stood up he looked out over the cab. "Hey, Skeet…there's a light in the road! Someone's coming!"

Skeet cradled Jackie under his arms, turned to look down the road for an instant, then dropped him to the metal bed. When Jackie tried to get up, Skeet stomped on his chest and held him down with his foot. As he hopped around to control Jackie, the light continued to move in their direction.

"That ain't no car! Shoot, Hoss, that's it. That's the Light, that Lands End Light, that ghost," Skeet said, his voice tentative.

"Nah, can't be. Ain't no such thing."

The Light moved closer. The two boys watched and Jackie listened. He knew of the ghost. His Grandpa Gabe told him it was the ghost of a runaway slave that came back to look for his family and was hanged on a road under one of the live oaks like the one above him. While the two boys watched the Light, the rain-starved thunder rumbled like distant artillery over the outer islands; strobes of light flickered visibly off to the east.

"Now you tell me, Hoss. That don't look like no headlights. Ain't no motorcycle neither."

"What we do now, Skeet?" Hoss asked, his eyes fixed squarely on the Light as it grew brighter and nearer. Skeet stepped toward the front of the truck to get a better look. He placed his hands on top of the cab and watched as the Light moved from one side of the road to the other, then back to the middle of the road. With each zig and zag, it appeared closer and it moved faster, now no more than a quarter mile from the boys.

"We just get the heck out of here!" Skeet yelled as he jumped over the side of the truck and scooted into the seat. Hoss jumped off the back, ran to the cab, and slammed the door behind him. Skeet flipped on the headlights and turned the key. *Click. Click. Click*, in rapid succession. The truck wouldn't start and the headlights grew dim. A second try. *Click. Click. Click*, this time the headlights flickered off. The Light was now less than a hundred yards away. *Click. Click. Vroom*! The engine raced and growled as Skeet pumped the accelerator. The headlights came to life. Skeet's heart pounded faster than the pistons under the hood. He gave the gas pedal everything he had, which sent up a ten-foot rooster-tail spray of sand, sticks, and shells as the truck peeled out from under the tree headed straight toward the Light. Jackie rolled to the edge of the open tailgate before the rope snagged on the rusted wheel well and stopped him.

"Turn around," Hoss screamed and braced himself. "You're going straight at it."

A fireball-flash killed the truck's motor before Skeet had time to hit the brakes. It didn't sputter or wheeze; the motor froze and died but the truck continued to roll, slower and slower. All the usual night sounds were gone; only the sound of tires on asphalt and rusty brake drums remained.

Skeet and Hoss looked at each other. Both took a deep breath before they looked out over the hood. The Light was gone. They spun around and saw Jackie in the bed working to free himself from the ropes. Beyond Jackie, farther down the road behind them now, they saw it again, the Light. They watched for a few seconds before Hoss yelled, "It's coming back!"

The Light was moving back toward them. Skeet tried to start the truck, but nothing happened, not even the promise of a *click*.

"Come on, Skeet. It's getting closer. Let's go."

"Shut up. I'm trying." Skeet fumbled with the key; his other hand pounded on the steering wheel. That combination didn't work. Nothing he tried worked.

Jackie sat up in the bed of the truck and shivered as the Light drifted closer. He pushed himself back toward the cab. At the wheel well he rolled to face the piece of metal that caught the rope. He pushed his face against it and snagged the sock out of his mouth. He gulped for air as he struggled to inch his way closer to the cab.

"Help! Take these ropes off. Help. Help me," Jackie screamed, donut-eyed. The fear that had effectively crippled him during the drive shifted from the boys protected in the cab to the uncertainty of the haint Light.

At a spot twenty-five feet behind the truck, the Light stopped and hovered. Skeet fussed with the key, his eyes out the back window; still nothing happened. The next time he turned the key, the Light moved. It drifted much more slowly, deliberately, and directly as the boys looked on. The Light seemed to focus its beam on Jackie huddled in a ball. Skeet and Hoss dropped down below the back window and waited. The Light came lower, then melted into a white-hot laser speck on Jackie's shoulder. The instant it landed Jackie felt a buzz and a momentary calm before it disappeared entirely. None of them dared to breathe. They could hear nothing but the sound of their own hearts in their ears. Then the pickup moved.

The truck began an eerie, smooth roll perforated by the creaky drag of the worn parts. Hunkered down below the dashboard, Skeet and Hoss stretched their necks to look above the dash and saw the Light in front of them moving away at the same rate of speed as the truck. As the Light moved faster, the truck rolled faster. Skeet stayed low. Unable to see the road, he grabbed the steering wheel. The truck jittered violently until Skeet released his grip. As the Light moved to the right, so did the truck. Then back to the left. Faster. The metal-on-metal grind and groan of the axle was drowned out by the rush of the road under the tires. Jackie leaned against the inside wall of the truck bed and watched as the Light shot up, then zoomed down the road, growing smaller and dimmer until the dot of light was gone. Without the Light, the truck slowly rolled, recklessly crossing the road, through an abandoned drainage ditch and landed nose first against a vine-covered stump.

"What the heck?" Hoss said. "We gotta get out of here before it comes back."

Skeet tried to start the truck. All he got was the familiar *click*, *click*, *click*. After several tries he said, "It ain't goin' to start. Come on. Let's hoof it back up the road. We can thumb once we get up there."

"What about our jigaboo?" Hoss said, looking toward Jackie.

"What do you mean?"

"We takin' him with us, ain't we?"

"What?"

"We can't just leave him out here. We're in enough trouble already. They find out we just left him out here all tied up, then they'll know what was happening."

"Ain't nobody goin' to believe him. He's better off than he would've been. Come on." Skeet hollered out the window, "You is one lucky coon tonight. You be good now. And you forget all what happened here, you got me, boy?"

Jackie didn't respond.

Skeet and Hoss hopped out of the cab and headed back up the road the way they came.

Jackie crouched low in the bed of the truck and watched. It wasn't long before Skeet picked up the pace and started to jog. Hoss chugged behind, unable to match Skeet's pace.

The only thing bigger than the silence was the roll of thunder, closer than before. Jackie watched the two white boys until he couldn't see anything of them; they disappeared into the night. He struggled more with the ropes until he was able to push one loop off his feet and then another and another. When his legs were free, he hopped off the truck and wrestled to free his arms. By the time he was done he figured the other boys had at least a fifteen minute head start. He didn't know where he was exactly, but he recalled where Gabe said the Light was on Saint Helena, so he elected to jog in the opposite direction, the same route the others had taken.

It wasn't long before he saw a light in the distance. He could tell it wasn't the same light that haunted him earlier. Though a light drizzle blurred his vision, the closer he got, the more he recognized the building behind the light. It was the Pritchard Praise House, where his parents were. His good fortune confused him. He couldn't let his parents know he was on Saint Helena. They would question how he got there and why. His only out would be to lie unless he squealed on Skeet, which he knew would only make matters worse. Negroes don't accuse whites; when they do, often they find themselves in deeper trouble when the facts seem to turn against them. His father would go to the police. Jackie knew that Chief Heimer would never believe him or his story.

When he slowed his walk to weigh his options, Jackie saw a figure come from the other side of the building, pass under the light above the wooden door, and run into the dark area by the woods behind the praise house. Whoever or whatever Jackie saw wore a strange shaggy suit and something over his head that was nearly the width of his shoulders.

Rather than face his parents just yet, Jackie chose to follow the figure into the woods. The thin streams of light that leaked out from the dilapidated praise house allowed him to find the path the figure had taken. Vines that could have been there since the beginning of time clustered together and covered the entrance into the trees. His movement was slow through a web of muscadine vines, a minefield of razor-like saw palmettos, and snares of twiggy yaupon holly bushes. He worked slowly down the path, using the flashes of lightning to mark his way. Fortunately, the occasional thunder and commotion from inside the praise house was enough to mask his movement. He had managed less than fifty feet when a flashlight beam illuminated the path some distance ahead.

Suddenly, a voice stopped him. *Praise Lord, now. Praise Lord.* It was the garbled tone of his Grandpa Gabe, repeated again and again from inside the tiny hall. All the other voices had stopped; only Gabe had anything to say. The voice, the strength of which he only heard at the praise house, caused him to hold up and listen.

Eventually, as he crept farther, light flickered through the brush. He worked his way toward the light and hunkered down for a better look. The figure with the flashlight was headed toward a small fire under some sort of table or altar. Around the fire he saw the figure he had seen by the praise house, but there were others. Each of them wore something over their heads; two had full head covers, masks that could have been papier-mâché or wood or clay. They were grotesque animal-like masks. One mask, worn above a covered face, looked like a hyena jaw that protruded out with more than a foot of sharp teeth. The mask had tusks of a warthog and antlers. Another figure had a different mask, one that resembled a crude water buffalo with spiked teeth. It had leather thongs that tied animal horns on the top. The third mask was a face, long and flat. It had a smooth, tall forehead and a feather headdress. At the bottom a beard of small shells strung like dreadlocks hung from the chin. The three of them wore tattered brown robes with dried cordgrass cuffs above their wrists and along the ragged bottom. They rattled like snakes as they circled the flames barefooted—high-stepping, crouching, and spinning with arms pumping and pushing, up and down, against the night air. Jackie looked twice to make sure it wasn't the hot embers from the fire that caused them to dance that way. A crack of thunder distracted Jackie, and then a fourth figure popped out of the woods.

The figure was a haystack with feet; it looked like something Bugs Bunny might hide in on the Saturday morning *Looney Toons*. The outer garment was covered in bands of cordgrass layered neatly above the knees. Over his head he wore a white hood, just a sack, not pointed like the KKK, but with the trademark cut-out eye holes. Jackie noticed how the others by the fire turned to give their full attention to the fourth member of the group. The grassy figure twirled, and as he walked forward, his grass torso fluffed out like a tutu. When the figure reached the others, arms emerged from inside the grass cover. Two hands, wrapped in cloth, held something that looked like a pot or a basket with a lid. Jackie shifted to his right to get a better look. When he did a tree frog landed on his neck. Startled, he jumped backward, off balance on one leg, and swatted at the frog, but he smacked a thorny vine instead.

"Ow!" The activity around the fire stopped immediately. The group of four froze, turned, and listened. Jackie tried to regain his balance but fell backward into the brush, no more than twenty yards from the fire.

Jackie fought to get on his feet. One of the figures— the one with the feathers and bells—ran toward the noise. Headed to blackness, Jackie bear crawled to get through the thicket, then worked his way up to his feet and thrashed blindly through the woods, his hands protecting his eyes but not much else. The bells on his pursuer's mask helped Jackie locate where he was. A flashlight beam began to search the woods around him. Jackie flattened. *Dear Lord, Jesus,* he thought. The briars and twigs in the underbrush pricked his stomach through his shirt. The light rain felt good on his back. When the beam scanned the path a safe distance away, he moved on, quieter now and cautious. His stealth paid off. The hunt lasted less than five minutes. The pursuer gave up chase and the flashlight beam headed back toward where Jackie had seen the fire, now no longer visible through the woods.

Lost and breathless, Jackie continued. He feared capture and worried he had gone in a big circle back to where he saw the fire. After what seemed to be hours and miles of battling trees, vines, and elements of the night, he broke out into a small open area near a road. With no idea where he was, he felt the freedom of the open pavement to walk down the middle of the road in the rain. He thought of what might happen to him now. He prayed for traffic, for a ride, but was fearful of who might be on the road at this time of night. He had not walked far or long before he came to a street sign that read Ernest Drive. It was a smaller street and not a name he recognized. Minutes later, off to his left, even without the aid of the moon, he recognized the ruins of the Chapel of Ease. Soaked and bleeding from both palms, he sighed with the relief. Now his biggest concern, other than Skeet and Hoss, was how to get home.

He had walked up the middle of the road less than a mile when lights from an approaching car captured his shrinking shadow on the pavement. Jackie stepped back as the lights approached, passed, then stopped. It was a sleek new Cadillac, like the one he had seen in the motorcade. A rear door opened. When a head emerged, Jackie saw it was a colored man. He waved Jackie toward the vehicle.

"Care for a ride, son?" asked the stranger, his voice deep and distinguished. Despite the events of the evening, Jackie had a feeling about this man, a comforting feeling. Though he didn't know him, he recognized him. He accepted the ride but clung to the door handle on the opposite side of the car. The man did not talk or ask any questions; he just stared at the headlights through the windshield. Jackie hopped out of the Cadillac once they crossed the bridge in town; from there he ran home, relieved to find the house remained dark with no sign of the family car. Jackie was safely in bed when his parents returned. His mother opened the door a crack, saw her son and smiled. She couldn't hear the *lub-dub* of his heart or read his mind. He lay there, still stoked by adrenaline, and wrestled with how he would deal with Skeet; he knew he had to do something.

CHAPTER 11

First thing Old Man Croft did after he opened the Western Auto store the next morning was to put his delivery boy, Eddie Newcomb, through the third degree about the missing truck. The acned teen offered neither a defense nor an excuse. He stood there and repeatedly gave the shrugged-shoulders seagull salute and, of course, never shared his secret hiding spot for the keys. Second thing Croft did was to call the police and report his truck stolen.

"Stolen?" The muscle in Chief Heimer's left jaw moved a little toward a grin, puzzled anyone would steal such a rust bucket.

"That's what I said, Otis. Stolen. The kid said he parked around back like usual and it's not there this morning."

"Okay, Stanley. Relax. Relax. I'll get on it quick like a bunny," Heimer chuckled. "Consider the crook captured."

The police chief dispatched one of his deputies to cruise in search of the vehicle. He also passed the word to the county sheriff's office, per standard operating procedure, since most of the islands were outside the city jurisdiction. The rumor mill cranked up later that morning when a local farmer from Saint Helena Island came into town to sell vegetables and mentioned to Stanley Croft that he had seen the truck straddled over a ditch nestled in the crook of a rotten tree out on Saint Helena. Croft passed that word back to the chief, who in turn passed it to the county sheriff's office.

The call went out to the patrol near Saint Helena with a resounding "ten-four," followed thirty minutes later with, "We got a ten-fifty-one out here. My ten-twenty is two hundred yards southwest of Family Lane on Lands End Road. Copy?"

"You got a what?" the dispatcher asked.

"We need a dang wrecker out here, Horace. This truck done sittin' in a ditch and took a bite out of some old tree. Send a wrecker out here." And so he did.

It didn't take but two weeks for Old Man Croft to get that truck repaired and back on the road. There were payments to collect. Chief Heimer didn't have the same motivation as Stanley Croft. In those same two weeks, the police had not interviewed a single suspect.

For the boys, Jackie included, it was two weeks of silence. There was no mention of the incident to each other or anyone else for that matter. There were a few standoff stares and hushed hallway discussions between Skeet and his cronies, but no words exchanged between Skeet and Jackie. During the dedicated research time, Skeet doodled or hid his brother's *Hot Rod* magazine behind textbooks while Ricky Clemonds and Jackie discussed how they could each look for a needle-in-a-haystack clue to the Gullah treasure at their respective libraries—Ricky at the county library and Jackie at the J.I. Washington Colored Branch of the city library.

Ricky was excited about research and a chance to go to the library. Alone in his own little world, he begged his mother to allow him to go to the library. She was surprised at his interest and concerned about his safety.

She agreed under the condition that she stay at the library while he was there since this was his first visit. When Ricky protested, she promised to remain out of sight while he researched, which seemed fair to him, though he had no earthly idea where to begin. He remembered very little of what Gene Skyles had said and had only a vague recall of what his research topic was. The only word that registered for him was "treasure." A librarian noticed him wandering aimlessly through the stacks like he was lost in a maze. He told her he was looking for treasure, but when asked, he couldn't tell which treasure.

"Do you mean *Treasure Island?*" she asked.

The mention of the two words together sparked Ricky to say, "Gold. Gold bug."

"Oh, the story. You need Edgar Allan Poe." She walked Ricky toward a different section in the stacks and pulled a very thin copy of Poe's story.

The librarian sensed Ricky had a special need, so she helped him find a table—within her view from the circulation desk—where he could sit and read. He thumbed through the short story until he ran across the page that showed the coded message. The pattern of the code intrigued him. He found it easier to understand than the text itself. But his interest wasn't in the story at all. He was interested in the latest copy of *Boys' Life*, his Bible on how to be a normal kid; he knew he wasn't because everybody had told him. He pushed Poe aside and brought the magazine back to his table. He liked the science fiction stories the best, but he always looked at the last page, where he found cartoons of the Tracy Twins and Pee Wee Harris, jokes, ads for stamp collectors, and gadgets like Cub Scout mini-flashlights or pocketknives and, best of all, magic kits. This was what normal kids wanted; that's what interested him most.

Jackie relied less on Poe or Skyles and more on his Grandpa Gabe for research. Since Gabe's suggestions were based on stories he heard on the plantation as a small boy, the details or facts—if they were facts—were somewhat fogged by time. The colored library wasn't very well stocked and all that Grandpa Gabe gave him led to dead ends. Desperate for anything, he asked the Negro librarian at the desk for help; she had nothing to offer. When he told her that he had to make a presentation at the PTA meeting the next day, she could say nothing but *I'm sorry.*

The following night, the attendance at the Beaufort Junior High School Parent Teacher Association meeting was light, as usual. The few concerned parents milled around socially in the kid-sized gym before the meeting started, most grumbling about the landslide victory of Lyndon Johnson over the local favorite, Barry Goldwater, two days prior. Jackie, seated in the back row of the auditorium stage, looked a bit like tar in a bread pan. The school board dignitaries and Principal Langhorn were front and center, closer to the parents. As the last of five student presentations, Jackie had the longest wait, plenty of time for whatever it was that was crawling around in his stomach to eat its way out. He fidgeted, looking for his parents while the adult speakers gave updates on enrollment, class sizes, curriculum changes, and programs. Late in the evening when it was his turn to present, he stepped up on the box behind the lectern and lit a fuse of controversy that hissed through the crowd. His parents, seated respectfully in the back, looked proud but weary. His mother flashed a timid, toothy smile and gave him a silent mini-applause. He read his one-page report with flawless grammar, without stumbling over a single word, despite the restlessness in the audience. At the end Jackie suggested that the Gullah treasure might still be somewhere in the Lowcountry. At his mention of gold and silver coins the audience whooped, cheered, and laughed. As the crowd funneled out of the gym, Jackie heard one outburst that stuck with him; he prayed his parents didn't hear the voice say, "You Gullah people are either real gullible"—then a laugh—"or just plain dumb."

Based on a summons from the principal midmorning the following Wednesday, Mary Alice Forten knocked on his office door promptly at three thirty. Over the first three months, she had learned every conversation with him had the possibility of turning ugly, not something she looked forward to after a day in the crucible of her classroom.

"Come in."

Though she hoped for the best—a congenial smile and *congratulations on great student presentations for the PTA*—she turned the knob and imagined herself walking into an inferno. When she opened the door, she saw that the principal was not alone. The room was packed with people. As requested, she had Jackie Eddings at her side.

"Have the boy take a seat out there. We want to talk to you first, Miss Forten," the principal said from behind his desk. He gestured for Jackie to wait. "Please come in and close the door."

Jackie took a seat on a folding chair outside the office. He could hear the principal as he began.

"Miss Forten, these parents have requested this session. They have concerns about your current approach in the classroom and the presentations last evening." Langhorn proceeded to introduce the president of the PTA, a member of the school board, and a set of concerned parents.

"Actually, Langhorn, my beef is more with you and this here school board," said Hank Newcomb, standing next to the desk. "See, I don't want my boy in the classroom with that colored boy. Nobody asked me if he could be in this school with my kid. I never got a say in any of this."

"Now wait a minute, Mr. Newcomb. You need to—"

"I don't need to nothin'. You get that colored boy out of this school. This school is for white kids, not them Negroes."

"If I may…" Bill Hammond, the school board spokesman stepped forward. "It was the school board who directed the integration of this school. That is the first step in changing our district policy. And y'all need to be prepared for much more in the future."

"That's the dumbest thing I ever heard," Newcomb said. "Them animals is goin' to screw up Skeet's education. That boy's had enough trouble already without makin' him go to school with them coloreds. And you"—he paused and looked directly at the teacher—"why does he have to work with that colored boy anyhow? There is plenty of white kids in that class."

The voices were loud enough for Jackie to hear every word. He had heard so much of this from classmates, now from their parents. At least one parent. Tears welled up in his eyes. He stood to open the door and tell them all that he just wanted to go back to the Negro school. As he reached to knock, his mother's words howled once more. *Da' be your school!* Then in a whisper, the voice of Grandpa Gabe. *Dey will be tough times, but you is de onliest person who can change all of dis for all de colored childrens.* Instead of the doorknob, Jackie put his hand on his forehead and went back to his chair. On the other side of the door, the eyes turned toward Mary Alice Forten, visibly shaken by the previous exchange.

"Miss Forten, tell me again, well, explain to us all, why you made these kids work in groups? Why'd you mix the groups? Why not let the Eddings boy do his project alone?"

Forten breathed through slightly parted lips while she composed herself. She had always been afraid of closed spaces, more so when they were filled with threatening people. Perspiration behind her ponytail dampened her collar and below. A queasiness in her stomach threatened. She kept her hands behind her back to hide what she couldn't control.

"I...I...I thought that was my job. I thought since Jackie Eddings was assigned to my classroom that I was expected to integrate him into the activities and experiences of the class." She swallowed to arrest the reflux in her throat. After a deep breath, she continued. "Students need to work together in the classroom, just like they will when they graduate. That's how society works. And, since there are Negroes as well as whites in society, I thought they should work together in—"

"There sure are coloreds, yep. They live in their society and we live in ours," Newcomb said. He had his head cocked away from Forten and twiddled his thumbs with his hands above his belt buckle. "They don't need to be doing things together in no classroom."

"But, Mr. Newcomb, I think students need to understand that society is changing." She looked toward the principal for support. What she saw was the long lame-duck forehead of a tired face weeks from retirement. Turning to Newcomb she added, "And they need to change old attitudes, too."

Bill Hammonds was slow to respond. "Well, Miss Forten, you are correct. Students should be aware of the changes in society, but sometimes those lessons are learned outside of the classroom."

Tongues of fire lashed out in her belly. As she prepared to argue her point, the principal spoke first.

"Another point to be made here, Mary Alice…Miss Forten, is about the students involved. Mr. Newcomb is correct. Robin Gundy has been through quite a bit. He has been through your grade level twice before. I know you are aware."

"Yes, Mr. Langhorn, I was well aware of Robin Gundy's background, which made it more important that he learn these life lessons in a structured environment, in my classroom, because nobody will take the time to help him learn these lessons once he leaves the school," she said, with a steeled look into the eyes of Hank Newcomb.

As the argument in the office grew louder and more pointed, Jackie's tensions eased, somewhat, comforted by the words of his teacher. How she hoped her efforts would teach Skeet to accept him and maybe all the Gullah people. He had not realized this before now. Maybe she could make a difference. Gradually, the comments drifted away from the direct issue of integration and became strictly racial.

"Tell me this then, Sydney…why in blazes is she teaching these kids about Gullah crap? That ain't history, least not American history. Gullah treasure? Ha, I ain't never heard of any treasure, any Gullah treasure, and I been here all my life," Newcomb challenged. He crossed his arms and leaned against the bookcase behind him, ready to launch into the principal if he dared defend the teacher.

"You know, Mr. Newcomb, I can't answer that. Miss Forten, care to explain your choice of that topic, please?"

Bill Hammond stepped forward and said, "Our curriculum does not specify exactly what topics can and cannot be addressed in the classroom."

"Mr. Hammond…" The teacher looked toward the school board spokesman with a nod, then, looking down, she stepped toward Hank Newcomb and drew a line on the floor with the toe of her shoe. Her hands, still behind her back, rested softly, one on top of the other. She looked up and said, "Sir, I am new to Beaufort and the Lowcountry. When I prepared my course outline, I attempted to incorporate the well-known history of the country, the South, and the local area. Part of the history is the incredible heritage of the Gullahs. It is what it is, Mr. Newcomb. They live here. You live here. We live here. If their history includes stories, maybe we should hear about them. Better yet, maybe we should understand them or maybe even solve them, if there are mysteries." Her tone was relaxed, forceful, and confident, a total reversal of what she felt when the session began.

"Look, teach," Newcomb said with a finger just short of the teacher's forehead, "I don't need no snotty-nosed kid right out of school tellin' me what my boy should or shouldn't know. You teach him all you want about history, but stick to the facts."

"Facts, Mr. Newcomb? We only know the facts because someone, sometime researched a topic and determined what the facts were. These kids are doing the research to discover the facts, then it becomes history, just like you want," she said, then took a step back.

"Okay, I think we understand both sides of this issue," Sydney Langhorn said in an effort to restore calm. "I will discuss this further with Mr. Hammond and the school board. Miss Forten, for the present time, you may continue with your group research projects, but before you begin another group assignment, I want you to bring it in here so we can discuss it. Is that clear?"

"Yes, Mr. Langhorn."

"Does anyone else have any other comments?"

Hank Newcomb puffed out his cheeks. He looked at the principal and then back toward the teacher before he grabbed his wife's hand. "Come on, Mailyn." He opened the door and pulled his wife through in a huff.

Jackie jumped up from his seat when the office door opened. He watched as the group exited the office. When he saw Miss Forten, she turned to the principal and asked if he wanted to speak to the boy.

The principal was curt in his reply. "No, not today, but close the door. I need to talk to you."

Mary Alice offered a warming smile to Jackie. "Wait here. I shouldn't be long."

"Miss Forten, let me set a few things straight with you. Have a seat." He moved to the front of his desk, pushed the large wooden nameplate aside, and sat on the edge. "I've been in this school for nearly forty years. I intend to be in this school for another two hundred and four days, not a day more and not a day less, and during that time I intend to be calling the shots. I don't need the school board in here telling me what to do. Is that clear?"

"Yes, Mr. Langhorn."

"And I don't need a teacher with less than three months behind the desk to think she can call the shots, either. Is that also clear?"

"Yes," she said. Though her response was quick, the crease in her brow suggested she did not agree.

"So I don't care how you do it, but I want these group projects to stop. At the very least, I want you to single out the Eddings boy and not have him working with a group of white kids. He can learn just as much on his own, right?"

"Well…"

"Right, Miss Forten?"

"I don't believe so, sir. You see—"

"I see, all right. I know how these kids work around here. This is, well it was, a very peaceful school. All the schools were. This integration thing has created issues. I don't suppose you heard what happened over at the colored high school last week?"

"No, sir."

"One of our school buses full of white students driving down Ribaut Road passed a group of colored kids and allegedly an occupant of the bus stuck a broom out the window and hit a colored boy in the back of his head."

Mary Alice cringed.

"Why would they do that, you ask? Why would the Negro kids up in the colored section of the Breeze Theater drop things on the white kids down below? That's just what kids do. And you want to go mixing them up in your classroom? I know how these kids think, Miss Forten. I tell you, the Eddings boy will do a fine job by himself if he is not asked to interfere, I mean, interact with the other students. Understood?"

"But, Mr. Langhorn—"

"I'm afraid there is no 'but' in this discussion Miss Forten. If you insist on group learning, Jackie Eddings remains in a group of one! And if I hear anything different, we'll be having another very short conversation. Now, you're a pretty young thing and will probably make a fine teacher, but you need to learn the basics. The basics here are exactly as I said. No questions. No buts. No changes. I don't know that I can make it any clearer than that. Do you have any further questions?"

"I would just like to say—"

"Questions, Miss Forten. Any questions, not comments."

"No, sir." From the moment the principal had instructed her to sit, her hands had been a nest of nonstop twisting fingers. She had not noticed this until she reached for the arms of the chair to stand. "Thank you for your time, Mr. Langhorn," she said as she reached to shake his hand.

She closed the door. Her first impulse was to massage her temples with her thumbs. She sighed and noticed the air outside the office was cooler but filled with the same vile mist of raging hormones, acne creams, and excessive perfume she had grown to accept in her first few months. She sniffled a few times as she strutted off, chin up.

"Oh, Jackie!" she said, startled when the boy trotted up alongside her. As they walked, she had a distant stare, her eyes focused more on thoughts than things. She said, "Jackie, do you have a copy of what you read to the PTA last night?"

"Yes. It's in my desk."

"Good. Let's go to the classroom. Would you get it for me?"

"Sure."

Two days later, on Friday the thirteenth, the *Beaufort Gazette* published the entire speech Jackie Eddings presented to the PTA. It appeared verbatim—misspelled words corrected—in the three-column, quarter-page, biweekly section entitled, "Items of Interest to the Colored Community." When the Gullah community read the column, and as the word of mouth spread about Jackie's report, the Lowcountry responded with a surge of crypt-searching, hole-digging, clue-hunting seekers of gold. Shovels appeared most everywhere, and for every shovel, there was an exponential increase in the number of holes that appeared in the most unusual, often private, sometimes sacred places.

CHAPTER 12

On the streets Jackie's presentation—his presence not his material—ignited a firestorm of mixed sentiments. Local gossip hubs like Harvey's Barber Shop, the Beaufort Beauty and Slendorizing Salon, as well as the United Five and Dime echoed opinions loud and long.

"A Negro boy speaking at a white school? My word, what next?"

"A treasure the Gullahs kept secret for all these years. Well, I'll be."

"And I can't believe the *Gazette* actually printed that column in the paper this morning," one shopper said to the checkout clerk. "Holy Moses."

The Clemonds family found themselves in the midst of the topic of the day. Weeks earlier in a conversation with the teacher, Ricky's mother learned Jackie Eddings was a Negro. Neither Cybil nor her preacher husband ever had dealings with coloreds, not at the church or otherwise. They had nothing against Ricky associating with Jackie, especially since he was the only boy who would talk to their son. Ricky's "special needs" singled him out as "different" to the other kids in his class much like Jackie was different, in a different way. When the bishop reassigned Elliott Clemonds to the Carteret Street United Methodist Church, he and Cybil knew it would not be an easy transition for their emotional son. A teenager in a

127

new town, a new school, new (to him) students. Fortunate to be placed on the same project team, Ricky was happy to have one friend, someone who would share time with him.

Cybil Clemonds was desperate to promote their friendship. She called Hestelle Eddings, introduced herself, and asked if Jackie could spend the night one Friday. Given Jackie's uneasiness with the boys in his class, Hestelle was reluctant to agree, saying, *Da's awful kind of you, ma'am, but…boys…I'm not sure da' would be good idea.* Cybil assured her the boys would be fine and explained that Ricky really had nobody else to play with. *It would be ever so kind of you to let Jackie spend the night, but I understand. I just thought it might be good for kids in school to see this kinda thing happen, relationships and all. Think about it, please.* Cybil prayed and a week later Hestelle called and agreed, though she had not mentioned it to Jackie.

Jackie refused to go. Given Grandpa Gabe's earlier warnings about white kids, he was definitely unsure about Ricky. At school there were protocols and norms. Miss Forten was gentle with him, always at his side to assist when he didn't understand simple things or became flustered, usually followed by an outburst of some sort. Even though they would be in Ricky's house and his mother would be there, Jackie was scared. *What would we talk about? We don't even talk de same. What would we do?* Once again Gabe had the words of wisdom Jackie needed to hear. "Ef de soul's hurtin', feed it! Feed da' child's soul. Pay dem others no never mind. Remember peoples is what dey do, not what dey thinks or says." On Gabe's words, Jackie changed his mind.

Though it was a short walk to Ricky Clemonds's house, Jackie was nervous about spending the night. Along the way he stopped at Grandpa Gabe's for a few words of encouragement. When he climbed the steps to Gabe's porch, a rusted nail on a bowed board moaned. A large bird with black iridescent plumage and a Bowie-knife beak, spooked by the noise, flew through the porch, then croaked from a nearby tree. *I'll fix da' step after fishing tomorrow*, Jackie thought.

Gabe didn't hear the squeaky step, the bird, or the creaky door hinge; he was sawing logs in his favorite rocker. Like most of the furniture in the house, the chair had been handed down through generations, held together with a combination of baling wire, stripped screws, and generous amounts of Elmer's wood glue. Jackie pulled the ottoman close, then moved Gabe's side table, a special wooden foot stool that bore the number "1848" crudely chiseled under the seat. Gabe once told Jackie that was the year it was made, but many of the stories Grandpa Gabe shared changed with each telling, and like his questions, were repeated as often as every ten minutes. He tried to waken Gabe, careful not to startle the old man because surprises were never good for a person his age. Jackie coughed and cleared his throat; that didn't bring Gabe out of his deep sleep. Determined not to show up at Ricky's house without Gabe's thoughts, Jackie got up and wandered around, cleaned the dirty dishes off the counter, washed them and put them away. He checked on Gabe's pet parakeet named Sherman in the corner of the kitchen, a minimal-care companion for Gabe who always looked like it had just finished an "air only" cycle in a laundromat dryer. Feathers ruffled every which way, the pathetic bird had plenty of seed, but his water bowl was a mess. When Jackie reached into the cage for the bowl, the cross-eyed parakeet lunged across and pecked Jackie's hand. He dropped the bowl and spilled water across the bottom of the cage, on the box beneath it, and onto the lacquered sideboard where the bird stayed.

"No!" he cried under his breath.

When he lifted the cage to wipe up the spill, he checked to make certain whatever was inside the box beneath it had not been damaged by his carelessness. He had never paid any attention to the box before. He dabbed the water off of the top, which read "vellum," then opened the box. It was filled with old letters and documents—fragments—many seemed too fragile to pick up. The water had managed to seep into one corner and onto one document, which he removed. It was a small square of paper. It would need time to dry.

Gabe snorted in the other room. Startled, Jackie slipped the delicate square into his pocket, placed the lid back on the box, and raced to get the cage, with clean water, back where it belonged.

"Hey, Grandpa Gabe, it's me. Jackie," he said extra loud for Gabe to hear from farther back in the house.

"What you doin', boy?" Gabe asked in a hushed voice.

"Just stopped by. Need your advice, Grandpa," he replied as he returned to his seat at Gabe's side.

Gabe dipped the rocker forward and let it ease itself back while Jackie explained his predicament. He finished with, "What do you think I should do, Grandpa?"

"Sound like dis white boy be your friend"—he took a deep breath—"so do like you do wid you colored friends."

Jackie sat back. He knew he had told his Grandpa about Ricky before and he also knew Gabe couldn't remember things. "Uh-huh, but remember I told you he's a little different, Grandpa Gabe. He act funny, strange funny, sometimes."

Breathlessly, Gabe mumbled between gasps, "We all be grains of sand…in da' sea of life. Some in dem tides, some on dem beaches. We all be different."

The words stumped Jackie.

"De spirit be in you soul, boy. Let it out. Be it in what you feels an' think an' what you do," Gabe added in short bursts between breaths, his head against the back of the chair.

"Da's all, Grandpa Gabe?" Jackie asked hoping for more.

"Go boy. You be fine," Gabe said. He offered a tight-lipped grin, closed his eyes, and dozed off. Jackie went on his way.

From the kitchen, Cybil Clemonds had one eye on the front porch step where Ricky sat. He glanced up momentarily when Jackie rounded the corner two houses down but quickly returned his attention to a ladybug on his sleeve.

"Hi, Ricky," Jackie said as he came up the walk to the steps.

"Hi back," Ricky replied. He nudged the bug with his forefinger.

Jackie watched but said nothing.

"Hi," Ricky repeated without looking up. He stood, careful to keep his forearm parallel to the ground so the bug wouldn't fall off. When he turned to go inside, the bug flew away.

"Bye-bye," he said, staring at his arm.

"Jackie, welcome," Cybil said from just inside the screen door as she opened it. "Ricky has told me so much about you. Please come in."

Ricky pushed to be first through the door, his forearm still cocked.

Cybil Clemonds let Ricky call the shots for the entire evening. He selected Swanson TV dinners, his favorite, especially when served in front of the television; no adults allowed, though mother was always close. Ricky's favorite television shows—*Lassie, Rawhide*, and his newest favorite, *The Addams Family*—were either at bat, on deck, or next in line for entertainment. The boys silently settled in at opposite ends of an antique camelback sofa covered with quilts. Aluminum trays of turkey breast and fried chicken oven heated with creamy whipped potatoes and mixed vegetables. Ricky chose turkey, which had the additional compartment with his favorite cranberry sauce. For Jackie, this was his first TV dinner, very much a treat. He ate slowly, sat uncomfortably, and snuck glances at Ricky, who had formed his potatoes into a rather crude pyramid. With the precision of a surgeon, Ricky used his knife and fork to grab peas, one at a time, and place them along each side of his potato monument. Each time he placed a pea, he said, "Ping." When all the peas had a place, he took the knife, spiked it through the center of his food art, and swirled the parts into a mix, a no-no in the Eddings household. Ricky ate the mix first, moved on to his favorite cranberry sauce next, then butchered the turkey into tiny pieces, but never ate a bite of it. When the TV shows ended, Cybil surprised the boys with a pan of Jiffy Pop for them to prepare on the stove and sent them off to bed.

Ricky decided they would build a tent out of blankets and a broom, then sleep on the floor, which turned out to be a dreadful experience. Every time Ricky placed the blanket over the broom, the tent collapsed. When Jackie stepped in to help, Ricky yanked the blanket away from him. Confused and helpless, Jackie stood and watched, annoyed by Ricky's constant jabber about how spooky *The Addams Family* was.

"Friday the thirteenth, not good. Thirteenth, not good," Ricky would say, then fall on the floor with a pillow over his head. He would pull his head out, look around the room, work on the tent, then repeat. Jackie tried to reassure him the characters were supposed to be funny, but Ricky didn't seem to hear a word; he just moved around the room like Jackie was invisible.

When the tent was finally ready, Ricky entered first. Jackie gave him a few seconds before he peeked through the flap. Ricky sat cross-legged with a flashlight pointed up toward his chin and his eyes cast down at the light source; the shadows stenciled an eerie mask on his face. Jackie crawled in and closed the flap. He reached into his pocket for a pack of Juicy Fruit gum. When he pulled his hand out, Ricky saw the tip of the wrapper and snatched it out of Jackie's hand. Along with the gum was the small square of paper Jackie pocketed at Grandpa Gabe's.

"What's this," Ricky asked. "It's old. Paper. Wet paper. Very old." Ricky peeled it open with the same surgical dexterity he used on the peas. "What's this paper?"

"I don't know. Something I found." Jackie's eyes could not get any wider.

Ricky stared at rows of letters, numbers, and symbols on the scrap of paper that fit in the palm of his hand. "A code. Like in *Boys' Life*. I saw this in *Boys' Life*," he said.

"Give it back, Ricky. It belongs to my grandpa."

"It's mine." Ricky pushed through the flap on his end of the tent and crawled to his closet.

Jackie picked up the flashlight and followed behind, whispering, "Ricky. Ricky."

"Mine. Mine," Ricky continued, his head buried in a pile of stuffed animals that filled the bottom of his closet. "Mine," he said again, his voice muffled by his cloth pets.

"Ricky, can I see it?"

"My secret code."

"Just for a second? Then I'll give it back," Jackie said.

"Promise?"

"Promise."

"Stick a needle in your eye?"

Jackie hesitated but knew he had to promise to get Gabe's paper back. "Cross my heart."

Ricky kept his head buried while his arm reached back with the paper in hand. Jackie quickly recovered it and used the flashlight to have a better look.

"Dem aren't words. Just letters and stuff."

"I know, I know," said Ricky with a giggle. He began to crawl backward out of the closet, pulling a flat box with stuffed animals riding on top. "If you want to know a secret you got to get back in the tent."

At this point Jackie didn't question. He had his paper and that's all that mattered to him. He crawled back in with the flashlight. Ricky backed in as well.

"Do you know what that is?" Ricky asked as he tossed the stuffed animals aside.

Jackie read the top of the box. "Ouija."

"My cousin's. My mamma doesn't know I have it." He ripped the lid off the box, threw it aside, and kept talking. "The lady at the library showed me the code from 'The Gold Bug.' She said that guy liked to trick people with his codes. He put them in letters, too, like a game." Ricky kept his gaze on the contents of the box. "Think this could be his code? Remember that man in our class? Or maybe a real *Boys' Life* code?"

"I don't know. May not mean anything. I can't ask my grandpa. He don't know I has it."

Ricky pulled out the game board, unfolded it quickly, and placed it between their knees. Jackie aimed the light to study weird images of the sun and the moon in the corners and the arch of letters with a row of numbers beneath them.

Ricky was as excited as a three-year-old on an Easter egg hunt. He fumbled with the one piece that came with the board. "Take this heart thing with the hole in it and you put it on the board like this." Ricky slid the planchette around on the board as he whispered his instructions. "Then we both place our fingers on the sides of the heart thing and we ask a question."

"What?" Jackie asked.

"Grr," Ricky growled. He slapped his thigh with the flat of his hand, his face puckered to cry. "We ask a question"—he jerked his head, still looking at the board—"and ghosts move the thing around and when it stops we look at what is under the hole, a letter or number." Ricky pulled at his hair with both hands and said, "Then we put all those together and that gives us the answer." Ricky grabbed Jackie's wrist. "Put your fingers like this."

Talking too fast to breathe, Ricky said, "Ask it to tell us what that piece of paper is? If it's a code, we can ask it to tell us what it says. No, wait!" He crawled out of the tent. Jackie could hear him open a drawer or something, then he came back with a sheet of tablet paper in his hand, talking faster still. "No, no, no...ask it if we can talk to Edgar Allan Poe or to Lizzie Doten because the lady at the library told me she talked to Poe's ghost. I wrote that on the paper."

"Ghost?" Jackie said, thinking about the Light and not sure that Ricky made any sense.

Ricky slapped his thigh again. "Come on. Come on. Put your fingers on this."

Ricky placed his fingers on one side of the planchette. Jackie followed Ricky's lead.

"Not so hard. Don't push it. The ghost moves it," Ricky said. He sat perfectly still, eyes closed and expressionless. "Okay, ask the question."

"What do I say?"

"Just wait." Ricky closed his eyes and reentered his previous semiconscious state. "Ouija, can we talk to Edgar Allan Poe?" he said in a deep, mysterious voice.

Immediately when he finished, there was a rapping, a knocking sound. Startled, the boys pulled their hands back like they had touched a hot coal. The planchette smacked the flashlight and blinded Jackie.

"Boys, are you all right in there?" Cybil Clemonds said from outside the bedroom door.

"We're okay, Mamma. Go away," Ricky screamed, his heart beating much quicker now than it had been an instant earlier.

"Okay, but don't stay up too late," Cybil said resisting the urge to barge in and reprimand her son's manners.

"We won't!" Ricky screamed in reply.

Ricky repositioned the flashlight. The boys repositioned their fingers on the slider and waited. Seconds later, it moved; their stomachs moved even more. The planchette slid slowly to the right, then drifted up toward the top of the board, then toward the left and stopped. Ricky looked down through the hole in the slider and saw the word "yes" positioned directly beneath. He looked up at Jackie's face for the first time since he'd arrived. Jackie was a shade lighter, his eyes locked on frozen fingers.

"Now what?" Jackie said. His voice trembled.

Ricky clapped his hands with his fingers splayed so wide they looked like ping-pong paddles. His eyes bulged. His fingers walked down his legs, back into position. Ricky's lips barely opened with enough time to say, "Are you Poe?" before the slider jerked to the far edge of the board so fast their fingers nearly came off the piece, then it carried their fingers back over the word "yes" before it froze. The boys heard something splash against the window.

Jackie flipped back the blanket enough to get his nose out. Nothing there. He looked back at Ricky still cross-legged and entranced by the board. He placed his fingers opposite Ricky's.

"Tell us what the code says," Ricky pleaded in a tentative, soft voice.

The planchette shook, moved, and stopped briefly above the letter T. Then it moved up the board and to the right before it stopped for a second over the letter H, then jerked to the next letter I, and dropped down and back left before it landed on the letter S.

"This..." Ricky repeated.

Jackie acknowledged with a slight dip of his chin, careful not to speak. Together they lightened their fingertips on the slider. Again it moved, but when it did, there was a thump, then a rolling sound, then another louder thump. Ricky pulled away from the board, looked out of the tent, and saw a baseball that had been on his dresser by the window as it rolled across the floor and slowly under his bed.

"What was da'?" Jackie asked as he jerked back his hands.

"Something fell, I think," Ricky said. He put his fingers back into the game with Jackie. Together they watched the heart-shaped marker travel the board to spell the word "clue."

"This clue," Ricky repeated and again, another noise, this time from the bookcase above his bed. Both boys looked out this time.

"It's my lucky horseshoe. It fell." He snuck out to retrieve his good luck charm. "I don't feel so good," he confessed from outside the flap.

"Maybe we shouldn't do dis no more. Something ain't good," Jackie said, crawling to join Ricky. "Put de game away. Let's just go to sleep, Ricky."

Ricky was quick to agree. He stashed the game back in its hiding place and returned to the tent with his horseshoe, which he promptly slid under his pillow. "Goodnight."

"Goodnight, Ricky."

Strange noises grated on Jackie's nerves. For half an hour he flicked open one eye to check on the sounds until he eventually fell asleep. It took Ricky longer. Late into the night while they slept—or thought they slept— Ricky saw the same friendly figure he had seen before, the one in the cloud. It was a little man. Unlike the chilled silence of his first visit, this time the dwarfish figure was doubled over in full belly laughter just outside the tent flap by Ricky's head.

"That game"—the figure laughed—"that Ouija game is pure poppycock." He curtailed his laughter only long enough to speak. " 'Twas not Poe, lad. 'Twas me moving ye hands." Again, he laughed long and hard.

Ricky looked back in the tent; Jackie was sound asleep even as the laughter grew louder.

"And 'twas me," he said with a bow, "who pushed thine ball and dropped thine horseshoe. It has no luck neither, lad. Ye want to talk to Poe, do ye? About treasure? Come now, lad. I be the guard." His British accent toyed with the inflection. "I can talk to him," he added as he hopped off the bed with his toes only inches from Ricky's nose. The air between smelled like wet dog and pluff mud, though neither was near. Ricky looked directly at the little man and noticed he could see through him to his closet. "I can ask Poe about the paper ye have, the one ye believe 'tis a clue. I can ask, but mind ye, that game board is not but an evil joke. Such foolishness I shan't stand." Without wind, clouds, sound, or fanfare of any sort, the figure was gone and Ricky slept on.

CHAPTER 13

A breeze of wet-earth autumn air and snowflake-winter chill whistled through the bedroom window left open a hair. The boys rose sometime between sunrise and pork fat in the skillet to hit the living room for Saturday morning cartoons. Cybil Clemonds served on-demand Eggo waffles and sausage patties in front of the tube. Ricky offered another food art exhibit. Jackie watched cartoons and tried to ignore him. He was successful until Ricky hopped 'round and 'round the room before he devoured the Eggo he'd nibbled into the shape of a frog.

"Ricky, I gotta go. I gotta go fishing with—"

"Bye," Ricky said, fixed on the screen where magpies offered less of a threat and infinitely more interest than Jackie.

Jackie poked his nose into the kitchen. "Thank you, Mrs. Clemonds. I needs to leave now."

Cybil remained bent over a cup of coffee at the Formica table. She smiled an exhausted smile in a way that formed slots in her cheeks. "You're welcome, Jackie. Thank you for spending the night. I hope we will see more of you…soon."

Jackie offered a yes-ma'am polite smile like his mamma taught him, and headed out.

Once in a while on Saturdays, Grandpa Gabe's friend Obadiah let Jackie and the Cockrill brothers—Anthony, Sumter, and Isaac—use his bateau for fishing. They never went far. Rowed a piece up the Beaufort River then poled the flat-bottomed boat through the marshes till they caught enough fish or shrimp for dinner and headed back to the dock. With the wind and chill, this was one of those days when their mammas would have to find something else for dinner; their luck on the water failed them. They tied up at the dock by the bridge to Lady's Island, grabbed their gear, and headed up Carteret Street toward home.

The Cockrill brothers were well known in Beaufort. Anthony, a sophomore at Robert Smalls High School, had already made a name for himself in football. He was a tall string bean, which made him an easy target for long balls down field. With hands nearly the size of serving trays, he caught most anything thrown his way, and when he did, he was gone. Nobody had ever caught him with a football in his hands. Sumter was the middle Cockrill. At twelve, he was too short, too round, too slow, and too lazy to be in sports. Like Ferdinand the Bull, he spent afternoons under Paul Bunyan, the prized live oak in the Greene Street Playground near their house in the North Quadrant. He was never really motivated to do much of anything but look at bugs and watch the other kids play, exactly what the first-grade Cockrill, Isaac, did. In the park the youngest Cockrill was always in a swing, playing Red Rover with his munchkin-sized friends, or twisting through the jungle-gym maze of galvanized pipe. Every evening the neighborhood could count on the familiar school bell that Earnestine Cockrill would ring to signal suppertime. She never had to ring the bell a second time.

Sunshades slapped against porch posts as the boys swaggered up Carteret Street, doing the sorts of things Negro boys did, mindful of white passersby who might take offense. Two-by-two, down the sidewalk, they goaded each other about girls, cooties, and Jackie's school.

"Jackie, you never answered my question whiles we was out. Did you say you spent de night wid de preacher man son? He retarded, ain't he?" asked Anthony Cockrill. He walked a distance behind Jackie to avoid the bobber, hook, and cane pole over Jackie's shoulder.

"No, he ain't retarded. He just a little slow maybe sometimes. Da' all. He has some trouble talking and thinking straight. He get nervous, but he all right."

"No, he retarded," said Sumter. "Ever sees him walk? He kinda slumped over and kinda drags his foot sometimes, don't he?"

Jackie didn't answer. He knew they were right, but he wasn't comfortable with where the discussion was headed.

"So, what you do over dey? Why you hang out wid dem white kids anyways?" Anthony ragged while he stopped to wait on Isaac, who as the youngest—for the privilege to go fishing with the big boys—had to carry the metal pail with only two fish but half filled with water. "I heared a couple dem white girls talking about him coming out of Bitty's Disc Den. One dem said da' kid were a certified moron."

"What's da'?" asked Isaac, who dumped out half of the water when Anthony turned away.

"He's not a—" Jackie started.

"Da' a stupid person. Somebody da' ain't smart," said Anthony.

142

"Da' mean Sumter be a moron." Isaac laughed. When Sumter turned to grab him, Isaac dropped the bucket and hid behind Anthony's legs.

"You gets you little black butt back here or I gets Sharmane Johnson to put cooties on you at school," Sumter said. He lunged toward his little brother.

"He ain't a moron. He ain't really retarded, neither. He just new and tryin' to make friends."

"And he picked you, de poor colored boy in de white school?" Sumter said. "Da' kid must be for sure cuckoo ef you aks me."

"His mamma asked me to come over."

"Why?"

"'Cause we are doin' da' project on de Gullah treasure. Him, me, and Skeet Gundy."

"Oh yeah," echoed Anthony. "Skeet Gundy."

As they passed the Lord Carteret Motel, Jackie looked over his shoulder into the parking lot and the corner room. "His mamma call my mamma. She explained how much trouble Ricky was havin' gettin' settled into de new school. My mamma told her I be havin' problems, too. I guess Ricky's mamma thought since we was both new and havin' problems wid de other kids da' maybe de two of us could be friends or somethin'."

Ahead they watched as a small boy came out of the library, looked both ways—several times—then crossed to their side of the street. It was obvious from his size and his gimp, it was Ricky Clemonds.

"What does ya know? It be you friend de moron," Sumter said with a sharp elbow jab to Jackie's ribs.

Anthony quickly looked around, noticed there nobody else in sight, and yelled, "Hey, Ricky. Wait up. Jackie here wants to talk to you."

Ricky turned to see who called his name. When he did, he saw Jackie send a signal with a shake of his head.

People. Colored people. Many colored people. A mob of colored people. Ricky leaned forward, head down. He tried to put more sidewalk between him and the others, but his limp was no match for the Cockrills, who seconds later surrounded him. Jackie hesitated but joined the huddle with Ricky in the middle. Ricky tried to slip around little Isaac, but Sumter cut him off.

"What's in da' lunchbox, Ricky? It Saturday. Ain't no school today? You pretending it a school day? You wants you pal Jackie to play school wid ya?" Anthony asked with a faux-sympathetic look on his face. He checked the streets for would-be passersby.

Ricky studied the cracks in the concrete by his feet. He clutched his lunchbox to his chest and inched his feet to move around Sumter, but the younger boy's bulk blocked him.

"What for lunch, Ricky?" Sumter asked with a mean smirk. When he reached for the lunchbox, Ricky wrenched his shoulder away from the hand. With the sudden jerk, he lost his grip and the small metal box hit the concrete; the Davy Crockett lid popped open. Jackie dropped his fishing pole and grabbed both the lunch box and the contents that lay beside it, a copy of "The Gold Bug" and a folded *Boy's Life* magazine.

"Da' sure do look like a good lunch, Ricky!" said the oldest Cockrill.

"Moron!" Isaac chimed in.

"Hush up, boy," Jackie warned. "Leave him alone."

Looking up, Anthony noticed a car as it turned and drove in their direction. He and his brothers put some space between them and the other two boys. Jackie handed Ricky the lunch box, then placed the other items inside. Ricky latched the lid and squeezed his prized possession to his chest. He closed his eyes so hard he saw stars.

The car coasted as it approached and slowed to a crawl as it passed. The driver was a teenage white boy wearing a baseball cap with a Confederate flag across the front. He glared at the two on the sidewalk, then shifted to stare down the other three before he stomped on the gas pedal, leaving some of Firestone's finest rubber tattooed on the pavement. A thick cloud of Quaker State blue smoke chased from behind.

"Let's go," Jackie said. He and Ricky began a slow walk up the sidewalk.

"Now why you go helping dis poor white boy, Jackie? Dey ain't doing you no good at da' school of yours," Sumter said as the three brothers stepped up to walk alongside the other two.

"Y'all leave him alone," Jackie urged.

"I need to go," Ricky said. "I need to go." His walk was incredibly slow; he never looked up. He seemed to navigate by counting the squares of concrete along the walk.

Anthony jumped to the front and stopped the group directly opposite the Methodist church on Carteret Street.

"Why you don't want to talk wid we other Negroes? You talk to Jackie, here," Anthony said, his deep voice cracking with puberty. He reached over and snatched at Ricky's arm but came up empty.

"You is a moron, ain't ya?" little Isaac asked, still lost by the meaning or the insult.

Ricky shook his head. "The books, they know where the Gullah treasure is."

"Then, I guess you be right, Isaac. He surely be a moron even ef he ain't even goin' to say he ain't," Sumter said, he too, reaching for the lunchbox. He leaned closer to Ricky and said loudly, "Fool. Dey ain't no Gullah treasure. You be crazy."

"No. It's real. There is. It's real. Real treasure. I know it. It's real," Ricky retorted with no fear in his voice. "The treasure is at that house. The Castle house. It's real. The little man. He told me. The treasure is real."

The words drew a laugh from the two older Cockrills. They could see the white kid tremble from tonsils to toes; they loved it.

"He be a moron, Isaac. You know'd da'," Sumter said. "He be talkin' to little peoples what ain't real."

Jackie's eyebrows rose. He stared and wondered why his mixed-up white friend would talk his crazy talk now. *Just be quiet, Ricky.*

Ricky wrapped his arms around his chest to protect his lunchbox; his body whipped uncontrollably. With closed eyes, without a breath, he sputtered, "He is, too, real. He's there to guard the—"

"Shut up, you moron," Anthony argued, leaning to whisper directly into Ricky's ear. "Dey ain't no treasure. Ain't no Gullahs got no treasures. Remember da' from your books. Dem white men took all da'." His nose tickled at Ricky's ear.

"Hey, boys. What you doing to my good pal, Ricky?" a voice hollered as a car rolled to a stop beside them. It was Skeet Gundy, riding shotgun in his brother's car, the car that had passed at a crawl. "You colored boys need something?" Skeet asked, dragging out the words with a peculiar drawl.

"No, Mr. Skeet. We just walkin' home. Jackie here saws Ricky and wanted to aks him somethin'," Anthony answered while his two brothers backpedaled away from the car.

"Well then, why don't you boys just mosey right along now, y'hear. Just move on up that sidewalk and get on home to your mamma." Skeet motioned with his thumb to provide direction.

Poles and pail in hand, the Cockrills hurried up Carteret Street, just enough to satisfy Skeet; Jackie stayed.

"So, Ricky, what's in the lunchbox, pal? We ain't got no school today. Where you been?"

Ricky turned his back to the speaker. He focused his eyes on the ground and the red brick steps of the house close by and tried not to be frightened. "I went to the library. I found the treasure. Yeah. I found the treasure," he mumbled, a bit more relaxed without people in his face.

"You what? Come over here, you idiot," Skeet shouted. He reached through the open window and pounded on the outside of his door.

Ricky turned to go to the car window, but Jackie grabbed his shirt. Ricky continued to pull to get to the car. Jackie held fast.

"Let him go, boy," Skeet warned.

"Leave him alone, Skeet. Just leave him alone."

"Hey, boy, I ain't telling you again. I'm talking to Retardo. I'll finish with you later. Now, let go of him."

Ricky squirmed to move closer to Skeet, but Jackie pulled him back and stepped in front, outside of Skeet's reach.

"Look, ya little coon, get out of the way or I'll move you out of the way," Skeet threatened.

Jackie stood his ground. When Ricky tried to step around him, Jackie corralled him with stiff arms.

Skeet pounded the side of the car again; his brother antagonized them from behind the steering wheel.

"I ain't warnin' you again. Step aside, boy!"

When Jackie refused to budge, Skeet grabbed the outside handle and opened the car door.

The midday sun blinded Elliott Clemonds as he stepped through the massive church doors across the street. He squinted. Through the slits in his eyes, he saw the car door open and Skeet's head pop up from inside. Seconds later he saw his son next to Jackie.

"Ricky, are you okay, son?" the reverend shouted.

When Skeet's brother saw the preacher hustle down the steps, he stretched out across the front seat, grabbed Skeet by his belt, and yanked him back in the car. The car sped off before Skeet could close the door. As it passed the three Cockrill brothers, Skeet flipped them the bird, though they appeared more interested in Jackie.

Pastor Clemonds emerged through an oily blue cloud similar to the one the car left earlier. "You okay, big fella? I thought I asked you to wait for me to walk you home."

"Yeah, Daddy. Just wanted to walk. Wanted to talk to Jackie."

"Who was in that car?"

"Skeet. The boy from school. Skeet Gundy. Kinda dumb," Ricky replied.

The name didn't register with the boy's father. "Guess they were in a hurry," he said as he watched the car disappear around Bellamy's Curve. "Mind if I walk with you boys?"

"Excuse me, Reverend Clemonds, sir. I needs to get on home. I'll see you later, Ricky."

Ricky waited until Jackie was several steps away before he fearlessly looked at the back of the colored boy's head. "Bye," he replied, raising one hand a tad.

Jackie broke into a trot. When he caught up with his colored friends, he stole a glance back toward Ricky and the reverend. The pair didn't bother to follow him and the others. Elliott Clemonds, with a Davy Crockett lunchbox in his left hand, tilted to his right to listen to Ricky as he limped the block and a half to their house.

Jackie had a few words with the Cockrills when he rejoined them. They didn't want to hear any of it. They shook him off the same way they shook off Skeet. They were still buzzed about the treasure.

"Hey, come on," Isaac said, "let's go into de library an look for treasure maps like de moron kid did. We can finds de treasure before him, can't we?"

To amuse his little brother, Anthony told Sumter to carry the bucket of fish home while he and Jackie took Isaac into the colored-branch library.

"I can't. I needs to get to Grandpa Gabe's house. I told Mamma I would stop to see him right after fishing. I gotta fix one of dem porch steps. I be late already."

After the group split and had gone their separate ways, Jackie heard the wail of a siren before he saw the ambulance round the corner from Prince Street on two wheels. He watched the red bubble on top as it weaved its way around stopped cars headed toward Bay Street.

Less than half a block away, he saw his mother. She was standing on Grandpa Gabe's front porch, her hands folded ready for prayer in front of her mouth. He quickened his pace to join her.

"Mamma, what's wrong?"

"Grandpa Gabe. De ambulance just took Grandpa Gabe to de hospital, Jackie."

The boy's heart stopped momentarily. "Why, Mamma? What happened?"

Hestelle Eddings didn't respond. She bowed her head, gripped herself in a bear hug, and rocked back and forth like she had a baby in her arms.

"What happened, Mamma?" Jackie pleaded. He peered around his mother and looked at the front room.

"Dey said he was robbed or it looked like he was robbed. He don't have nothing. Why would somebody try to rob Grandpa Gabe?" she said as she sobbed and rocked.

Jackie moved closer to the door. He saw his grandpa's favorite chair and beyond that on the floor a pile of papers.

"Dey think it be his heart. A heart attack. He might die, Jackie. Grandpa Gabe might die." She staggered to lean against the pillar by the porch steps, where she bawled into her hands.

Jackie looked closer at the mess on the floor by the chair. Papers and a familiar box, the box where he had found the scrap of paper he shared with Ricky.

Maybe it was a clue. Maybe somebody else knew.

CHAPTER 14

For five days, Hestelle Pritchard Eddings paced, wall to wall, in an oversized utility closet converted into an undersized two-bed hospital room where Grandpa Gabe lay, briefly conscious, seldom coherent. Outside the walls of the Beaufort Memorial Hospital, scores throughout the Lowcountry made ready the checklist for what appeared to be the inevitable funeral service. Foods prepared. House cleaned. Burial cloths—both white and black—cut. But when the patriarch of the Gullah community knocked on the pearly gates, Saint Peter told Gabe to go back and finish his work; it wasn't yet his time.

Jackie had not been allowed to visit his grandpa during those days, but on the fifth day his parents took him to the hospital. As they entered through the side door marked "Colored Entrance," menacing thunderheads boomed off to the east over the Atlantic. Inside Jackie was dazed by the spotless quiet. He noticed how bright and white things were—doctors in long white smocks, nurses in long white house coats over their clothes; all the people wore white. The halls smelled of bleach and heavy starch. He walked to the end of a white corridor. He entered a white room. There he saw two colored men; one was Grandpa Gabe. His mother told him he had to talk softly because the other colored man in the room was in great pain. The doctors had to saw off his left leg below the knee the day prior as a result of complications due to diabetes.

Jackie became squeamish when he stepped inside the door and saw Gabe in the first bed. He stood motionless and watched the blankets that covered his grandpa rise and fall ever so slightly. His eyes wandered to monitors that flashed and beeped, visible signs of Gabe's waning existence. His eyes were closed, buried deep in sockets of coal-black, cheeks vacuum sealed over angled bones, the picture of a man who, in his ninety-sixth year, carried the legacy of a Gullah culture threatened by despair and greed. Most men his age, especially colored men, died decades earlier, sacrificed in war and persecuted in peace, segregated into a second-tier society deprived of social status and the freedoms that came with it.

Jackie surveyed the sterile confines of the room. Stark. Basic. White. On one wall, a photo of the Lady's Island Bridge in a thin black frame. On the wall in front of the bed, a Coca-Cola calendar with a glossy picture of a girl in her white graduation cap and gown surrounded by five guys, all offering her a Coke with words that declared, "Things go better with Coke." They were all white. The rows and columns of days beneath the caption were May and June, months that had passed a half year earlier. A partition divided the room, nothing more than a metal frame on wheels with a white curtain, a simple solution for privacy and to muffle the incessant moan hidden on the opposite side. When Jackie dared to peek at the bed around the screen, he saw how the covers draped over the right foot and slumped sharply to a nub below the left knee. The man, much younger and lighter than his grandpa, covered his eyes with his forearm to darken his world of pain.

Irvin Eddings waited outside the room, only two guests allowed at any given time, hospital rules. Hestelle Eddings listened and counted each labored breath from the only chair in the corner. It wasn't like the other chairs Jackie saw in the halls. The chair was a salvaged leathery thing that hung low to the ground from decades of use. The webbing, what there was, could barely support the weight of the cushion and certainly not that of a concerned family member with tired feet. Other than frequent visits by Gabe's personal physician and friend, Dr. Palmer, only family members had braved the segregated restrictions of the hospital.

They had been in the room nearly fifteen minutes before Gabe opened his eyes. He was groggy, but the tips of his mouth perked upward when he saw Jackie. He was pleased. Hestelle moved from her chair to be closer. She fluffed pillows and placed them behind Gabe's back, then held the back of his head while she touched a small Dixie cup to his lips for a sip of water. As he rested she stroked the wrinkles and the deep dimples of his cheeks, roughed by gray stubble. Though he was able to talk, she was conscious of his weakened state; she brushed his lips with her finger to keep him quiet. Heavy tears lingered in the corners of her eyes as she softly shared news from the neighbors and other well-wishers. Several minutes passed before Gabe rolled his head toward her and uttered, "Stelle...let me talks to de boy." He gasped for a breath. "Alone."

"Sure, Grandpa. Sure," she said, forcing a pained smile. She motioned for Jackie to come to her side of the bed. She turned away from Gabe's ear and gave her son instructions. "Now, just listen to Grandpa Gabe. Don't you be asking him a bunch of foolish questions or make him talks a lot. He be very weak, Jackie. Understand? He need to rest. Just listen to what he have to say. And, ef anything happens, ef he needs anything, you come and gets me right away. Okay? I be right outside de door wid your daddy. Okay? Understand?"

"Yes, Mamma," he affirmed with a series of nods.

"Okay." She turned back toward the bed and removed a pillow to allow Gabe to recline peacefully. "Listen to dem nurses here, Grandpa. Dey make you well so you can goes home soon." When she bent down, two heavy tears dripped on the old man's forehead. She kissed them away, rubbed her hand across the top of his head, and ended with a loving pat on his bony shoulder. As Hestelle walked out of the room, Jackie moved toward the head of the bed to be closer to his grandpa's muted, strained voice.

"Come here, boy," he whispered.

Jackie leaned into the mattress closer to the old man.

Gabe lay there, his head cradled in pillows, his deep-brown eyes fixed on the ceiling. He struggled with short sips of air between his words. "I has dis box. It be from my parents and dey parents, dey story," he said before he closed his eyes.

"I be missing something, boy." Through the slits below his eyelids, Gabe tracked the hazy path of a fly that butted, persistently, against the clear glass globe above his bed. He coughed and continued, his voice a deliberate but breathy monotone. "Da' box be de oldest of all dem things I has. Small things my daddy touch and his daddy…"

Jackie listened as the voice trailed off. He looked toward the ceiling and followed the same fly as Gabe. He listened to the moan from beyond the screen.

Gabe broke the silence, his eyes still closed. "You know da' box, boy?"

154

Jackie looked down at the head on the pillow. "No, Grandpa," he replied.

Gabe fought for a deeper breath. "You know de box I has?"

"You has lots of boxes. I don't know about da' one." He hated to lie to his grandpa. He was sure it was the box where he had spilled water early, but he was afraid to admit his accident which got Gabe's precious papers wet.

"De one under da' bird cage?"

"A box under da' cage?" he said with feigned surprise.

Gabe drew a deep breath. "You opened da' box."

"Nu-uh, Grandpa. I never saw da' box."

Gabe slowly rolled his cheek toward Jackie. His eyes, tunneled deeper in his skull. "I saw you, boy."

"I don't know what you mean!" While he struggled with the words, Jackie avoided Gabe. He shot a glance toward the monitor beyond the old man's head, then up to the fly above.

"I heared you say something"—he chopped his words for air—"an' saw you move da' cage." He stared hard at Jackie. "In da' television…I saw you put something in you pocket."

"No, Grandpa. I didn't take nothing. Honest." Fear left a dull headache in its wake. He wished his mamma would appear, or a nurse or somebody. He had never felt this way around his grandpa. His mouth went dry. Sweat beaded on his brow. Goosebumps popped up on his arms. He imagined his nose grow longer.

Gabe rolled his head away. The fly was gone. He stared at the filament in the light, refusing to blink or breathe.

"Grandpa? Grandpa Gabe? Grandpa?" Jackie leaned his ear over Gabe's lips. The only sound Jackie heard was the rhythm of his own nervous heart. Even the monitors with their incessant beeps shared the silence.

Jackie turned for the door, then heard Gabe exhale two shallow breaths in rapid succession.

"Mamma?" Gabe sniffled. "Mamma? I sees you," Gabe said longingly. The muscle in his left jaw rose enough to show he had smiled. "Yes, Mamma…I knows, Mamma…Massa Lembath he say…I look, Mamma…I look." His voice trailed off to a quiet mutter. Jackie watched and listened as Gabe rolled his head side to side and mumbled words—responses—for minutes to a voice Jackie could not hear.

He rolled his head toward Jackie. "Jackie," Gabe managed. "Come…"

Jackie snuggled as close as he could.

"Grandpa, I looked—" Jackie started, moved by courage to confess.

Gabe's withered voice choked out two words. "Don't lie." Short breaths, gasps with little air. His eyes still closed, he choked, "I look through da' box. I put de letter in my bib. Dey were no scrap." His head turned away. "I dumped all dem boxes. Da' scrap. It be missing. I waked up here."

He hiccupped and took three short breaths. Jackie was torn. He wanted to go for help, but he couldn't leave his grandpa, not now. He might not ever hear his voice again. He wiped away tears that blurred his eyes.

"Grandpa Gabe, I—"

"My bibs. Find dem. De letter. It be in dem," Gabe said. He rolled his head. His eyes opened and pointed toward a coat tree in the corner by the closed door. Jackie reluctantly left the bedside and backpedaled to the pole, never taking his eyes off Gabe. In the bib on the front of a ragged pair of coveralls, Jackie pulled a flimsy dog-eared and stained piece of paper.

"Did you finds dem?" Gabe asked with a hurried gasp when Jackie returned.

Jackie unfolded the sheet. The handwriting was script he had never seen in school, even in his new school. The penmanship was fancy with curves and looped letters, much better than Jackie's handwriting. He scanned the body of the letter when his eyes noticed the signature, one bit of writing he thought he could read. Edgar A. Poe. The letter, it was signed by Poe. Ricky had said—

"Did you find it, Jackie?"

"Yes, Grandpa Gabe."

"Da' paper in you pocket and de let—" Suddenly, Gabe choked and began to cough. This time Jackie didn't hesitate. He refolded the letter, shoved it into his pocket, and reached for the doorknob.

"Mamma! Mamma!"

Hestelle Eddings heard Gabe choking and rushed past Jackie into the room. Irvin grabbed his son by the shoulders and turned him out toward the hall.

"Nurse!" Irvin called. "We needs a nurse. Help!" he yelled.

Two nurses quickly came to the room.

"Ma'am, I'm sorry but you're going to have to leave now," one nurse said as she nudged Hestelle toward the hall.

"No! Grandpa!" she cried. "Grandpa!"

"We'll take care of him. We need you to leave now. He needs his rest."

Hestelle looked over her shoulder to the other nurse who stood over her great-grandfather, her hands flying about. When they reached the hall, the nurse closed the door behind Hestelle, who dissolved in her husband's arms. From inside the room, they could hear the nurses, then a page for a doctor over the hospital speakers. While Gabe clung to life, Jackie waited with his parents. In his pocket he held the letter, in his head he held the secret, and in his heart he held his unconfessed lie.

CHAPTER 15

O n the drive home guilt churned inside Jackie's stomach. He saw how lying to Grandpa Gabe affected him and how he may never be able to confess the truth. Back in his room, Jackie closed the door and cried facedown on his bed until his tears came out dry. A bird outside his window croaked. He lifted his head and looked around; he was safe and alone. He sat up and looked over and over again at the letter and the scrap spread on his bed. As much as he tried, he couldn't seem to grasp the complete meaning behind Poe's words and phrases, if in fact they were his. The mere fact that the letter—the paper itself—was over one hundred years old amazed him. It was the oldest thing he had ever seen. The words, Poe's words, were written nearly one hundred and fifty years earlier.

After dinner, the Eddings family made their weekly pilgrimage to the praise house on Saint Helena Island. The community would be there to pray for old Gabe; Jackie knew he had to be a part of the service and the "shout."

Stars poked through banks of fast-moving clouds beneath a moon that hung full in the night sky, bright enough to see colors at a distance with shadows near and far. When they approached Penn Center, Irvin Eddings slowed. Jackie saw the crowd of black cars like the one that gave him the ride weeks before, a Volkswagen van, and an old school bus near the large meeting hall. People moved about freely, back and forth across the road in the moonlight. His father passed the main entrance and turned into a narrow gravel drive on the opposite side of the road. A small sign directed him to the Gantt Cottage. Irvin parked in front of the building and told Jackie to stay with his mother. Two Negro men walked up to the car, shook Irvin's hand, and the three of them went inside. The two greeters—unfamiliar faces to Jackie— came out almost immediately, but Irvin didn't reappear for five minutes or more. When he returned to the car, he didn't say anything. He just drove off, down Lands End Road the short distance to the Pritchard Praise House.

The grassy field around the small building was dotted with cars. A solitary bulb above the door cast a dim silo of light that barely illuminated the two steps into the chapel, but the ample moonlight made it easy for the Eddings family to join the others inside.

Irvin Eddings walked several steps behind his wife and son. As he did, he noticed a figure on the far corner of the tiny gathering place. The figure teetered with both feet on a wobbly two-foot stump, hands cupped around both eyes; it appeared the figure was peeking between the slats or cracks of the wooden wall. The older Eddings stepped away from his family and toward the rear of the building to get a better look. About that time a man in a hat carrying a long object came through the open front door and headed around the other side of the chapel. Irvin stopped. The figure on the stump flattened against the wall when he saw the man in the hat pass the rear wall, headed toward the woods.

"Hey!" Irvin Eddings shouted.

The two figures both responded. The man in the hat looked briefly toward Irvin before he hurried into the woods. The figure on the stump wobbled and hit the ground with a thud, then ran away, fast.

"Irvin, come on!" Hestelle yelled. "Dey is waiting for us inside. Now come on."

Irvin Eddings didn't bother to pursue either of the figures. The service tonight was meant for Grandpa Gabe. He owed Hestelle's family that respect. He hesitated and watched the figures for another few seconds, long enough to recognize one distinguishing feature about the figure on the stump. It was a white man.

He joined his family and took his place inside among the other worshippers. Like other praise houses, seating was assigned based on long-standing traditions within the community. Hestelle Eddings, as a direct descendant of the Pritchard family line, had seats on the front bench reserved for her. Handshakes and hugs with words of comfort and encouragement welcomed them as they made their way to the front.

A petite lady, not much taller than Jackie, warmed the crowded one-room building with an a cappella gospel hymn, the first of many for the service. The gospel music, with all the old people singing off-key, embarrassed Jackie; he simply mouthed most of the words. He bowed his head, chin to chest, and thought about Grandpa Gabe. Between the hymns several members of the congregation jockeyed to recite favorite scripture passages from the Bible—James 2:2–4, Leviticus 19:19 and others—but only two bothered a glance at the written word; all the others needed no text. The verses emblazoned in their memories rang with "hallelujahs" and "amens" aplenty to invoke heavenly light on Gabe and sundry topics pertinent to the times.

After the readings and hymns, the group pushed the benches tight against the walls and formed a circle. An elderly lady, dressed in white from top to bottom—head wrap to high heels— launched into her raspy rendition of "I Feel Like Praising Him." With energy akin to a freight train leaving the station, the hand-clapping, cane-tapping, foot-stomping ring shout crescendoed. The overflow crowd had little room to shuffle and twist their bodies in the customary fashion. The hot, humid air inside the century-old building quickly filled with a suffocating mix of rose water, lavender, Old Spice, and mold, almost too stale to breathe. Cries and shouts propelled the counterclockwise movement. Shoulders held stiff. Feet scuffed. Hips wiggled.

The slow, jerky rotation allowed Jackie and a handful of others to slip out as their part of the circle moved past the door. All the early departees, except Jackie, were quick to crank up their cars and leave. Out of the stuffy room, greeted by the tannic smell of burning leaves, Jackie breathed a sigh of relief as he wandered about the grassy lot, shadow cast long under the full moon. He needed less music, prayers, shouts, and cries. He needed the twinkle of the stars, the touch of the breeze, the peace of the night. He found it there, but for a very short time. In the distance, through the moss-shrouded oaks, pointed palms, and towering pines, he saw a light. He remembered the light that threatened him weeks earlier. The masks. The chase. The long walk in the dark. The ride from a stranger. He turned away and walked back toward the chapel, thinking of Gabe, but images of the costumed figures returned. Another look back over his shoulder was all it took.

Like a moth to a flame, he jogged across the field, into the woods, and down the same path he had used before, being more careful this time, curious more than scared. And they were there. The same strange costumed figures. He saw them, three of them, before a bag covered his head. It happened so fast he couldn't react. As the hood went across his head and over his eyes, he looked toward his feet. Even in the woods, dense as the underside of a woolen blanket, the moon volunteered enough light for him to tell there was a person and the person wore coveralls with spartina grass cuffs, like the others. He squirmed to free himself, which did no good. Whoever bagged him had slapped his mouth with a paw or a mitt. Even if he could scream, the ring shout in the praise house filled the air with "Lordy be" this and "Lordy be" that, "hallelujahs" and "amens"—not even the angels could hear their own harps. When the figure cleared the wood line near the light, someone or something else grabbed ahold of Jackie's feet. They wrapped and tied his ankles with heavy twine and placed him on a seat, a stumpy log. He pushed to stand, but two large hands crunched his shoulders down while another pair tied his hands behind his back. In the end, someone cinched a soft muzzle around his face, which made it impossible to yell. With the bag over his head and his mouth tightly covered, each breath became more of a challenge, so much so, starved for oxygen, Jackie passed out.

He had no idea how long he was unconscious, but when he opened his eyes, Jackie could see everything. His captors had removed the bag from his head. The gag across his mouth had a new taste. The hood itself was gone, but now he wore something new, something hard on his face and forehead. When he shook his head, it felt like a mask, tall and round, like a plate. Attached to it out of the corners of his eyes he could see rope or strands of hair knotted up like dreadlocks. They had stripped him of his street clothes. The adrenaline that coursed through his body warmed him against the chilly night air. Over his shoulders and chest he now wore an open weave fishing net like a poncho. Twine, pulled tight around his stump seat, cut into his shins. He was powerless, unable to say or do anything; he listened and watched as the figures—assumed to be men based on their voices alone—danced around the lighted pit in front of him. At first he questioned why hadn't he returned to the shout and Grandpa Gabe. But the siren call of curiosity lured him back into the woods. Unlike his first encounter in the woods, he had tried to be more careful, but this time it seemed like they had a plan. A surprise. An ambush. And then? But the masks and brown suits confused him. He understood pointed hoods and white capes. This was different. His imagination raced, and not toward pleasant endings.

The dancers moved in a similar fashion to the ring shout. Counterclockwise, feet shuffled, shoulders cocked, arms in constant motion—up, down, out, and in. Jackie couldn't understand what he heard. It sounded like the Gullah the older Negroes spoke, but his parents and teachers had discouraged his use of that language the day he started school—years before he attended the all-white school—which made it nearly impossible for him to interpret their somber incantation. The haystack figure with a burlap hood stepped away from the others and pulled out a large knife, the size of a machete or cleaver. He began to gyrate in a separate dance, beckoning to the others to approach him. One by one they did. Each danced with patterned strides. One approached while the other two, on their knees, bowed low, continuously. The ritual dragged on for an eternity—or so it seemed to a wide-eyed Jackie—but the moon had moved in and out of clouds for only fifteen minutes.

Then the dances stopped. The haystack raised his arm with the knife and walked behind Jackie. Jackie screamed as hard as he could, but the wad in his mouth muffled the sound to nothing. He twisted and squirmed on the stump. He couldn't detect any movement in the thicket of vines, scrub oaks, and palmettos back toward the woods. His stomach gurgled. Bubbles lodged in his throat. Anxious for any movement, he turned back toward the three prostrate in the sand on the far side of the small clearing. He pulled his hands against the twine on his wrists until the pain became too much. He snorted for air but sat motionless.

From the corner of his eye, Jackie saw the fourth figure slip out of the woods; it was the haystack. Over his shoulder he dangled a metal chain stringer with small dead animals, each on a separate hook. Moonlight between the clouds revealed the carcasses of a raccoon; a rabbit, maybe two; a squirrel; a marsh rat; maybe a cat, and an opossum. The breeze had picked up. A one-word unintelligible, subdued shout from the haystack energized the others. They hoisted their heavy-masked heads from the sand, rose onto all fours, swaying and chanting louder and louder as they hoisted themselves to their feet. Jackie reenergized his efforts to free his hands and feet with the masked figures closer and closer around him. One figure, the one with the water buffalo head, pushed hard on Jackie's shoulders to hold him. The haystack stomped forward to within a foot of the stump. When Jackie looked away, another figure, the one with the warthog face, grabbed the boy's chin and yanked it upward to force him to watch. The haystack unhooked the marsh rat and snapped it on the net Jackie wore over his bare chest. He flinched when the cold fur rubbed against his skin. The large hands on his shoulders crunched down harder while Jackie watched the raccoon and all the other lifeless critters become a part of his mantle. The foul odor of blood and rot nearly caused him to vomit.

The moon now hid behind the edge of a cloud. Drumrolls of a storm thundered in the distance. Lightning axed through the sky over the outer islands. The winds bent treetops. The smell of rain was all around, but it had not started at their site. Two of the figures, the haystack and the character with a beard made of shells on strings, conferred away from the others.

"Get da' boy. We needs to go now," haystack said. "Church be over soon."

"Wait," the water buffalo cried. He approached Jackie, tilted his head in a peculiar manner, and said, "Where is the clue? The small paper you stole from the old man?"

Jackie, held firmly by two grown men, was too exhausted to respond and had scant energy to think. *How does he know Grandpa Gabe had the paper? How does he know I took it?*

"Huh? What?" Jackie replied from his daze.

The mask came closer. "I said…I want to know what you did with the sheet, the clue?"

Jackie didn't respond. The voice sounded familiar, or so he thought.

Haystack pushed the water buffalo aside and nodded. A minute later the water buffalo returned with a primitive spear. He flashed it menacingly close to Jackie's eyes. The hand around Jackie's jaw and cheeks grew tighter.

With the tip of the spear just below Jackie's Adam's apple, the water buffalo spoke again. "I asked you, where is that sheet? You know exactly which one I mean."

With his chin, jaw, and cheeks strained, the tip of the spear was the only incentive he needed to choke out his reply. "Da' man from Virginia. De Poe man. He talked at my school, to my class. He has it," he gurgled, adding to his string of lies.

"Why?"

Jackie remained silent.

With that, the spear tip dropped to the ground, his chin fell free, and some of the pressure on Jackie's shoulders disappeared. The haystack stood firmly in front of Jackie, the spartina grass of his costume flapping in the gusts from the east. The others fumbled behind Jackie before they untied his feet and yanked him off the stump. When they grabbed his elbow to turn him, Jackie ripped loose of their hands and lunged to run away. That's when he realized they had tied a rope to his wrists. His arms shot up behind him in a most unnatural way. The collection of dead animals hooked to his chest thumped against his skin.

Veils of rain under a rolling barrage of thunder and volleys of lightning emptied the praise house, people running from cover to cars, their Bibles over their heads. Gusts of wind drove rain sideways. Strobes of lightning replaced the illumination of the earlier full moon; the distant flashes cut a Sleepy Hollow-silhouette of trees on the edge of the field.

Well-wishers held Hestelle Eddings hostage while the storm raged. Eventually, only her husband and Titus McTurion, the praise house leader, remained.

"Irvin, where's Jackie?" she asked.

"He was in de back during de shout. I saw him. I know I saw him dey a while back."

Irvin placed his Bible over his head and looked out the door. The rain and wind nearly blasted the Good Book out of his hand. "Jackie! Jackie Robinson!" he yelled against the force of the rain. The storm muffled his voice, audible to no more than fifty feet from the building. He stepped outside and looked around. The field was clear except for his car and Titus's.

Irvin tucked the Bible under his arm, cupped his hands, and cried again with more volume, "Jackie!"

"Maybe he went home wid someone else. Dis here rain, ya know..." suggested the preacher.

Hestelle pulled her head back and creased her brow at the suggestion.

"Probably. Someone probably told him not to wait for us out in de storm so dey grab him and dey took him on home," Irvin said. Soaked completely, he wiped the rain off his Bible. "I'm sure da' boy ain't out dey in dis rain."

A mother's instinct nudging her, Hestelle didn't want to agree, but did nonetheless. "Da' boy and me goin' to have us a talk, uh-huh."

The Eddings dashed to their car. Irvin unlocked the passenger door for his wife first. The instant Hestelle's door slammed shut, lightning exploded in a fireball atop a tall pine in the woods beyond the praise house. The ground surge popped the light above the door and scared the bejesus out of Titus McTurion, who shook so hard he couldn't get the padlock through the hasp and chain to lock up the praise house. When he did, he bolted for his car. Halfway there, lightning lit up the field with pyrotechnics only Mother Nature could provide. Had he bothered to look up, the flashes would have exposed a quartet of weird-looking creatures as they marched two-by-two deeper into the woods with one scared, near-naked colored boy.

CHAPTER 16

The Eddings arrived home to a dark and empty house. Hestelle checked Jackie's room. He was not in bed or reading. She looked for a note, but found none. Nor did she see any likely signs of his return, like water tracked in from the storm or wet clothes on the floor. Hestelle and her husband made a list of the people they recalled seeing at the service and called each one, starting with those most likely to have given Jackie a ride home. Nobody gave them the news they had hoped to hear. One man, Charles Baker, confessed he and quite a few others had left the shout early. When he left he remembered that he saw Jackie standing just outside the praise house. *That was before the storm hit*, he said. The Eddings wondered why nobody else mentioned leaving early.

Outside, the storm exploded into a sound and light fury rarely experienced in late November. Inside, a stronger emotional tempest devastated nerves and hope. Hestelle bawled constantly, constrained only briefly during calls to friends who might have news. An hour passed, then two. The couple hopelessly waited for word from Jackie or anyone who might have seen him. At midnight they called for help.

"My son is missing," Irvin Eddings said to the officer or clerk or whoever it was that answered the phone at the Beaufort Police Department.

"How do you know he's missing?" a desk clerk replied in an obvious yawn, awakened by the phone.

"Because he ain't home," Eddings said, short of biting a chunk out of the phone.

"Well, has anyone seen or heard from him?"

"No! He's missing. Nobody's seen him. Nobody know where he is."

"Okay, let me get some details. Hold on. Let me get a pencil."

Irvin Eddings waited until the voice returned.

"Name?"

"My name is Irvin Eddings," he said, flustered by the question.

"Not your name, your son's name?"

"Jackie Robinson Eddings."

"Hmm, sounds familiar. Age?"

"Fourteen."

"Height?"

"Five feet, seven inches."

"Weight?"

"Hundred and ten or so."

"Hair color?"

"Black."

"What color eyes?"

"Brown."

"Oh, skipped one. Race?"

"Negro."

There was a pause in the questions. Irvin waited.

"Ain't your boy the one was in here a few weeks back?"

"Yes, sir."

"Ain't he the colored boy in the Beaufort Junior High School?"

"Yes, he is an' he's missing. We don't know where our son is."

Again, the clerk paused and Irvin waited. Hestelle came up behind him, placed her hands on his shoulder, and listened. Irvin turned to see tears still watered her eyes and dripped from her cheeks.

"Well, that boy of yours sure—"

"My boy is missing. Can you help us find him? Please, sir?" Irvin pleaded.

"I'm going to need some more information."

"I'll gives you any information you needs. Just find our Jackie."

The desk clerk nursed a cup of cold coffee he'd brewed up three hours earlier, as he went through the standard missing person checklist outlined in the manual. It was all right there. All he had to do was ask the questions, which he did reluctantly in a third degree that lasted fifteen minutes.

"Okay, I have all I need. We're kinda shorthanded right now. Some of our folks are taking off early for the holiday next week. I'll talk to the chief and see what he wants to do."

"You mean you can't...or you won't start looking tonight?"

"Ya see, no can do there, Mr. Eddings. I can't be issuing an APB—all points bulletin—for every call like this I get. I gotta run this by the chief," the clerk said. He remembered the last time Jackie was in the office after the boat vandalism questioning. The chief told his friend Geordie Swanson he would keep an eye on this kid. The clerk figured the chief would want to know about this report before the dispatcher started any kind of search. The boy might be hiding something. Chief better know.

"Yes, sir, I understands but my boy be missing and dis storm…he could be hurt. An accident. Somebody might have…I mean…he might done been—"

"Ten-four there, boy. I get what you're getting at, but rules is rules. We'll call you just as soon as we have something for you. You have a good night now."

The lights remained on all night at the Eddings' residence, flickering a few times due to the storm, but never going out. Hestelle pressured Irvin to call the police station all night, but Irvin waited until morning. Rather than call, Irvin Eddings stopped by the police station, waiting long enough for the chief to have a cup of coffee.

"Chief Heimer, there's a Mr. Eddings here to see you," the dispatch clerk said with his nose just inside the chief's door.

"Mr. Eddings, yes. Send him in," Heimer grumbled.

Irvin entered and waited for the chief to motion him to sit.

"I remember you and your boy. My dispatch clerk showed me the report from last night. Your son made it home yet?"

"No, sir."

"Hold on, let me get something. Hold on." The chief got up from behind his desk and strolled out to the front to pour another cup of coffee. "Oo-ee. Sweet jeezus, that's hot," he shrieked when he sipped from the cup as he walked back to his chair. He gave a thumbs up to the older gal typing in the corner.

"Okay, so the boy was last seen at the Pritchard Praise House on Saint Helena?"

"Yes, sir."

"And you've asked folks that were there if—"

173

"Yes, sir." Then Irvin made a connection with the peeper. "And dey is something else about de praise house. I didn't mention dis when I called last night, but as we was walking into de service, I saw dis man snooping through de back."

"A guy?"

"Yes, Chief Heimer. Dis man were standing on a stump and peeking in through de cracks in de side, like he were spying or something. I jus' knows he was hangin' around. I ran him off but he may have come back. He may have did something wid my son."

The chief spent time getting more details. He grilled Irvin Eddings about the guy on the stump, but the best description he could offer was a basic tall, thin, and definitely white.

"Okay Mr. Eddings. I think I have it. I'll see what we can do." Otis Heimer rose from behind the desk and opened his office door. "We'll let you know as soon as we have something. Go on home. We will handle it from here."

After Irvin Eddings left the office, Chief Heimer spent the balance of the morning with a crossword puzzle, the latest *Sports Illustrated*, and a brief review of the storm damage reported on the log from the previous night before he left for an early lunch.

"Hey, Geordie," the chief said when he saw Swanson walk out of the Rebel Grill rolling a toothpick in his front teeth. "How's tricks?"

"Can't complain. Besides, nobody would listen. What's new with you?"

"That colored boy of yours, the one on your boat? Kid's missing, least his parents ain't seen him," Heimer said, holding open the door. A couple walked out. "Called last night during the storm. Said their boy was with them at the praise house, then they couldn't find him there before they left, and he never showed up at home. Kid picked a bad night to run away. That storm was a killer."

Swanson hesitated for a second. "Kid never did seem too bright. Your guys out looking for him? Praise house, hmm. Fine place to lose your kid. This ever happen before?"

"Running reduced holiday staff this week. I issued an APB to the squad cars to keep their eyes open. Can't afford too much manpower on a runaway colored boy." He smirked.

"Trust me, I'll let you know if he shows up on my boat again...looking for a place to sleep or something else." Swanson laughed.

"Hey! Thanksgiving. Got plans? Why don't you come over to our place? Just me and the wife. Nothing fancy. Lots of food. Plenty of beer," the chief added while he gnawed on a cigar clenched in the corner of his mouth.

"Hey. Sounds good. Thanks. What time?"

"Bears play the Lions at noon. Come early. We can watch the game on the tube."

Geordie Swanson gathered himself in a rigid military posture, clicked his heels together, rendered a snappy salute, and left.

CHAPTER 17

Per their adjusted schedule Cliff Gilbert dialed the FBI switchboard that night and requested to speak to Coyote. As usual it didn't take Coyote long to get into details.

"I don't want to hear your buts. Forget it. What did you see?" the voice snarled.

"What?"

"I said...what did you see at that church thing?"

"A bunch of people. Negroes. All dressed up and headed into that dinky chapel out in the middle of nowhere."

"And? Was that it?"

"And that was it," Mole replied.

"Anything suspicious? Any unusual activity?"

"Well, not there. Not while I was looking."

"What do you mean 'not there'? How long were you there? You told me the nineteenth was the day they—"

"I was there maybe ten minutes, but before I got there, on my way, I hung out in the woods until it got dark. There were these guys in costumes milling around in the trees. I couldn't figure out what they were doing."

"Costumes?"

"They were weird, creature things. Animals, but weird. Big heads. Masks they wore over their heads."

"And you didn't think to mention that?"

"I thought maybe they were part of the church thing. Could have been. I didn't know." The mole shifted the phone to his other ear and continued. "After sunset cars started to arrive. When it was dark enough, I worked my way up to the back of the building as best I could with all the headlights around the field, the parking area. I found a stump and stood on it to watch what was going on inside."

"And…?"

"It was a big love-in kinda thing. Eventually, one colored lady, an older woman, started singing. That's when I heard some guy holler at me; at least I think he was hollering at me."

"And…?"

"So I started running," he said without a word about first falling off the stump.

"Did he get close to you? Close enough to identify you, you think?"

"No. There was another guy. A colored guy who was leaving. The guy that hollered started toward him and stopped."

"Did you get a good look at that colored guy, the one leaving?"

"Sir? No, sir. He was headed toward the woods out back. I was headed toward the road over on the side."

"Okay, so go back. What was all the talk about a kidnapping? Last time you reported—"

"Not sure. Guess maybe I misunderstood."

Coyote was patient to correct Mole's statement. "No, you were flat wrong or stupid. You know there's a kid missing? A colored boy last seen at the praise house. Is that your kidnapping?"

"I don't know. Could be. Never heard about the kid. Can't say as I saw any—"

"Right, except your report told us you heard talk of a kidnapping and it would be November nineteenth at that location."

"Yes, sir. And I heard those guys in the costumes. They talked about a kidnapping. They made it sound like somebody special, someone important, not a kid."

"Wait. So the guys in costumes...the ones in the woods? That night? You heard them say something about a kidnapping?" Another pause, longer than the last. "You heard someone mention kidnapping at Penn Center? A kidnapping at the praise house on the nineteenth. Then, on the nineteenth at the praise house, you hear the masked guys mention kidnapping again? So which is it, Endelson? The kid or someone else? I can't go back to the Director and tell him all of this was just some crazy local shenanigan!"

Mole swallowed hard and dissected his words before he slowly spoke. "Sir, all I know is what I heard. I heard the masked guys in the woods mention a kidnapping. And, like I told you, at Penn Center weeks ago, I heard someone, I can't say who, mention a kidnapping, too. I can't say who any of those guys were talking about or even if they were talking about the same thing."

"Crap. I've heard enough. Get your head screwed on right and sort all this out."

Before Endelson had a chance to say anything, the line went dead. He could tell by the tone which ended the call that he had no questions.

CHAPTER 18

It was six days later Chicago quarterback Rudy Bukich had just completed his third touchdown pass of the second quarter when the motel room door crashed against the wall. Three characters in masks appeared and flipped the lock from the inside. It took two seconds for Gene Skyles to register the attack and half a second more to spring to his feet, trapped in the narrow space between the bed and the bathroom wall, his half-empty bottle of beer now draining across his naked toes. A face with the beard of shells stood tall on the bed; the masked hyena blocked an escape along the wall; the water buffalo guarded the door and spoke.

"We want the clue. The boy told us you have the coded message," the buffalo said.

"I don't know what you're talking about. What boy? Who are you?" Skyles said, stoically rigid while his eyes leaped wildly between his uninvited Thanksgiving Day guests.

When he denied them, the mask of shells used his forearm to plaster Skyles against the wall. With both arms free, Skyles grabbed the attacker's wrists and hiked his knee into his groin. With the same leg, he pushed off the wall to shove his weakened opponent onto the bed. A split second later, the hyena mask snatched Skyles from behind but misread his victim, who spun hard to his left and caught the second attacker just below his ear,

179

though not hard enough to break the bear hug he was in. Still sucking for wind, shell-face rejoined the brawl and wasted no time putting Skyles in a headlock. With two bodies hanging on him, Skyles pushed off the wall a second time. The pile of bodies landed on the bed. The mask with the shells let loose of his head and knelt over the other two. As he bent down to smother his victim's face with a pillow, Skyles lifted his head slightly and rammed into the chin of the heavy mask. The collision sent a buzz through his head, his eyes rolled backward, and he blacked out for an instant, long enough to allow the two aggressors to pin his arms to the bed with their body weight. When Skyles came to, he blinked the pain from his eyes and saw both masks over him in a ghoulish nightmare. The third visitor, the water buffalo, had moved away from the door and closer to the bed.

"We have no intentions of harming you, Mr. Skyles," he said as he stepped to the foot of the bed. His posture—arms crossed over his chest—suggested otherwise. "We want only to retrieve the coded clue."

"I told you, I don't have what you are looking for. I've never even seen it."

"We know that's not true. The boy said—"

"I'm not sure who you're talking about, but whatever you're after, it's not here."

"We'll be the judge of that."

Unable to break free, Skyles rolled his head and eyes as he watched the water buffalo begin; he started with the desk. Stacks of notebooks, papers, a small tape recorder, files, and texts; he checked them all, page by page. He grabbed the Samsonite briefcase next to the desk and dumped it on the floor. He smoothed things across the red shag carpet like a miner panning for gold, each paper item checked front and back. He emptied desk drawers and inspected the same way. He opened every container, large and small. Coat pockets. An empty suitcase. A bag with a belt, a tie, and a Lipsitz receipt. He pulled the King James version of the Bible from the nightstand shelf and thumbed the pages to allow any extra markers or pieces of loose paper to drop to the floor; nothing fell. The water buffalo had not replaced a thing; the entire sleeping area looked like a scene from Hurricane Gracie, despite Skyles' repeated pleas.

Two knocks, a pause, and another single knock alerted the hyena to slap a hand across his victim's mouth. The eyes of all three intruders, as well as Gene Skyles, turned toward the knocks. The door opened a crack, only long enough for a voice to say, "Make it quick. Need to go. Car's in back in the bushes, hidden, where I dropped you." The words were not Gullah or with any accent at all. Skyles strained to catch the face behind the voice. Out of the corner of his eye, Skyles saw the voice came from a Negro man with a dark gray coat sleeve.

The water buffalo opened the bathroom door and a pungent, sweet odor of burning marijuana wafted out. Seconds later, Skyles heard the flurry of things smack against the wall or shatter on the floor; then the water buffalo reappeared.

"We're not through here, Mr. Skyles, so let me warn you. Don't mention this visit to the police. Doing so will only place the boy in more danger. Surely you wouldn't want to bring any harm to the boy." He turned toward the desk covered with notebooks, years of research notes plus a few rare original documents. "It appears you have invested a good bit of time in your work, proof of whatever...of something dear to you. It would be a shame to lose all of those...facts, wouldn't it?" He turned back and stared into the blank, wide-eyed stare of the researcher. "Trust me, if you mention this visit to the police, not only will the boy suffer, but so will your research. Those papers…I promise you…you will watch them burn, every last one of them. Be smart. Remain quiet."

The speaker moved to the door. "We're leaving. Not a word. Not now. Not later. Not ever." As the door opened, the other two masked figures crawled off the bed and headed out. The water buffalo followed and gently closed the door behind.

Skyles lay stunned. He felt like he had to safely disarm a ticking time bomb. Rapid, deep breaths eventually rewired his logic. He lifted his head and realized the damage was worse than he feared. Clothes draped the chairs and dresser. Papers littered every horizontal surface and the trash can. When his surreal visitors didn't return, he pushed himself up. His arms ached, but they supported him while he sat for a longer look. He stood, grabbed the beer bottle, now empty, and walked to the bathroom where he found another pigsty of broken glass, liquids, and papers. His reflection in the mirror explained the jackhammer inside his skull—a crusty crimson blob scabbed above the wrinkles on his forehead. He soaked a washcloth in warm water and wiped away the blood. As he patted a towel to his forehead, the phone near the bed rang and startled him; his stomach flipped. He reached for the phone but pulled back to let it ring a third time.

"Hello," he said cautiously, certain the caller would hear the pounding in his head.

"The boy is at the praise house."

"What? Hello?" He waited. "What'd you say? Who is this?" he asked, taken aback by the message. The voice was familiar, recent. There was no reply. The dial tone returned.

He hung up the phone. The pain in his head was still there. He rubbed his forehead, then his eyes, then the back of his neck. His visitors had been quite clear that he should not contact the police, at least about their visit, but what about this call? Based on his work with Mary Alice's class and having heard Jackie Eddings was reported as missing, Skyles put two and two together and assumed the visit had something to do with Jackie. The clue or code they were after was something Jackie had or needed. With their warning he decided not to risk a phone call; instead, he went straight to the Eddings' house.

He drove the six blocks from the motel to the boy's house without passing another car. He passed two couples on Carteret Street having a grand old time apparently walking off their Thanksgiving Day feast. At the house he left two wheels on the pavement but parked most of the car on the edge of the leaf-covered lawn.

Irvin Eddings answered the knock. He opened the wooden door but left the screen closed between him and the white man on his porch.

"Mr. Eddings," Skyles said with his hand conspicuously placed over the wound on his forehead.

"Yes."

"Excuse me, Mr. Eddings, my name is Gene Skyles. We met at the police station a few weeks ago. I need to talk to you about your son. May I come in?" he said, looking around to determine if anyone might have followed him from the motel.

Under a week of stress and leery about answering to a strange young white man, Irvin Eddings replied, "What abouts my son?" His face betrayed his surprise, shock, and concern.

"I believe I know where he is."

Irvin Eddings nudged the screen door; Skyles pulled it open and stepped just inside where the sweet smell of baked goods in the oven distracted him.

"Who is it?" Hestelle yelled from the back of the house. Nervously, she walked out, wiping her hands on her apron. Rather than sitting helplessly idle on a holiday without her son, Hestelle Eddings had baked an apple pie, Jackie's favorite, hoping that simple act would bring her boy home.

"Mrs. Eddings," Skyles said with a nod in her direction as she entered. "My name is Gene Skyles. We met a few weeks back at the police station. I'm a student doing research and I spoke to your son's class at the junior high school. A few minutes ago I received a phone call in my motel room. I'm staying at the Lord Carteret. The caller said your son was at the praise house."

Hestelle Eddings gasped and covered her mouth with her hands.

"Who was de caller? Is you sure? Dis be real?" Irvin asked.

"I'm not sure. It was a man, but he didn't identify himself. I can't say for sure what he said is true."

"Why dey call you?" Irvin Eddings asked.

"I don't know," Skyles replied with no mention of his visitors.

"Does de police know?"

"No. I came directly to you. Maybe you should call them."

"Irvin...baby...let me gets my sweater. We needs to go." Tears rolled down Hestelle's face as she ran out of the room untying her apron.

"Let me calls de police," Eddings said, moving toward the phone.

"I have my car out front. I can drive. Grab what you need."

"Call the hospital. Have them tell Gabe. Tell them we'll visit later," Hestelle yelled from another room.

"Hestelle, we needs to find Jackie. We can do all da' later. Come on," her husband replied as he dialed the police.

Irvin Eddings talked to the dispatcher on duty. The clerk went on and on, question after question. Finally, Irvin Eddings cut him off. "Alls I knows da' call came in and said my boy, Jackie Robinson Eddings, de boy what been missing for days, be out at de praise house, de Pritchard Praise House on Saint Helena. I'm going to get my boy," then he hung up.

Gene Skyles paid no attention to the speed limit on the Sea Island Parkway or down Lands End Road. If anyone stopped him, the bigger question would be why a white man was chauffeuring two Negroes around in the back seat of his car. In the distance the wail of a police siren grew louder and louder. As they approached, they saw an awkward figure upright against the door.

"Baby, baby," Hestelle cried as she flung open her car door before their forward motion stopped. Irvin opened his door at the same time.

Still dressed in the netting covered with dead animals and wearing a mask which sat high on his forehead like a headdress, Jackie was gagged at the mouth and held upright by a rope that ran through the hasp on the front door of the praise house.

Jackie opened his tired eyes. He straightened his stance and pressed his back against the door.

Irvin Eddings tugged on the cloth gag in his son's mouth until it was free.

"Mamma! Mamma!" Jackie cried. "Mamma."

"Oh, baby. What has dey done to you? Oh, baby! What has dey done?" Undeterred by the vest of carcasses, Hestelle Eddings caressed her son's masked head, then fought her way through the tears to reach for his hands, tied behind his back.

"Mamma, I was so scared. I was so worried," Jackie sobbed. "Mamma, is…is Grandpa Gabe okay now?"

"Oh, praise de Lord Jesus, he be still alive," she said choking as she wept. "And my baby, he alive, too." She wrapped her arms over his shoulders and pulled him tight against her chest. Irvin managed to get his fingers between the strands of rope and free the boy from the hasp.

The reek of rotten meat forced Skyles to turn away and take a deep breath before he joined in untying Jackie. Once the boy was loose from the building, they took him to the side where Skyles and Irvin Eddings tugged at the ropes around the boy's wrists and waist. As they worked the final knots loose, a sheriff's car turned off the main road and headed toward them across the grassy field. The unlucky patrolman who pulled duty on Thanksgiving was a perfect double for Barney Fife from *The Andy Griffith Show*, down to the cockeyed way he wore his cap. He got out of the car—gumball still in full flash-and-twirl with the siren at full strength—and headed toward the group. He suddenly stopped short.

"What the heck is that smell?" he said with a high-pitched drawl. He covered his nose and mouth with one hand, the other on the grip of his pistol in a belt that sagged like one on a gunslinger in a TV western.

Gene Skyles wrapped his hands around the bottom of the net vest. As soon as the boy's father pulled the mask off Jackie, the young researcher yanked the net off and over Jackie's head. He walked a few steps away from the others and with a two-handed backhand flung the vest as far as he could. Hestelle and Irvin weren't the least bit concerned with the foul odor and slime left on Jackie; they just wanted to hold their son.

While the family embraced in their teary reunion, Jackie rambled about masked figures, nights in the woods, and little sleep; Skyles stood nearby to answer the patrolman's questions. He explained exactly what they saw when they drove up—the ropes, the mask, the net, the dead animals. The patrolman knew that Irvin Eddings had placed the call to the police and wondered why Skyles was there. Skyles simply said he happened to be at the Eddings house when they called the police. At that the Barney Fife look-alike cranked in his chin and puckered his brow; he was not too keen on the Thanksgiving Day integration. He eavesdropped on the whimpering kid before he closed his notepad, hopped in the cruiser, turned off his cruiser light and left; he never bothered to secure any evidence—ropes, the gag, fingerprints—and definitely had no interest in the vest.

Gene Skyles leaned against the side of his car and watched as the Negro family huddled, hugged, and talked next to the praise house with tears that never seemed to stop.

"Mr. Skyles…" Irvin Eddings called as the Eddings walked intertwined three abreast toward the car. "Would you care to joins us for dinner?"

Gene Skyles was surprised to hear the offer after all this family had been through over the past week. His plan for a quiet Thanksgiving with a parade, a football game, a large bag of potato chips, and a few beers had burst into a nightmarishly bizarre rescue of a lost child, and now he had been asked to sit down at a table with a Negro family on Thanksgiving Day; he wasn't exactly sure what to make of the offer.

"Dem church peoples, dey brung us fixins. Da' preacher's wife, da' Clemonds lady, she brung us a turkey already cooked. An' some cornbread. We ain't have much appetite till now, but now we's goin' to celebrate," Irvin said. On the other side of Jackie, Hestelle Eddings smiled a weary overdue smile.

"We be thankful for sure," Irvin Eddings added as he helped his son toward the car.

"And apple pie, Mamma?" Jackie asked with a wad in his throat.

She nodded with a grin that marked her relief far short of her happiness. The pie she made for Jackie was the magic that brought him home.

"I need to meet Miss Forten later. She was preparing a little something. Besides, I hate to barge in and all. You folks have had—"

"Not be barging in at all, Mr. Skyles. You found our boy and we be so thankful for da'." Eddings smiled and closed the door, his son nestled between both parents in the back seat.

"Well…sure. I'd love to," Skyles agreed as a gesture. Besides, it was Thanksgiving, the day every red-blooded American male should eat at least two overstuffed meals. His menu of chips and beer in the motel was not a proper tribute to the Pilgrims. He took his seat behind the steering wheel. "I'd like that."

"Well, I'll be," Chief Heimer said. He hung up the phone, grabbed two long-necked beers, and walked back to his living room to join Geordie Swanson. "I done heard it all now."

"What are you mumbling about, Otis?" Swanson questioned, his eyes glued to the game.

"That Eddings boy is back, well...was found."

"What? Found? Really. Where was he hiding?"

"Yeah, that was my dispatch clerk. Said the kid showed up at that praise house out on Saint Helena talking about guys in weird masks who hauled him off. Said the boy was wearing some crazy headpiece or something and a net covered with dead critters," the chief said, passing a beer to Swanson.

"Who found him? You have squad cars out looking for the kid? Over the holiday?"

"Not a chance. Clerk said the boy's father called in. Had received a tip, a call or something that said the boy was out there, so dispatch checked in with the sheriff's boys and they sent a car that way. Found the kid, his parents, and that guy Skyles out there." Heimer tried to direct his attention to the television, but his guest continued to question him.

"Skyles? Skyles! You mean the kid from Virginia doing research?"

"Yeah. Beats me how he got involved, but"—Heimer took a swig of beer—"yeah, well, we done solved another one. Case closed."

"Closed? You're not going to track down what happened to that kid or who was involved?"

"Geordie"—Heimer chuckled before taking another, longer swig on his beer—"we're talkin' about a colored boy, remember? The one that was on your boat—allegedly on your boat."

Geordie Swanson hesitated, then joined Heimer in a good laugh. "Gotcha. Understood."

"What'd I miss?" the chief asked. He settled into his chair with the grace of a walrus on a toadstool. He pushed the lever to prop up his feet on his recliner and picked up his armchair quarterbacking right where he left off.

Irvin Eddings had Jackie squirt himself down with the hose outside the house so he wouldn't take his road-kill, dead-meat bouquet inside to mix, mingle, and ruin the house filled with the lingering aroma of apple pie. In the inside shower, the fresh, earthy smell of the bar of pumice soap and the warmth of the hot water only washed away Jackie's perceptible trauma, but it was enough to bring a relaxed smile to his face. Dreams of home were more than a psychological refuge for him over the past seven days. They were channels of strength between Jackie and Gabe. To hear he was still alive meant the world to the boy. Though his senses spurred the growl from his stomach, he was anxious for supper to be over so he could go see his grandpa.

Dinner was a bit awkward. Both parents fought the urge to question their son, who seemed more content with eating. Their faces glowed with the sentiment of the day, thankful and relieved to have their son safely home. Despite their invitation, they found it strange, maybe a bit awkward, to share the holiday and this homecoming with a white stranger at their dinner table, in their house.

Jackie had eaten with white kids for months at school. It wasn't all that different for him. He knew Gene Skyles and they shared snippets of small talk, but for most of dinner, Jackie was quiet. After the meal Hestelle suggested that the men should go in the living room and talk while she did dishes. Irvin offered to help and sent

Jackie and Gene Skyles into the other room to relax and chat while they waited for dessert.

"You know...we were all worried about you, Jackie, especially Miss Forten," Skyles said.

Jackie looked down. He had not said anything since they left the table. He fidgeted with his hands and scratched his neck. After Skyles spoke, Jackie crossed his arms on his chest.

"I was blindfolded almost de whole time out in de woods on Saint Helena. We never drove anywhere. I couldn't see anything." He continued to look at the floor.

"Why you? Who would do that to you?" he said, then quickly added, "If you'd rather not talk about it, that's okay."

"I don't know," Jackie said, asking himself the same question. "I don't know who dey was. When de blindfold was off, dey wore masks, all four of dem." Jackie quivered as he spoke, the ordeal still very real and still very much present in his mind.

"Masks? What kind of masks? Like robbers? Like the Lone Ranger or hoods?"

"No, sir, Mr. Skyles. Like weird animal heads an' all. Big wooden things," he said, glancing up at Skyles, then back to the floor.

Skyles could feel his stomach churn. He had questions to ask, but had to resist. He simply said, "Oh!"

Both Jackie and Skyles drifted into thought, unwilling or afraid to extend the brief conversation—Skyles lost in the words of the buffalo mask and Jackie with thoughts of Gabe.

"Mr. Skyles, can I come an' see you dis week?" Jackie asked, breaking the silence.

"Sure. Any time, Jackie," Skyles said. He smiled to comfort the boy who rested his eyes on the floor.

"I wants to talk about Edgar Allan Poe, da' all. My grandpa had something about de Gullah treasure an'—"

"Treasure and Poe? Interesting," Skyles said, trying to lighten the mood. "Like 'The Gold Bug'?" He chuckled. "Sure, Jackie. What do you say we meet, maybe at Luther's Pharmacy on Bay Street? I'll buy you a soda. We can talk."

Jackie chewed on his lower lip. He knew meeting in a place like Luther's, in public, was not a good choice for a Negro boy. He hesitated on his reply long enough for Gene Skyles to understand the dilemma.

"Better yet, why don't I take you out to Span's, you know, the malt shop. We can talk awhile," Skyles said and noticed the beginnings of a smile cross Jackie's face.

"Can we do it Saturday afternoon, maybe?" Jackie asked.

"Of course. I'll stop by around two. How's that work?"

"That would be good, Mr. Skyles," Jackie said, glancing up for a second.

"Apple pie anyone?" Hestelle Eddings asked, loaded down with a tray filled with plates, forks, and one hot homemade apple pie that had Jackie's name written all over it.

CHAPTER 19

The switchboard operator exhibited definite signs of holiday carb overload trying to make the connection, but after several tries the conversation opened without any fanfare.

"*Sí, señor*," the voice replied to the Coyote code name.

"Happy Thanksgiving, sir," James the "Mole" Endelson said at the opening. "I hope you had time to be thankful."

"Get on with it."

Endelson held the handset in front of his face and mouthed a few choice words not meant for Coyote's ears. "Since last week, the activity has slowed. The group that visited a week ago spent only one night. Most were gone before midmorning. A lot of talk about the Nobel Peace Prize."

"Forget that. Speaking of last week, you mentioned masked guys in the woods and the kidnapping and all. Well, they found that boy, and he said masked guys took him, guys in masks like you described."

Endelson smiled *I told you so* into the phone.

"So, yeah, you had the kidnapping thing down. Great work. Too bad it was just a local kid. And what about the other kidnapping conversation? What else?" Coyote urged.

"Still talking about Zorro's request to meet with the Director."

"Not a chance. The Director came out and publicly charged Zorro with being 'the most notorious liar in the country' and 'controlled by Communist advisors.' So they can forget any meeting."

Endelson continued. He sensed Coyote was not in the mood for expository chatter. "Discussions were limited. Large group sessions. Principal topics were voter registration and outreach. Mainly Mississippi. A lot about crowd manipulation."

"Come on, kid. You're killing me. Places, dates, times, names? Facts, Endelson. Don't Dick-and-Jane me, son."

"Usual names popped up. Young, Williams, Palmer, but none of them were there."

"Local involvement?"

"They mentioned another potential staff retreat next year, September," he reported. "Several discussions with a Robert Caplin. Sounded like he was an attorney. Topics were random, but many calls."

Mole wrapped up his report in short order, anxious to be rid of Coyote's abrasive holiday spirit.

Coyote massaged the back of his neck while he digested the mole's basic incompetence.

"Okay. Listen up. I hear they have a great Christmas parade in Beaufort, sort of a nice, hometown festive event. It's on Sunday, next. Plan on going. While you're in town, I need some legwork. Back channel message that came in said "Footprint" will be at Beaufort National Cemetery. Go there after you watch part of the parade. Check out the area, especially the monument to the Union soldiers there, the one that looks like the Washington Monument. Can't miss it, I'm told. Check around. See what you find. Plan to be there at three thirty that day. No questions. Check in per schedule."

"I'm not sure—"

"And, by the way, Happy Thanksgiving." Coyote dropped off the line.

In the midst of a long holiday weekend, Geordie Swanson had no treasure hunting excursions booked. Normally, he spent weekends in a dual role, split personality as a flamboyant tour guide and the erstwhile reincarnation of a smiling Captain Ahab for his crew of able-bodied (and paying) gold seekers. On this Friday, he had the day to himself and opted for a "walk-in" visit to the office of Robert Caplin, Esquire.

"Mr. Swanson. Surprised to see you, sir. Welcome," Robert Caplin said, his hand extended as Geordie Swanson walked into his office.

"May I offer you a glass of cold water, Mr. Swanson?" Edreca Witsell asked with a low voice before she returned to her two-chair, one-desk outer office. As a middle-aged mother and legal secretary, her body had thickened and her kinky hair had resigned itself to a premature gray.

"No, thank you," Swanson said. "I'm fine." The sun through the single window was bright in his eyes.

"Please, sir, have a seat." He motioned toward a small two-seat sofa that showed its age. "To what do I owe the honor of this visit?"

"Mr. Caplin, I appreciate your willingness to talk. I had some time on my hands and took a chance that you might have the same, given the holiday and all," Geordie said.

"I have a window. Can't say I have time on my hands because of the holiday. A day's work is never done and, because of the holiday, I have one day less to see clients. But I can spare a few minutes. What may I do for you?"

"I wanted to talk to you about the Eddings boy."

"Great to hear he is back," Caplin said with a smile. "What a heart-wrenching experience. To be gone for such a long time. Seven days I believe it was?"

Geordie Swanson was impressed and curious to hear Caplin already knew of the boy's return, which had occurred less than twenty-four hours earlier. "Yeah. I happened to talk to Otis Heimer. Seems the boy is okay," he said, his eyes focused on a strange object on a shelf behind the lawyer. "A few weeks back, when we met in Chief Heimer's office, you were defending the boy on the charge of trespassing and vandalism…of my boat, that is."

"Yes. I remember." He lowered his voice and adopted a more curious tone.

"Well, I'm still concerned about what the boy was doing on my boat. I can't seem to find a few things. Then, out of the blue, he turns up missing. I think there might be some connection there."

"It sounds like Chief Heimer would be the one to question on that," Caplin said. He glanced at his watch, then reached for a pen from a cup on his desk and began to write.

"Not sure Otis plans to do much. Had dinner with him yesterday and seems now that the kid is back, Otis considers the case closed."

Caplin looked up. "Well, Mr. Swanson. I've known the Eddings family a long time. Their Jackie is a good boy. He's strong, a smart kid, that's why they selected him to be the first Negro to attend Beaufort Junior High."

"Well, my experience with that colored boy is different," Swanson said with a stern look directly into the eyes of the colored attorney. "I'm sure you understand."

Caplin offered a slight nod, straightened his back, and folded his hands on his desk.

"So did the boy tell you anything when you talked to him that day?" Swanson baited.

"As you know, that would be confidential information, Mr. Swanson, restricted under the attorney–client privilege of the law," he answered. "But, between the two of us, I can assure you, the boy has said nothing about the incident or his intentions, actions or otherwise."

Geordie took a deep breath and looked away. On the wall next to the door where he entered he saw another strange object. "Say, your honor," he joked, "you've some interesting treasures in here. That's my line of work, you know…finding treasure. What's that doodad behind your desk there? And the one over by the door?" he asked. He used both hands to point to the objects that caught his eye.

Caplin looked over his shoulder and used the pen to point at the object behind him. "Well, this is a ceremonial sword from Africa. A very old and dear friend of mine gave that to me a number of years ago. It's from the Mende people in Sierra Leone. This particular piece is probably hundreds of years old." Geordie Swanson shook his head and curled the corners of his mouth in a curious smile. "Nice."

"And that, the little figure, is a carving. Also from Africa, from the Temne people. They're also from Sierra Leone. West Africa. Not sure how old that is. Sure looks old," he explained.

"Interesting. Yeah, looks old."

"Just my small way to stay in touch with my Gullah roots. Most Gullahs are descendants from people in Sierra Leone. And your ancestors, Mr. Swanson? Your roots are from…" He clenched his hands and tucked them under his chin.

"England, my good fellow," he said in a robust cockney accent. "Interesting objects. Treasures. Very classy art, Mr. Caplin. Very classy," Swanson said as he looked around the room for similar items. "Any other treasures in here? Better guard them, ya know. I'm always looking for treasures, gold mostly," Geordie Swanson said with a wink. He craned his neck to eye the room, corner to corner. A diploma from Morehouse College. Another from Howard University Law School. Between his college diplomas was a class photo from Robert Smalls High School and beneath that, portraits of two Presidents of the United States, Abe and LBJ.

"No, sir. This is my office, not a museum. I like to have a few things around to keep me grounded in who I am, where I came from and where I'm headed. The colored people around here have a great need for my time," he replied, pen in hand. He snuck a look at his watch a second time. Swanson acknowledged.

"I've taken up far more of your time than I intended." He stood. "I can certainly appreciate your schedule. Mine is far more predictable. Someday it may even be more profitable," he said with a laugh. At the door he turned back toward the lawyer. "Guess I'll be seeing you around town then, Judge."

Before Swanson could leave, Caplin stepped closer and offered his hand. "Anytime, Mr. Swanson. Anytime."

Swanson shook the attorney's hand and ventured one last look at the coat tree in the corner "Nice hat! Really like that hat!"

Three days later the Bureau tapped the Negro lawyer's work phone and his home phone, a party line he shared with two other families; their teenage children made for interesting listening for analysts.

CHAPTER 20

J ackie didn't talk much on the drive from his house to Span's on Saturday. He was polite to offer short answers to Gene Skyles along the way, his mind still preoccupied with images of masked figures that flickered on and off in a dimly lit silent movie. When they arrived, that movie ended; images dissolved like a puffs of smoke.

Span's was the local hangout for Negro teens around Beaufort. Short on cash? Span's offered credit on signatures alone. Cedric Span—built like a man who worked in a meat locker or loaded semis for a living— knew every colored teen in the area. He wore Elvis ducktails behind a Fats Domino face with a smile of ivories bright enough to make Ray Charles see. He loved his kids and trusted they would never stiff him on what they owed. He accepted their payments may take a while—sometimes a good while—but he had never lost a penny.

The tiny parking lot in front was short on cars but long on youth. Small groups of teens—girls with girls and boys with boys—stood safe distances apart in the adolescent exchange of shy, flirtatious glances with occasional comments that both tantalized and tormented, most of which fell silent when Gene Skyles walked by. Inside Span's the buzz was all about the white man who walked in with Jackie Robinson Eddings, the poster child for integration of Beaufort Junior High.

Skyles saw two empty stools at the counter, but Jackie preferred to sit in a booth and headed to a corner, concealed by a half-wall to the restrooms. Skyles looked for the ever-present sign that read "Coloreds," but he never saw one. He did note that as he slid into the bench, all heads and eyes came his way. Feeling slightly insecure, he smiled and looked across to Jackie.

"What would you like? Do you have a favorite?" Gene Skyles asked. He pulled out a chocolate-stained sheet of paper from under a saltshaker, but for his selection he eyed the chalk board next to the large red button Coca-Cola sign that hung over the counter. Jackie ordered a Brown Cow—root beer float with chocolate ice cream; Skyles went traditional with a hot fudge sundae. While they waited for their order, he opened the conversation.

"Jackie, can you keep a secret?" he said hoping to relax Jackie and grab his interest early on. Jackie lifted his eyes off the table. Skyles leaned forward to get under Jackie's stare. "Now, if I tell you, you need to promise not to tell anybody. It'll just be our secret. Just ours." Jackie nodded.

Skyles narrowed his eyes to a sliver, hunched his shoulders, leaned over the table, and said, "Somebody broke into my room at the motel." He paused and, keeping his low profile, scanned the room, then looked back toward Jackie. "They wore masks like you described the other day. The kind your kidnappers wore. Weird animal heads." He pushed back in his seat when the waitress appeared with their order. In her gray houndstooth dress and starched white apron— trademarks of Span's—she offered a silent smile on a face barely older than the teens at the counter. Jackie punched a straw into his glass and took a sip before he leaned back against the bench with his hands in his lap. He didn't say anything; he stared at nothing in particular, his faced washed with dread and wonder.

"They were looking for a coded clue. Do you know anything about that?" Skyles said to bring Jackie into the discussion. He leaned forward and quietly added, "They said you gave it to me."

A pause offered time to think. "I...I did," Jackie confessed. He bowed his head.

Skyles, still leaning over the table, waited for the boy to look up.

"Dey was holding me. Tight. It hurt. I told dem no, first," he said and raised his chin, his eyes glazed over in an unfocused stare. "Then dey held dis spear right by my throat." He grabbed his Adam's apple and rushed to say, "I thought dey was going to stab me. I was scared. I had to say something. I was afraid dey go to my house and hurt my mamma or dad or maybe go see Grandpa Gabe. I'm sorry, Mr. Skyles. I told them you had it. I'm really sorry. I didn't mean—"

"Jackie! Jackie! It's okay. It's okay," Skyles reassured. "So these guys in my room, there were three of them and I think another outside. They tore up my room pretty good." He leaned back, pushed his empty dish aside, and folded his hands on the table. "They told me not to tell anyone or..." he paused and stared at Jackie. Jackie pulled back against the bench again, tears welled in his eyes. "I haven't told anyone except you. Please. Please, don't tell anyone, not even your parents. I don't want to alarm them further. They've been through too much already. I will look into this. I promise. Don't worry."

A group of teenage boys strolled into the malt shop. Though their size was more basketball-like, they wore dark green Robert Smalls High varsity football jerseys. The entire room erupted in applause and cheers. "Go Generals!"

Despite the distraction, Skyles tried to bring the conversation back to the table. "Jackie, do you have some coded message or something? What is it they want?"

Jackie hesitated. He looked from booth to booth to see how many people were still looking in their direction. "I has seen dem masked guys twice, Mr. Skyles. De first time I snuck up on dem near de praise house. De second time, dey caught me. I think dey knew I was there." He sounded nervous and scared.

"There? Where? At the praise house?"

"Yes, sir. Then dey took me in de woods." He stopped there. Again, he broke eye contact and bowed his head, and after a short while, he began to whimper.

"Jackie, okay. This message, this note. What is it?"

"It's de reason I wanted to talk to you. I don't know what it is. I can't read it."

"Where is it?"

"I has it," Jackie said. "Dey is also a letter. I can read da' but it don't make no sense. Dey is a name at de bottom and I think it looks like it says Poe."

The researcher's eyebrows rolled high on his forehead, then dropped to a vee. "You mean it looks like it says Poe on the letter?"

"Yes, sir. It does."

"May I see the letter? Do you have it?"

"Not wid me, but I can gets it pretty easy," Jackie answered, not ready to turn over his treasured note without more thought. "I can bring it to you."

"When?"

"I can bring it to your room at de motel later today," he said. The knot in his stomach loosened but remained. He sat back in the bench, more relaxed.

"That'd be great, Jackie," Skyles said, working through the surprise. "That would be great."

"Mr. Skyles, I'm sorry about dem guys in your room. I—"

"It's all in the past, Jackie. All of it. Finish your ice cream and I'll take you home. Okay?"

"Yes, sir," Jackie said, building on a smile. "Da' fine."

Jackie ran up the porch steps to his house when Skyles dropped him off. When the screen door slammed behind him, his mother was quick to welcome him home.

"Jackie Robinson Eddings, how many times has I told you not to let da' door slam?" she hollered from the kitchen, the source of deep-fried something.

Jackie stuck his head in. "Sorry, Mamma," then tilted his head back and looked down his nose toward his mother standing in front of a cast iron skillet filled with boiling oil and floating batter.

"Sweet tater fritters," she said before he could ask.

"My favorite. Thank you, Mamma," he said. He went to his room and opened a beat-up cigar box where he kept his special things—baseball cards, S&H Green Stamps, some loose change, the coded note, and the letter his grandpa had given him in the hospital. Gingerly, he placed the two tattered pieces of paper inside his school copy of *Animal Farm*, an English assignment. With book in hand he ran back through the house and out the door, which slammed behind him. Hestelle Eddings dropped the slotted spoon in her hand and charged the door.

"Jackie Robinson, you come back here. I told you—"

"Mamma, I needs to go see Mr. Skyles. It's about school, Mamma," he hollered, walking backward away from the house.

"You come back here, baby. I never said you could go nowheres. And I told you not to let de door—"

"I'm sorry, Mamma. I won't forget again. Promise," he said, then turned and broke into a trot down Duke Street headed for the Lord Carteret Motel.

"You be back here in time for dinner. You hears me?" Jackie raised his hand with the book and kept running.

"Hi, Jackie. Come in," Gene Skyles said from his motel room doorway. "Have a seat." He gestured toward the bed as he closed the door. He grabbed the chair from the desk, spun it backward, straddled the seat, and held the sides of the tall wooden back. Jackie immediately opened his book and pulled out the fragile pieces of folded paper.

"Mr. Skyles, dis is what I have. Can you tell what dem are or what dey mean?"

Skyles moved to the side of the bed opposite Jackie and reached for the papers. He placed both on the bed, then opened the smaller square like he was peeling a hard-boiled egg. With the paper flat in front of him, he took several minutes to stare at the mix of characters— letters, numbers, and Greek alphabet symbols:

(щ53&HΣ27Ψ6.ΨΔ!43ΨLHΔ..(щ8β7.ΩΩ.βΔΨ
Ψ9Ωщς..3ф&L969Ψ../!&7Υщ!β2.ΣΔ.β8Lβ3
!276Ψ..93βΨ.ββ&!Δ3.Ψф3фL27&Hщ7!L
6.Ω/3Υ&3ΨL2Σф.ΨΩ(Δ..(63βL2щLфΨ.ΔΩ6щ
(щ7ΥΨф.Σ8.Ω.L3L2.βΔщ&Hβщ!L!L.Ω.щ8
Ψ..(6щΩщ&.ΣL3.Δ4!

His eyes drifted left to right. Jackie watched, certain Skyles would identify the source, the code, and the message. It took a few seconds while he wondered and imagined in silence. The bed creaked when the researcher adjusted his seat, slid the scrap of paper toward Jackie, and looked up.

"I don't know, Jackie, I'm not sure what this is. I mean, it looks like a code, a message, something; that I can be pretty sure of, but I'm not sure it's Poe. It could be anybody."

"Look at dis other paper, Mr. Skyles."

"Sure," Skyles said. He slowly unfolded the larger paper with the same care as the first. This time when he had it open, he didn't hesitate.

"This is Edgar Allan Poe. A letter signed by him," he said, looking up at Jackie. Though he had seen dozens of authentic letters signed by Poe, this one opened his eyes wider and wider as he worked his way through the text.

"Where did you get this, Jackie?" he asked, his mouth cast in an oval of surprise. "It could actually be quite valuable if it's an original letter signed by Poe," he said, his eyes refusing to blink.

"My Grandpa Gabe. He had it," Jackie replied.

The more Skyles stared and read, the more certain he was that the letter was original. He read it slowly:

The Secret of the Gullah Treasure

Charleston
Dec. 9. 1828

My Dear Sir,

By way of beginning this letter, for a month I have struggled with illness, dismal privation, and the plague of evils which consorts them. Even until today I remain dangerously so, and quite unable to write normal correspondence of any sorts, even an ordinary letter. Throughout my miserable existence I have thought how deeply and sincerely I deplore the attacks which you have addressed to myself so personally and individually. There are but a few things which could afford me more pleasure than the opportunity of holding you up to the ridicule of public scourging for your written lies about my character and person.

That said, it is with all due respect, nevertheless, I remain inwardly compelled to do you a very great favor. You need be under no uneasiness about your money. I believe there is due you your wager of 2100$. Now, I do not intend to object to this insistence at present, for that would lead me into a virtually incessant dialogue, besides being out of place in me.

I am reminded that I am your debtor and my conscience rides me to address your due. Money, beyond doubt, can be wagered and won, but this is not the totality of the need you require. As I have no money myself, I have enclosed what is known by many in Charleston and from your fields on the island of Ste. Helena, to be of greater value.

Pray do not think me careless of my promise to see to the debt you so publicly demand albeit against my innerself after these eight months. For were it not for the tales of an old Negro by name of Jupiter, I scarcely doubt my words would offer such a generous prize. The public forum be my judge, but to you, sir, my debt is paid locked by cipher for your safe keeping.

Yr. Ob. St.
Edgar A Poe

Mr. William Lembath

He studied the markings, the style, the wording in it before he looked up. "And how did your grandpa get it?"

Jackie thought for a moment, embarrassed to admit what he knew. "He told me it was one of de few things he still had from his mamma. She be a slave, a house slave in Beaufort." Again Jackie paused and looked away. "He say when dem white peoples left Beaufort after de Yankees came in de Civil War, his mamma an' dem other slaves dey took things from de master's house. Dis is de onliest thing he had. It be one of de few things he have da' his mamma had."

While the boy talked, Skyles marveled over the good fortune of this paper treasure. More and more made sense. Poe was a gambler, a miserable gambler. It was his obsession with gambling that led to his ruinous debt, which haunted him throughout his entire life. And then the name, Lembath. It was a familiar name. He looked up at Jackie, still facing away. "Freddie Lembath!" he said. "Jackie, do you know Mr. Freddie Lembath?"

"Yes, sir. He sells taters, collards, and things from a cart up and down de streets. Sometimes he brings dem to Grandpa Gabe."

"That's the guy. I remember him. I met him when I visited your school that day. Is he related to your grandpa?"

"No, sir. I don't believe he be," Jackie answered.

"And you said your grandpa's mother was a slave for Mr. Lembath? Do you know if she was in the Lembath house on East Street, the one across from the Castle?"

The mention of the Castle tightened Jackie's stomach. "I don't really know."

Skyles dropped his head back as far as it would go while a huge, open-mouth smile blossomed across his face. He chuckled and dipped his chin to his chest, let out a deep sigh, then chuckled again. "This might be the key to my research, Jackie. See, I know this man, this Mr. Lembath, at least I know of him, and of his family. They've been part of my research." He walked to his desk. He rummaged around a bit and pulled out a notebook. While the researcher thumbed through his notebook, Jackie took the square of paper with the clue on it and held it up to the light. He paid no attention to Skyles as he jabbered on excitedly.

"In my notes I have a hunch...the dengue fever...and unmarked graves at the church in Charleston, very old church, the Circular Congregational...and records here for the Lembath family...with this letter, this connection to Poe...I just might be able to prove that Anna Belcher Lembath is the Annabel in Poe's poem...and explain why he dared not use her entire name."

"But what about dis clue?" Jackie said, handing the torn paper back to Skyles.

"Oh, right." He shook his head to clear his flash of euphoria. "Let me take another look."

The Poe expert switched gears from his impromptu hypothesis to concentrate on the odd collection of marks on the paper, desperate to find a pattern. He had seen many Poe secret writings in his research. He had studied Poe's simple substitution methods and key-phrase technique, but reeling from the excitement of what the letter offered his research, Skyles made neither heads nor tales of the cipher.

"Jackie, I don't know. Off the top of my head, I would say this is probably a clue Poe wrote, but I can't make any sense of it. How about if I keep this clue and—"

"No, sir!" Jackie blurted out. "No, sir, I can't let you have dis. It be Grandpa Gabe's and I needs to get it back to him, ya see—"

"Okay, okay. Maybe I can copy these symbols and see if I can figure it out. Would that help? Would that be okay?"

Jackie grabbed his head and let his hands slide down over his face and back onto the bed. "Okay. You can copy it, sure. I need to go. My mamma said I had to be home for dinner."

Skyles pulled a pencil from his briefcase and quickly copied the symbols, character by careful character, in the notebook where he had notes on "Annabel Lee." When he finished, he gently folded both papers.

"Jackie, those are valuable papers. Even if we can't figure out what that one means, those documents are worth money to a museum or collector or researchers like me. Make sure you take good care of those."

"I ain't selling dem papers, Mr. Skyles. Dey belongs to my Grandpa Gabe. Dey is all he has from his mamma," Jackie said as he stood to leave.

"I understand. I understand." He stood and opened the door. "I'll let you know if I come up with anything."

Jackie nodded. Once out the door he broke into a jog and headed north on Carteret Street to be home in time for dinner; tears of disappointment trickled down his cheeks.

CHAPTER 21

M a'am. My instructions are right here…" The ambulance driver checked the clipboard. "From Dr. Joseph Palmer. 'Patient's Name: Mr. Gabriel Sampson Pritchard. Action: Released. Release Notes: Return patient to residence via hospital ambulance. Notify family before release. Meet family at residence. Address: 504 Prince Street, Beaufort.' "

Hestelle Eddings had received the earlier phone call but was surprised and upset by how the driver and assistant—a Mutt and Jeff pair of white males—planted Gabe in his rocker like they were offloading a bag of mail at the Greyhound Bus station. She looked back over her shoulder and watched as Jackie adjusted the quilt over Gabe and turned on the television.

"Mamma, is Grandpa Gabe okay?" he asked as he walked to join his mother.

"Says here, doctor's note, that the old man suffered or suffers from myocardial ischemia," the driver explained straight off the sheet of medical mumbo jumbo.

"I heard all da' before and it don't make no sense to me," she replied, drained by days of helplessness and dread. She rubbed her temples, briefly, then looked back at the driver and politely asked, "Can you tells me what da' means?"

"Means he had a heart attack. Simple as that." He closed the clipboard folder and tipped his hat. "I'll be headed back."

"Wait!" She grabbed his forearm. He looked down at her hand, which she quickly pulled back. "Are dey any instructions for what we needs to do for him?"

"Nope. Just let him rest. Don't let him do anything strenuous. Doc Palmer said he would be by later on." With that the driver was out the door, down the steps, and on his way.

Hestelle rejoined Gabe behind the chair; Jackie sat on the ottoman in front.

"You heard da' man, right, Grandpa?" she said, brushing her hand through the kinky gray hair that stubbornly remained.

Gabe bobbed his head.

"I gots to get home to cook. I'll bring supper over here tonight, so don't you be dancing around in da' kitchen, ya hears me?"

Again, Gabe bobbed his head.

"Jackie goin' to stay here wid you till I gets back. Okay?"

Gabe bobbed his chin and lifted both his hands inches off his blanket in surrender.

Hestelle kissed the top of Gabe's head and motioned for Jackie to follow her to the door.

"Now you watch him. Don't let him do nothin' 'cept go to de bathroom an' you help him. You got da'?" she said, her finger in his chest

"Yes, Mamma."

"Ef he need water, you gets it. You understand?"

"Yes, Mamma."

"Ef anything happens, you come get me rights away."

Jackie nodded.

"I be back later, couple hours probably."

"Un-huh," Jackie replied.

When his mother walked out, Jackie repositioned the quilt over Gabe's shoulders. The hospital medication eased the old man to sleep. Jackie nodded with each rise and fall of Gabe's chest, hypnotized by the movement and pained by each dry, raspy breath. As he looked on, he reminisced about all the things Gabe had done for him and for so many others. He recalled the stories Gabe had shared. Then he remembered the night, in the hospital, when he had lied to his grandpa. The lie. He scrunched his eyes as if he had been kicked or stabbed. The devil in the lie conjured up the masked figures in the woods. He fought to clear his head, then he remembered. The masked creatures had given him a message, words they said were meant for Gabe and only Gabe. *What were the words? What did they tell me?* He concentrated on that moment. He had to recall one moment, one phrase, from his horrifying weeklong experience. Words of that message. Exactly as he heard them. That one time, only once, at a time and place when he was sure he was about to die. He focused. He had to get it right.

The quilt slid off Gabe's shoulder. His eyelids rolled open in a drowsy down-the-nose stare.

"Grandpa Gabe?" The ottoman wheezed when Jackie bent over to get closer. Gabe's skin was pallid, a dull gray-black. A smile soon crystalized across the old man's face. "Grandpa, how do you feel?"

Gabe closed his eyes, which worried Jackie. When he reopened them, he said, "I be home and you be here." Jackie hopped off his seat and held a glass of water close for Gabe to sip. He watched the lump in Gabe's throat ride up and down when he swallowed. Most of what touched his cracked lips dribbled down his chin and onto the quilt. When he finished Gabe reached his hand out from under the quilt and touched the boy's as he wiped the water off the quilt.

Jackie sat still on the ottoman for several minutes. His throat tightened. Nausea from uncertain fear bubbled inside him. He remembered exactly where he was, how he felt, exactly what he heard when the haystack creature told him exactly what to say. "Grandpa Gabe, I was told to give you a message."

Gabe simply nodded, a slight dip of the chin.

Jackie recited the words slowly and verbatim so Gabe could hear. The message was short, seven words, none were English. They were words Jackie rehearsed and remembered by sound, not words Jackie had ever spoken to anyone except the masked creatures. When he finished, Gabe opened his eyes ghostly wide. Jackie could see the lacey red veins that crowded the coffee-bean irises of the old man's eyes. Gabe's hands crept from under the blanket onto the arms of his chair. His shoulders rolled forward off the backrest.

"Where you hear dem words?" Gabe asked amid deep breaths. "Who telled you dis?"

Jackie could not look Gabe in the face. Speaking loud enough for Gabe to hear over the noise from the television, he dropped his head and looked at the floor and explained how his captors made him recite the words and how they responded each time he spoke them. When Jackie finished, Gabe asked, "Was you scared?"

"Yes, Grandpa."

"Did dey hurt you?"

Jackie wanted to say yes but realized the pain was fear and loneliness, not physical.

"Not really. I was cold and hungry a lot of times, but—"

"What did you learn?"

The words went straight to Jackie's heart.

Through all of the questions, Jackie couldn't bring himself to look at Grandpa Gabe. He fidgeted in his seat and gazed about the room and, even with the television noise in the background, he realized how peaceful life was within the walls, in this house. He looked at the bird in the cage, the boxes in the corner, dust in webs by windows, the old paintings on the walls, the mantel with small brass-framed pictures of him with his parents lined up along the edge, pictures of Gabe much younger. The house smelled of mildew and mold, of decay. To Jackie it smelled like a dying old man.

"I learned what it means to survive."

Gabe closed his eyes, fell back against his chair, and didn't move for quite some time.

"Grandpa, do you have other old letters like de one you showed me? De one from de hospital?"

Gabe started to speak but stopped suddenly. He looked at the boy and nodded without expression.

"You said…" Jackie continued, but the old man was gone. The quilt on his chest rested, fixed and flat. Gabe didn't move. The silence in the room was complete, even the noise from the television seemed to disappear. Jackie had never heard Death before. He eased himself closer.

"Grandpa?" he cried. And again, louder, "Grandpa Gabe?"

The old man snorted and flinched in his chair, his breath light, slow paced.

Jackie continued to call, but aside from the movement in the quilt, Gabe did not respond. Jackie dashed to the phone to call his mother. When he picked up the receiver, he heard voices, other members of the party line.

His voice trembled when he spoke into the phone. "Excuse me. I need to call my mamma."

"Boy, you gets off dis line right now," a rude male voice responded in an ugly tone.

"But it about—"

"I said"—he cleared his throat and continued slowly, an octave lower—"you gets off da' phone right now. I be having a private conversation."

"But—"

"Don't 'but' me, boy. I says hang up!" he harrumphed.

Jackie hung up the phone and went back to Gabe's side with an eye on the clock in the kitchen. Five minutes passed, then ten. Gabe's breathing remained shallow. Jackie went back to the phone, but turned so he could still see Gabe. When he lifted the handset, he heard voices, again. He gently replaced the receiver in the cradle, and as he did the voice from the speaker said, "I'm still on this line."

Jackie stared at the old man in the rocker. He remembered Gabe's final nod before he passed out. *There must be other letters*, Jackie thought. There had to be more and he couldn't wait for Gabe; he had to find them.

With an eye on Gabe, he started where he found the initial clue, under the birdcage. That box was no longer there. He tried the chest of drawers in the corner. Many old clothes and newspapers. A stack of discolored lace doilies, a worn horse blanket, a broken frame, some playing cards, but no papers. In the corner, partially hidden by a long woolen overcoat, Jackie saw a stack of boxes, six in all. He grabbed the top box. It was a tall tin box that read "Sunshine Saltines" on the outside. It was heavy, much heavier than saltines would have been.

Indeed. Inside, the tin was half full of pennies, every one of them a dull gray color, and all seemed to be the same year, 1943. Jackie put the tin aside and grabbed a box made of wood and paper. The seal around the edge, though broken, read "American Cigar Company, Charleston, S.C." Inside was a Charleston newspaper from 1945 with a headline that said the Negro workers chanted, "We shall overcome," as they walked the picket lines by the plant. The next box was a red Bingo box. The corners, once taped, were ripped, the lid barely able to stay on. Inside were metal tiles with numbers on them. Underneath those were cardboard Bingo cards, just as he expected, but beneath the stack of cards there was something else, papers not related to the game. All of them were folded. To his eye and to his touch he was sure they were old, like the one Gabe had shared, the letter signed by Poe. Jackie lifted them, one at a time and unfolded each. Every one of them bore the name of William Lembath. Some referred to him as Dr., others as Mr. or simply William. They came from Philadelphia, Savannah, and Charleston. The penmanship was difficult to read, a sloppy mix of cursive and script. The sentences made no sense, as a whole, but, rightly or wrongly, he thought Gene Skyles needed to read these letters, to see these words, to see if they solved Skyles's hypothesis that the real Annabel Lee was a daughter of William Lembath of Beaufort. One particular letter caught Jackie's eye. At the very top it read "Circular Congregational Church, Charleston." It would have not been of any significance had Gene Skyles not mentioned that name the day before in his motel room.

Several other items sat in the box, memorabilia mainly. Jackie checked on Gabe—no change. He continued to rummage through the other items in the Bingo box.

Cards. Labels. Some small rocks. A ripped photo with worn edges and missing corners, but with a faint penned identifier scribbled on the back that read "Hattie." The figure in the center was a tall Negro woman dressed in a full black dress, buttoned tight up to a white Peter Pan collar that lay flat at the base of her neck. She wore a pleated white apron tied around her waist and draped nearly to the ground. She stood in the dirt; beyond her was a large stone house. Jackie remembered that Grandpa Gabe had mentioned his mother was called Hattie, though never with a last name. He held the photo in his hand and admired the simple beauty of the face, then in the background, even without the giant live oaks, Jackie recognized the solid block structure of the Castle.

Gabe's first cough startled Jackie. The Bingo box and all the contents fell from his lap. He bent over to gather things when Gabe began a steady cough, a spell that wouldn't stop. Between each cough, he wheezed.

"Grandpa!" Jackie raced back to Gabe, who had doubled over with spasms. "Grandpa!" Jackie screamed. He dropped to his knees, his hands on top of Gabe's quilt.

"Do you want water? Anything? Water?"

Gabe nodded.

When Jackie left to refill the glass with water, Gabe continued to cough. He rolled his head to the side to keep the boy in sight. With his head turned, Gabe spied the Bingo box and the papers scattered on the floor. By the time Jackie returned, Gabe was rigid in a catatonic stare.

"Grandpa, here. Take a sip," Jackie begged.

Breathless, with the back of his head against the chair, Gabe wouldn't move. A finger-length drool oozed from his mouth. When Gabe didn't respond, Jackie pulled back the glass and waited. Finally, the quilt moved.

"What you done, boy?" Gabe muttered with barely enough strength to air the words.

Jackie didn't respond. He wasn't sure if Gabe had noticed the papers on the floor; he moved to the side of the rocker to block the view.

"De box. Da' box. How... Why?" Gabe rolled his head toward Jackie. He breathed hard.

"Grandpa, I was—"

"You was what? Da' be"—the coughing resumed—"my box, not yous," Gabe charged.

"I...I was trying to aks, Grandpa Gabe, then you fell asleep. I thought you nodded da' it would be okay to look for other letters, letters like de one from de hospital."

"I never said—"

Jackie's sense of room and space and peace had abandoned him. "But, Grandpa, da' letter. I showed it to da' man, de man from school, Mr. Skyles. He said it was valuable. Maybe an original letter from Edgar Allan Poe and worth a lot of money."

"Who—" the only word he could speak before the spasms returned. He squinted with each labored cough.

"Edgar Allan Poe. He be a famous—"

"Dey my letters. I telled you—" Gabe managed before his next spasm. He closed his eyes to avoid conversation.

"But, Grandpa...but Mr. Skyles thinks dem is real an' may even have de clue for de treasure da' Poe wrote about," Jackie said, his words coming faster and faster like a downhill locomotive. "An' dem letters, de ones in de Bingo box, dem..." He hesitated and noticed the forlorn look on Gabe's face. Jackie knelt down next to the chair again and placed his hands on the quilt over

Gabe's knees. "I'm sorry, Grandpa," he said with a sigh, his face aching with contrition.

"Bring da' box," Gabe said. He pulled his hand out from under the quilt and gestured in the general direction of the mess on the floor.

Jackie gathered the papers with the same soft touch he had used to open them.

"What dem say?" Gabe asked, unable to read the letters, not because of his physical state, but because the man never learned to read.

"Dey don't make much sense, Grandpa. De names, though. You recognize de names?" Jackie asked, pulling the ottoman close as a seat.

Gabe grew weary. This exchange had been his longest since before the hospital. He rested his chin on his chest and added, "I knowed dem names. Dem stories from my mamma."

Jackie started with the photograph. He placed it in Gabe's lap in a spot visible from his lowered head. Gabe pulled his other hand out from under the quilt and tilted the small scrap image to see it better. His hands shook as he allowed himself the pleasure of recall.

"It says Hattie on de back, Grandpa. Is da' your mamma?"

The old man filled his aching lungs. His brow dipped as his lips quivered; the very edges curled upward.

"She a pretty girl," Gabe said. Jackie watched. Gabe offered nothing more, no explanation, no words, but his face told Jackie all he needed to know. He embraced the moment. The peace and reflection was better medicine than any doctor could offer. When the time passed, when the reunion ended, Jackie continued.

"Grandpa Gabe, dem letters?"

"Dem was my mamma." He paused, taking a breath after a few words. "She told me...dem was in de house...where she be a slave."

"De name in de letter is Lembath. De Lembath house over by de Castle. Is da' where she worked?"

Gabe didn't respond. He closed his eyes. Jackie thought he had fallen asleep.

"She told me...de Great Skedaddle...de box she kept. Dem letters. I puts dem in da' red box."

Jackie's head was spinning. The names in the letters might be helpful with the clue and for Mr. Skyles.

"Can I take dem letters to de man from school?"

"No," Gabe choked and immediately began to cough, another spasm that bent him forward in his chair. Jackie sat and waited, praying Gabe would be all right and that he would change his mind.

"Bring da' man here," Gabe said when his fit stopped. "Dem letters dem stay here, in dis house." Gabe rested a while, then continued, "Ef he want dem letters, he need be here."

"Knock, knock," a voice said as the screen door creaked open. They never heard footsteps on the porch or the squeaky board on the step.

"Gabe, how you feeling?" Dr. Palmer asked. "I see you made it back home okay. Did they take good care of you like I asked?"

Jackie stood up next to Gabe in the rocker.

"I see you have your personal assistant here with you. Jackie, how are you doing, boy?" the doctor asked. He placed a small black leather bag on the floor and extended his hand for Jackie to shake, which he did.

"I hope Gabe's been behaving himself."

"Yes, sir, Dr. Palmer. He been coughing a lot, though."

The doctor noticed the old papers on the floor in front of Gabe and Jackie.

"Catching up on old correspondence, eh?"

"Some old letters. Grandpa Gabe and I was going through is all. I plan to have Mr. Skyles look at dem. Dey might be from Edgar Allan Poe."

"Poe?" Joseph Palmer questioned. "Now, how would those letters be here or, better yet, why?" the doctor asked.

"Dey is old letters Grandpa Gabe has from his mamma is all. Grandpa said Mr. Skyles can come over an' look at dem."

Dr. Palmer's smile melted rather quickly. He pulled his stethoscope from his bag. He nonchalantly plugged the ends into his ears. "When is he coming over?"

"I still needs to aks him."

The doctor peeked at the letters. He reached to pick up one for a closer look. He scanned it briefly, then picked up a second one. Still holding the letters at his side, he added, "Not sure that's a good idea. Your grandpa is sick. He's had a very difficult week"—he hesitated—"and so have you. How are you feeling? You look better than you did when I examined you on Friday."

Jackie nodded. "I be okay," he smiled, half-heartedly. "Well, I won't bother Grandpa Gabe about dem letters now. Grandpa doesn't want me to take dem out dis house." Jackie looked at Gabe who had dozed off. "De letters, dey is memories from Grandpa Gabe's mamma. Dey might also help Mr. Skyles wid his research an' he might help me wid my school project."

"Project?" Palmer asked. "By the way, how is school? Kinda different there? You being nice to those white kids?"

"Yes, sir," he said and looked away.

While Gabe dozed, Dr. Palmer listened to his heart the best he could and checked his pulse, or so it appeared to Jackie.

"Not much more I can do here now. I need to take off. Let Gabe sleep." As the doctor repacked his bag, he said, "It's not a good idea to bring that man here, Jackie. Gabe is real sick. In fact, I don't think you should even mention these letters to him, that Mr. Skyles."

Jackie was unsure what to say. "Okay, Dr. Palmer. I'll tell Grandpa Gabe."

"He needs his rest. You take good care of him. Tell him I'll stop by again tomorrow if I can."

The doctor held the screen door and eased it closed without a sound. Gabe continued to sleep. In the meantime Jackie packaged up all the letters and other items. He placed everything back in the red Bingo box and returned it to the pile with the other boxes, making sure he returned things to their original position. He knew Gabe would notice. For a ninety-six-year-old man, he was funny that way.

By the time Hestelle Eddings returned Gabe had slept well over an hour with Jackie at his feet watching television. He was anxious to visit Mr. Skyles and to bring him over to his grandpa's house, despite the doctor's orders. Maybe, just maybe, the letters had something more that Skyles could use to break the ciphered clue. And if he was able to unscramble the code, maybe it would lead to the Gullah treasure. The letters appeared to be the only lead or hint of the truth behind the Gullah treasure. He had to know. He had to show Mr. Skyles these letters.

CHAPTER 22

With his eyes glued to the classroom clock the reading, writing and 'rithmetic of Monday classes passed slower than usual. As soon as the bell rang, Jackie gathered his books and headed for the door. He broke into a trot in the hall and sprinted to the Lord Carteret Motel. He knocked on Gene Skyles' door then dropped his books on the ground and bent over with his hands on his knees to catch his breath. After a few seconds without an answer he stood and knocked a second time, longer and harder. *Come on Mr. Skyles, answer de door. Please!* No answer. He squeezed his eyes shut, flopped against the wall, took a deep breath through his nose then puffed his cheeks out like balloons while he exhaled, slowly. While he waited he watched leaves and abandoned newspapers square dance across the parking lot in mini-cyclones revved by the afternoon winds. He rolled to his left and knocked a third time. Still nothing. Discouraged, he grabbed his books and headed home.

"Where has you been, boy?" Irvin Eddings said as soon as Jackie opened the door.

"Daddy, can't dis wait?"

"No," he said with a stare hot enough to burn through Jackie's chest. "What took you so long?"

"I ran all de way from school," Jackie said without a mention of his side trip to see Gene Skyles. "Can't dis wait for an hour? Even thirty minutes? I needs to see Mr. Skyles."

"I told you, I wanted you home immediately after school and da' is what I meant, boy. Come on. We going to see Chief Heimer."

Jackie dropped his books on the sofa; his father grabbed a hat. They walked the three-quarters of a mile to the police station without sharing words. Jackie wasn't sure of the purpose for this visit; his concern was only how quickly he could get back to see Gene Skyles to tell him about the letters at Grandpa Gabe's.

"Have a seat," Chief Heimer said as he closed the door to his office. There was only one chair in front of the chief's desk. Jackie took the opportunity to stand behind the chair and allowed his father to sit and protect him from the chief. He placed his hands on the back of the chair, bowed his head and listened.

"Okay. Mr. Eddings, I believe it is. And this is your son, Jackie Robinson Eddings, as I recall." The chief sauntered around the desk, slid into his chair and grinned. "As I recollect we met somewhat recently."

"Yes, Chief Heimer," Irvin Eddings answered.

"What brings you to my office this time?" the chief asked, expecting a confession for the earlier charges of breaking and entering, trespassing and mischievous behavior on Geordie Swanson's boat with no mention of the boy's disappearance.

Irvin Eddings looked down. He fumbled with his hat in his hands for a bit then looked up with an expressionless face. "Chief Heimer, sir, I wants to know what you found out about whoever it was da' kidnapped my son?"

The question didn't settle well with the chief. *Why you uppity Negro jackass! What do I care about who kidnapped your*

226

boy? Who knows. The boy may have just run off and dressed himself up. He may have made up this whole thing. And, what difference does it make? He's back. I have better things to do with my time.

"Well, uh…Mr. Eddings…I assure you we're working on your son's case," he replied, boldly.

"And has you found him or dem? Does you have anything?" Irvin asked.

Heimer folded his hands on his desk, leaned back far in his chair, and scoffed, "You see, Mr. Eddings"— Heimer cleared his throat—"we have many citizens in Beaufort; they all need our protection every day." He let his eyes wander, then addressed his visitor. "Since your son is back, you see, finding who did what to your son is not as important to us as other calls that come in."

Irvin Eddings came out of the chair. "Wait a minute, Mr. Heimer—"

"Chief Heimer, Mr. Eddings," the chief said as he leaned forward to correct his colored guest.

Eddings held his tongue; he let his eyes and the tremor of his body convey the depth of his anger. When he sat down, Heimer rocked back in his chair.

"Chief Heimer," Irvin said with emphasis, "as I sees it de safety of my son is more important than anything da' happens here."

Otis Heimer cocked his head while he drummed his fingers on the desk. "All a matter of opinion, Mr. Eddings. All a matter of opinion. Your opinion says…drop everything and figure out where my son was. Have you asked him?"

Irvin Eddings looked across the desk, his forehead wrinkled to form one dark uninterrupted eyebrow. He looked over his shoulder toward his son.

"I mean, your boy's been in trouble here before. Who's to say he didn't plan to run away from home but chickened out?"

"Mr. Heim…uh, Chief Heimer, my son wouldn't do da'." Irvin Eddings responded eye-to-eye emphasizing his point. "Somebody took my boy. Somebody kept him for a week and somebody should do something about da'."

"Well, we are, Mr. Eddings. Rest assured we are," Heimer said. He rolled his chair back and crossed his leg. "We'll continue to investigate this, but let's hear from the boy."

Otis Heimer hoisted himself out of his chair. He pushed his thumbs under his wide belt and walked toward Jackie. The boy shifted to the side of his father's chair as the chief moved in his direction. Otis Heimer placed one hand on the back of the chair and leaned down toward the young Eddings.

"So tell me, boy, what happened out there in the woods?"

"Nothing, sir. I mean I was blindfolded and somebody took my clothes and made me wear dem animals and—"

"And what did this person or persons look like?"

"I don't know, Chief Heimer, sir. I was blindfolded," Jackie said, cautious to show the respect for authority he learned in his previous visit.

"Now, boy, let me help you see things a little better. The report says there were four guys who wore masks, big masks. They looked like animals," Heimer said, leaning even closer.

Adrenaline pricked for control of Jackie's entire body, except for the words he managed to choke out. "Sir, I don't—"

"Don't you lie to me, boy. Ya hear?" Otis Heimer lifted his head to stare down Irvin Eddings who had started to lift out of his seat. The look settled the boy's father and the chief continued. "You see those kinds of people or things in the woods?"

Jackie felt like he was going to vomit. His heart pumped faster than it had when he was in the woods. He caved.

"Yes, sir. I seen masks like da', but I seen dem before."

"Another time?" Heimer said in surprise. "You saw them some other time?" he continued, toying with the boy.

"Yes, sir," Jackie replied, his brain working harder than his heart to cover his story.

Irvin Eddings remained still, gripped by a confession he had not heard before.

"When? Tell me about this other time, boy." Heimer egged him on, hoping to coax out the truth that there never were any people in masks at all.

"It was de night de Western Auto truck be stolen," Jackie started. Words began to flow out of his mouth well before his brain could approve. "Two white men. Dey pulled me out my house and drove me in da' truck."

"What?" Black-and-white fireworks inside Irvin Eddings's head launched him out of his seat. He turned and tossed his hat on the chair. "Why didn't—"

"Hush!" The chief put his hand up to hold Irvin back; he needed the boy to focus. "Pulled you out of your house? Where were your parents?" the chief said with a look toward the boy's father.

"Wait! I wants to know about dem whites. What was dey doing, son?" Irvin pressed.

"Just answer me, son. Your parents were where?" the chief insisted, loudly, his eyes first on the father, then on the son.

Jackie eyed both men and continued. "It was Thursday. Dey was at de praise house. I didn't go because I had school work."

"And they took you where?" the police chief asked.

"Dey tied me up and took me to de Hanging Tree on Saint Helena."

"Dey did what?" Irvin Eddings yelled. "Why ain't you told me dis before?"

"Hold on, Eddings. One case at a time. Let's hear more about the masked guys."

It was as if the chief had kicked a grizzly. Irvin Eddings turned back toward Otis Heimer, baring his teeth.

"I wants to hear about dem whites." Once again, he locked eyes with the chief and, without turning, said to his son, "What happened?"

Jackie chewed on a fingernail for a second, then picked at it with his other hand.

Heimer wouldn't break the stare. He took a step closer, toe-to-toe with the boy's father. "I said...one case at a time, Eddings. Did you not hear me, boy?" The chief tugged on his belt and held the stare, then very slowly reiterated word by word, "One case at a time. Now, sit down. You came in here to ask about the kidnapping case. We're going to work through that and then maybe..." The chief scowled and walked back behind his desk with his eyes locked on Irvin Eddings. "Continue, boy."

"They was fixin' to do something when de Lands End Light appeared."

Heimer motioned to Irvin Eddings, "Sit!" He knocked on his desktop with his knuckles and shook his head. "That ain't an option. I said sit!"

Irvin Eddings squinted, the venom of animus shared in his response. He took his seat.

"So you saw the Lands End Light. And then you saw these masked guys?" Heimer laughed. "Eddings, this boy of yours has quite an imagination."

Irvin, first checked the chief, then looked at his son and softly said, "Why didn't you say nothing about dis before, Jackie?"

"I—I—I was scared to."

"Who were dem whites?" Irvin asked his son. Eddings was back on his feet. He shoved his hands deep in his pockets and began to pace.

"I don't know," Jackie lied. He knew if he mentioned Skeet's name or Hoss Lassiter they would make life bad for him at school or find some way to finish what they started. He remembered Skeet warned he was not finished with him yet.

"What did dey look like? Was dey young or old or what?" his father pressed.

"I don't know, Daddy. All I know is my hands and feet was tied and dey had a rope in de truck." He looked at his father, then at the chief. "After de Light appeared it flew over us and de white guys got scared. Dey tried to get de truck to go but it wouldn't then it did, but de truck got stuck. Dey left me in de back of de truck and dey took off. I had to get myself untied and—"

"Okay. Hold up right there," the chief blurted to stop the boy. "I told you, one case at a time. You answer my questions, boy, not your father's. I want to know about the masked guys. Were they there, at that tree?" Heimer asked. He tapped his pencil.

"No, sir. When I got untied, I walked to de praise house. When I got dey I was waiting for my parents to come out and I sees dis masked thing go across de field into de woods so I followed it," Jackie said. His stomach had settled; his brain was in control of the story. "I went into de woods and da' when I saw dem, de masked creature things."

"Doing what? What'd they say?" the chief asked, the pencil scribbling across the sheet.

"Dey sorta dancing or praying. I ain't sure. Dey was a ring shout in de praise house and I couldn't hear real good. I tried to get closer and da' when I fell. Somehow dey heard me fall and chased me."

"Chased you?" Irvin asked from the corner.

"Yeah. We ran a ways through de woods. I hid but dey came closer. When I finally found my way out de woods, everybody had left de praise house so I walked home."

"From Saint Helena? You walked home?" the chief asked in amazement.

"Yes, sir," Jackie replied.

"You didn't thumb or get a ride?" As soon as he asked the question and looked at the boy, he knew the colored boy had no chance for a ride. Coloreds didn't drive off the island after dark and, at that time of night, the only whites who would pick him up would probably have intentions other than a ride into town. He was surprised to hear Jackie change his story.

"I mean, well...yes, sir, Chief Heimer. I got a ride."

"Who? How?" Heimer asked, shocked.

"It were a black car da' stopped. A colored man told me he give me a ride to de bridge and he did."

Heimer wasn't sure what to make of the car or the driver or the ride. He moved on. "Okay, these white guys and the truck. What did they look like?" the chief asked with a nod toward Irvin, then back to the young boy.

"Dey was white. One kinda thin, de other kinda fat," Jackie said, being as nondescript as possible.

"Old or young?" Heimer urged, his pencil eager to add notes.

"I don't know," Jackie said. He closed his eyes and added, "Young sorta. Maybe."

"Young sorta. Well, I'll be. And you don't know who they were and you have no idea how old they might have been?"

"No, sir," Jackie continued in his lie.

Irvin Eddings stepped forward. He stood in front of the chief's desk, but turned toward his son, blocking the chief's line of sight to Jackie.

"When was dis?" Irvin asked.

"Weeks ago. After school started," Jackie replied, then looked away.

"That's what integration does," the chief said, confident he had secured the motive for whatever it was these truck thieves had in mind.

"Ever see dem around your school, son?" Irvin asked.

"I'm de only colored boy in de school. Dey white peoples around everywhere, all de time," Jackie answered without another lie. He refused to lift his eyes off the floor.

Irvin moved back and started to pace behind the chair. In the office he managed five short steps before he had to change direction.

After several minutes of noodling on his pad, the chief leaned back and spoke. "Okay, Mr. Eddings, I thank you for coming in today. I can certainly appreciate your concern for the welfare and safety of your boy." He placed his pencil back in a cup. When he stood, his hairline, in fast retreat, and wide-set eyes made him look like a beluga whale in khakis. He laced his fingers in front of his chest and stretched his arms forward to crack his knuckles. "I can take it from here. I'll report back to you in a few days. Give me a week, Eddings. One week and we can knock out both of these cases," Heimer said with a nod of confidence.

Jackie looked at the chief, then back at his father.

Irvin Eddings was totally confused. He wanted to argue with the chief, but given what Jackie just revealed, he needed to talk to his son first. "Yes, Chief Heimer. One week. I be back to see you then. You calls me sooner ef you finds something, anything," Irvin said. His face reflected his disapproval of the chief's attitude. He looked at Jackie. "An' ef my son can help wid more details, tell me and I bring him back."

Irvin Eddings reluctantly but politely extended his hand toward the chief, who hesitated but returned the gesture. When Irvin Eddings nodded toward his son, Jackie turned and headed to the door.

"Tell Chief Heimer thank you, son," Irvin said.

Jackie turned back toward the desk and the man with a badge who had caused him to lie more than any other person on Earth. "Thank you."

When the chief dipped his chin and raised his index finger to his forehead in a one-finger salute, the visitors walked out the door onto a sun-starved sidewalk.

The confession and revelations of the previous thirty minutes left Irvin Eddings confused and frazzled, a pressure cooker of emotion. Words—bitter and sweet, harsh and soft, measured and free-wheeling—stacked up behind numbed lips, down a throat still burning with bile. They walked three blocks side by side before a voice in Irvin's head broke through. At the Red Bird Taxi office, there was a bench on the side of the building, the usual spot for drivers to collect, share smokes, and swap stories. It was empty. Irvin seized the opportunity to stop and talk to his son.

"Jackie, I be disappointed in you," Irvin Eddings started, seated alongside his son on the bench. His tone was the male cry of a heart that ached. When he heard his father's words, Jackie didn't look up. He stared at the patch of mud by his feet and wished it would suck him down into the earth.

"Why'd you not tell me about dem whites?" There was a pause of disappointment that hung longer than the fear behind it. "I ain't going to ask you now. Makes no difference, do it?" Irvin Eddings stopped again. Looking straight ahead, he pulled his hat from his head and held it between his knees. A pair of large black birds, larger than crows, flew past.

"You had reasons." He waited. Jackie didn't speak. "Something about da' school? You ain't had no problems till you went dey."

Irvin bent well forward and passed the brim of his hat through his fingers an inch at a time until it had gone one full circle.

"Jackie, dey is a lot who hate you out dey right now. Ain't your fault. People be mad. Mad cause you be a colored boy sitting next to dey white child, in de same classroom, de same school. Haters da' ain't going to change overnight, but you can change dem." He ran his fingers along the crown of the hat, shaping and reshaping while he shared his soul. "Dey say you ain't smart enough to be dey. Da' you just ain't de same as dem white childrens. But you is. An' so be every colored child in dis Lowcountry. To dem you ain't one colored boy. You is all de colored childrens. You gotsa be smart. You gotsa be strong. You gotsa be firm. It weren't no accident you be sent to da' school. Show dem, dem white kids, da' you can do de same work as dem, da' you fit in, you belongs."

Jackie picked at his fingernail and let his father's words soak in deeper. Irvin took a few calming breaths while he shifted his shoe and watched the mud mound up along the sole.

"I think dem whites was goin' to lynch you. I think so," he said, turning his head toward his son, then back looking at his shoe. "And da' scare me. And…you know what scare me more? It scare me more da' you didn't tell me or your mamma. You can't let da' happen. You be a man soon enough, on your own two feet, but till then Mamma and me be here to helps you. It ain't fear da' bring you to us. It be love."

He looked over toward his son. This time Jackie returned the look. Their eyes met briefly before Jackie looked away.

"Daddy…" Jackie choked, "I understands."

His two words were enough to foster a smile on his father's tired face. He reached over and rubbed his son's head.

"Dis project wid de white boys. De preacher's son and who da' other boy?"

"Skeet Gundy."

"Yeah, Skeet. Start wid dem. Work wid dem and make da' project good. Make dem your friends and dem others be friends soon."

Jackie understood, though exposing Skeet might change things for his father. Friendship with Skeet would be more of a challenge than finding a Gullah treasure.

"Okay, then go. You says you wanted to see da' Mr. Skyles."

"Yeah, it be about de Gullah treasure project," Jackie said with his own smile back.

"Then git! Don't be late for supper. Mamma don't like it when you not home on time, you knows da'," Irvin said.

Jackie jumped up and jogged off toward Carteret Street. Irvin Eddings watched. The boy never looked back; Irvin didn't expect him to. When Jackie dropped out of sight around the corner of the post office, Irvin stood and stepped toward home—alone. He had not gone but a few steps before he suddenly stopped, reversed direction, and charged off to the law office of Robert Caplin.

CHAPTER 23

J ackie tossed, turned, and wrestled with his bed sheets all night. The interrogation by Chief Heimer and his father's sermon-like appeal smoldered in his head like a peat bog. But the excitement Gene Skyles showed fired up the teen most. Skyles was ready to run to Grandpa Gabe's the instant he heard of the letters, but Jackie confessed his grandpa probably needed a little warning given his physical and mental state. Before Jackie dashed home for supper, they agreed to rendezvous at Grandpa Gabe's after school the following afternoon.

The next day, based on his father's prompting, Jackie shared his news with his project teammates. When he mentioned to Ricky that he had found letters by Poe and that Mr. Skyles was going to look at them, Ricky became predictably unhinged. Hunkered down at his desk the entire day, he doodled pencil drawings of treasure chests and large bugs with eyes, hairy legs, and pincers. Skeet, on the other hand, gave Jackie his usual dirty look with predictable hostility.

"Now ain't that exciting," Skeet said, his wrinkled scowl inches from Jackie's nose. "Guess I'll be getting ready for another treasure hunting trip, eh? Like the last time? Remember that one, boy?" He thumped Jackie in the chest with his index finger. "I ain't forgot. I ain't goin' to forget. And I ain't finished," he whispered. He walked away but added, "Oh, we goin' to find us some treasure all right, boy. We going to find us a great reward."

By the time Jackie had walked from school to Ricky's house, Cybil Clemonds had picked up her son, driven him home, asked him about his day, and succumbed only once to his pouty tantrums. This time she settled for an ice cream sandwich from the Good Humor truck, despite the fact that it was December.

"Hello, Jackie," Cybil said when she answered the knock on the door. "What a pleasant surprise. Come in."

Ricky was on the floor seated no more than three feet from the television, lost in concentration.

"Ricky, look who came to visit. It's Jackie," Cybil said.

"Hi," was the monotone response and it came without taking his eyes off the screen.

"Well, Jackie, have a seat. You boys can watch cartoons for a while."

After his mother left, Ricky held out his ice cream so Jackie could see, but continued to watch cartoons. "Look, a horse. I took teeny, tiny bites and made a horse."

Jackie drew back a bit and looked at the food art in Ricky's hand, though what Ricky described as a horse looked like a melted ice cream sandwich to Jackie.

"Did you ask your mamma? Can you go to my grandpa's house?"

"Hey, Mamma, can I go to Jackie's grandpa's house?" Ricky yelled from the living room.

"What, darling?" She stirred the contents of a bowl under her arm when she moved to the doorway.

"Mrs. Clemonds, I told Ricky I found some old letters at my Grandpa Gabe's house. Dey might be real."

"What kind of letters? Just letters?"

Jackie looked at Ricky, who didn't bother to join the conversation, nor did he laugh at the cartoons.

"No, dey is letters written by Edgar Allan Poe," Jackie said. "Mr. Skyles, de man from Virginia is going to look at dem and tell us ef dey is real. Dey could be valuable. Can Ricky come wid me to Grandpa Gabe's? Mr. Skyles is coming over soon."

"That's so interesting. And you want Ricky to go with you to watch Mr. Skyles?"

"Yes. See, ef de letters is real dey might help us wid our Gullah treasure project. And, Mr. Skyles thinks dey might help him wid his project, too," Jackie explained.

Ricky shoved the uneaten butt-end of the horse-shaped ice cream sandwich in his mouth and immediately started slapping his cheeks with his hands, mumbling, "Cold. Cold. Cold." He kicked his heels into the floor until the ice cream melted and he could open his mouth. He stood up and turned off the television.

"Okay. We can go," he said and turned toward the front door.

"Ricky!" his mother shouted. "Where do you think you are going, young man?"

"Grandpa's house. Got to go now. Need to see Mr. Skyles."

Cybil turned to Jackie in the never-ending battle of control with her son. "He can go with you, Jackie. Just make sure he stays with you, in the house, please." She resumed stirring her bowl. "Ricky, be home for supper. Your favorite tonight. Pot roast and peas. Don't stay too long, honey, okay?"

"Yeah," Ricky said, going out the door.

Cybil looked at Jackie a few steps behind Ricky. "Be careful going over there," Cybil Clemonds warned. When

Jackie turned back to wave goodbye, he saw her nod, wink, and smile.

The boys marched through the front door without bothering to knock. Jackie knew his grandpa often took naps—planned and unplanned—during the day; he didn't want to disturb the old man. Inside, Gabe was curled up, asleep in his rocker, but there was another guest in the back of the room. Startled by the boys' silent entry, Freddie Lembath fumbled to close a cloth sack he had over his shoulder and to reposition things in the corner.

"How you be, boys?" he said, stacking a few boxes. His words whistled through the gap of missing teeth. "Didn't hears y'all come in. Just here waitin' for Uncle Gabe to wakes up. I brunged dem sweet taters, squash, and fresh collards. I knows he likes dem so I brunged dem for him. I puts dem here just so you knows I brung dem over. I dropped a tater down here." He pointed to the corner, then continued to place the vegetables from his cloth sack on the top of the chest near the boxes in the corner.

"Thank you, Uncle Freddie," Jackie said, pulling the ottoman close to his grandpa. He shared the seat with Ricky, who faced away toward the television to avoid eye contact with anyone.

"Where are the Poe letters? You said your grandpa had Poe letters," Ricky said. With his finger he traced the pattern in the ottoman cloth visible between his legs.

"Dey in de box in da' corner," Jackie replied, pointing.

"I want to see them. I want to see them now," Ricky insisted. Freddie Lembath eyed Ricky while he finished unloading the vegetables, then toddled closer to the boys.

"I should wait to ask Grandpa Gabe," Jackie said. He looked at Gabe who showed no signs of waking.

"I want to see them. See them now," Ricky screamed. "The Poe letters. I want to see them. You promised." He started to bounce up and down on his butt.

Jackie waited.

Ricky continued to spring up and down, then started hitting himself in the head with the palms of his hands. Jackie was afraid Ricky would become more violent if he didn't see the letters. Gabe had allowed him to look at the letters before and he did agree to let Gene Skyles look at them. He knew where they were.

"Okay. Okay." Jackie placed his hand on Ricky's shoulder; Ricky pushed it off.

"Show me the letters! Show me the letters!" Ricky bounced harder. Jackie put both hands on Ricky's shoulders and pushed down, hard enough to keep Ricky from bouncing.

"Excuse me, Uncle Freddie," he said as he walked to the stack of boxes. With more care than he used the last time he moved the boxes, he gently placed the top boxes aside to get to the red Bingo box. When he opened the box, it was empty.

"Dey gone! All dem papers, dey gone," he screamed. He turned to show Ricky the empty box.

Ricky turned a nonchalant look toward the box.

"No Poe letters. You said you had letters. No Poe letters," Ricky screamed. Then he returned to tracing the cloth pattern on the ottoman.

"Dey was right here," Jackie explained. "I put dem in here like Grandpa Gabe told me."

The commotion was enough to roust Gabe. He rolled his head toward Jackie's voice.

"Dem boys here, Gabe. You catchin' forty winks on us?" Freddie Lembath joked.

Gabe glanced back to the side toward Freddie Lembath in time to see him wink and wave the palm of his hand.

"Grandpa Gabe. Dey missing. All you papers. Dey gone." Jackie lifted the empty Bingo box and tilted it for Gabe to see.

Gabe closed his eyes and took in a deep breath.

Jackie dropped the empty box and returned to his grandpa's side; he saw a tear roll down Gabe's cheek.

"Dey was all I had."

"And Grandpa Gabe, de letter, da' Poe letter. Mr. Skyles say—"

"Come closer, boy," Gabe whispered.

Jackie bent down near his grandpa's lips. He could feel the air on his ear when the old man said something nobody else could hear. When the old man leaned his head forward, Jackie fished his hand behind the seat cushion and pulled out the worn Poe letter. He closed his eyes and breathed a sigh of relief before he smiled, sat down next to Ricky, and opened the letter. Freddie Lembath had a different reaction.

"What be da', boy. Lets me sees da'," he said, reaching to grab the letter. Jackie turned away and bumped into Ricky.

"An old letter, Uncle Freddie," he said, not offering a look.

Freddie stepped back with his hands on his hips. "Just wants to sees da' is all. You knows I can't read."

Footsteps on the porch and a knock on the door drew everyone's attention.

"Hello. Anybody home? Jackie, are you in there?" Gene Skyles said outside the screen door.

Holding the letter in his hand like a baby bird, Jackie got up and opened the door.

"Hi, Mr. Skyles. We're in here," he said and added in a whisper, "Grandpa Gabe is really tired and he lost his papers."

Skyles looked at the boy. "You mean—"

"But I have de letter, de Poe letter an' de cipher note."

Skyles smiled at Ricky Clemonds, then looked over at Freddie. "If I remember, you're..."

"Freddie Lembath," said the farmer with his toothless smile before Skyles could finish.

"That's right. We met one day over by school." He smiled at the older colored man on the other side of the Gabe. He recalled the Poe letter and nodded.

"Grandpa Gabe," Jackie said running his hand across his grandpa's shoulder as he passed behind, "dis is de man I told you abouts. Dis is Mr. Skyles."

Gabe opened his eyes long enough to see the white man in front of him. Then he closed them again.

"Mr. Pritchard, Jackie showed me the letter—" Skyles started.

Jackie nudged him and told him to speak louder.

"Mr. Pritchard, Jackie showed me your letter and I believe it is authentic. I believe it was signed by Edgar Allan Poe himself. This would be the only known letter in existence signed by Poe while he was assigned to Fort Moultrie." The news didn't make the old man budge. "That letter could be worth quite a lot of money."

Gabe moved his head, not up and down but side to side.

Skyles frowned and turned to Jackie. "Mind if I take another look at the cipher clue, the one in the letter?"

Jackie went back to the bird cage. He lifted the cage and pulled out the box under it where he had hidden the cipher note. He handed it over. Skyles studied it for a while and recalled the first time he had seen it at the motel. Since then he found something in his research notes he thought might help. He eased down and sat next to Ricky on the ottoman. Ricky jumped up and watched Skyles pull two sheets of paper from the briefcase he brought with him. With his notes on the floor on either side of the cipher, he ran his fingers down each row and column, back and forth between the code and his papers.

Ricky was spellbound by the papers and intrigued with the way Skyles ran his fingers across them, almost like he could feel each symbol. Ricky plopped down on the floor for a closer look. Leaning on his elbows, he rested his chin in his hands and consumed the clue like it was an episode of the *Hardy Boys*. But his fascination didn't last.

"So what be da', Mr. Skyles?" Freddie asked. He moved closer, his mud-caked shoes over the edge of the researcher notes. Skyles touched the colored man on the ankle and looked up with a concerned frown. The talkative farmer stepped back, closer to Ricky, who decided the bird cage would be more interesting. He hopped up, walked over, and made faces at Sherman, the bird.

Jackie stood back a few steps and waited patiently. Grandpa Gabe slept. Freddie Lembath continued to talk nonsense.

"I hads a dream about all dis. I dreams about da' Gullah treasure," he said. He talked, nonstop, for over five minutes. The background gibberish made it difficult for Gene Skyles to concentrate. From time to time he would cast an infuriated look toward the old guy, but he didn't want to intrude; he felt uneasy correcting the colored man in another colored man's house. His fingers moved slower and slower between the papers.

About the time Lembath finished, Skyles straightened up. "I don't know, Jackie. I can't figure this out. I thought I had some things here that would help, but they don't," he confessed, pulling at his hair and looking directly at Freddie Lembath, who offered a grin worthy of any professional hockey player.

"Da' likes my dream," Lembath said. He looked at Jackie. "Sees I don't thinks dey is de treasure. Da' project? Da' is a trick for de colored boy in da' school."

Skyles smiled and jumped in. "No. The project is to do research, not actually to find the treasure. Sorry, Uncle Freddie," he said, still irritated with the colored man's endless chatter. He stood and added, "By the way…your last name. That's your family name? Have you always had that name?"

"Yes, sir, Mr. Skyles. Da' be my family name. We was a slave family and da' be de name of de master back when dey come to de Lowcountry," Lembath answered. He shifted the sack over his shoulder.

"And your family, they worked for Mr. Lembath back in the eighteen hundreds?"

"Yes, sir, Mr. Skyles. Dey did, up until de war anyways," Lembath replied in a drawl that made the last word four syllables long.

"So Dr. Lembath, William Lembath, the one in this letter. He was their owner?" Skyles asked.

"Who da'? Yes, sir. I reckon so." Freddie shrugged, clueless and uninterested.

Any researcher would find it incredibly fortunate, truly remarkable, to discover an original letter with Poe's signature—an authentic but uncertified signature—and, almost simultaneously, meet a man whose ancestors were slaves for the letter's intended recipient. Skyles was unsure what to make of the coincidence.

The brief history quiz ended when Gabe began to cough and wheeze, each episode distorting his face. Jackie picked up the glass of water on the stool next to Gabe's chair. He placed the glass near his grandpa's lips. Gabe snatched sips between coughing spells. Soothed by the drink, Gabe's eyes wandered about the room and stopped on Freddie Lembath. Totally awake for the first time since Jackie and the others had arrived, he looked to his longtime friend.

"Dem papers dey all I has of dem."

Freddie nodded a gums-aplenty grin. "You be okay, Gabe. You be okay."

"We'll find dem, Grandpa," Jackie said. "But Grandpa, Mr. Skyles can't do da' code. He say it don't make sense."

Gabe rocked his head in agreement.

"I best be move along now, Gabe," Lembath said, the first to head out. "I left dem things to eat. I be back later in de week. You takes it easy an' listen to da' Doc Palmer, y'hear?"

Gabe lifted his wrist from the arm of the chair as a farewell wave.

"Jackie, I'm sorry about that cipher. All the confusion in the room. Maybe I can work on it back in the motel, from my copy," Skyles said. "Mr. Pritchard, it was nice to meet you. I think you have a very valuable letter here," he added as he placed the aged sheet of paper on the quilt in the old man's lap. "Jackie, stop by in a couple days. Maybe I will have something for you."

"Sure, Mr. Skyles. Thank you for coming over."

When Skyles pushed open the screen door, he turned. "Jackie, I would still like to get a photocopy of that letter somewhere in town. I'll check and let you know. Good night." Skyles helped himself out.

As Gabe rolled his head toward Jackie, pain forced his eyes shut.

"Grandpa, we got to go. Ricky needs to get home. We promised his mamma. Ricky, time to go."

Ricky continued to make faces at the bird. Occasionally, he strummed his finger across the bars on the cage. Sherman just sat there.

Jackie walked back and tapped Ricky on the shoulder.

"I gotta go. I gotta pee." Ricky grabbed his groin with both hands, and his feet started a side-to-side dance like he suddenly stepped onto a bed of hot coals.

"De bathroom is through da' door," Jackie said, pointing across the room.

Ricky limped to the bathroom, closed the door, and flipped the latch.

"Grandpa Gabe, where could dem papers be? Nobody would take dem." He wondered if Gabe had misplaced them.

Gabe looked into Jackie's eyes, smiled, and reached from under the quilt to pat the boy's hand.

"Grandpa, Mamma, she be by shortly. I'll tell her as soon as I gets home. She'll have supper for you."

As the boys began to walk off, Gabe coughed. Jackie turned back. Barely audible, Gabe said, "De box." Jackie hurried back to the rocker.

"Bring de red box."

Jackie pulled the Bingo box from the stack of boxes and gave it to his grandpa. Gabe reached for it with both hands and set it on top of his cover between his legs, careful to keep it in his sight and close.

Under the glow of early streetlights, Jackie shadowed Ricky home. His limp slowed their walk, but they made it home in time. When he stepped into his house, Ricky turned back toward Jackie. He looked down at his fingers twisted like snakes in a pit. Ricky looked up, his head wobbling like a Slinky. He chewed on his lower lip, but managed to say to Jackie, "I'll crack that clue…just like the *Hardy Boys*." That's all he said before he closed the door in Jackie's face.

CHAPTER 24

"R"icky, dear. It's time for dinner. Put your book away, please," Cybil Clemonds said.

Ricky made it home from Grandpa Gabe's house ten minutes before dinner. The house, filled with the fragrance of pot roast simmering in the oven, was a warm and cozy contrast to the chilly December breeze outside. But Ricky was not distracted by food or weather. He immediately sat at the table and pulled out his new *Highlights* magazine. Next to jigsaw puzzles, which he completed light-years before most people could form the border, Ricky was a whiz at the hidden picture images in the games section of the magazine. When his mother reached for the magazine, Ricky jerked it off to the side and continued to concentrate on the picture.

"Do as your mother asks, son," Elliott Clemonds said, taking his seat at the table. Cybil started to grab the magazine. Ricky whisked it off the table onto the floor. Cybil closed her eyes and bit her lip, a practice she had adopted over the years. She stood silently for a moment, her hands on her hips, before she reached down, picked up the magazine, and tucked it under a bowl of fruit. She remained silent while she served plates to the table.

"Tell me about your day, son," Elliott asked.

Ricky didn't respond. He was hunched over his plate like a surgeon in the operating room; using his knife with scalpel precision, he moved individual peas to form letters to spell "bug."

"Ricky, your father asked you a question," Cybil snapped, still peeved over her son's actions before she served the plates.

Ricky reacted, but it wasn't the reaction Cybil had hoped to see. He dropped the knife and dipped his nose closer to the plate. With both hands on the table, he drummed his fingers, not a harmony of anything musical, but a simple response to voices and images sparking in his head.

Cybil, quick to process Ricky's actions, redirected her comments. "Elliott, Ricky's colored friend, Jackie, took Ricky to visit with his Grandpa Gabe. They have a clue on the Gullah treasure project."

Elliott finished chewing and cut into his pot roast. "A clue? Interesting. Ricky, remember, son, this Gullah treasure idea is a research project. It's not history or anything real. It's folklore, kinda like Paul Bunyan. So be careful not to believe too much," he warned.

The finger drumming rolled on, accompanied by a low-level mumble.

"Son, I didn't understand you. Please sit up straight," Elliott said.

Ricky mumbled more and then audibly spoke, "There is a treasure."

"I just don't want you to be disappointed, that's all. These kinds of things hurt you."

Ricky mumbled again.

"Ricky! Look at your father when he is speaking to you," Cybil demanded. "Sit up and look at your father. Now!"

Ricky stiffened. He used his fork to smear the food around his plate then pushed back from the table and crossed his arms. Turning, he looked dead-square into his father's eyes and let his emotions bark his response. "There is a treasure. We have the clue. I know the code."

Elliott sensed the frustration and again cautioned his son, "You mean like the story you read in class? It's just a story, Ricky."

Ricky placed his hands over his ears and gyrated in his seat.

"Ricky…"

Cybil quickly moved to her son's side. She pressed her hands against the sides of his shoulders to stop his rocking while she looked back at her husband with a puckered scowl. "Ricky, why don't you go start your homework? Maybe you can eat a little more later, or I will fix you a snack. Popcorn maybe."

His parents made no other effort to correct their son; they remained silent and waited him out. The boy stopped his display but continued to hyperventilate. When Cybil took a step toward him, he stood up, flipped his chair backward on the floor, and stomped off.

In his room, Ricky leaned against the inside of his door and slammed it closed with his butt. He looked around and saw the Level-Five disaster area of his room. In customary teen defiance and total disregard for the constant corrections of his mother, it was always a wall-to-wall heap. The closet door remained open unable to close due to flow of toys from inside. Bookshelves crowded with figures of G.I. Joe, cowboys and Indians, plus a flotilla of model aircraft carriers, submarines, and various USMC landing crafts. His dresser boasted plastic models of the *H.M.S. Bounty* and a Caribbean pirate ship built with the same set of steady fingers that formed words out of peas on a plate. Clusters of assorted rocks, feathers, shells, a baseball, and his lucky horseshoe filled in voids. His small two-drawer desk—the one his mother covered with decoupage clips of nursery rhyme characters—was covered with coloring books, sketch pads, colored pencils, stacks of jigsaw puzzle boxes, and another plastic model of the Invisible Man in a supine position with miniature lungs, kidneys, and stomach removed.

On his bed lay his school bag, untouched and undisturbed since he returned from school. He opened the latch and turned the bag upside down to empty the contents—a math book, a history book, and an English composition notebook where he had entered his research notes on the Gullah treasure project, though filled primarily with doodles of beetles and other bugs. He started to write comments about his afternoon with Jackie and Mr. Skyles, but two lines into the comments, he turned the page and began doodling again. Images meant to be bugs, treasure chests, and pirate flags looked more like oval flowers, breadboxes, and labels from bottles marked as poisonous. When he recalled his father's words at the table, he gripped his pencil like an ice pick and scribbled a free-form mess on the sheet until he wore a hole through the paper.

Schoolwork bothered him. He rolled off his bed and rummaged through the field of make-believe around the closet. Buried beneath the mess, he knew he would find the Ouija board. Hidden from his parents, it was at the bottom of the mound, in the corner of the closet. He had not used it since the night Jackie slept over. He pushed his books aside, placed the board flat on his bed, and with a feather-light touch, placed his fingers on the planchette. Fearful of what his words might do, he closed his eyes and whispered, "I need to speak to Edgar Allan Poe." He gasped when he felt the marker piece move under his fingers. *Or did it*, he thought. He opened his eyes and saw the heart-shaped indicator had not budged from where he had placed it. His pulse ratchetted back to one beat above normal. He posed his request a second time without taking his eyes off of his fingers. Nothing budged. He relaxed his wrist, thinking his touch was too heavy. He took several deep breaths before he addressed the talking board a third time. "Will Mr. Poe talk to me?"

This time he had no doubt the planchette moved. It slid fast across the board, stopping over an area with no letters or markings. After a pause, it zipped back across the board to where it started, then again back across to the unmarked space. Ricky was too scared to breathe. He watched and waited, his light fingers still riding the wild movements. For a moment they stopped without revealing any answer, then they began a slow slide toward the upper right corner of the board where they rested above the word no.

He tried again. "Why not?" he asked, louder.

This time planchette vibrated, visibly shook under his fingers, then ever so slowly started to move diagonally back toward him. When it crossed the letter "U" on the board, the planchette flew out from under Ricky's fingers, off the board, and hit him square between the eyes. He scooped both hands under the board and flipped it in a high arc that nearly hit the ceiling. Frightened, he struggled to catch his breath.

When the board landed, the overhead light flickered off for a full second, then back on. It flickered again. After the second flicker when the light came on, Ricky noticed a luminous cloud outside his window, a fog that had not been there before. He cocked his head to the side like a curious puppy and stared at the light on the other side of the glass. Like steam from a tea kettle, the fog seeped over, under, and around the sash then began to take shape inside his room. Ricky slid off the back side of his bed and peeked just above the wad of covers on the mattress. He tucked his nose behind his school books and watched the cloud by the far wall as it hung— restless as a kitten tied in a burlap sack—until the fog melted away, leaving behind the hazy shape of a little man with a rather large head. He wore tight breeches— one leg yellow, the other purple—and a tunic of red and green. He had a shaved head covered by an orange cowl and on top of that a three-pointed cap in red and blue with bells on the tips of three floppy horns. On his feet he danced lightly with slipper-like velvet shoes that curled at the toes.

"Quiet, lad. I bring ye no harm," the little man said. Ricky watched, silent, fear-frozen, and astonished. "Certainly ye remember me. We met a ways back and we have talked several times since, though ye never knew 'twas I." Ricky edged up from his crouch, amused by the colorful dwarf and his strange accent.

"Well then, let me remind ye. 'Twas ye with two other lads. One ran away and the second held thy hand and pulled ye away. Remember, lad?" he said.

Ricky nodded his head ever so slightly—yes.

"Of course, lad, the dreams. Ye thought them only dreams about the Castle where I live. And the treasure. Surely ye remember the treasure and how ye wanted to talk to the poet Poe." The mention of Poe's name got Ricky's attention. "And the bewitched game ye possess. Surely ye believe not in such falderal, do ye?"

Ricky nodded his head—yes.

The dwarf stifled a hearty laugh. "Dear me. Those times ye placed thy hands upon that board piece"—he

255

chuckled lightly—"I moved the piece around." He stopped and laughed harder and raised his hand in a wave. "Such foolish questions. Poe talking to you? Poppycock. He is, forever more, eternally silent, unable to help ye with a code."

"He's got to," Ricky said loud enough for his parents to hear. He shook his head and echoed, quietly, "He's got to."

Again, the dwarf laughed. "Remember when ye walked into the cloud by the Castle? Remember the warmth and bright light around ye? 'Twas I who opened the gate to the hereafter for ye to see, but thy friend pulled ye back too quickly."

"It was you? At the Castle?"

The jester did a jig, then bowed. "At thy service, my lad. My name is Gauche."

"I know," said Ricky, looking directly at the ghost. "I learned all about you."

"Poppycock," Gauche chortled. "The same old rubbish about me being from France and traveling with that fellow Jean Ribaut. Why, I would never bow before that outspeckled inisitijitty, a gentleman of four outs, I say." The dwarf jester took a seat on Ricky's desk and continued. "No, lad, I am a Brit. I set sail in October of 1564 as jester for Sir John Hawkins aboard the seven-hundred-ton *Jesus of Lubek*, which he had leased to carry the captured slaves from warring African tribes to this land. On his return to England, he would carry a cargo of gold claimed from the ship, the *Santa Clara*, which the Spanish *Tierra Firma* Fleet abandoned in a terrific storm. For his efforts Sir Hawkins siphoned off a wee bit of the booty and buried it here so as not to share it with Her Majesty the Queen. I, thus, await his return."

Ricky's eyes bulged beyond his brow. "There is treasure here," he screamed, then cringed before he plastered his mouth with his hands. He crawled the short distance from behind his bed and peeked out his door. He could see his parents deep in their fervent nightly Bible reading, unaware of sounds from their son's room.

"Tell me where that treasure is?" Ricky insisted.

"Sure 'tis not mine to offer. Sir Hawkins would not approve," the jester quipped.

"But he's dead and not coming for the treasure."

"Oh, but time will bring him forth. Like myself, 'tis but one small step between worlds," the dwarf said as he hopped off the desk and climbed atop the bed, closer to Ricky.

"Send Edgar Allan Poe. Why doesn't he come?" Ricky asked, bewildered and definitely confused.

"I have met this fellow, Poe. A nice chap. A bit odd. Loved to play cards; Loo, was it? Though he was not very good."

"But why won't he talk to me?" Ricky said on his knees aside his bed.

"Poe was not a belligerent sort. He preferred to pummel others with cryptography. He would never share the secrets of his craft."

Ricky repeatedly banged his forehead against the mattress and growled in a low tone. "You gotta help, Mr. Gauche."

"Patterns are puzzles. Find a pattern." The dwarf bounced off the mattress and moved back toward the window. "Oh, dear royalness. I have been away from my Castle far too long. Go I must. There I shall be for ye, Sir Richard, my friend. And enough with thy preposterous board game."

With that pronouncement, the room grew cold as a renewed fog slithered across the floor. When it reached the ghostly feet of the jester, it climbed to encircle him in a mini-tornado. Silently, papers, feathers, socks, underwear, magazines, and more whirled wall to wall, floor to ceiling. His plastic models fell from their stands. The boxes of puzzles burst open, pieces flying in the mix. Ricky scrunched tightly against his bed with the pillow over his head lifted enough for one eyeball to watch the chilly twister disappear with his visitor. The fog evaporated. The room was again calm and messier than before.

Ricky squeezed his head between his palms and screamed into his pillow, "Come back! Come back! You need to help me!"

"Ricky, are you all right?" his mother asked, opening his bedroom door only enough for her voice to enter. "Was it a dream?"

"No, I saw him," Ricky said, rolling to his side, the pillow still grasped in his hands.

"Saw who, dear?"

"That ghost. The one from the Castle. I saw him."

Cybil Clemonds had addressed dozens upon dozens of these appearances with Ricky through his youth, his imaginary friends. "It's all right, dear. He didn't harm you, did he?"

"No. He wouldn't help me."

"Help you? Help you with what?"

"The clue. I wanted to talk to Mr. Poe," he sobbed.

Cybil pushed the door open and joined Ricky on the edge of the bed. She reached under his shoulder and placed her hand on his trembling back. "I know, son. Maybe your little friend will change his mind and bring Mr. Poe another time. You should get your sleep, dear.

Things will be all right. Everything will work out fine. Don't you worry about a thing." As she rubbed his back, she could feel his muscles release the tension. She looked around the room—the space she had religiously tried to get Ricky to clean—and noticed things seemed a bit out of place, more so than usual. His school books were flipped open and upside down on the floor, his papers were completely across the room, and beneath them she saw something that disturbed her greatly. It was the edge of the Ouija board buried under layers of puzzle pieces. She squinted harder. She rationalized how silly the game was but feared the potential damage it might have on her delicate son. "Ricky…" she started, then hesitated. *Now is not the time to question him about the board, maybe tomorrow after he's rested*, she thought. She lifted her hand and sat upright.

"Get ready for bed, darling. We'll check your homework in the morning." She kissed him on his forehead, then eased herself off the bed. At the door she turned for another quick inspection of the room and the edge of the game board before she walked out.

Ricky lay in bed for a few minutes after his mother left. He picked at his fingernails and mumbled to himself. It took some time, but eventually it felt safe for him to get up and change into the Davy Crockett flannel pajamas his mother had made for him when he was ten. He had grown only a smidge since, but the shrinkage pulled the sleeves almost to his elbow and pant legs well above his ankles. Regardless, Ricky refused to wear anything else.

He turned off the overhead light and climbed into bed. The clouds that passed through the moonlight washed the wall above his dresser with shadows of models and other toys around the room, shadows that formed hazy, weird shapes, not of the models, but of letters and strange symbols which confused him. He ducked under the covers, hidden from the shadows, but the symbols lingered in his head like a snow globe. The harder he tried to shake them out, the more clearly they appeared. He rolled onto his stomach and covered his head with his hands, to be darker still. The darker the space, the brighter the symbols became. He began to cry. Numbers and solutions for math equations would often float through his head but nothing like this. These hurt. *No, no, no,* he cried, nose deep in the mattress. He rolled back and forth. His fear grew deeper, the symbols, brighter. A bright light from behind his eyeballs burned laser-like into the center of his skull. He screamed—*ahhhhhh*—muffled entirely by his bed. He rolled over on his back, panting, gasping for air, eyes closed, tears streaming down both sides of his puffy face. The burning and pounding in his head stopped. The tears stopped, too. But when he opened his eyes, the burning light was back. This time it was projected on the wall, not in his head. When he focused, he realized what he was seeing on the wall were numbers and symbols, the ones he had seen in his head, but they were stationary now and formed in rows, like text. What he saw was a visual image from his memory, an image of the clue Mr. Skyles had studied on the floor at Grandpa Gabe's. That glimpse—permanently fixed in his head—was now on the wall.

Moonlight had lost control of the night. Spikes of lightning etched the sky. In the distance, thunder jackhammered clouds. Outside his window he heard the trees dancing in the wind. Rain would follow. Ricky tossed things aside and frantically dug through the clutter to find a notebook and a pencil. He snatched his silver Mickey Mouse flashlight—always in the same spot under his bed. Lying on his side, flashlight aimed at the pad, he created an exact replica of the clue Jackie gave Gene Skyles hours earlier, letter for letter in identical format. When he had written all the characters on the pad, he held the flashlight on the paper for less than a minute, then began to write again. This time he was writing in broken code, the text of the clue itself.

CHAPTER 25

Though it took hours, the Sandman eventually broke through Ricky's excited force field. He was locked in a deep sleep when his mother knocked on his bedroom door the next morning.

"Time to get up, Ricky," she said, opening his door a hair.

Ricky pulled the covers over his head.

"Ricky, dear, get a move on it. We need to check your homework, don't forget."

In the aftermath of the strange happenings the night before, Ricky managed to find a shirt and pants—the same combination from the previous day—which he labored to pull on before he managed a zombie-walk to the kitchen for breakfast.

Cybil inspected her son as he walked in. She placed a bowl of oatmeal on the table and stopped Ricky before he sat down. On her knees, she was able to rebutton Ricky's shirt so buttons and holes matched; his effort left one side longer than the other.

"I broke…" Ricky mumbled while his mother adjusted his clothes, but the sudden yet fuzzy recall of his father's ridicule the previous night caused him to reel in his tongue in midsentence.

Cybil leaned back to look up at her son and continued to work on the shirt. "Broke what, dear?" She worried this would be a confession of some significant magnitude. Over the years, especially after his episodes, Ricky had been known to destroy any number of things, some as trivial as all the pencils in his school bag and others as severe as a treasured vase presented to her at her husband's ordination.

"I broke...I broke..." Ricky brushed his mother's hands aside, finished buttoning his shirt properly, and sat down at the table.

"Broke what, dear?"

"I want Wheaties," he said, pushing the oatmeal as far away as he could reach.

"I made you oatmeal."

"I want Wheaties."

Cybil closed her eyes and rubbed her forehead with her fingertips before saying, "All right, dear. I'll get you some Wheaties. Take out your homework papers and let me see them, please."

Cybil reached into a cabinet for the box of cereal while Ricky rummaged through his book bag for the papers he had collected off the floor. He grabbed a handful, placed them on the table, and spooned the cereal into his mouth.

"You didn't finish your English work. Did you read the story? You didn't answer any of the questions on this sheet."

"I did the math, Mamma." When he talked the flakes and milk tumbled out over his lower lip, back into the bowl. His mother gave him a disgusted look.

"I can see that and I am proud of you for doing those problems, but you didn't finish your other assignments, dear. English is important. And this history worksheet, you were supposed to draw some maps. Now I know you like to draw Ricky, so why didn't you finish that sheet?"

Ricky wiped milk from his chin with his sleeve. "I can do those maps later. I need to go. I need to go to school." He stood and struggled to get his arm in his jacket sleeve. Cybil waited, not ready to offer any assistance. When his hand was free, she handed him the papers and reached for her coat. "Tonight, young man, you will do your work as soon as we get home, no questions. Do you understand?"

Ricky didn't acknowledge her. He simply walked off, plowed through the front door, and stood on the porch with his head down, book bag in one hand and his Davy Crockett lunch box in the other.

Ricky Clemonds hobbled into school and down the hall looking for Jackie. He was completely out of sorts, out of his shell, and out of character. He walked up to every group he saw and stuck his nose into the crowd to see if Jackie was with them, forgetting Jackie had no other friends. Kids turned and stared. Some laughed; others taunted him. None of it seemed to matter; for Ricky, his immediate quest was to find Jackie. It ended when he reached Miss Forten's classroom.

"Easy code," he said as he took his seat at the desk behind Jackie. "Easy code."

Jackie looked over his shoulder. "What easy code?"

"Easy code. I broke the code." Ricky snickered.

Jackie turned in his seat to face Ricky. "De code? De Poe clue?"

Ricky averted his eyes to avoid Jackie. He looked at the floor, then up at the ceiling while he rambled. "That ghost came. I asked to talk to Poe on the Ouija board. The ghost guy said no and…" He was breathless with all his chatter. His fingers extended and joined, tapped uncontrollably against his cheeks. "He disappeared and then I saw these letters and then I saw the code you gave Mr. Skyles and then I wrote down the code and then I knew what it said." He looked back at the floor and took a deep, deep breath while he silently clapped his hands. "I broke the code just like the Hardy Boys," Ricky said with a toothy grin reflected in his desktop.

"You never had da' clue, Ricky. What you talking about? Slow down. Talk slow."

Ricky stuffed his books and papers into a rat's nest of failed English papers and science quizzes in the cubby under his seat. "I just saw it."

Jackie frowned. "But I just handed it to—"

"The paper on the floor. Letters and numbers and things. I took a picture with my eyes."

Jackie checked the front of the room. Two boys were at the chalkboard drawing their version of Kilroy graffiti directly behind the teacher's desk. "But da' was code. What you mean you got de clue?"

"I know the code!" Ricky no longer whispered, though, as usual, the other students paid no attention to him, except one.

"Oh boy. Sicky Ricky got the clue," Skeet said as he walked in the door. "Hear that everybody?"

All eyes turned to Skeet. He walked across the back of the classroom, thumping each of the boys in the backs of their heads. "No, you get a clue, Ricky Retardo. There ain't no stupid Gullah treasure. Ask your boy there. He knows that, too." He shoved the back of Ricky's head with his palm and sat down in the desk behind him.

"I saw that, Robin Gundy," Mary Alice Forten said as she walked through the door with an armload of books. "See me after school today. Do you understand?"

Skeet curled the corner of his upper lip and mouthed a few choice words under his breath.

Jackie leaned his head over his shoulder and whispered to Ricky, "I'll come over to your house after school."

Skeet, unable to wipe the smirk off his face, responded in usual fashion. "I'll be there too."

Cybil Clemonds, still pondering the Ouija board she had discovered and Ricky's incomplete homework from the night before, sat her son down the instant they returned from school. He sat in the kitchen, his head cradled in his hands, supported by his elbows on the table while his mother busied herself with supper, one eye on her son, whose only movement was to check the clock above the sink. When Ricky heard the knock, he pushed away from the table and gimped to the front door.

Cybil, close behind him, wiped her hands on her apron. "Go back and do your homework like I asked. I'll see who's there." She made it to the door before Ricky, but the boy grabbed the knob and opened the door.

"Jackie! So nice to see you again," Cybil managed before Ricky nudged her aside.

"Hi." Ricky greeted his guest but watched a tortoiseshell cat stalk a pigeon across the lawn.

"I promised my mamma I would stop by de United Five and Dime and pick up some sewing supplies she needed, but I came as soon as I got home," Jackie said.

Cybil was unaware what was going on. A planned meeting? Regardless, she welcomed the visit by Ricky's only friend. "Well, please come in, Jackie. I told Ricky he had homework to do, so you boys may have only ten minutes, then I'll have to ask you to leave, so Ricky can finish his assignments," Cybil said with a stern look toward her son.

As Jackie stepped into the house, out of the corner of his eye he spied Skeet on the sidewalk. Skeet waved and offered a huge grin. He turned and walked backward away from Carteret Street. "Hey, boy. See ya later," he yelled, then moved on.

Jackie politely stood just inside the door. Cybil Clemonds left the boys and went back to the kitchen.

"So…" Jackie said.

"So what?" Ricky echoed looking at the ground.

"So let me see it."

"See what?"

"You told me you had de clue, Ricky. You said you knew what de code say."

"Yeah."

"Well, where is it?"

"I hid it in a secret place." Ricky walked away; Jackie followed, headed toward Ricky's bedroom.

The appearance of the room remained the aftermath of the tornadic night before. Ricky began ripping through the piles of toys, comic books, and clothes under a layer of puzzle pieces. He nosed around, grabbing things, tossing them over his shoulder, frantic, like a dog with a bone to bury. He worked his way around the room from desk to bookcase to dresser to closet and back to his desk while Jackie stood by the door. Ricky fell, frustrated, on the opposite side of the room, where he sat cross-legged, rocking back and forth; his knuckles battered bone against bone on his forehead.

Jackie was unsure of what to do. "Ricky, do you have de clue or were you—"

Ricky jumped up, went to his desk, and grabbed the Invisible Man model. He flipped the plastic figure over onto its front, chest pointing down, then banged it on the desk until all the organs fell out. There with the kidneys, ribs, and heart was a marble-size piece of paper. His fingers dug at the wad until it unfurled into a page ripped from his composition notebook.

"Here."

Ricky handed Jackie the paper. The characters—reminiscent of first-grade-level handwriting—made no sense. The paper was covered with the same strange collection of symbols that Gene Skyles had inspected, but beneath each character Ricky had written down the letter each symbol represented, although there was no punctuation, just lines of letters. Ricky stood on his bed to look at the note over Jackie's shoulder.

"Ricky, it's time for you to get back to work on your assignments. I'm afraid your friend is going to have to leave now," Cybil Clemonds shouted from the kitchen.

"Let me take dis to Mr. Skyles. I'm sure he can unscramble dis."

"Like the Hardy Boys," Ricky cheered.

Jackie folded the note and put it in his pants pocket as he walked out of the bedroom.

"Thank you, ma'am," Jackie said with a tilt to his head. "Have a good evening, Mrs. Clemonds."

"Oh, you are quite welcome, Jackie. Ricky truly enjoys your visits," she said, hiding a sigh of delight.

"Good night. See you tomorrow, Ricky," Jackie added as he bounded off the steps in the dark headed home, deep in thought about Ricky's apparent discovery. As he turned north onto East Street, two arms grabbed him from behind and another fat hand slapped over his mouth. When he tried to scream, a fourth hand poked at his side with a small blunt object.

CHAPTER 26

Boy, I told you I'd come by Ricky Retardo's house tonight. You saw me and you didn't even invite me in," the voice said in a pouty singsong. "That ain't very nice, boy. You and Retardo trying to keep all that treasure for yourselves?" Skeet Gundy pulled Jackie closer to his hip and jabbed deeper into the boy's side. "Now that just ain't right at all. I mean that's downright terrible. Guess that calls for a little something terrible in return, now don't it, Hoss?"

Hoss Lassiter pressed the palm of his hand deeper into Jackie's face.

"Well, you is one lucky negra, Jackie boy, 'cause I happen to have a truck so we can go for another ride."

Jackie kicked and stomped on toes to get free. The three boys hip-bumped half a block up the street as Jackie struggled. A block later they slipped in behind the Sea Island Supply Company. Skeet had parked the stolen Western Auto truck near the trees on the lot, beyond the headlights of any street traffic. Hoss slammed Jackie facedown onto the hood of the truck and held him there while Skeet tied Jackie's hands behind his back. When he went to tie the boy's ankles, Jackie kicked out with his leg and caught Skeet in the groin. Skeet groaned and kneed Jackie in the back, then pulled a rag from his pocket and gagged him. From his other pocket, Skeet yanked out a familiar pointed white hood, which he pulled over

269

Jackie's head, the two eye holes intentionally positioned on the back side. They shoved Jackie into the seat of the truck between the two of them, then drove off, unnoticed in the dark. Around Bellamy Curve they turned into Pigeon Point. At the park Skeet stopped the truck.

"Okay, boy. Let's have some fun. Hoss, get this coon out of my truck."

Hoss Lassiter hopped out and, without a word, the truck lurched forward, the passenger door slammed shut, and they were moving again.

"Hey, Skeet, stop! Wait! I thought we was—" Jackie heard Hoss cry from outside the truck, his voice fading as the truck backfired its way down the street.

"Change of plans, Hoss. Won't be needin' you after all. This is just between me and my Jackie boy here," Skeet yelled with his head halfway out the window. "Just you and me tonight, boy. Just you and me. Ha, ha, ha, ha, ha, ha." He turned his eyes back to the road ahead and laughed with maniacal pleasure.

For Jackie there was no way of knowing how far they had gone or in which direction they had traveled. He slid forward, stiff in his seat, to relieve the pain on his arms bound behind his back. His fingers picked at the twine around his wrists. He considered turning and kicking Skeet with his bound feet but realized that would probably cause him to lose control of the truck. He talked himself out of turning enough to open his door, the reality of which would land him on his head in the middle of some road somewhere, still tied and blindfolded. So he waited and prayed that somehow, sometime, somewhere Skeet would let down his guard and he would find a way to get free.

Jackie relied entirely on the movement of the stolen truck. They had traveled straight, in silence, with only two stops, which Jackie figured were the two traffic lights on Boundary Street, headed out of town. After ten minutes or more, the truck slowed. A backfire sent shivers through Jackie. Each time the truck strained or jerked or backfired as it slowed Jackie felt his stomach percolate up into his throat. After a sharp left turn, which pushed Jackie up against the door, he felt a rumble under the tires. By the feel and the sound, the first bumps were obvious railroad tracks, followed immediately by a sudden turn to the right, then a rutted sandy or worn-gravel road. Minutes later the truck skidded into a hole that nearly swallowed the front tire and bucked Jackie's head into the roof of the cab. Before Jackie had a chance to regain his balance, he felt Skeet drape something over his head.

"Time for you and me to take a walk, Jemima boy."

Skeet popped his door and moved deliberately to the other side of the truck. He jerked open the passenger door and gave a mule skinner tug to tighten the lasso now around Jackie's neck.

"Move it, Sambo, or I'll drag your bony black butt until there ain't no skin. Buzzards would like that," Skeet shouted.

Jackie slid out of the truck. Off balance when he landed, he wobbled and fell back against the truck. Skeet tied a rope to one of Jackie's ankles before he released the twine that had been around both ankles during the ride. With one rope around his neck and another around his ankle, Jackie was hardly in a position to do anything except what Skeet wanted.

Skeet ripped the white hood off Jackie's head. "See, I don't want to deny you a chance to watch what's

271

happenin' here, boy, no sirree. We's goin' to have us some fun. Now you just walk nice and slow through that patch of trees right there. Nice and slow is all. Nice and slow or I'll break your leg. Now move it, boy."

Jackie looked around; a pair of wayward moths dive-bombed his head. There wasn't much of a moon and nothing he could see looked familiar. Trees with their long necks and big heads grew sideways on either side of the road. He inched down the overgrown path for twenty feet before it entered the woods. The stand of trees was no more than fifteen feet deep before it opened up again. Jackie's eyes opened wide. On his left, in the moonlight, he saw where the railroad tracks emerged from the trees around a bend and ran a short distance to another bend off to his right.

"Hold it right there, coon." Skeet pulled out some of the slack in the rope around Jackie's neck and tied it to a tree. With the second rope in hand, Skeet said, "Okay, follow me."

When Jackie refused, Skeet whipped Jackie's leg out from under him. He landed on his hands and arms tied behind his back, which wrenched his shoulders and slammed his head into the cinders near the rail. The rag in his mouth muted his cry. Jackie choked.

"I said follow me, boy!"

Jackie got to his feet and shuffled toward Skeet nearer the tracks, looking back to the rope tied to the tree as it tightened.

"Now sit down there between them tracks," Skeet said, pulling the wad out of Jackie's mouth.

"You ain't goin' to do dis, Skeet," Jackie said, coughing for air.

"Don't you be tellin' me what I is or ain't goin' to do, boy. Shut your mouth. Hear me? You make any noise and I'll shove that rag and a lot more back in there. Now, sit down."

When he hesitated Skeet put his entire body into a tug that upended Jackie and dropped him square between the two rails. As soon as Jackie hit the ground, Skeet tied his end of the rope around a signal light on the far side of the track. Both ropes were tight enough to keep Jackie from moving in either direction. And there he stayed, hands tied behind his back, ankles pulled tight by one rope and his neck choked by the other.

"Skeet, let me up. I didn't do nothing. We wasn't going to keep de treasure. I was just visiting Ricky because—"

"Shut your trap, boy. You ain't comin' to my school. You ain't goin' to get no treasure. You ain't even goin' to see your mamma again, boy." He tormented Jackie with another maniacal laugh and retreated back down the path. "Should be a train by here to pick you up soon enough."

"Skeet! Hey—Skeet, come back! Help! Don't do dis!" Jackie screamed. With his free leg, he kicked, which only tightened the two ropes more. He rolled from side to side while his fingers blindly searched for a way to free his hands. Every time he moved, the cinders under him dug deeper and deeper into the exposed flesh on his hands. One cinder, then a second, then another and more. Razor-sharp chunks brought razor-sharp pain until his fingers throbbed too much to move.

"Help me! Somebody...help!" Lying quietly, tears steadily flowed down his cheeks. With every painful throb in his hands, he cringed and sobbed to a point of near unconsciousness. At times he held his breath and listened. He waited for the rumbling of the track, which never came. He thought of his parents, only his parents, and of Grandpa Gabe. Not of school or Ricky or the treasure. Not even of Skeet or "why?" He thought of his family. He recalled his time in the woods with the masked figures; the pain was much greater now, the threat much more apparent, immediate and deadly. But his thoughts always returned to his family.

Though it felt like he had been there all night and daybreak would come soon, it was only an hour before Skeet returned. Jackie remained silent as Skeet staggered out from between the trees.

"That train ain't picked you up yet, boy?" Skeet asked as he approached Jackie. His speech sounded as if he had a pregnant slug for a tongue. "Shazam! Guess it don't go to your daddy's packing plant at Port Royal till later on. Sorry, boy. Since I'm here I'll just have to give you another ride." He bent over to untie the rope from the track light but straightened quickly. "Ooo-doggies. This place is spinning out here tonight."

When he bent down the second time, he lost his balance and face-planted in the grass. He rolled over on his back and laughed while he carried on a one-sided conversation with the green train signal light before he got back on his feet and untied the rope.

"Now, you just stand up nice and easy, boy. Don't hurt that pretty neck of yours or it'll get longer. And remember, I still got a rope around your ankle so I can put you right back down there on them tracks and you can wait for that train. For sure it will come," Skeet said, unsteady on his feet. He motioned for Jackie to stand; this time Jackie followed instructions.

Skeet stumbled as he walked back across the tracks, but there was enough slack in the rope that his fall did not affect Jackie. Skeet walked Jackie back to the tree with the other rope and untied it.

"Go on"—Skeet gestured with a nod—"back through them trees like when we came in. And keep your trap shut or this noose gets tighter." He gave a gentle tug to the rope around Jackie's neck.

Jackie moved on ahead of Skeet. The truck was still parked on the edge of the road where Jackie saw it last. Skeet opened the door and pushed a seat full of beer cans to the floor.

"Get in, boy." He gave Jackie a two-handed shove into the cab of the truck. "Dang, them hands of yours sure look like they hurt. You should take better care of yourself, boy. Them get infected and you'd probably lose both them."

When Jackie's feet cleared the door, Skeet tossed the two ropes in behind him. He leaned against the truck and worked his way around the front. Taking a healthy swig from a can of beer on the dashboard, he slammed the door and tossed the can out of the window. He grabbed the rope looped around Jackie's neck and tucked it under his leg, a ready restraint in the event Jackie tried anything.

"Okay, Jackie Robinson, let's see if I can remember how to get back to that tree where we was before." The thought of the tree Skeet mentioned tied a noose around Jackie's stomach and memories of the same around his neck.

"Skeet, why are you doing dis? I ain't—"

Skeet gripped the steering wheel hard and rammed the brakes. "Shut up, you little Geechee jigaboo." His eyes flickered as he screamed. "You just sit there. And if you don't be quiet"—he paused and looked around the area outside the window—"I finds me a tree right here and we have us a little party." A ghoulish grin swelled across his face. He turned his head back to the road and sent out a rooster tail of sand and rock that arced ten feet into the air when he crunched the gas pedal to the floor.

Jackie was afraid to move or speak. He watched as Skeet drove down a narrow, sandy lane that took them to a paved road. Clouds now offered very little moonlight, enough for Jackie to see there were no houses, no trailers, no buildings, no lights and, definitely, no cars, which may have been a fortunate thing since Skeet, unskilled at driving in the first place, was showing the effects of the empty beer cans on the floor and the one he held in his left hand.

"Nothin' like a little party with your friend. Here's to you, Jackie boy." With that, Skeet dropped his head back and chugged the beer. As he did the truck veered off the pavement and rattled through the high-cut weeds on the berm.

"Ooo-doggies. This here road keeps movin' all over the place." Skeet tossed his empty beer can out the window, clenched the steering wheel, and punched the gas pedal to the floor. The truck snagged the asphalt, hopped back on the road, and lunged across the centerline. Skeet zigged back to the right and nosed the truck down his own lane. "Now that's some kinda fun. Like riding a bull." He teased the accelerator with a toe-tapping flutter. Jackie braced with his legs, but his upper body bounced back and forth. He moved as close as possible toward the door despite the tightening noose around his neck. Skeet reached down between his knees and pulled out another beer. With one hand he held the can; the other pulled the tab on the top. With no hands on the wheel, the truck drifted on its own, this time completely off the left side of the road. The front tire on Jackie's side traveled in a rut that ran along the edge of the pavement. Skeet whipped the wheel to the right.

When he did, the asphalt ripped a chunk from the sidewall of the tire and robbed the drunken driver of what little control he had.

"Look out!" Jackie screamed, but Skeet's bloodshot eyes had no time to focus on the deer that stared at the headlights. His reaction time, slowed by the alcohol, never had a chance to find the brake pedal. The entire front end of the buck—all eight points and two front legs—came through the windshield and nearly pinned Skeet to his seat. The truck made a 540 degree spin before the front tires caught the edge of the pavement and flipped the truck completely. It rolled twice and landed on its side against a tall oak which hung over the road.

On its first revolution Jackie was thrown from the cab. Blood dripped into his eye as he sat dazed—but conscious—surrounded by shards of glass and twisted metal in the grass twenty-five feet from the truck. The momentum and gyration of the truck caused the ropes to wrap around Jackie's legs like a cocoon.

"Help! Help! Skeet." No response. There was barely enough moonlight to see the truck and not enough for him to find Skeet. From where he sat, he smelled gasoline and sensed he had to move away. The slightest motion—eyelids to toes—was taxed by pain. Being tossed around and out of the truck, he could count every bone in his body as he stretched. Still tied, he began to roll. After three revolutions Jackie looked back and noticed the broken glass of the truck mirror off to the side, closer to the truck, but still a safe distance away. Jackie saw it as an opportunity to free himself. He changed direction and rolled, then sat up and scooched to the mirror. He took a piece of broken glass out. With his hands aching from the cinder cuts he began to blindly saw the twine around his wrists.

"Skeet! Skeet! Where are you? Help!" He yelled as he worked. He heard nothing. No voice. No response. Nothing. From his new position, with a closer look at the truck, he spied a flame that flickered under the smooshed hood. He worked faster, harder, to free his hands. And then he heard a *pop*.

The sound came from the general area of the flame. In the aftermath of the collision, the sudden and unexpected sound was hardly audible, but the instant Jackie looked up to identify the sound, a horrendous fireball shot up ten feet and engulfed the truck in seconds. He watched in panic as the fire weaved its way through the dead underbrush along the road. He sawed deeper into the strands of twine. They loosened. He sawed faster, his eyes fixed on the flames. "Skeet, come back! Help me!" Finally, the bonds snapped. He tugged his arms free and took time to gingerly touch his wrists, carved by the cinders at the railroad tracks.

"Skeet! You still here?" he yelled as he wrestled with the rope around his legs from hips to toes. No reply.

Freed, his adrenaline fought a losing battle against the pain. Ligaments that would not—could not—fully extend. Muscles that failed even the slightest test of strength. Bones battered and bruised. Jackie tried to stand, but his knees buckled. He began to crawl, looking back briefly to measure the progress of the fire. At the road, he leaned against a tree to rest and catch his breath. While there, he looked up and down the road for someone, anyone, who could help him; he found nobody. He worried that if someone did come along he could never explain the stolen truck. His ankles, sore from his struggle with the ropes, left him dead-footed, but he had to get away from the smoke and fire. He had to leave the scene. Had to find help.

With the tree as a support, he made it back on his feet. He swallowed hard, but his mouth was dry and rough as sandpaper. He gripped the tree, managed three deep breaths that offered more pain than air, and prepared to walk away from it all when a heart-stopping scream caused him to grip the tree harder. The scream, filled with agony but no words, had to be Skeet, there, somewhere. With his back against the tree, Jackie rolled to face the torturous cries. Skeet had to be in or around the truck and threatened by fire.

Jackie knew that Skeet brought this on himself. Whatever it was that caused Skeet pain was nothing compared to what Jackie had been through and the things Skeet had intended for him. The thought of what might have happened made Jackie more aware of his own pain. His entire body—scrambled inside a tumbling truck and launched out the side door—shouted at him.

Above his pain, Jackie hollered, "Skeet. Skeet." When he heard a response—a second gut-wrenching cry—the tips of his mouth rose slightly and his cheeks puffed out. Spasms of comfort rushed through him while he leaned against the tree and watched the fire consume the taunts, jeers, ridicule, hate, embarrassment, and bigotry Skeet directed at him. A morbid sense of euphoria warmed him more than the flames. Briefly, only briefly, did he feel sorry for Skeet.

He cradled his forehead in the palms of his hands, but as the screams continued, he slid them to cover his ears and he began to cry. Finally, when the screams became too much for him to welcome, he stood, pushed off from the tree, and began a slow crouch-walk away from all of it, blinded by tears of sorrow or pity or thanksgiving; he wasn't sure.

His pace remained tortoise-like at best. He teetered from tree to tree. The screaming drifted farther and farther behind him, but another voice grew closer and stronger; it was Gabe. By the time he reached the seventh pine, Gabe's whispers convinced Jackie there was no time to reflect or judge or think. He had to get to the truck. He had to find Skeet.

The space between Jackie and the burning truck was open. The few small trees that had been there were knocked down by the rolling truck. Without the trees for support, Jackie crawled. He felt every one of the cinder cuts on his hands each time he touched the dirt. He stayed low to the ground and shielded his face from the waves of heat and the cloud of toxic smoke. Concussion from a small explosion deep inside the truck rocked him backward. The blast deafened him momentarily, replaced immediately by screams, each more panic-filled than the last.

"Help me! God help me! Somebody help me," Skeet hollered. The cry originated to the left of Jackie, toward the rear of the truck, away from the flames. He closed in on the voice.

"Skeet! Skeet! Keep hollering, Skeet," Jackie echoed in reply.

"Here! Over here."

Jackie draped his shirttail over the right side of his face as he moved closer to the truck. He put his chin on the ground and, like a hunter, stalked the blinding flames, the heat far too intense to rush head on. Through narrow slits under singed eyelashes, he could see the carcass of a big buck lying stiff just inside the wood line on his right, beyond the fire. Twenty feet farther, the burning truck lay on its side. Beyond the truck, fire tiptoed along branches of several small trees that had crashed to the ground. That is where Jackie saw the back of Skeet's head, trapped beneath those trees.

Another explosion dropped Jackie flat on the ground and launched a flaming block of metal from the front of the truck that landed close enough for Jackie to smell the acid. He rolled to the side, away from the burning truck battery, where he took a few precious seconds to catch his breath after the near miss. With the pause, he thought about all the gasoline in the tank of the truck. Like the battery, he expected the truck to be the next—and possibly the last—blast he would hear. But the next thing he heard was another pain-filled cry from Skeet. He pushed up to his knees and yelped when he placed his hands on a thorny vine in the sand.

Finally, he saw Skeet. He was pinned on his stomach with three small trees across his legs, his arms trapped under his body. Jackie crawled close, grabbed hold of Skeet's leg, and pulled. Skeet howled like a wounded animal.

"Stop! Stop! I'm stuck. I'm hurt." Skeet moaned.

Jackie climbed around the trees that were on Skeet and saw his other leg tucked beneath the trees, positioned at a weird angle, his foot facing in a direction not meant by Mother Nature.

"You going to be okay, Skeet" Jackie said, calmly, choking on the smoke and flames that seared his lungs. "I can gets you out. It goin' to hurt. You gotta move when I tells ya." Jackie stomped on the branches close to Skeet's face to put out the closest flames. Then he took off his shirt, wrapped it around the top tree, and pulled it off the others. Skeet screamed. "Goin' to be another minute. Just wait."

Jackie dropped the tree to the side. The next two trees, bigger than the first, were on Skeet's legs. Jackie tried to lift the top tree, but it was more than he could manage. He moved back toward Skeet's feet.

"Skeet, I'm goin' to sit here an' lean against dis tree so I can use my legs to push dem trees up off your legs." Skeet groaned. "When I say so, you gotta move out de way. Can you crawl?"

"I can't feel my leg."

"Just roll, then. Can you roll?"

"Maybe. Hurry up," Skeet pleaded.

Jackie pulled his shirt on, then leaned against a large pine next to Skeet's legs. Using the tall grass around the base of the tree to anchor his weight, he pushed up against the trees. Skeet cried, "Stop! Stop!"

Jackie eased up.

"I'm hurt, boy. Don't hurt me no more." Skeet was now crying full tilt. "It hurts."

"Ain't no other way, Skeet. Ain't nobody here but us and dis truck going to explode. We needs to get out of here. I going to push again. Dis time when I tells you, you roll toward me. Hear?"

"Do it. Do something!"

Jackie took Skeet's response as an affirmative and steadied himself for another push.

"Ready? One. Two. Three!" Jackie pushed harder. This time he leaned back further, grabbed some tall grass, and lifted his butt cheeks off the ground for extension. The trees lifted slightly. "Roll, Skeet. Now!" Jackie grunted.

Skeet screamed, flopped one turn, and landed face up in front of Jackie. His twisted leg moved just enough to be clear of the logs. Jackie pushed the downed trees aside and again used the tree to get to his feet.

"Ow! Stop! Stop!" Skeet howled when Jackie grabbed him under his arms.

"Shut up, Skeet. I'm going to get you out of here," Jackie said, angered that his rescue seemed unappreciated.

Jackie tripped several times as he dragged Skeet to the road a safe distance from the flaming wreck. As they moved, Skeet cradled his right arm with his left across his chest. His legs dragged limp; neither seemed to work. His right leg slid through the sandy brush. It was turned inward and flat from the knee to his toes.

Jackie collapsed at the base of a tree opposite from where he dropped Skeet. Exhausted, he rolled his head to look up and down the pavement. Still no headlights, house lights, or street lamps anywhere, just the glow from the burning truck, which was beginning to fade around the red-hot metal.

Jackie panted and asked, "Skeet, where are we? Where was you going?"

Still a hostage to the alcohol and roughed up by the trauma, Skeet drifted in and out of consciousness. "Shut up, ya jack-mouthed negra," he mumbled, slumped over at the waist.

"Which way does we go on dis road? Skeet?"

"I don't know," he finally grumbled. When he straightened his back, he cried another animal howl.

"I don't knows where we—"

"Just go. I don't care, just go, boy!" As soon as he said it, he bent forward and upchucked remnants of the six pack of beer he drank earlier. He coughed and gagged, vomited a second time, then howled.

Jackie was beat. His shoulders ached to a point that he could barely lift his shredded hands, so swollen he couldn't make a fist. Again, the whisper inside his head moved him. He worked his way to his feet, then hoisted Skeet with a jerk.

"You tryin' to kill me, boy?" Skeet said, his head still abuzz from the beer. "You hurt me, boy, and I'll finish what I came here to do soon as I'm able."

With that Jackie let loose. Skeet landed hard on his tailbone. Before he could continue his fall, Jackie jumped in front of him and grabbed Skeet by the throat. He reeked of vomit.

"You was goin' to do what? You is goin' to finish what?" His grip grew tighter and tighter. "You was goin' to kill me, was da' what you was goin' to do, Skeet? Huh?" Jackie hands ached, but he squeezed and pressed his thumbs against Skeet's Adam's apple. Skeet, too broken to struggle, tried in vain to breathe.

"You stole da' truck. You drove out here and you died out here, da' is what peoples will think. Dey never know who choked de Lord's life out you and left you." Jackie pulled Skeet's nose closer to his and stared into Skeet's panicked eyes. He held him tight, his thumbs deeper and deeper into his throat. The last bit of flames flashed a dim light across Skeet's face, enough for Jackie to watch Skeet's eyelids quiver and close. Then the voice whispered once again.

Jackie dropped him. For several minutes, Skeet lay flat in the dirt. He wheezed and wailed to catch his breath. When he did Jackie grabbed him by the throat again. "Now I'm goin' to help you." He let loose of Skeet and shoved him to the ground.

Jackie bent down to pick up Skeet but returned upright. "Ef you don't listens to me or ef you don't do as I say, I going to latch onto da' neck of yours and finish what you came here to do, to kills somebody. You got

da', Skeet? And there ain't nothin' you can do about it."
Still short of breath, Skeet said nothing.

Since Skeet couldn't recall any houses along the road
to this point, Jackie continued farther down the road
with hopes he would find somebody, a house or
something, soon. Though much shorter and not quite as
muscular as Skeet and pained by the tumbled thrashing
of the accident, Jackie draped Skeet over his shoulder in
a fireman's carry and began to move down the pavement.
With every step, Skeet groaned. With every other step,
Jackie winced. He breathed heavily. His foot placement
was deliberate and slow. After fifty feet he stopped to
adjust the body on his shoulders. Skeet responded with a
scream.

"Shut you mouth, Skeet. I told you I don't wants no
screaming in my ear." Jackie wiped away tears, puffed,
and tightened his grip.

They continued down the road. The farther Jackie
walked, the colder it got, the blacker the night became,
and the more often Jackie had to stop to catch his
breath. Skeet remained quiet, motionless; even his groans
ceased. Finally, Jackie spotted a mailbox. He wanted to
quicken his pace, eager to find a house, but his body
didn't dare move any quicker. The name on the mailbox
read "Frazier." Jackie headed down the gravel allee. It
soon vanished into the woods bordered on both sides by
mammoth live oaks with no sign of a house, only the
drive which faded into blackness about fifteen feet away.
Dismayed and too exhausted to waste steps to find a
house that he couldn't see, Jackie paused long enough to
shift his hold on Skeet. He returned to the road.

A dog barked ahead in the distance. He recalled the
last incident he had with Skeet and a dog; there was no
alternative but to continue around a bend in the road

toward the sound. His risk paid off. Less than two hundred feet around the curve, he saw another mailbox. As he approached he could see a small shanty, one apparently never introduced to paint. There were no lights. At this time of night, Jackie didn't expect people along this rural stretch of road to be awake. He hesitated to think what a person answering a door in the middle of the night might do when they saw a Negro boy carrying a bloodied and broken white boy. A white person could easily think there was a fight and the Negro kid had done something horrible. If a Negro answered, they might hesitate to offer aid for the white boy, fearing they would be charged, the appearance of which would be justified in most white courts.

The single 40-watt bulb blinded Jackie when it flicked on above the door. He eased his eyes open and saw a thin, elderly black man in a threadbare nightshirt. Before Jackie could explain anything, the screen door opened and the old man struggled to help the two boys inside.

CHAPTER 27

The ambulance crew sent for Skeet was unwilling to also take Jackie. The elderly Negro man who opened his house when he saw Jackie on his steps walked a fine line between begging and threatening the driver and medical technician—both white—to have pity on the colored boy who carried the white boy to safety.

"We have rules. Rules is rules. Got to follow the rules." The driver grinned, then went back to filling out a form on his clipboard.

"Dey ain't goin' to send no other ambulance out here for da' boy, least not no time soon. Not way out here," the old man said.

The driver tossed the clipboard through his window, pulled a toothpick from behind his ear, and walked to the rear of the ambulance. While the technician secured the gurney inside, the driver closed the rear door. He walked to the passenger side and said, "Get in boy. You sit real low in that seat and don't you say a word."

The ordeal that began a little after sunset the evening before ended well before the sun had a chance to wink over the horizon the next morning. A groggy-eyed medical team worked to reset Skeet's broken arm, insert pins in his leg, and suture up a checkerboard of cuts on his forehead. Aside from the bruises assumed—though not checked—under Jackie's swollen black skin, aside from his hands, the hospital staff surmised Jackie had no apparent injuries of consequence. His true source of pain came from the police chief's barrage of questions.

The evening before, worried that Jackie had not returned from Ricky's house, Hestelle Eddings called Cybil Clemonds and learned Jackie had left their house over an hour earlier. She immediately called Grandpa Gabe; there was no answer. With one arm still wrestling for the coat sleeve, she shouldered her way through the door and ran, under the light of street lamps, to Grandpa Gabe's house two blocks away. She yanked open the screen door and nearly buried the doorknob in the wall when she charged into the house. She gagged at the sight of Grandpa Gabe unconscious, lying on top of a sea of old papers surrounding his chair in the living room. Screaming, she rushed to his side and rolled him onto his back. She felt a weak pulse, but he did not respond to her screams. She grabbed the phone, pulled it to her ear ready to dial, and heard a voice on the other end.

"Bacon fat, Evelyn. You's gots to add more—"

"Sharleen! Sharleen!" Hestelle screamed. "Get off de line please. It's Gabe. I need to get an ambulance here," she yelled. Sharleen Botume shared the party line with Gabe.

"Sure. I'm so sorry, Hestelle," she said and quickly hung up.

Hestelle dialed the hospital and, despite her panic, convinced them she needed an ambulance. Then she called her husband, who grabbed his hat and drove to Gabe's place, where the two of them paced and prayed on their knees for twenty minutes waiting for the emergency vehicle to arrive. It looked exactly like the last ambulance that had carried Gabe to the hospital. This trip, the Eddings' family Ford was a short bumper distance behind.

Through the night medication helped Gabe rest peacefully in the small room earmarked for Negroes at the end of the second floor hall. Hestelle waited, watched, and worried about Grandpa Gabe and her missing son. Between the two of them, Hestelle and Irvin went through three dollars in dimes calling friends and looking for Jackie. In the end, they called the police.

In a twist of serendipity early the next morning as Irvin Eddings passed the emergency room headed to his car to retrieve a sack lunch he had left from the day prior, he heard Chief Heimer ask Jackie a question. He darted into the room. Jackie cried and shared a short-lived hug of relief before the chief interrupted and pushed for more questions. Irvin Eddings barely had time to mention Gabe before Heimer jumped in.

"Look, Eddings. I'm conducting an investigation here."

"My son be missing. I need to know why and what happened. Why he be here?"

The sleep-deprived, coffee-starved chief turned slowly toward his questioner. "When I'm finished. Leave. Get out."

Before he backed through the swinging door, Irvin Eddings told Jackie that Grandpa Gabe was back in the hospital, second floor, the same small room as last time.

Irvin and Hestelle Eddings were awash with emotions, but sensed interfering with the chief's questioning—for now—would only create more problems. Relieved to know where Jackie was, they kept watch over Gabe and made frequent trips down the back stairs to check on their boy. A little after six o'clock, after the chief had finished with Jackie, the Eddings drove their son home, eager for details of his disappearance. The ham-bone soup Hestelle had prepared for supper the evening before sat cold on the stove; the aroma still lingered throughout the house. They had all been through a lot, especially Jackie. There was nothing more to be gained by a lengthy interrogation, at least not until they had some rest. They sent Jackie straight to bed, allowing him to skip school, to sleep and to avoid any curiously anxious rumors of his white classmates.

By noon, Irvin Eddings was standing in front of Chief Heimer's desk, hat in hand.

"You sees, Chief Heimer, my boy was kidnapped, again, by a white boy. He done nothing wrong."

"Hold up there, Eddings. There are plenty more facts in this here crime. This is a crime, you know," he said, his voice rusty and parched. He cleared his throat and continued, "Stealing a vehicle. Grand theft auto, they call it. Destruction of private property. Under age driving. Driving without a license. And beer cans in that area. We found the Western Auto truck, ya know. Your boy mentioned it when I talked to him initially. Yessir, it was in bad shape. Definitely ain't goin' to be on the road again. That thing is just a heap of burnt up metal."

"Yes, chief, sir. But you sees my boy all he did was save de life of da' white boy. My boy ain't done nothin'—"

"Hold your horses, boy. I'll be the law around here. Don't you go tellin' me how to do my job. You got that? I'll do the decidin' on who did what and who done wrong. You understand me, boy?" he said, popping out the last word in a burst of sourness that literally smacked the face of the colored man in front of him.

Irvin Eddings nodded sheepishly, his hat in hands waving like tail feathers behind him.

"I think my boy be lucky he alive," Eddings mumbled.

"Well, now…that might just be true, and that might be plain luck, ya see, if your boy was drivin' that truck."

"My boy ain't never drive nothing, Mr. Heimer, sir, I means, chief, sir."

The chief scowled. "You ain't sure what your boy been doin' there, Mr. Eddings. You got no control on that boy of yours. Why…he was standing here in front of me just weeks ago. Now you're tellin' me you know for sure he wasn't breakin' into people's boats and things?" the chief needled.

Irvin Eddings inhaled and, as he exhaled said, "Yes, sir."

"Well then, I suggest you just run on home and let the law work this here incident. Your boy…we'll see if your boy did anything. We'll know here right soon, I reckon. I'll take care of this. I'll take care of this right quick," Heimer said, shaking his finger. "You just watch that boy of yours."

As Irvin Eddings passed through the door, Otis Heimer cried out, "By the way, I heard the folks at the hospital say your Grandpa Gabe came in last night. Hope things turn out okay for the old fella."

Later that afternoon the chief meandered into the Beaufort Memorial Hospital, opted not to take the steps, and rode the elevator to the second floor. There he sauntered into a large bay of beds, shooed out the pimply faced candy striper with her skirt hiked up well above her knees, and lifted the patient clipboard at the foot of the bed closest to the double-door entryway. "Robin Gundy. Well, I'll be," he chuckled. "All these years I thought your name was Skeet. Ain't that a hoot. It's really Robin, like Robin Hood? Steal from the rich and give to the poor. That you, son?" the chief said with a grin somewhat stereotypical of a southern lawman. Skeet, anchored by plaster casts on one leg and the opposite arm, closed his eyes to avoid the unwelcomed interaction.

"Robin, you got some explainin' to do."

"Chief Heimer, sir, I can't help much. All I remember is wakin' up in this bed," Skeet replied with cocky juvenile self-assurance.

The chief's head rocked back and his face scrunched up as if someone pulled it with a drawstring. "What do you mean?"

"I mean, I remember being at the Bitty's Disc Den lookin' for the Zombies new number one, and then...poof, Chief Heimer, I was here in this room all beat up and covered with cement." Skeet knocked on his arm cast with his free hand. He cracked a smile at the expense of pain that created a starburst of wrinkles at the corners of his eyes.

"Wait a minute. You mean you don't remember stealin' Stanley Croft's truck and drivin' it out to Burton? You picked up that colored boy, drove off and ended up in a tree, on fire. You don't remember any of that happenin'?"

"No sir!"

The chief walked closer to the bed and leaned over the arrogant teen. "Don't go playin' no games with me, son. You're on thin ice here. That foster home of yours will be like paradise compared to where you might just end up. You best be tellin' the truth." He stepped back to pull up a chair from the corner of the room. He turned it backward and leaned over the back rest; his fried-food-enhanced belly pushed his belt buckle between the slats.

"I'm goin' to ask you one more time and don't be givin' me any of your lip. Tell me about last night. Did you steal that truck?"

"I told you, Chief. I don't remember nothin'. That's the honest to God's truth. If I'm lyin', I'm dyin'," Skeet answered with a pathetic lost-puppy look on his face.

The chief sensed otherwise. "Guess I'll just have to ask that colored boy who carried you to that house out there. You remember that?"

"No, sir."

"You remember that colored boy? That Eddings boy?."

"I ain't done nothin' with no coloreds. Can't stand them jigaboos."

The chief flashed a surprised smirk at the boy's choice of language. "So you don't remember showin' up at some house last night? You don't remember that colored boy carryin' you on his shoulders? You don't remember what you was doin' out there in the first place?"

Skeet fell back against his pillows with his eyes on the ceiling above him. "All I know is I am here in this bed and my leg hurts 'cause they said they had to put a pin in it or something. I don't know why. I don't know how. Now can I go pee?"

The chief hoisted his flabbiness out of the chair. He walked out the door and flagged down a nurse to help Skeet, then turned back toward the bed. "You think real hard about what happened, son. I'll be back and you best have more to tell me, ya hear?"

Skeet simply rolled his head away.

Rumors about Skeet's absence spread throughout his school faster than head lice in a daycare. The day after the chief's visit, Skeet had his stepbrother tell Hoss to escort Jackie to the hospital after school. Jackie, significantly smaller than Hoss, could not argue or escape the persuasion Hoss used. Besides, Jackie had approval from his mother to visit with Grandpa Gabe, whom he had not seen since the incident.

"Boy," Skeet said when Jackie walked through the doors, "we got to discuss what you is going to tell the chief."

"I'm going to tell him de truth," Jackie said. Hoss slid in behind him.

A wisp of a nurse appeared in the doorway behind Jackie. She stood all akimbo; her starched white uniform and pointed little cap added an air of authority.

"What are you boys doing in here?" she scolded in a peach-fuzz southern accent. "You know you're not allowed in here without an adult," she added with an extended look at Jackie.

"Ah, they ain't hurtin' nothin'. They're my classmates. They brought my homework and books and stuff," Skeet offered as he waved the boys closer with his free hand.

"Well, they can't be in here without an adult," she repeated.

"My parents will be here anytime now. Let 'em stay," Skeet said.

She looked at Skeet and back at Jackie.

"He's the only colored boy in our school, and we are working on a research project together."

She looked back at Skeet and said, "Okay, but if your parents aren't here in ten minutes, these boys will have to leave."

Skeet agreed. "Promise."

When the nurse left, Hoss nudged Jackie closer to the bed.

"Okay, here's the deal, Sambo. I'm tellin' Chief Heimer you made me steal that truck and drive you around to look for that stupid Gullah treasure thing. You got that? You better tell them the same thing or else."

Jackie couldn't believe this was the same boy whose life he had saved less than two days before. The same boy who he made promise to shut up. The same screaming teen who winced with every labored step Jackie took down the darkened, deserted road in the middle of nowhere. To Skeet, the fact that he owed his life to Jackie made no impression; he never acknowledged an instance of that, nor would he. Not in front of Hoss and certainly never to Jackie. Jackie aimed to refresh Skeet's memory. He figured Skeet might have been too delirious to recall all that happened. But with Hoss at his side, he knew Skeet would never agree or even consider what Jackie had to say. He bit his tongue.

"So now what you say to that, boy," Skeet said.

"I'll tell de truth," Jackie said, assured Skeet did not really know what the truth was.

Skeet paused briefly, then said, "Well, the truth, as you recall it, better be just like I said, boy, or you and me is goin' to have another meeting. You hear me?"

Pinched by Skeet's lack of post-trauma memory and the unwavering loyalty Hoss had for Skeet, Jackie nodded. "You know da' ain't right, Skeet."

"Boy, you don't tell me what's right. I was there. I know what's right. I was just tryin' to help you. I might even tell Fats Heimer you was drivin' that truck and that you ran it off the road. Don't be tellin' me what to say or what's right, boy."

"There ain't no way I was goin' to steal no truck or drive no truck. I wasn't even goin' to—"

"Boy…you was in trouble once with the law and they been watchin' you. Just 'cause you have your little colored butt in a white school don't give you no special privileges. You still a Negro down here. You ain't got no rights."

Jackie knew that was wrong, but also remembered the words of Grandpa Gabe. He kept his mouth shut.

"You go on now and get on out of here, boy, and don't you forget what I jus' told you. You do good by me and I let you slide. You cross me and you can bet we be seein' each other one more time right soon as I get out of here."

Jackie eyeballed Skeet. He wondered what had ever moved him to go back to the burning truck or why he bothered to lug Skeet away from it or seek help at all. Nothing had changed between them and, in his mind, it appeared nothing ever would. He turned and stepped to leave, but the fat, hairy arm of Chief Otis Heimer pushed him out of the way to allow Hank and Mailyn Newcomb, Skeet's foster parents, to enter the juvenile ward. All three of them, individually, gave Jackie the once-over as they passed by. Jackie quickly broke eye contact and followed the worn white tiles of the floor.

"So, Robin," Heimer said with a smirk, "have you given more thought to our conversation yesterday? Any more details you can recall?"

"Sure do, Chief Heimer. I feel so much better. Things are much clearer today," he said in an Eddie Haskell voice.

"You remember things today, do you?"

Skeet nodded his head.

The chief looked at Hoss Lassiter and motioned toward the doors with his head. The chubby teen said, "Aye, aye, Chief," and walked out of the room.

"And?" Heimer continued, arms crossed, propped on his ponderous gut, looking down at Skeet.

"Well, Chief, I remember now. I borrowed the truck. I guess that wasn't good of me, was it? But that colored boy, the one that just left, Jackie Eddings? He told me to do it," Skeet rattled on with the phony alibi he had outlined for Jackie. "See, we are doing this school project, me and the colored boy and another kid, Ricky Clemonds; he's kinda retarded. See, we are supposed to find a lost treasure. The Gullah treasure, which Negroes around here believe is somewhere, but it's kept sorta hush-hush. All I remember is the Negro boy said we needed wheels, because he knew where the gold, the treasure, was. So I borrowed the truck. Just for a bit, you see. I didn't mean to keep it or anything. That colored boy said just drive out to Burton. I figured it was some Negro secret or something, so I just did what he wanted and that's all I remember until I woke up in here." Skeet sighed and rolled his head, looking up at the ceiling.

"You mean to tell me you'd do something that colored boy would tell you? Who is the dumb one here, huh?"

"Now, Chief. Listen to my boy," Hank Newcomb chimed in. "I told you Skeet wouldn't just up and take no truck. I mean my boy Eddie works for Old Man Croft. He ain't goin' to bite the hand that feeds him. That just ain't right."

"Skeet's been a good boy, Mr. Heimer," Mailyn added. "We ain't never had no trouble. He minds well. He does his chores. He's respectful to me and Hank."

Otis Heimer rubbed his receding hairline with stubby fingers that looked like flesh-colored kosher pickles. He looked over at the parents, then back to the teen.

"Son, you ain't got an ounce of brain in that head of yours if you listen to the colored folks 'round here. Them folks barely able to talk let alone think and make no sense when they do. Now why'd you go listenin' to him?" the chief asked, but he raised his hand and continued before he allowed for an answer. "See, that Eddings boy…he was placed in your school 'cause the law says we had to do it. Ain't nothin' special 'bout that boy. Ain't nothin' special 'bout any of them colored people. They ain't goin' to last in your school. In two years all this will change and that colored boy he'll be back in that colored school; you just wait and see." The chief moved to the other side of the bed, grabbed the cast on Skeet's arm, and gave it a hard shake.

"Ow!" Skeet screamed.

"Trust me, son. Don't do nothin' stupid again. I'll see what I can do 'bout Old Man Croft. Somebody owes him a truck. Sounds like you'd be the one"—Heimer looked over at the Newcombs frozen across the room—"unless that colored boy was the one who stole that truck. Right?" He walked back to join the couple. "I have a meeting with the Eddings and their boy in 'bout an hour. Guessin' he'll confess when I ask him a few things."

Hank Newcomb flipped his wife an underhanded wave to shoo her to follow the chief. Before leaving, Mailyn Newcomb leaned over the metal hospital bed to kiss Skeet goodbye, only to have him roll away and pull the bedsheet over his head.

CHAPTER 28

Even the heavy wooden door tested by many tropical storms that had lashed the Beaufort Police Station for decades was little match for the late autumn sidewalk twisters that blasted leaves through the opening when the Eddings family entered.

"Y'all go on in. Just give me a minute here," Chief Heimer said as he stepped between Jackie and his mother. Out the door, he walked to the water cooler, pulled a Dixie cup from the tube on the side, downed two refills, and tossed the cup toward the wastebasket that had already runneth over with identical flowered cups.

"Okay, let's talk," Heimer said, wiping his wet hands on the faded, latte-colored pants hiked well above his ankles to accommodate his overaggressive waistline. He spun his chair into position before he plopped down—gravity-assisted—without offering a seat to his visitors. He ratcheted forward in his chair. His heft had flattened the wheels to a point where they slid rather than rolled.

"So I talked to the Gundy kid…" He started in a protracted, monosyllabic drawl, his eyes still on the deskwork. "He tells me you told him to steal that truck, boy." He cast an intimidating stare down his nose toward Jackie.

"My boy never did no such thing, Mr. Heimer," Irvin Eddings responded.

"Chief! It's Chief Heimer and I'm talkin' to your boy," the chief challenged.

The older Eddings lifted his chin and rolled his eyes toward the ceiling to avoid a second outburst that would surely not help his son.

"What you say to that, boy?"

"Chief Heimer, I didn't steal no truck and I didn't tell nobody to steal no truck," Jackie said, the words squeezed passed the lump in his throat.

"Now that don't seem to square up with what your buddy said. Not at all." He pulled his glasses from his forehead to the tip of his nose and scanned an unorganized collage of papers that littered the desk. "Says here in my notes that you told him you knew where that Gullah treasure of yours was and that you and him were going to go get it"—he folded his hands on top of his notes— "and that if he met you down behind Von Harten Brothers that evenin' that you would take him to it."

"No, sir, I didn't say nothin' like da', Mr. Chief, sir."

"Don't you lie to me, boy," the chief said, pounding both hands flat on his desk hard enough to make pencils fly. "I ain't got time for games, boy. You been in here before and I been watchin' you."

Jackie felt a queasiness so strong it made his knees shake.

"The Gundy kid had a little trouble rememberin' exactly what happened 'cause of how he hurt his head and all. I coached him a little and his memory came back just fine, boy. Maybe I need to do the same with you, eh?"

"Chief Heimer, I think my son—"

"Hey, you just shut your mouth. I don't need no uppity Negro to tell me how to do my job. I told you before, I was talkin' to this here boy and I'm still talkin' so don't interrupt me. Is that clear there, Eddings?"

"But—"

"I said…is that clear?" Heimer pulled his glasses off his nose and laid them on the desk, his eyes fixed laser-tight on Eddings.

Irvin Eddings remained expressionless, his face more stoic than the granite on Rushmore. "Yes, sir, Mr. Chief."

Locked in his stare, Otis Heimer eased his hands onto the armrest of his chair and leaned back to full tilt. "Okay then, boy, you wanna explain now what really happened?"

Jackie snuck a glance toward his mother, then toward his father and finally back toward the desk, low enough to avoid the chief's eyes.

"Mr. Chief, see I was at Ricky's house and—"

"Where? Ricky? Ricky who?" Heimer asked coming forward.

"Ricky Clemonds. He lives over on North Street. We was working on da' project, de Gullah treasure project."

Heimer snickered to hear Jackie suggest any belief in the treasure. "Go on."

"And I was leavin' Ricky's house when Skeet and dis other kid, Hoss, grabbed me an' took me to da' truck.. Dey put a hood over my head and tied my hands."

With each statement, anger twisted his parents tighter. Irvin clenched his fists hard enough to turn his black knuckles white. Hestelle held her breath until her head began to pound.

"Skeet stopped once and when Hoss got out da' truck, Skeet took off and left Hoss behind. I didn't know where we was or where we was goin', but down the road somewhere Skeet stopped and he took off de hood and tied me to de railroad tracks. Da' is when he said a train would be by soon to pick me up."

"Oh! Oh!" Hestelle Eddings cried out. She moved to hug her son. The chief raised his hand.

"Just stay put. Let the boy talk." He motioned for the boy's mother to step back. She hesitated until Irvin looked her way. "And then what?"

"Then no train came. Skeet came back and put me in de truck. I saw dem empty beer cans on the floor when he started driving. Not sure what he was going to do, but dis deer jumped in front of de truck and—"

The chief cleared his throat. "Stop right there, boy. Let's go back. Let me help you with some details I think you missed there. Seems we saw you snoopin' around the Western Auto a while back. Bet ya never noticed Deputy Francis when he drove by that day, now did ya? So you cased that truck and figured out how to start it. Hotwired I guess. Easy to do on them old trucks. Gotta hand it to you, boy"—he chuckled—"never thought you'd be smart enough to hotwire a truck, but doggone if you didn't fool me there." The boy's father chomped on the insides of his mouth when he heard the chief's audacious accusation.

"And then you met that Skeet fella and drove off to wherever. That deer thing, or whatever, maybe just dumb-kid reckless driving, you ran into the tree, and that truck caught fire. You figured if you saved that white boy's life you'd be some hero and everything would be forgiven. Ain't that right, boy? Everything would be okay 'cause you saved a white boy's life?" Heimer said, his head cocked to look at the boy, his squinty eyes filled with hateful curiosity.

"No, sir. Da's not it at all, Mr. Chief," Jackie replied, now looking up at the fat white man behind the desk.

Heimer recoiled and said, "Boy, are you questioning me?"

"No, sir, Mr. Chief. It's jus' what you said didn't happen da' way." Jackie thought a minute about how to tell his story. He knew enough not to mention his initial flight, leaving Skeet to burn. "I mean, de truck was on fire and I could hears screaming. When de truck rolled I flew out and was left a good ways away from it and de fire. I crawled into da' fire and pulled Skeet out. He was hurt bad. There was no cars around and I knowed I had to get help so I carries him to a house, first house I come to."

Heimer slammed his desk again. "You know that ain't so, boy. You know that ain't the truth."

"My boy don't lie, Mr. Heimer. He be tellin' you da' white boy was goin' to kill him. If da' train don't come he probably goin' to lynch him up somewheres," Irvin Eddings said quickly before the chief had a chance to shut him down.

The outburst drew another stare, this time a wordless guilty verdict. The chief's hands pressed on the desk, poised to launch when a knock diverted his attention to the door.

"Chief Heimer. So sorry. I apologize for being late...again. As you recall this boy and this family, they are...well...clients of mine and—"

"I don't believe you were invited here, Judge," Heimer said, irritated by the interruption.

"Oh, no sir. Don't believe I need any invitation. See by law—you know, your laws—my clients are entitled to have counsel present at all times during interrogations and for investigations. Let's say a little bird told me they were here in your office, so I figured it was my law-abiding duty to be here with them," Caplin explained.

Irvin Eddings stepped back to allow Caplin to move in front of the desk. Jackie's mother pulled her son toward the back of the room, closer to the door.

In a silent huff, the chief slid his hands about the desktop, flustered by the intrusion. His plan for questioning the boy had to change, but he was at a loss on a new approach. He leaned back in his chair and drummed his pudgy fingers on the armrest. "Seems your client, Mr. Caplin, stole a truck and possibly kidnapped a white boy."

"Facts, sir?" Caplin questioned, slapping his hat against the side of his leg. "Surely you can substantiate your accusation with evidence, Chief Heimer. Care to share the facts?"

"I told your clients. They heard the facts. Too bad you weren't here to hear them yourself."

"Well then, I suggest we recess for now, sir, to allow me to hear those facts as my clients heard them as well as to hear their side of the story, one which you may not have heard or elected not to hear," the colored lawyer said, his head cocked to the side.

"Your boy there," Heimer stuttered, "I mean, your client, could probably use a little time to refresh his own memory on the facts. I believe after he thinks it over a bit, the evidence will prove my side of this case." He slid forward in his chair, interlocked his fingers, and placed his hands on the desk. He looked around the room for a brief moment, avoiding the eyes of the others, then nodded toward the lawyer. "Request granted. We can hold off for a few days."

Caplin smiled and returned the nod as he looked toward the boy and his parents.

"Next time, Judge, you be here from the start. I'll have someone call your office to arrange the meeting. Do we understand each other here?"

"Oh, sure. Most certainly, Chief Heimer. Very considerate of you to allow the law to influence your procedures here," Caplin said as he turned the Eddings family toward the door. "If you'll excuse us we will be leaving."

"Hold it right there, Judge. Last time I checked this is still my office and I believe I am in charge here."

Caplin stopped and turned back toward the desk.

"You know this boy has been in trouble before. Don't let him lie to you like he tried to lie to me. I ain't goin' to put up with no lying from him or you or anyone else 'round here. And when this boy starts accusing that white boy of lyin' or tryin' to kill him, you just forget he ever said that." Heimer leaned more forward with his elbows on the desk. "This better not cause no trouble in this town. That whole lynchin' thing? That word best not get out," Heimer concluded, tilting his head toward the door, a subtle suggestion that the four Negroes were dismissed, a cue they followed without parting words.

CHAPTER 29

In the days that followed, Jackie reflected less on the recent events in his life and school and the treasure and dwelt on Grandpa Gabe, who remained at Beaufort Memorial in a winner-take-all grudge match with the Grim Reaper. Gabe was still unconscious when Jackie stopped by his room after the meeting with Skeet. Three days later, after Gabe's condition improved, since Hestelle was busy baking cookies she promised for a bake sale at church, she told Jackie he could ride his bike to the hospital to visit Gabe.

Jackie's bike—a hand-me-down collection of layered rust on metal, commercially referred to as the Hawthorne Flyer, the best Montgomery Ward had to offer—was a tenth-birthday gift his father bought from a classified ad. The beast of a bike made pedaling an M-48 tank sound easy. With almost no air in the fat rear tire, cranking the distance with two bruised legs became too difficult. Jackie pushed the bike along the last half mile of sidewalk to the hospital where he leaned it against a tree on the backside of the building and entered through the entrance marked "Colored." The middle-aged white receptionist grilled him with a barrage of questions. Given Gabe's condition and the fact that Jackie was part of the immediate family, she overlooked the hospital rule that required an adult to escort child visitors under the age of fifteen. She kept an eagle eye on Jackie to ensure he took the back stairwell at the end of the hall up to the second floor where Grandpa Gabe rested, alone and unattended.

The space, the same converted utility closet, was one of four spread throughout the hospital at the ends of the halls. All identical. All with the word "Negro" crudely stenciled in black above the door, each with a paint-starved metal bed squeezed inside four windowless walls. No bedside table or nightstand. No stand for flowers or cards. A clipboard hung from the bed above the stainless steel pot that eliminated the need for a colored bathroom.

"Grandpa Gabe," Jackie said softly from the door before he entered. The old man didn't move. Jackie stepped closer to the bed and, adding volume, tried again, "Grandpa?"

The old man's body remained still, but his eyes opened slightly in a distant drowsy stare.

"Grandpa Gabe, it's me, Jackie. How do you feel?"

Gabe worked the corners of his mouth into a ghost of a smile and allowed his eyelids to drift closed as he rolled his head at a glacial pace toward the sound of the young boy's voice. His eyes reopened. Jackie sensed the pain as Gabe's arm—a wrinkled pitch-black limb that looked like tar on a twig—slid out from beneath the starched white hospital bedding.

"Grandpa Gabe, are you going to be okay?" he asked, bent close for Gabe to hear.

The response came slowly, breathless syllables coated with pain, spoken as if each was his last. "Boy, I done seen life, much life before dis. I 'spects I sees more still. You's the one be concerned 'bouts youself."

Jackie looked steadily into the hollowness of his grandpa's eyes. "What you mean, Grandpa?"

"I heared you been in trouble. I knows you didn't do nothin' bad but bad be lookin' for you," Gabe said, his words less pained, more pointed.

"I don't understand, Grandpa Gabe."

"Da' white boy done tried to kills you." He rolled his head away from Jackie and stared at the ceiling.

Jackie didn't know how to respond. He wasn't sure how Gabe would know.

"You ain't telled nobody, has you, boy?"

"Yes, sir. I told de police. Mamma an' Daddy knows."

"Ain't telled nobody else, has you?"

"No, sir."

"What you goin'to do wid da' white boy now?"

"I'm goin' to make him pay, Grandpa Gabe. I'll finds a way. I'm goin' to show him I ain't willin' to die, not from him, not from nobody."

"You know why he want to kill you?" Gabe let his head roll back toward Jackie. "He don't like you skin. He think you ain't as good as him 'cause you skin be black." Gabe stopped. The lump in his throat bobbed up and down as he swallowed. "He think we colored people is animals, don't he?" Gabe bent his wrist and pointed at Jackie with a pencil-thin finger, skin stretched tighter than canvas on a portrait. "An you's gotta be careful. You's gotta remember, it ain't jus' you he be after; it be all colored peoples, even me." Gabe rolled back and stared at the ceiling once more. He started to talk but no words came out. He tried again. "I knows, boy, I knows. I done seen dis for years." He closed his eyes and continued, "I sees dem buckruh, dem white peoples takes everything from us." A cough. "Dey takes our land, our mules, our money…" Gabe went silent again.

Jackie leaned closer to catch his next words. "But dey not takes our pride. We be a proud people and we goin' to stay proud, you hears me?" Gabe fought for air and rolled back toward the young boy he loved so dearly. He whispered slowly, "Jackie, you gotta be proud. Show dem you ain't no animal, da' you be better than him. Be strong. White peoples"—he paused—"dey don't believes dis white boy try to kill you. Dey won't believe you. Dey think things be fine here."

"But, Grandpa, ef I do nothin' he'll hurt me again. I mean—"

"Listens to me, boy, an' you listen good." When Gabe's voice rose above his strained whisper, he began to cough; his finger beckoned Jackie closer.

Nearer the pillow, Jackie noticed something black protruding. Gabe's lips quivered when he whispered, "He ain't goin' to hurt you. I know he ain't."

Jackie couldn't remember the last time he doubted the old man, but on this he had to fight the urge to argue. Instead he reached toward the pillow and, from beneath it, pulled out a feather, a striking piece of plumage—long and pointed with an iridescence that flickered even under the soft light from the single bulb overhead.

"Grandpa Gabe, what's dis?" Jackie asked, holding the feather where his grandpa could see.

It was either fear or wonder or both that caused Gabe's lower jaw to twitch, leaving words trapped inside his mouth. Jackie looked at the feather, then back to Gabe. He sensed something strange, a feeling or emotion.

"Grandpa Gabe?"

"It look like a feather," Gabe replied, noncommittal.

"What's it for?"

Gabe didn't respond.

"How did it get here? How did it get under your pillow?"

"Haints I s'pose."

Jackie shied back. "Haints?"

In due time Gabe spoke, his voice surprisingly strong; his lips did not tremble in the slightest. "It be de raven feather."

Jackie waited for more.

"It mean something to happen."

"Something good? Something bad? What?"

Gabe closed his eyes again. The seed of a smile began to blossom across his sealed lips.

A nurse in a starched white uniform appeared at the door. "I'm afraid you're going to have to leave, child. This poor old man is tired and needs his rest," she said with a sugar-coated southern drawl, but with a look that, of itself, was the constant reminder that colored people just needed to do as they were told. Jackie immediately stepped toward the door then turned back toward the bed.

"Bye, Grandpa. I'll come back with Mamma on a visit, soon."

As he walked out of the room, before he turned left to go down the back staircase, he looked to his right and saw Skeet Gundy down the hall. The mere sight of him made Jackie's throat tighten. He busted through the stairway door and took the stairs two at a time, hopped on his bike, and straddled the Hawthorne home.

With Jackie out of sight and no hospital staff visible on the floor, Skeet wheeled his chair to the end of the hall where he read the letters above the door. Acting on a hunch, he wheeled into the room where Gabe dozed, too exhausted to notice. Skeet lifted the clipboard from the foot of the bed. The emergency contact name and address confirmed his guess that the patient was Jackie's Grandpa Gabe.

Later that evening Jackie and his parents visited Gabe. While Dr. Palmer spent time with the parents in a small conference room, Jackie and Gabe spent time together. They continued their discussion of earlier in the day, but also talked about the letters and the Gullah treasure project. When it was time to leave, Gabe whispered, "Bring da' white boy Skeet 'round to sees me so we can all talks about da' project. An' bring da' clue, too."

Hestelle Eddings overheard her great-grandfather and lanced him with an ugly stare.

Hours later, while the night shift settled back for their mid shift meal, Skeet slipped out of bed and into his chair. Days in the hospital had allowed him ample time to master wheeling his chair with one arm and using the plaster-bound arm to brake his forward movement before his pinned leg—supported and extended like a battering ram—met with anything immovable, not to mention he could make his joy rides almost silently across the tile floors. If he encountered a staff member, he would flash a toothy grin their way, which bought the lanky teen complete access throughout the hospital.

As he approached Gabe's room, Skeet looked around. The coast looked clear. He aimed his extended leg toward the door and wheeled through the threshold.

"Nah, nah, nah, baby. Now where are you going there, honey?" a voice called out. Skeet stopped short of the door. Down the hall, an elderly nurse had stepped off the elevator, pushing a small cart. "Now, you know you are not supposed to be on this floor, young man. What do you think you are doing?" She walked up directly in front of him with her hands on her saddlebag hips.

"I was—"

"Help! Nurse! Nurse! Help. Help me!" came a cry from the other end of the hall. "Help me, please. Someone help!"

The nurse quickly abandoned her cart and hurried to the opposite end of the hall, but hollered back to Skeet, "Get on back down to your ward, baby. Go on. Get." Skeet shook his head, smirked, and rolled through the door.

In the room, Skeet looked around. He checked beyond the curtain that divided the room; there was no other occupant. He looked around and decided what he really wanted was the old man's flat pillow. He wheeled the chair parallel to the bed as Gabe slept. With his free arm, he yanked the pillow from beneath the old man's head. When he did, the long black raven feather harpooned between the toes on Skeet's bare foot. Startled, he shook it off to the side. Pillow in hand he scooted forward in the chair, twisted, and stretched out over the colored man's head.

"Say there son, better be careful with that leg of yours," a voice said from behind him. Skeet spun around and dumped the pillow in his lap as a tall Negro man of medium height and build dressed in a long starched white coat entered the room. "You know those chairs sometimes roll when you don't want them to. You could end up on the floor, or even worse, on top of my patient. What are you doing in here, especially this time of night?"

"Oh, he's the grandpa of a school friend of mine, Doc. I come to check on him at nights," Skeet said amid his zero-turn pivot. "Ya see, the staff here, they ain't too sharp at night and I worry 'bout my friend's gramps."

Before his initial, well-timed comment, Joseph Palmer had hesitated long enough outside the door to grasp Skeet's intentions. "And the pillow?"

"He looked uncomfortable so I was just fluffin' it up a bit. Thought that would make him feel better," he said with a tone that was less than convincing.

The doctor lifted the pillow from the boy's lap and eased it back under Gabe's head without him awakening. "Very thoughtful, young man, but I believe the medical staff is far more qualified than you to make those adjustments. This man's very ill and I'm sure your friend would rather you not do anything to harm his grandpa. Wouldn't you agree?"

"No, sir, Doc. No, sir," Skeet said, able to hold his tongue for the moment.

After a quick check on Gabe, Dr. Palmer reached down and grabbed the handles on the wheelchair. Skeet looked back over his shoulder at the bed as the wheelchair rolled out into the hall.

"What's your room number?" the doctor asked.

"I can get myself back," Skeet answered, grabbing the large wheel with his hand.

The chair stopped abruptly. After a deep inhale, Palmer tilted his head back and closed his eyes before he said, "Son, I took an oath to care for patients and nobody ever mentioned anything about color. Please tell me where your bed is. Otherwise, I'll have to call the nurse and let you explain what I saw and what you claim you were up to."

Skeet didn't want to give the nurses any reason to pass word to his doctor. He told Palmer he had a bed in the juvenile ward, then remained silent until the doctor wheeled him to his bed as the only occupant of the bay.

"I sure hope my friend's grandpa will be all right," Skeet said with a false air of sincerity.

"Oh, I believe he'll be just fine. I'll ensure he's safe and trouble free until he's released. You get some rest, son. And what was your name again?"

"Gundy, Doc. Skeet Gundy."

"Goodnight, Mr. Robin," the doctor said.

Skeet was surprised the doctor used his real name. "How'd you know my name?"

"It's in your records," the doctor said as he offered the cocky teen a hand back into the bed, then left the boy alone. Under the influence of bleach-scented sheets, Skeet wrestled with his casts to get comfortable. He hadn't abandoned his plan, but scuttled his efforts for the night before he dozed off.

CHAPTER 30

It had been two hours since Dr. Palmer wheeled Skeet back to his bed. When the Negro doctor returned to the hospital, he made the required stop at the duty desk by the juvenile ward on the first floor, a requirement for medical nonresidents and for him as a Negro doctor. After a brief chat with the duty nurse, he asked her to sit and monitor a patient at the other end of the hall while he went upstairs to check another patient. With the duty nurse as his proxy, Palmer went to the second floor. At the nurses' station, he met with Nurse Callahan, the nurse who had stopped Skeet by Grandpa Gabe's room earlier. He asked her if she could assist him with another patient on the first floor.

"Well, Doctor," she said, reluctant to leave her post and even more reluctant to listen to a Negro and—doctor or not—nonresident. "I really should stay here."

"This will only take a few minutes. Things appear to be rather quiet here now. If you would, I most certainly need your assistance."

Deborah Callahan stepped out from behind the counter and followed the doctor to the elevator around the corner. It took a few moments for the car to make the trip up from the first floor. When it arrived, the two of them entered and went down.

While Dr. Palmer visited with Nurse Callahan on the second floor, a group of three entered the juvenile ward

315

in silence and immediately gagged Skeet. Wrapped stiff in plaster, Skeet presented little threat. Besides, what he saw terrified him. Each visitor wore a large strange mask and shaggy coveralls. Unable to talk (or scream) Skeet's eyes widened and his chest heaved. Two costumed creatures wrapped his legs tight with a sheet and snatched him out of his bed while the third—the one who looked like a hyena—grabbed the wheelchair. Exiting the room they took the stairwell to their left and ascended to the second floor, then quickly entered the room marked "Negro."

Unceremoniously, they placed Skeet in his chair. One of the three picked up the wooden wedge used as a door stop and jammed it down in back of Skeet's head to tighten the gag in his mouth. When they had him positioned where and how they wanted him, they faced him close enough to hear Gabe whisper, "De Gullah treasure be true." After a few short, heavy breaths, he leaned forward to be closer to Skeet. One of the masked visitors placed the pillow behind him for support. Gabe panted and continued to whisper, "Dey be a treasure. You best help da' Gullah boy find it. Ef you do anything or even think 'bout hurtin' da' boy, dey be a hex upon you."

Gabe's neck went limp. His chin dropped to his chest. One of the creatures grabbed Skeet by the shoulders and slammed him against the back of the seat; the others rushed to Gabe. They tilted him back, leaning slightly past vertical. Only his eyes moved, rolled open. His left arm fell limp off the edge of the bed, then trembled as he raised it enough to motion with his index finger. He pointed toward the black feather on the floor in the corner, the feather Skeet kicked away earlier. The hyena took the feather to Gabe. The old man clenched it like a dagger and rolled his head to stare at Skeet seated in the grips of one of the costumed visitors.

"De raven bring de hex," Gabe slurred. "When he leave him feather, best beware."

The eyes behind the masks noticed Gabe lift his right hand in a subtle wave. Dismissed, they whisked Skeet, undetected, back to the juvenile ward. Before removing the wooden wedge and the gag, the hyena placed his hand around Skeet's throat, leaned forward, and rested the full weight of his mask on Skeet's face.

"Nevermore," he said with a deep Gullah accent, his breath a vapor of seafood and garlic.

Skeet hadn't dared a blink during the five-minute ordeal. The moment the creatures left, Skeet passed out, or simply fell into a deep sleep.

Pestered with senseless dreams, he awoke a few hours later. *No old marble-mouthed jigaboo's going to stop me with none of his hoodoo voodoo* talk Skeet said to himself, sitting upright in bed. *I'll show him and that Geechee boy of his how a hex works.* He scooted toward the side of the bed to swing his chair under him. When he did, the ward entrance doors mysteriously closed on their own. The air across the ward chilled, not unheard of for December, but neither of the windows in the room was open.

"Skeet," a voice summoned.

Skeet looked around. The only light in the room came from the "Exit" signs, hardly enough to see anybody that might be in the room, especially at the far end. There were ten beds in the ward and Skeet's was closest to the door.

"Skeet."

It came again. This time it seemed closer but still all around him, like an echo. In the distance, he thought he saw something, a body in the bed farthest away; then it disappeared. Hair all over his body—even those covered in plaster—stood on end. He scanned the room and saw the body again. This time on a different bed, opposite side, closer. He stared directly at the form and it disappeared. He shook his head, afraid he was seeing things, imagining the voice and the body.

"Skeet!"

The voice called once more. This time it was no longer an echo. It came from behind him, from the other side of his own bed. He twisted as fast as he could; with the casts he wasn't that quick. There was no body, no form, but there was a sign. On his bed was a long black feather, the same type Gabe had warned him might appear if the hex was on him. He flipped the sheet with his good hand and the feather drifted to the floor. When it landed, Skeet heard another strange sound. Not a voice, but the call of a bird, though deeper and raspier, almost a growl. A bird—black and much larger than a crow—flew up from the floor where the feather had landed. Then a second. Then a third. All in a squawk. Then more. One bird mutated into six or more, a flock of huge black birds calling. Their squawks eerily mimicked his voice, reciting his name. "Skeet. Skeet."

"Somebody get in here. Y'all come in here," he hollered, his breath a frozen mist from his mouth. When the doors didn't budge, he screamed louder, but, with the noise from the birds, he couldn't hear his own desperate cries. Finally, he noticed the doors shake. Someone from outside pushed and pulled against them. He screamed again but the birds drowned out any reply. He heard—or thought he heard—a faint voice from outside the doors say, "Open the door, boy. You come and open these doors right now." Skeet was in no position to move to the door. The birds circled his head, occasionally flying close enough to scratch his scalp. When Skeet made a move toward his chair, one of the birds buzzed past his nose, followed by another, then another, pushing him back against the pillows. He parried the attacks with his arm cast and flailed vigorously with his other arm. His heart raced faster and stronger, but his arms grew heavier and moved slower. Finally, the birds moved away from his head and formed a revolving sphere next to his bed. Remarkably, they flew in close quarters without ever touching each other. Huge birds in frenzied flight, faster and faster until the mass of feathers formed a black cloud still boiling with activity but no longer solid. The color drained from the cloud, black to gray to a mist and from the mist a figure appeared.

"Blimey! 'Tis thee," the dwarf figure said in a voice that sounded vaguely like one of the Beatles. "Thou art the wanker from the Castle, aren't thee?"

Skeet wouldn't, couldn't speak; his brain was a mush of half-chilled Jell-O.

"Thou art the chap that turned thy bum and ran when I presented myself. Thou left thy friends behind. And the dog!" The figure started to pace alongside the bed, wringing his hands in a nervous tick. "Come on. Thou hast cocked up this one now. What do thou say for thine self?"

Skeet remained speechless. His mouth was dry and butterflies tickled in his throat.

"I don't have all night. Speak up thou simple prat. Thou was scared, wasn't thou? And thou left thy friends or was they not friends? It was thou who took them there and thou was going to nick that treasure for thy self, eh?"

Still no response from Skeet.

"Speak thou pimply prat. Talk to me lad or I'll bring back the birds," he said as he sprang in one bound from the floor to the top of the bed, where he sat crossed-legged with a Cheshire cat grin and sang, "Tra-la-la...The birds with black feathers that flock close together. Tee-hee, dweedle-dee...Ravens behavin' and cravin' the flesh, appetite delight for fright." He stopped abruptly and floated, prostrate, toward Skeet's head, out of reach. "They won't be so friendly next time, Skeet Gundy."

Skeet had visions of scenes from the movie he saw a year ago at the Breeze Theater, Hitchcock's *The Birds*. "I don't know what you're sayin'," Skeet said, each word a stutter, some more prolonged than others.

The floating figure shot straight upward as if the ceiling sucked him into the dark void, and then he appeared at the far end of the ward, a shadowy figure walking slowly back toward Skeet.

Someone outside the ward pounded on the doors; they shook but didn't open.

The figure paced forward. His footsteps were loud, much too loud for his size. They sounded like a horse as it clomped from the dark into the shadows just outside the light that filtered in through the ward doors, which no longer rattled.

"Thou was going to steal the treasure, wasn't thou? Ha, ha. And not going to help thy friends, were thou now?"

"Yes."

"And then thou planned to hurt my friend Ricky." The visitor coughed a bit to clear his throat.

"No. No."

"But thou planned to hurt the Negro boy, his friend, Jackie Eddings."

"I...I..."

"That would hurt Ricky. And now thou plans to hurt the colored boy's Grandpa Gabe. That would hurt the colored boy, which would hurt Ricky, even though thou hast been warned." The tiny visitor now stood at the foot of Skeet's bed. Too short to see above the bed frame, the dwarf levitated to face Skeet at eye level.

"Thou art a maggot and daft as a bush. Such a twit thou art. Though I am a mere bard, my storytelling is true and does not portend frivolity, for in my world I see all, but in thy world, the old man sees all. Thou shouldst not test him. His powers of hex are real. The birds are but a sign. So much more can happen to thee. Dost thou understand?"

With a blink of an eye, the dwarf transformed into a raven and flapped his wings like a duck landing in a pond as he stood on the metal rail at the foot of the bed.

Skeet managed to scoot back, plastered hard against the head of the bed. "I'm not going to hurt nobody. Nobody. I promise."

The bird evaporated into a mist that drifted to the bedside where the tiny man appeared again. "And thou will help my friend Ricky Clemonds find the treasure?"

Skeet nodded his head to agree.

"There, there, lad," he said raising his hands to calm Skeet. "And his colored friend, he will be thine friend, too?"

Skeet hesitated. The experiences of his night flashed through his head—the colored doctor, the masked visitors, the raven feather, and the stubby bard. All of them prodded him closer to believing the Gullah "thing" was real. The history. The hex. The treasure. It might all be real.

"Yeah, sure. He can be my friend," Skeet choked out.

As the sound of the last consonant left his lips, the colorful jester was off the floor and on top of Skeet's chest on all fours. His foul breath smelled like he had not brushed his teeth since the sixteenth century.

"No, lad. Say it properly. Thou will be his friend. That colored boy, Jackie, will be the boss, not thee." The jester did something to his face. It turned red; the veins under his skins moved about and his skin wrinkled and dried, then dissolved to nothing and left only a skull under his fanciful cap. His breath now smelled even worse. Skeet turned away.

For such a small figure, the bard weighed heavily on the boy's chest. And the closeness of his mouth made Skeet want to vomit. "Sure, yeah," he said, coughing the words.

"Say the words, lad. Say it!" the little man insisted.

"Sure. Yeah, sure. I'll be his friend. He can be the boss. Sure."

"All right then," the dwarf said, straddling Skeet on the bed, his face returned to how it originally appeared. "We have a deal. Two things before I go." The figure hopped off the bed and leaned against the iron bedpost near the boy's feet.

"Remember these two things. First, the hex is real." He spread his arms out like wings and levitated two feet off the ground. The room grew colder as the chubby dwarf floated toward the darkened end of the room. "And second. Don't forget, 'Bird, bird, bird—bird is the word!' " he sang as he chuckled a hideous laugh and disappeared, absorbed by darkness at the far end of the ward.

CHAPTER 31

Sunday morning the weather literally turned south in Beaufort. An unusual deep dip of the polar jet stream paralyzed the Lowcountry. The blast of Arctic air brought a thirty-degree swing in the daytime temperature. The balmy sixties on Saturday gave way to highs only in the thirties on Sunday. After church Jackie bundled up, mounted his rusty but trusty Hawthorne Flyer, and pedaled back to the hospital, where he timidly asked the receptionist if he could visit Skeet. She scowled, then questioned him on the whys and wherefores of his request before she pointed him to the nearby juvenile ward. Jackie realized Skeet had not moved since he saw him with Hoss days after the accident.

Despite the late morning hour, Skeet was still dozing, the combination of teen circadian rhythm exacerbated by fatigue from the previous night's events. Jackie stopped at the foot of Skeet's bed. A wave of ill feeling washed over him. His stomach twitched. Flashes of the blindfolds, ropes, train tracks, and trees reeled through his head. When he kicked the bedpost, Skeet flinched and stared at Jackie long and hard, then shrouded his head with the blanket.

"What do you want?" His tone filled with animosity.

"My grandpa's upstairs and he wants to see us…together," he replied in a tone icier than Skeet's question.

Skeet pulled the sheet back over his head and processed what Jackie said. The mention of Gabe drew sweat inside his casts; he grudgingly agreed.

The two boys moved toward the elevator together. When Jackie grabbed the handles to push the wheelchair, Skeet swatted his hand away and pushed on the big wheel with his one free hand.

At Gabe's room, Skeet told Jackie to go in first. He watched the colored boy pass through the door and approach the bed. Skeet stopped his wheelchair in the doorway and checked for creatures in masks. Jackie nudged Gabe to awaken him. Gabe rolled his head toward the sound of Jackie's voice, and a moment later noticed Skeet in the wheelchair by the door. Gabe mustered a slight smile and winked.

"I sees you has a friend wid you," Gabe said with an ever-so-slight nod toward the door. Skeet dropped his chin and grunted as he pushed hard on the wheel to pull up next to Jackie, still half expecting the creatures to pop out from behind the curtain in the middle of the room.

"Like you asked, Grandpa Gabe."

"You bring da' clue?" he said in a dry, raspy voice. He squinted; his eyes ached for restful sleep.

Jackie pulled out a wad of paper he had been fiddling with in his pocket. He looked at it and didn't remember it having any color to it. He unrolled the scrap and froze, briefly, then dropped the paper. He jammed his hands back into his pockets.

"What're you doing?" Skeet asked clearly annoyed.

Jackie continued to feel around in his pockets. Skeet looked down and saw the paper on the floor was the wrapper from a stick of Juicy Fruit gum. He looked up at Jackie and laughed.

"Where is it?" Jackie mumbled. He turned his pants pockets inside out. The contents—leaves, a broken match stick, a few stones, and a nickel—fell to the floor. He pinched down the very corner of his pocket and felt a wad. He dug at his pocket. This time he pulled out a ball of lint. "No!" he cried. "Where'd it go?" He dug to the tip of his other pocket and found nothing, not even lint. Then he remembered. When he was in the old man's house waiting for the ambulance to pick up Skeet, he moved the wadded clue into a watch pocket. He thumbed into the pocket and pulled out the balled-up clue from Ricky Clemonds.

"What do it say?"

Jackie studied the letters just as Ricky had written it and then read the note slowly with hopes Gabe would understand:

beyondcharl esfortd eepwa t er
rive runtili tsnakeswh e ntwo
shal lowr unsgo southandeast
l ooknorthcu tb elowthetur tle
beakru n toth eendwestst ep
 eleven ro ds.

"I can't read dis. It just be letters, Grandpa." Jackie scanned the lines of the message; Skeet leaned to look but Jackie turned the paper away. Jackie studied the paper intently for several minutes and never shared it with Skeet. In the end, he was able to splice the string of letters to form words.

"Grandpa, I think it say, 'beyond charlesfort deep water river until it snakes when two shallow runs go south and east look north cut below the turtle beak run to the end west step eleven rods.' "

Gabe's face went blank. "Read da' again, boy," Gabe said in a breathy whisper. He closed his eyes and listened.

Jackie reread the clue. When he finished, nobody spoke.

"Charlesfort? Da' be Charleston," Gabe offered, each word separated from the others with a breath.

Skeet pushed back in his seat and leaned against the cast on his arm. Like most things he heard or saw that involved Jackie, nothing made sense. He was more concerned with the old man. Since he was summoned to the bedside, he feared every facial twitch or slightest movement in the old man's hand could saddle him with a hex.

"Not sure, Grandpa. Maybe," Jackie answered cautiously.

"Could be here, too," Skeet added. He wheeled his chair to the foot of the bed.

Jackie turned toward Skeet. This was the first time Skeet had offered anything toward the project.

"Ain't that that place out there, the end of Parris Island?" Skeet said, his head bent back, staring at the ceiling, unwilling to address either of the two Negroes in the room. "Out there where they say somebody built a fort way back centuries ago. The French or the Spanish. One of them. Weren't that what they said in history class? I heard that somewhere." Skeet turned with an arrogant cockiness that belied his less than scholastic achievements.

"Da' too, could be," Jackie said, nodding and looking back toward his grandpa. "I remembers da', Grandpa Gabe. So maybe not Charleston. Maybe here by de marine base because da' fort was on de Beaufort River, da' 'deep water' an' it winds around into Beaufort," Jackie said. "Da' could fit. Right?"

He got no response from Gabe who laid there with his eyes closed. Skeet offered an *I-told-you-so* look.

"Then it says, 'When two shallow runs go south and east.' What shallow runs? Does it mean the river gets shallow somewhere? Somewhere south or east or where?" Jackie dropped the paper on the bed, crossed his arms, and shook his head.

"Hey, boy, come here," Skeet said as he began to turn his wheelchair back toward the door. Gabe opened his eyes and formed a circle with his lips like he was blowing out a candle.

Skeet caught the look and added pleasantly, "Jackie, give me a hand." For the first time Skeet used Jackie's name in a tone that came across as nothing less than friendly. "Out here. On the wall. There's a map," Skeet said as wheeled himself into the hall. "I can't reach it. Take that thing off the wall and bring it in."

Jackie had a pained look on his face, uneasy about removing the wall hanging, but, after checking for hospital staff, he did as Skeet suggested. He placed the framed nautical chart on the bed, down opposite Gabe's head so he and Skeet could study it. The chart was full of numbers, depth soundings labeled in feet up and down every waterway shown. The depths of the Beaufort River were, by far, the deepest but grew smaller or shallower closest to the shores and along the marshes.

" 'Shallow runs,' " Jackie softly echoed over and over, leaning above the map with his hands on the bed.

"Shut up," Skeet said, "just shut up!"

Jackie stopped talking and noticed Skeet couldn't get close enough to the map to read the depths. His chair was too low to trace the patterns of land, water, and marsh.

"Put that frame here in my lap so I can see..." He caught himself from saying "boy." Instead he said, "Jackie."

Jackie placed the frame in Skeet's lap and leaned it against the bed.

"See here, the river is pretty straight until it gets here, by town, then it winds around."

"Yeah, looks like a snake," Jackie chimed in.

"No foolin'. So shallows from there..."

The boys studied the depths.

"Dey get shallow by de shore, but de shore don't run east and south; it goes all over. These here creeks. See all de creeks da' comes off de river, dey get shallow. And here dey are two da' run east and south, sorta," Jackie added, pointing to a spot on the map.

Skeet shook his head and pointed to another spot. "Yeah, sure. And here." He slapped the chart with his flat hand and started again. "And here...and here," he said repeatedly as he slid his finger along the blue trace of the river to other points that matched the nebulous wording of the clue. Jackie simply looked.

"It say, 'look north. Cut...' So from dem places ef we look north dey would be a cut. You know, like through de marsh or something, not over land."

The boys checked the map again. For each location they pointed out, they looked north. Two spots showed cuts through the marsh, but they could not decide which cut best fit the clue.

Jackie noticed Gabe tapping the sheets with his arthritic finger. "Show me da' map," he whispered. He rolled to his side and pointed toward the floor below his eyes.

Jackie placed the frame on the floor near the head of the bed. Gabe motioned. "Closer so I can see." Jackie lifted it closer to the mattress, less than a foot from Gabe's chin. He was too weak to hold his eyelids open; they drifted shut several times before Gabe spoke, very slowly.

"When I be a boy I fish dey, by da' turtle beak place." He closed his eyes and ran his tongue over his cracked lips. "Ain't heard da' no more."

"Where, Grandpa? What spot? Dis one?" Jackie said as he pointed. When Gabe opened his eyes a slit, Jackie moved his finger. "Or here?"

"Da' spot. Da' first..." Gabe's soft, breathy voice faded.

Jackie sensed Gabe was tiring. Then he moved his finger back down to the spot lower on the chart and imagined the geography as a turtle.

"That ain't it. Ain't no turtles there," Skeet said. He looked at the old man with scorn. "He don't know anything."

"Skeet, he didn't say dey was turtles and dis here clue don't say dey was turtles, it say—"

"I heard what it says and I—"

Saliva driveled from the corner of Gabe's mouth as he rolled his head to the left. His eyes bored into Skeet. Gabe groaned. He took in a deep breath before his lips moved. "I sees de turtle. I ain't says dey is turtles dey. I says it be look like de turtle beak. Look, boy. Look da' map."

Skeet shuddered when the Negro referred to him as a boy. He pushed Jackie out of the way with his extended plastered leg to wheel closer to the talker. "I says I don't see no dang turtle and there ain't no turtles there, ya crazy old coon." Skeet leaned as close as he could get to

Gabe's ear. "You ain't got no mind, nor no memory. You're just a crazy old man what has this boy of yours all jazzed up 'bout somethin' that ain't real…and you know it!"

Jackie grabbed the handles of the chair and yanked it back away from Gabe. Skeet held fast to the wheel to keep it from rolling. When Jackie pulled harder, the locked wheels slid across the floor. Skeet grabbed hold of the bed sheets to keep from moving back. The farther Jackie pulled, the more he exposed Gabe's bare chest, the ribs protruding like a washboard covered with tobacco leaves. Jackie wrestled the sheets out of Skeet's hand and recovered Gabe.

"You just as dumb as him, boy. You believe everything that old Gullah man tells you. That ain't no clue. There ain't no treasure. You been nothin' but trouble for me since that first day," Skeet added, forgetting how Jackie had saved his life only a few days ago. "And you better do as I told you with the police, boy. I warned you."

Jackie stepped back from Gabe and pushed against Skeet's broken leg. "It be too late, Skeet. I already told de chief exactly what happened."

"He won't believe you, boy."

"Oh, he did 'cause I told him how you jumped me, tied me up, blindfolded me. I told him all da'. Then I told him how you forced me to go wid you onto da' Mr. Swanson's boat da' time when I got caught and you ran away. I told him you broke into de Castle and ran away. I told him you made me and Ricky go wid you," Jackie said. He slapped Skeet's leg-cast. "I told de chief everything. I told him 'bout de time out on Lands End, too. And I told him every time you does something you fail an' run away. You always be runnin' away." Jackie could feel his heart beating in his ears. "You just a chicken, Skeet. A big ole chicken."

Skeet pushed halfway out of his seat, toppled, and landed back in the webbing of the chair. He tried a second time. This time Jackie elbowed him back down. Skeet's eyes went totally round.

"Why, you dumb nig—"

"Shut up, Skeet. Just sit dey. You goin' to help wid dis clue and—"

"I ain't helpin' you with nothing, ya—"

Gabe drowned out Skeet's words with a hack capped with one cautionary word, "Hush!" The coughing didn't stop. He barked and hacked and struggled for minutes. Jackie gently patted on his back like his mamma did for him when he had a cold, but it didn't help. Gabe wasn't able to breathe. Jackie stuck his head out the door to find a staff nurse. For a Negro to holler for help in a hospital would be like yelling "Shark!" from the bottom of a pool. He ducked back in the room. Gabe lay back against the pillows. His chest jerked with deep, stubborn movements, cheating death one short breath at a time. As he lay there, eyes closed, Gabe's withered hand appeared, from under the starched sheets, holding a raven feather. With a slight twist of his wrist, Gabe slashed in Skeet's direction. Skeet froze.

"You be scared, Gundy boy. What you scared of?" Gabe's words stumbled out between lips that never seemed to open and cheeks that crowded his tongue. From anyone else the voice would be nothing more than a hushed mumble; from the colored man fighting from death's doorstep, it was the breath of life finding its way home. A pause. A breath. "You scared 'cause people be hateful at you ef you ain't mean to dem." Pause. Deep breath. "You scared of school 'cause you don't know nothin'…an' you fail…jus' like you…scared of colored people…'cause you don't knows us…an' you fail," Gabe said with extended pauses between words.

He waited to continue. His breathing grew slower, shallower still. Something more than strength lifted his head off the pillow. His eyes, resurrected from behind their lids, found Skeet slouched in the wheelchair.

"Stupid old man," Skeet fired back with flared nostrils and wide unblinking eyes. "Ain't nothin' true 'bout what you say." He grabbed the wheel of his chair and pivoted toward the door. Jackie grabbed the handles and spun the chair around to face Gabe.

"We de same color on de inside…just as you is. Ain't no difference." Pause. Breath.

"Dey be a place…where de mens wid black skin own dey own thoughts." Pause. Breath.

"Where dey walk…an' work…an' bring life to dis here world." He coughed.

"Where dey farm de earth…an' raise dem cows. Where dey…praise de God da' saves dem." Pause.

"Dat same God…what white peoples praise."

Gabe's words roiled in Skeet's head. He grabbed the wheel again and tried to yank away, but Jackie held tight and pushed the chair closer to the bed, just outside of arm's reach. He tilted the chair back and bounced the chair a few times to settle Skeet, who swatted at Jackie to get free. When he saw Gabe slice the raven feather in his direction, he stopped, and stopped breathing.

"De raven visit you?" Gabe whispered. "You say you obey?"

Skeet began to breathe long, deep breaths through his mouth. His heart ticked faster and faster, racing fear.

"You be scared of de truth…'cause of da' place"— Gabe nodded—"da' detention home place."

Skeet turned away, then looked up at Jackie, who now stood next to the wheelchair. He had never been cornered by two Negroes. He did what he could to avoid their eyes, but there was no escape. The more he looked around the room, the more he looked inside his own head.

"You be scared of da' detention home place," Gabe said again, slower. This time he lifted the feather in his hand and tipped it toward Skeet.

The walls seemed to close on him. As the room shrank, it began to lose its color; eventually it went completely white. Everything went white. He stared open eyed, blinded by the whiteness.

When Gabe spoke, Skeet heard words reverberate in his head. *You leave now an' de hex go wid you.* As Gabe's voice echoed, then faded, the events of the long night played out like a three-ring circus in his mind, and the sounds of a weird honking calliope grew louder and louder. His mind's eye saw the feather in Gabe's hand grow into a living, breathing raven. And the whistles from the calliope soured off-key into deafening croaks of the angered bird, all sights and sounds meant only for Skeet. Skeet tilted his head back to witness the wrinkled, jittery lips of the old man. His words dragged out, a slow speed deep voice like a single record playing at album speed, 33 rpm. *You be scared.* Skeet swallowed hard and began a slow, penitent confession.

"I ain't got no place to go. I ain't got no family. My pa—my real pa—beat me all the time." He followed his words with a deep exhale. "He told me that there weren't no room for colored 'round here. They was animals an' I should treat them like animals. He told me if I didn't treat them like animals, he would treat me like one." Skeet looked away and ran his tongue across lips. "Only way to survive was to fight back. That made it worse." He rubbed his eyes with his hand, then looked up at Jackie. "The chief is going to tell the probation people and I'll be sent back up the river," Skeet said, lost in the thought. He turned back to Gabe. "Yeah, I'm scared. Scared I'll go back and not get out again. Scared that hex, the birds, all that will mess with me."

Jackie stood away from the chair, unaware of what prompted Skeet to open up. He waited for Gabe.

"I can change. I will change. And I can make my friends change, too," Skeet said, wiping his eyes with his free forearm. "If I try, try hard to believe in the treasure thing, and if I help find the treasure, can you help me?" His face was raw-red from the tears—and fear. Lost for words, he waited, rolled closer, then slowly reached forward and placed his hand on the back of Gabe's, conscious of the outstretched feather.

"Follow de clue," Gabe said as he slid his hand and the feather back under the sheets.

Jackie didn't hesitate to refocus the session. He lifted the frame and placed it back in Skeet's lap.

"Here, dis be where Grandpa Gabe say de turtle's beak be. See here," he said, tracing what appeared to be the beak of a loggerhead turtle common to coastal beaches in the Lowcountry. Skeet was quick to agree.

"If that's the beak, this here would be the cut, maybe, like the clue says," Skeet added, pointing to a small branch of a waterway that pointed north off the river. He pulled back and studied the chart. "I know that spot. That's the inlet that runs up alongside the Castle. Yeah, it runs right up there."

Jackie stretched to look around Skeet.

"But what do it mean, 'west step eleven rods'?" Jackie asked.

The two boys pondered the chart trying to make sense of the words in the clue.

"Beats me," Skeet said as he shifted in his chair. Using his elbow, he lifted his backside off the leather web. He sighed at the brief airing. "You sure that code is right? I mean—"

"I don't know. It be what Ricky said. We might should ask Ricky. Maybe rod is a code word, too," Jackie suggested. He looked at Gabe, his breath steady and relaxed.

"What in the Lord's name do you boys think you're doing? Who said you could take that frame off the wall?" the nurse asked from the hall outside the room. "And what are you doing to that poor man?"

Jackie recognized her; she was the nurse that ran him through the third degree every time he came to visit Gabe.

"This is a very sick man. You boys shouldn't even be in here," she said, entering the room. Deborah Callahan gave Jackie a not-so-gentle shove away from the bed. She grabbed the frame with one hand and a handle on the back of Skeet's wheelchair with the other. "Now y'all get out of here"—she turned toward Jackie—"and don't let me catch you with any more stunts like this. You hear me?"

Jackie nodded.

Outside the room Jackie hesitated and looked back at his grandpa. He suddenly remembered his lies to Gabe. When he stepped back toward the room, Nurse Callahan blocked his path.

"Where do you think you're going, young man? I said go. Leave the poor man alone. Push your friend here back to his bed and you go on home. Now!"

Jackie snuck another look around the wide-bodied nurse, then snatched the handles of the wheelchair. They took the elevator down to the first floor and back to the vacant ward. Alone in the large bay of empty beds, Jackie felt it fitting to lie to Skeet and tell him he had not said anything to the chief, not yet anyway, but the chief wanted to see him back after the weekend.

CHAPTER 32

The drop in the temperature made the Christmas parade more colorful and seasonal, though the kids had hoped for snow. Floats of all shapes and sizes, bands from local schools, and dignitaries wearing Santa hats with kids bundled warmly rode in open convertibles, waving and throwing peppermint candies at red-cheeked children along the route. More than the December breeze chilled James Endelson as he read names off the granite obelisk in the Beaufort National Cemetery.

"Family?" a voice said.

Endelson turned.

"Any of those Yankees relatives of yours?" a large man said as he walked around to the other side of the monument.

"No," Endelson replied, thinking it an odd question from a southern stranger.

"Any named Coyote? Does that ring a bell, kid?"

Endelson's eyes lit up. The voice. It was Coyote. "*Sí, señor*," Endelson replied, authenticating with the Spanish affirmation. He moved to put a face with the voice.

"Stay over there. Listen. If anybody comes this way, I'm walking off. You stay here and make conversation with them."

"Yeah."

"Give it to me. Things are moving fast."

"Wiretap confirmed the target, 'Footprint.' Well, lots of talk about Senator Thurmond. Due here in a couple weeks. Calls from the lawyer." Mole quickly summarized the calls.

"Where was he calling? Who was on the other end?"

"Not sure. Like I said the calls went to several numbers, including the hospital."

"Facts! That's why you're out there, kid. I need to know. You have blown this before. I don't need no puny uncredentialed, untested, rookie snoop feeding me bogus poop for the Director. Other sources told me about Thurmond. I need you to get facts. Thurmond is coming to this cemetery."

Endelson could see the man across from him flailing his arms. He leaned to look around the stone; the man with the voice turned his back.

"Okay, here's the deal, Sherlock. You get to work. Get to know this cemetery. I don't care what you tell those people at Penn Center, you get down here and memorize every tombstone, every monument, every hole in this place. All of that and plan to be here when it goes down. *Comprende, niñito?*"

The speaker didn't wait for a reply. He stepped around the base of the monument. Endelson recognized him immediately. It was the *Wile E. Coyote* treasure hunter. "If you screw this one up, you can dig that low profile of yours six feet under," Geordie Swanson said as he walked past Endelson and kept walking headed for the main gate.

"Go ahead, Coyote," the switchboard operator said, barely audible above the static in the phone line.

Before Coyote could speak, the voice on the other end said, "I have two minutes and only two minutes. Don't waste my time. Give me facts, no more of the hearsay you've been sending in over the wire."

"Yes, sir. Facts. Our wiretap picked up those specifics you'd asked about earlier."

"Go ahead."

"The tap intercepted a conversation that talked about Senator Thurmond. Mainly discussing how he switched parties and the impact that has had on the coloreds."

"And?"

"There was some interference with the tap, but the lawyer was talking to another male, may have heard the voice somewhere earlier. Will have the lab parse the tapes and identify the voice."

"Did you do a trace on the call? At least nail down the other end. Where he called?" the Director asked.

"The call came in from a phone at the Beaufort Hospital. A check of the line located it at a nursing station, not an office. Could have been anybody, but will have the lab do more analysis on it."

"What else?"

"The interference and background noise presented some problems, but we do know the discussion was about a kidnapping plan. The plan, to quote the caller, was to 'enlighten him' and 'make him see things their way.' I assume the 'him' referred back to Senator Thurmond."

"Can't let them do that."

"Yes, sir, we know. They mentioned snatching him once the crowd forms. Senator Thurmond is scheduled for a visit to the National Cemetery in Beaufort after he visits Charleston. That would be their best shot at this. Sounds like they have details for a distraction and escape."

"The last time you gave me a kidnapping report it was wrong. Flat wrong. I want a tail on that lawyer—what was that name again—twenty-four hours a day starting the minute the senator arrives in South Carolina."

"Yes, sir. His name is Robert Caplin. He's a well-known and highly active colored attorney here, well-respected by the Negroes in this area," Coyote said.

"Okay, well, you're not to let him get near Thurmond. 'Only dead fish flow with the tide.' I want you out in front of this one. If they kidnap Thurmond, we'll be the laughingstock of the country. He's got enough to handle with all the peckerheads on Capitol Hill clamoring down his throat about his intentions with his party switch, Communists, Martin Luther King, and all. Keep me posted. Gotta go."

The dial tone hummed in his ear. Coyote cradled his phone and had a follow-up meeting with a close friend, Jack Daniels.

CHAPTER 33

After school for days, Jackie would sit with Grandpa Gabe at the hospital. When Gabe slept, Jackie went over the code, trying to make sense of what Ricky had shown him. Finally, on Monday, Jackie pummeled Ricky with questions to make sense out of the decoded clue. The more questions Jackie asked, the more frustrated Ricky became. Loud voices shouted mixed-up messages inside Ricky's head. Finally, they were too much for him. He grabbed his head, got up, crawled to the corner of his room, sat with his back toward Jackie—cross-legged, Indian style—and gnawed on his bottom lip.

"That's the answer. That's the answer. That's the answer," he said, a mantra of some sort to meditate on the code. Over and over Jackie asked him how he knew it was the answer. Ricky simply bobbed in his place, munched on his lip, and repeated his assertion until Jackie decided he wasn't getting anywhere and went home.

Tuesday, Jackie tried again; this visit proved more profitable. Ricky recreated what he had shown Jackie earlier, the code pairings he had used to crack the code. Jackie was amazed that Ricky, who found it difficult to tie his shoes without assistance, could design a key that would unlock the cipher. Jackie specifically asked Ricky about the last line in the code, the reference to the word

341

rod. Neither of the boys could make sense of the term; Ricky's mother was at a loss as well. None of them considered looking in the dictionary for a standard usage. They assumed the definition to be something related to fishing since the clue was based on water and a river. It wasn't until the next day when the boys visited Gene Skyles at the motel that it all became clear.

"A rod is a unit of measure," the researcher told them, dictionary in hand. "According to this, a single rod is about sixteen and a half feet. So, if we substitute that for the word rod in Ricky's clue, it would say 'west step one hundred and eighty-one and a half feet.' "

The three of them looked at a map that Jackie had picked up at Griffin's Sinclair Station on Bay Street—they were free. It showed the small inlet that ran off the Beaufort River and up near the Castle.

Though it gave them a general idea of where to look, they needed to confirm their assumptions on the ground. Skyles suggested they visit the Castle. They could explain to the Dansons their interest in walking around in the yard and possibly a request to dig in order to uncover the treasure. Jackie cringed. He recalled the last visit to the Castle—the dog and the cloud that sucked up Ricky.

"No, we shouldn't go dey, Mr. Skyles," he said, his innards quickly cinched by the suggestion.

Skyles raised his eyebrows and said, "But, Jackie, this really looks like you are onto something here. It's your research. You need to go there to—"

"Well, but…dey has a dog."

"Big dog. Yeah. Mean Dog. Can't go there. Big dog," Ricky said. He stepped backward and pressed himself against the wall.

Skyles looked from one boy to the other.

"How did you..." he stopped short. He recalled the session in the police station when Ed Danson reported someone had vandalized the Castle. He turned to Ricky. "When did you go there?"

"A ghost lives there. Yeah," Ricky said. He bowed his head and bobbed his chin against his throat. "A good ghost. Gauche. Yeah. Good Gauche. Gauche is good ghost."

Jackie didn't say anything. He opted to just shrug his shoulders and act just as lost as Skyles.

"I know they have a dog, a big dog. I've seen Mr. Danson walk him. Don't worry. I'll go with you. I'll talk to the Dansons. But I think, since this is your project, you two need to be the ones to investigate your lead, like my research and the leads I find. I need to track those down, too. Maybe Miss Forten would want to go since she assigned the project. She might have an interest, too. Ask your parents if I can take you there tomorrow after school."

The boys nodded. Ricky clapped his ten fingertips together with his eyes closed. His smug grin offered a different expectation than Jackie's look of dread.

The Castle, in daylight, was a work of art nestled in natural beauty. The vastness of the lawn. The huge brick structure with massive stone columns. The boxed hedges and palmettos in the side garden. The enormous live oak, largest in all of Beaufort. Though Jackie recognized all of this, his attention was continuously drawn toward the right side of the house where he and Skeet had entered through the windows, and near the marsh grass where Ricky's ghost had materialized, if there was a ghost; for Jackie it was a cloud.

Edward Danson leaned against the door of the Castle and puffed steadily on his coveted, smuggled Cuban cigar as Mary Alice Forten introduced herself, Gene Skyles, and the two teenage boys who stood farther back on the porch near the staircase. After her introduction she immediately launched into the purpose for the visit, which Danson didn't fully appreciate.

"This is some kind of joke or something, right? I mean—"

"Sir, I promise you this is far from a joke. This is education," the petite redhead replied. Undaunted, she planted her two feet a comfortable distance apart in line with her shoulders—erect and squared. With her arms at her sides, she looked dead into the eyes of Ed Danson and laid out her instructional objectives for the project assignment. Throughout her pitch Danson shot glances over her head, more interested in the two teens, especially the Negro. "I've seen you before, haven't I, boy? At the police station. Didn't I?"

Jackie feared Danson would notice. He shoved his thumbs into the waistband of his trousers behind his back, looked at his feet, and replied, "Yes, sir."

Before Skyles could confirm that meeting, Mary Alice glanced back at Jackie, then spoke up. "Mr. Danson, I am sure that was all a mistake and—"

"Little lady, don't tell me what it was. This is my house. Someone broke in, damaged property," the owner said as he pointed toward Jackie.

"Sir, I am sure that was a mistake. Jackie Eddings is a fine boy, eh…a fine student. He would never—"

"Well, child, I beg to differ with you. The police think this boy was involved."

"Sir, I was there in the police station for that meeting as well," Skyles said, drawing the fire away from the teacher. "As Miss Forten said, it was probably a case of mistaken identity and—"

"There was proof, wasn't there, boy?" Danson said with his eyes only slits below a brow that looked like one long wooly pully caterpillar.

Jackie turned his head to the side when he heard the jingle of a dog collar from inside the house. A moment later Hitchcock appeared at the door and sat next to his owner's feet. Ricky took a step back and hid behind Jackie, but never lost sight of the dog.

Forten wasn't sure of how to proceed. "Sir, please, whatever happened in the past was certainly a misunderstanding or an innocent mistake, but these boys and another classmate currently in the hospital were given a group project in my classroom. They have researched for months. I know they have done a remarkable job with this piece of local folklore."

"Miss Forten did you say?" Danson asked.

The teacher nodded.

"Miss Forten, my family has been in this house since the end of the Civil War. You are standing on hallowed ground here. I am the caretaker of my family's good fortune and I'm not about to dishonor them by letting some teens"—he looked up and added—"and a vandal come onto my property and destroy a century of tender loving care," he stated amid puffs behind the red glow of his cigar tip.

"Mr. Danson, I appreciate what you and your family have done to preserve the history and charm of the Castle. That's part of the reason I assigned this project." She looked back at the boys, still standing well to the rear. She turned back toward Danson, standing taller than she had before. "I want these young men and all of my students to appreciate the history of the Lowcountry and the folklore of the Gullah people. I intentionally gave this project to an integrated team to promote racial harmony, understanding, and acceptance. The students on this team have done an exceptional job of research, best of any team in my class. We're all excited about their efforts and they are ninety-nine percent certain they know where the treasure is."

A great blue heron startled Ricky when it lifted out of the marshy inlet next to the Castle. He poked Jackie, but Jackie wouldn't turn to watch the six-foot wingspan flap slowly through the yard.

"Integrated? Now why in the world would you want to integrate these kids? And isn't he the only colored boy in the school?"

"It may seem a small gesture, but it's a big deal for these kids to see how Negroes perform. To learn that they have talent, too, and, given the right chances, they can perform just as well as white kids." She voiced her defense without taking her eyes off Danson. "It's a giant step for this school board…and it's the law."

"Just so you know, Miss Forten, I was not and am not a supporter of that school board's decision. I think things were going along absolutely fine the way they were."

Mary Alice quickly returned the discussion to a more personal level. "Mr. Danson, you like history, I mean, you must. You live in it." She smiled.

Danson looked over his shoulder, down the porch toward the far end of the house, and nodded.

"And history said during the Great Skedaddle slaves rounded up precious items abandoned by the white folks when they ran out of town. Those slaves buried a lot of things. What's to say they didn't bury things right here?" She turned and gestured with her arm outstretched toward the lawn behind her.

"Well, they did bury things here, under the outbuilding, out where the cookhouse, well the kitchen, was," Danson said in a protracted southern drawl. He wrinkled his nose to fend off a sneeze. "And the Yankees used that building as a morgue. May have even planted some of them dead Yankee soldiers right here, too."

"The boys' research suggests the treasure buried here—what they believe is buried here—could be much older than that," Gene Skyles interjected from the side. "Sir, I don't believe I have mentioned that I'm a PhD candidate myself and I know how tough it is to research. I can vouch for these boys both in their approach and their character and—"

"Where?"

"Sir?"

"Where are you in school? What are you researching?" Danson asked.

"Oh. I'm at the University of Virginia, researching writings of Edgar Allan Poe," Skyles said, again hoping to divert the discussion away from Mary Alice.

"Virginia! Good god, son. I should close this door right now. This is Tiger Country. Clemson Tigers!" Danson said with a wry but snobbish expression. "Now I'll tell you this whole thing is nuttier than a screen door on a submarine. I must admit I appreciate your work with these kids, Miss Forten, and your project idea just might be a good step forward, but there won't be any digging on this property." Danson turned to go back inside.

Mary Alice grabbed Danson by the arm before he could get through the door. He turned and scanned her body from head to toe.

"History is what this town is, Mr. Danson. You and the Castle are history. This town under seven different flags, that's history," she rushed to say, her calm, cool, collected persona drifting away with the cigar smoke in the late autumn breeze. "This town is about Reconstruction, about Penn Center, and the Port Royal Experiment. This is our history and these kids need to know and learn to appreciate it."

Danson blew a cloud of smoke over his shoulder and bent forward to be closer to the teacher. "And I am not a part of all of that," he grumbled. "If you owned this place and had put all the work into it, would you want kids digging it up looking for buried treasure of all things? Come on, Miss Forten. Grow up." He reared back and took a hefty drag on his cigar.

"I can control the digging, Mr. Danson," Gene Skyles said, coming to the teacher's defense. "I've been on digs. I can control all the efforts. We can cut squares of sod. I will bring tarps and all the dirt will go onto tarps, then all will be replaced without any noticeable damage."

Danson leaned against the door frame and watched squirrels bury nuts along the wrought iron fence by the street. Finally, things seemed to sink in. He looked down at Skyles, then paused in thoughtful silence before he said, "How much digging? What are we talking about? How will it be done?"

"The boys, with their fathers, will dig down, three maybe four feet in a trench." He knew they would probably dig deeper and wider, but for the sake of gaining Danson's approval, he underestimated the effort. "Only a shovel-width wide. If they don't find anything, they'll replace the dirt and sod and select a different location nearby."

"Trenches? How many?"

"Well, that depends on what they find."

"They're not going to turn this yard into a checkerboard. No way. No how. Limits. Set limits."

"Okay, sir, no more than a dozen."

"A dozen?" he huffed. "Six. You get six trenches. If you don't find it, you're done." Danson took a deep drag on his cigar. "What's in this treasure anyhow? What's it worth? I get to keep what they find, right?"

There was an extended pause where facial expressions communicated the unspoken words.

"Mr. Danson, this is the boys' project. They are fairly certain the treasure is located here. The contents of the treasure remain unknown," Mary Alice Forten said. "The treasure could be trinkets or memorabilia, pre-Civil War. It could be gold or silver or both." She hesitated and looked back at the boys, then back to Danson. "It was their assignment. They did the research. Whatever they find, whatever is in the treasure, should be theirs, wouldn't you agree?"

"Agree?" Danson barked. "Not on your life. No deal, little lady," He came out of the doorway and onto the porch. His aggression forced Forten and Skyles backward toward the steps. "This is my property and what you find on my property is mine. Simple as that."

"Mr. Danson, if I may," Skyles spoke up. "In my research I've run across many situations similar to this where the current property owner felt entitled to any items of value found on the property. Seems reasonable, but sir, that's not the case."

Danson scowled.

Skyles continued, "I'd like to offer something a lawyer gave me when I first encountered a similar situation." Skyles pulled his notepad from his jacket pocket. He thumbed through a number of pages, then stopped. "According to the law, it states 'property which is verifiably antiquated gold, silver, or money that has been concealed for so long that the original owner is either dead or unknown is considered a treasure trove and not necessarily the property of the owner.' " He closed his pad.

Ed Danson puffed harder on his cigar. "Not necessarily how I see it."

"I can only cite what the law reads. I don't write it myself," Skyles retorted.

"We'll see about that, Mr. Skyles. I'll have my attorney provide his opinion. We can discuss this further tomorrow. Right now I need to walk Hitchcock. Tomorrow. Same time."

Mary Alice Forten stepped forward and extended her hand with a determined look. "Yes, sir. That would be fine," she replied without asking the others in the group. After a quick, firm handshake, she turned and led the foursome down the stairs, across the brick walk, and out the front gate.

Danson puffed on his cigar *The kid is nuts. They're all nuts. And suckers. Maybe both.*

CHAPTER 34

Edward Danson watched the group stroll up the Castle walk the following afternoon. Slumped deep in a white wicker armchair, Danson had them join him—and Hitchcock—at the end of the porch. Forten and Skyles eased themselves into two chairs similar to Danson's; the boys sat next to them on the porch floor. The dog crouched with a soft and steady growl by Danson's feet.

"I assume you've talked to a lawyer," Mary Alice Forten said with no cordial greeting and only a half-smile.

Danson flicked the ash from his ever-present cigar and responded in similar fashion. "I did and he said the treasure is not my property." Ricky began to clap with hands balled up until Danson finished speaking. "But the land is and I say no digging."

"Why no digging? We found it. It's ours," Ricky grumbled.

Jackie pulled on his jacket sleeve. "Shh!"

Forten turned toward Ricky, then back toward Danson in his chair. "Why? Why the change? Yesterday you seemed to be okay when Mr. Skyles outlined how he would control the site and efforts."

"Because…" Danson labored on the word like it was a clarion announcing what was to come. "It's my property and I want to know more about this project, this crazy notion of a Gullah treasure. I want to hear how and why you think you need to dig here before I agree to anything,"

Mary Alice exhaled and started. "I assigned the Gullah treasure project to this group because Jackie is the first Negro student to enter Beaufort Junior High and I thought he could share—"

"Wait. This isn't your project. You said it was the boys' project. If you think they've done their homework and this guy here—what was your name again?" Danson asked, conveniently not recognizing Skyles.

"Gene Skyles, sir."

"If Mr. Skyles here thinks these boys have done good research, let's let them tell me."

Ricky looked at Jackie and immediately pulled his knees to his chest, wrapped his arms around them, and ducked his chin in behind.

"I want this colored boy to tell me about his project," Danson said with sour eyes. "What can you tell me that I don't already know, boy?"

Jackie looked at Mary Alice. She smiled and winked back. He stood and began to speak. "Sir—"

Danson came out from behind his smoke screen and said, "Sit down, boy. Tell me what this is all about."

"Mr. Danson, sir, our project was to research de...uh...the Gullah treasure," Jackie started and went on to explain everything they had learned about the legend. He touched on how they connected their ciphered clue to Edgar Allan Poe, then Gene Skyles stepped in.

"So, you see, I have an interest in this research project, too. A Poe connection," Skyles added.

"Poe! And the boy says you have a letter you think Poe sent to Mr. Lembath in Beaufort, huh?"

Skyles and the boys all nodded.

"Well, see that house there, straight out across the yard on the other side of the street?" Danson said, pointing with his cigar to the white house on the corner opposite the Castle. "That's the Lembath House. Owned by William Lembath. One of the first houses down here on The Point. Built even before this house. But, go on, boy."

Jackie finished his explanation, ending with the last line of the clue and how they believed the treasure was somewhere at the Castle.

"So you say the treasure...you think it is right here?" Danson said, waving his arm off to his right toward the prized ornamental garden in the side yard.

"No, sir. With the clue that Jackie just read to you, we calculated the distance from that point there, by that bush"—Skyles pointed toward the marsh inlet to the left—"in about one hundred and eighty feet in this direction, so probably on this side and just beyond the live oak there." He motioned toward the front lawn beyond the massive tree that shaded nearly everything.

Danson pointed to the front yard and began to cough. He pounded his chest with his fist and strained to say, "Nasty habit," choking and fanning the air in front of his nose. When he stopped, he took a series of short puffs and continued, "That's the area?" Skyles and the boys all nodded. "I'll let you dig there but I want you to share what you find, a fifty-fifty split."

"But the law... You just said..." Forten said with a raised voice, stunned by Danson's selfish offer, but she stopped when she heard Hitchcock's muffled growl.

Jackie cast a scornful look at the large white man. "Let's go, Ricky."

"No. I want to see the treasure. You said there was treasure. Show me. Show me the treasure," Ricky screamed. He stood up and started stomping his feet.

"You told me this man would give us the treasure. I want to see the treasure. We found it. It's our treasure. Show me the treasure."

Mary Alice stood and placed her hands on Ricky's shoulders to settle him. He stopped moving; she patted his back and continued.

"Wait a minute, Jackie," she said.

"But ef dis is de Gullah treasure don't da' mean we know who de owners is? De Gullah peoples, right? An' da' treasure belongs to dem, not Mr. Danson. Not nobody else," Jackie said to Forten. He looked over at Skyles and then looked at his hands. He felt a quiet sadness, the disappointment of failure. He recalled the voices raised in prayer, the shouts of the Gullah families inside the praise house. He thought of the Gullah people and the history of those that shouted there a century or more before. He thought on what his Grandpa Gabe had said about how he endured so much as a child and his parents and their parents even more. The treasure—if there really was a treasure—wasn't his to give away, to give to Danson. But he also remembered what Gabe had told him, that he had to work with the white people, the buckruh he called them.

Jackie looked at his teacher. "De Gullah people built dis town. Dey stayed in dis town. Dey rebuilt dis town. An' it was all taken from dem. De treasure could never be big enough to repay my Grandpa Gabe and all de Gullah people for what dey lost. Maybe it's better not to know, not to find it than to give it away. It belongs to de Gullah people. It's dey treasure." Jackie was sure of his words and spoke with more spirit than he had ever shown before.

"Hold on," Skyles said, calmly, eyeing Mary Alice.

"We did our project, Mr. Skyles. Miss Forten told me today she was going to have de *Beaufort Gazette* publish our research paper. I just needs to add we found it but we weren't allowed to dig."

"Now you wait right there, boy. I offered you a deal," Danson argued.

"I ain't de one to make de deal, Mr. Danson. I am one Gullah boy and I don't speak for all dem others." An impish smile blossomed on Jackie's face. "I am sure dey will finds a way to dey treasure once dey know where it is."

Hitchcock rolled over on his side and sniffed the bottoms of Danson's slippers. From inside a cloud of sweet tobacco smoke, Danson thought for a moment, a long moment. His eyes shifted around in a worried look as if they were tracking a mosquito in front of his face, then they closed and popped open quickly. Danson stared at Jackie with a frown that flipped upward in a smug grin. His eyes lit up. "I'm not going to be the one who sits here in this house, in the Castle, and argues that what your Gullahs or whoever buried here is mine.

"If that legend's true and that Gullah treasure is here, then you take it and you be sure the Gullah people get it." He used the stub of his cigar to point to Jackie. "You take it and you make it the biggest dang find in this town since the Great Skedaddle." He paused then shook his cigar at Jackie a second time. "And you make sure that teacher of yours there gives you an A-plus for your research."

"Me, too," Ricky added. "Me, too. I get an A-plus, too. I know the code and Gauche knows that, too."

Danson turned to Ricky with a curious look. "You bet, little fella. You get an A-plus, too."

Two days later on Saturday, while Skeet continued to convalesce in the hospital—Jackie had not bothered to keep him informed—Gene Skyles escorted the boys, along with their fathers, back to the Castle. Jackie pulled Ricky's Radio Flyer red wagon, loaded for a major dig— two D-handled shovels, a pick mattock with a taped wooden handle, a painter's tarp, and a coarse hemp rope that had seen its better days. Gene Skyles offered to help dig. Though he had no tools, he brought a new twenty-five-foot tape measure, wooden stakes, and a large ball of cotton twine he bought at Fordham's Hardware on Bay Street.

When they arrived, what they saw through the wrought iron gate took their breath away. The lawn beyond the live oak looked like the surface of the moon. Several shallow craters with piles of sand and shells littered what had been a manicured mat of green grass. The gate creaked as they slowly pushed through and spotted a large hole. It was over four feet deep and nearly six feet square. Scattered around the hole were bits of rotten timbers. Along the edge of the hole, two feet below the surface, they saw more chunks of aged, blackened wood.

"No treasure. No more. No more treasure," Ricky said, shifting in his normal sway. The fathers looked at each other, then at their sons. They stepped back from the hole to let the boys get closer. Jackie sat in the dirt; he couldn't take his eyes off the pit. Only one other person had a reason to dig up the perfect lawn, and only Ed Danson had any idea why he should. It had to be him.

Jackie jumped up, his face washed with dread. He headed for the stairs to the porch, his father Irvin close behind. Jackie suddenly stopped and looked at his father.

"What is it, boy? What's wrong?"

"It's Grandpa Gabe. I heard him. I heard him telling me—"

"Irvin! Oh my god! Oh Lord. Oh my Lord! Irvin?"

From the sidewalk on East Street, they could hear Hestelle Eddings's hysterical screams. Running, her dress flapping high, she rounded the corner in front of the Castle.

"Irvin? Jackie?" she screamed, looking around the property for her family. With only two Negroes present, she ran to them and collapsed to her knees, her head on the ground.

"Stelle, what?" Irvin begged as he reached down to help her to her feet.

Tears streaming down her face, gasping for air, she closed her eyes and leaned her head back and cried, "He's dead. Grandpa Gabe is dead."

CHAPTER 35

A t half past ten that night Joseph Palmer, Gabe's close friend and physician, along with Obadiah Whytsom, escorted his body from the hospital to his house. Met by scores of people, they placed his casket on the floor in the living room. The box, nothing more than four pieces of wood lined with a black cotton cloth, remained open to allow friends a proper farewell to Gabe, now little more than a skeleton vacuum sealed in ebony-foil skin. Before his body left the small room in the hospital, members of the Farmer's Club washed it, rubbed it with herbal oils, and dressed it in a white sheet, all done with much protest by the hospital staff. Around the room and throughout the small house, the mirrors had all been turned to the wall to deny any reflections of the corpse. On the stand close to where Jackie had found the box with the Poe letter, Robert Caplin had placed a bowl of water, a funeral ritual Gullahs believed to ward off the spirit and keep the ghost and other haints out of the house. From a low three-legged stool on the porch, Freddie Lembath, the vegetable vendor, thumped a haunting dull beat on a gourd drum to announce Gabe's death. In the shadows of the tree next to the house, a raven croaked its eerie reply.

Far more mourners than could fit in the tiny house appeared—tuh help shum cross obuh de ribbuh—so many that the modest front yard gave the appearance of a campsite. They drank, danced, gambled, and played games all night. Family, friends, guests, and curious but respectful others sang, prayed, preached, and shouted over the body, for without this celebration and a proper funeral the next day, the Gullah people believed Gabe's spirit would forever wander the Lowcountry, unable to enter the fourth and final stage in the circle of life, a transformation and rebirth where he would reunite with his ancestors.

Shortly after sunrise, the funeral coach from Wright-Donaldson Funeral Services snaked its way from the small house on Prince Street, across the swing bridge, and on to an overgrown, private cemetery on Saint Helena Island. Seven cars—with headlights on—managed an uninterrupted motorcade without escort by the police or sheriff's office who both pointed a finger toward the other as "their responsibility."

The open gate to the Pritchard Plantation leaned from one hinge, a sign of the times. The hearse plowed through the stubby overgrowth of oaks, hollies, sago palms, and palmettos along the seldom-used rutted lane toward the foundation of the plantation house—in its day one of the grandest sites on the island though it no longer held that privilege. Along the forsaken allée, monstrous live oaks appeared to bow in polite respect as the wooden casket of a friend they knew when they were mere saplings passed by.

With the shambles of the old house barely visible in the distance, the string of cars turned toward a private cemetery, worthless land Oliver Prichard set aside for the dozens of slaves he owned well before the Civil War. Rusted cars and piles of shells clustered near the remains of a barbed-wire fence marking the burial ground in the woods. The lead vehicle stopped before passing into the cemetery to allow the family time to ask their ancestors for permission to bring old Gabe in. When the spirits moved them, the Eddings family stepped out of their car and walked forward to the overly polished Cadillac Landau hearse. Other early arrivals joined them from the woods and many climbed out of the packed cars that followed from town. Dressed all in black, all with hats—men and women both—this was a Negro funeral. Only two white faces appeared, Mary Alice Forten and Gene Skyles. A third white face remained well to the rear, concealed and out of sight, but able to watch everything and everybody in the graveyard; it was Geordie Swanson, who kept his eyes on one attendee, Robert Caplin. Swanson had spent the night watching the lawyer from a safe distance away from the wake.

Pastor Titus McTurion hadn't even welcomed the mourners before the wailing shattered the stillness. Heads turned, only briefly, as cries rang throughout. Dozens of people stood packed tight, broken grave markers at their feet, congregated to witness the casket perched on shoots of bamboo. Women dabbed tears with perfumed white lace handkerchiefs.

"We come together today," the preacher started, "to bear witness da' our brother, Gabriel Sampson Pritchard, has done crossed over de river an' we, though sorrowed and saddened, bless his journey wid de loving reflection of de smiles he showed us."

"Ohhhhhh, Brother Gabe," a pained voice cried from the rear. "Lord have mercy on his soul," cried another.

The exchanges continued throughout the service. Every few words spontaneous cries rang out from the assembled. Titus McTurion paced his comments and blessings around the outbursts in an impromptu graveside eulogy of a man who had touched each of their lives from the day they were born. Untold numbers of shouts of "Amen" and "Oh Lord" coupled the sentences like conjunctions into one extremely long passage. When the pastor closed the worn black leather booklet he used at far too many committal services, for Gullahs decades younger than Gabe, a lone voice piped up and gave rise to a chorus in a familiar spiritual. Moved by the moment, the crowd swayed like a dune of sea oats as they sang. As the tempo increased, the ground began to heave when everyone—man, woman, and child—stomped their feet to shouts of praise. Body after body broke out of the mass and approached the casket. One couple passed a baby over the coffin. Others placed bottles, broken bits of colored glass, bleached seashells, and plates on the edge of the site. Dr. Palmer and a well-dressed Negro lady at his side poured pills from Gabe's medicine bottles into the grave. The pots used to wash the body were left to place on top of the grave. While people all around continued to sing and dance—only a small number slipped away—Hestelle Eddings, her torso covered by a long black lace veil, softly draped her hand over her nose to contain her cries. With her other hand she placed a long-stemmed white lily on top of Gabe's wooden box. As his mother walked away, in tears, comforted by her husband and swarms of other sympathizers, Jackie stayed behind, near the casket, lost in thought. He stood there and cried, proud and unembarrassed while others stepped around him, tapping on his head or shoulder, whispering their emotion-filled sentiments.

Five minutes or so passed. Geordie Swanson watched as the colored lawyer emerged from the well-wishers and approached the young boy. He watched as Caplin placed his hand on the boy's shoulder and gave a gentle squeeze, grabbed a wad of the boy's jacket, and motioned with a finger for Jackie to follow him away from the crowd. They headed toward an opening in the woods where the ramshackle remains of the plantation's last slave cabin, now little more than a shack, denied gravity its demise. Swanson thought it interesting that Caplin was with the Negro boy who, according to his friend Chief Heimer, had been involved in some way or another in several recent happenings around town.

Swanson had to move to keep Caplin in sight. The woods with the wait-a-minute vines, briar thickets, scrub oaks, and deadfall made it impossible to follow. An alternative was along the edge of the woods in full view of everybody in the cemetery, where he might encounter people as they returned to their cars tucked in the woods. His best choice was to move directly across the field. With luck he might go unnoticed.

His luck was not good. No sooner did he come out of the woods than Titus McTurion noticed. When the preacher stopped in the middle of a conversation with two of his congregation, all three turned their heads to watch this large white man striding across the field. Lucky for Swanson they did not say anything; he continued to move until Gene Skyles, escorting Mary Alice Forten back to the car, spotted him.

"Hey, Mr. Swanson," Skyles hollered with a wave. He excused himself from Mary Alice and ran over to Swanson, who stopped and shot a quick glance toward Caplin and the boy as they passed through the opening into the woods.

"Hey, I wanted to tell you the kids think they found that treasure. Remember? From that class when we talked? They were assigned to—"

Geordie Swanson hesitated, speechless, concerned that if he responded it would open a more casual and lengthy conversation he could not afford to have.

"Glad to hear it," was all he said. His head swiveled toward the woods and back, then toward the teacher, still a ways off, but headed toward them. "Looks to me like your teacher lady friend could use some comforting there, stud. Why don't you scoot on back to her? I gotta run."

Before Swanson could take a second step, Skyles stepped sideways to look back at Mary Alice. His movement inadvertently blocked Swanson.

"Sure," Gene Skyles said. "Just thought as the resident treasure hunter in Beaufort you might like to hear —"

"Yeah."

"Mr. Swanson," Mary Alice Forten yelled as she stepped closer. Half out of breath she continued, "I didn't see you earlier. Glad I caught you. So sad about Mr. Pritchard. I know he meant the world to the boy, Jackie, I mean."

Swanson looked up toward the woods. Nothing in sight.

"I'd like to have my class get a tour of your boat. Do you think—"

"I'd be glad to do it. Call me next week, but I need to go," Swanson said. He stepped around Skyles and continued his long strides toward the opening in the woods.

"Geez. Guess I'll just call him."

"Why is he here, I wonder?" Skyles questioned.

The white couple, as well as several of the Negroes still mourning in the cemetery, watched Geordie Swanson's thin tie flap over his meaty shoulder as he broke into a slow jog away from the crowd and through the gap in the trees.

Inside the tree line, Swanson paused for a quick look around for any sign of the lawyer and the boy. He glanced back toward the cemetery, where the pool of grieving Negroes continued to console one another. Unsure of what they might suspect if they saw a white man skulking in the woods, he continued on slowly toward the shack, the most likely place for the two to be.

Like most slave cabins, the bleached-gray front had a one-step porch, mostly weeds, and an opening the size of a door, though none remained. On the vine-covered side closest to Swanson, there was a hole where a window might have been. He crouched to the side and circled away in case someone might be inside watching. The intercepts from the wiretap led him to believe there was something shady going on with the lawyer, a good reason to approach slowly. When he heard the mumbo jumbo of voices inside, Swanson inched closer. He had no need to look in the window hole; cracks and spaces between the rotten slats offered more than peepholes. What he saw sent shivers up his spine.

The boy was positioned in the center of the floor on a stool that teetered atop a stack of debris; there was no sign of Caplin. A crude vest made of hemp rope and spartina grass replaced the shirt, jacket, and tie the boy had worn at the funeral. His head was covered with a helmet mask that looked like a beehive with a grass skirt. The lower front of the mask had a tiny face carved into it. A web of hemp straps that crisscrossed his lap pinched deep into his forearms and cinched against the tops of his legs. Swanson couldn't tell if the boy was gagged under the mask or just too petrified to make a sound. The voices came from the four figures who danced around the makeshift altar.

He remembered the chief told him the boy had been kidnapped before. He also remembered Mole, James Endelson, told him about the masked creatures he had seen in the woods by the praise house that night. The descriptions matched: hyena, water buffalo, a haystack, and some weird face draped in shells. Even with his trained ear, Swanson couldn't make out what the grassy creatures were saying. It was Gullah, no doubt; he had heard it regularly near the Piggy Wiggly in town. Geordie Swanson wondered what, if anything, any of this had to do with Caplin and Senator Strom Thurmond.

When the water buffalo stepped toward the pieces of the broken door on the floor and pulled out an ivory handled machete that he wielded like the blade of a helicopter, the others stepped away and started a freakish chant, arms raised overhead. Swanson's stomach gripped his Adam's apple and tied it to his knees.

"Hold it right there! FBI," Swanson yelled from outside the porch, badge in one hand, the other holding his standard issue .38 caliber Smith & Wesson aimed dead-center on the water buffalo. "All of you...keep your hands where I can see them. You...with the knife! Bend at the waist and place that blade nice and easy on the floor then back away...slowly!"

The beast-creature followed the instructions.

"Now, I want you to spread out, slowly. No quick moves. Leave space between each of you, then sit down with your legs straight out in front of you, spread wide, keep those arms high." They all did as he asked.

Swanson looked up at the boy but kept his revolver on the four others. "If you can hear me, boy, nod your head." Jackie nodded. "If you can talk, say something."

Silence. "Are you gagged? Nod your head." Jackie nodded. "Okay, well you're goin' to be okay just sit there. I'll take care of this. Just sit there and be quiet."

Swanson shook his head. Of course the boy was going to be quiet; he was gagged and tied up to a point he couldn't move anything but his eyeballs behind the mask.

He squeezed in behind his captives, out of their view, still unsure how they could see anything through the masks. He reached forward with his free hand and pulled the shell-face mask off. It was a skinny colored man with skin as black as any piece of coal he'd ever seen. Something told him he'd seen the face before. In town? On the water? Then it struck him. The guy from the dock. A shrimper. Obadiah Whytsom.

"You don't be doin'—"

"Shut up! All of you. No talking. Got that?" Swanson ordered. He dropped the mask behind him and moved to the next set of raised hands and tapped one arm with the snub-nose revolver. "Keep them up!" he said, then pulled off the second mask. It was Freddie Lembath. Swanson recognized him from the night before. He was the guy banging on the drum on the porch. Swanson didn't know his name, didn't really care to know it, yet. Lembath didn't move or make any comments; he did as he was told and kept his jittery hands high, higher than the others.

Swanson moved down the line to the "thing" that looked like a haystack. Lifting the mask, he was surprised, somewhat, to see the face of his mark, the Negro lawyer, Robert Caplin. "Ah, so we meet again, counselor."

The lawyer turned his head to the side to get a glimpse of Swanson.

"Keep your head and eyes to the front, Mr. Caplin. No need for you to go gazing around. Nothin' back here but us bulldogs and we aren't the least bit interested in turning this here show into a shootin' gallery. Convenient and all, being as we're here by a cemetery, but just do as you're told, Judge, and nothin' is going to happen to you…yet."

Caplin looked back to the front. His face, though Swanson couldn't see it, was one-dimensional, void of even the slightest emotion.

Only the water buffalo remained. As he stepped sideways toward the final masked figure, Geordie Swanson noticed the machete across the floor. Before he lifted the last mask, he stepped around and kicked the machete farther into the corner. Stepping back, he unveiled the last of the wooden-headed conspirators. Another Negro man, a familiar face he recognized. "Well, if it isn't our friendly local medicine man himself. The one, the only, Dr. Palmer in person. Why, I never would have recognized you in that getup. Nah, the machete was a giveaway. Anybody that can handle a blade like that is either a big game hunter or a doctor," Swanson chortled.

He stepped out from behind the foursome, weapon aimed for business. "Okay, all of you. Look straight ahead and slowly…very slowly, lower your hands. Place them behind your head." In unison, they did as they were told. Geordie Swanson looked toward Jackie. He hesitated and looked back toward the ghillie-suited quartet.

"Okay, Judge, I want you to crawl over to the kid, stand up, get that stupid mask off him, and get him down. Don't try anything fancy. At this range I can hardly miss." He waved the barrel of the .38 pistol toward the boy.

It took less than two minutes to get Jackie down from the pile, ungagged, and out of his hideous outfit.

"Listen up. We're all going to walk out of here together, nice and peaceful-like. Doc, why don't you lead the parade, and Judge, I want you right here in front of me. Boy, you get your shirt and jacket back on and stay next to my left side. And, if one of you mokes makes any kinda move, anything at all that I don't like, I'll plug ya. Put your right hand on the shoulder of your buddy in front of you and when I say move, let's get going." Swanson waved his fingers toward Jackie, urging him to get dressed and join him. "Okay, move!"

The cemetery still resembled a slow-motion ant hill. If Swanson didn't know better, he would have thought he was at a fish fry and not a funeral. It wasn't until Edreca Witsell gasped, "Dear Lord!" that the buzz over the grounds hushed, all eyeballs focused on a sight so reminiscent of the chain gang many had seen in years past, minus the shackled ankles.

"Y'all stand back. Just stay where you are," Swanson yelled to the curious crowd that formed along the path. "Where's the hearse driver? Open that thing up. We're going to take us a ride back into town."

A voice some distance away answered, "You ain't takin' nobody, nowhere."

Swanson eyed the crowd with no hope of identifying the speaker, though heads turned toward the far side of the cemetery gave some indication who it might be.

"FBI. I'm takin' these boys in for some discussion involving a kidnapping and attempted assault, possibly murder."

"You's just some fool white treasurer hunter. Ain't no FBI," another voice shouted.

Swanson flipped his badge out, high above his head. "Now stand back. Get that back end open."

"Just stay back. Everybody! Just stay back!" Robert Caplin yelled.

"Hush!" Swanson snapped.

The hearse driver opened the tail of the converted Cadillac and the four Negroes climbed in.

Swanson spied Hestelle Eddings standing near the vehicle, her hands covering her mouth. "Boy, head on over to your mamma. Go on."

Jackie ran, landing in his mother's arms.

"Drive this group to the Beaufort City Jail, pronto. They're invited to a session with Chief Heimer and me. I'll follow in my car. You make one wrong turn or stop or any of them gets out and I'll turn your tires into Swiss cheese and the five of you will visit the chief."

In town, Senator Strom Thurmond appeared on time, as scheduled, at the National Cemetery to a marginally interested crowd of twenty people, all whites, and a half dozen protestors, also all whites, and one Cliff Gilbert, who would later report exactly what he saw—facts, only facts. The senator's address took less than fifteen minutes, ran incident free, and then he was on his way by motorcade to Hilton Head for another gratuitous overnight with a generous but concerned constituent.

CHAPTER 36

When Geordie Swanson marched his costumed captives into the police station, the dispatcher called the chief at home to explain what Swanson had told him.

"I'm busy," he barked into the ear of the dispatcher at the other end of the phone line. "Put them in the drunk tank for tonight. I'll see them in the morning." He hesitated. It would give Chief Heimer great pleasure to hold the black attorney and the other three Negroes in the D-cell overnight. "And you tell Swanson to head over to my house ASAP. I want to talk to him."

Throughout the afternoon and evening, Robert Caplin made several polite requests for their release, all of which went unanswered. The dispatcher, a rookie officer filling in for the normal weekend desk clerk—a sweet young thing who said she had to do some Christmas shopping—allowed the detainees one phone call each, because he saw that on *Perry Mason* once. Caplin instructed each of them on who to call and he did most of the talking. None of the calls were local, which really didn't settle well when the chief found out.

After meeting with Geordie Swanson at his house Sunday afternoon—at the expense of missing much of the pro football game of the week—Heimer learned the whole story behind his treasure-hunting buddy. Sworn to secrecy, Heimer was taken aback by the undercover FBI operation in his own backyard and that Swanson was on assignment directed by Hoover himself to monitor Martin Luther King Jr. and activities out of Penn Center. The chief ranted and raved about how he'd been duped by the Feds, how they violated his jurisdiction, and how they should've coordinated with him if there was to be a clandestine operation in his territory. In reality, Otis Heimer wasn't sure which frosted him more—the fact there was an undercover operation in his area or the fact he didn't recognize Geordie Swanson was somehow involved with the law.

Through the two hours of back and forth, neither Heimer nor Swanson could make the connection between King, the kid, Thurmond, and the four stooges in their masks. Heimer did accept the fact that Swanson stopped a crime or what appeared to be a kidnapping. Unfortunately for Swanson, it appeared the mention of a kidnapping overheard on the wiretap turned out to be four goons and a colored boy, not Senator Strom Thurmond. He knew Hoover would have words—if not more—for him.

By Monday morning, Otis Heimer's spirits had improved. He was anxious to get to the office and interrogate the four creature-clad Negroes. He had visions his work would contribute to the ongoing FBI surveillance, but by the time the chief finished his questioning of the four overnight guests, his head ached. In each case, the Negroes selected Caplin as their attorney and, therefore, all the answers came from Caplin, which frustrated Heimer. Time and time again Caplin refused to answer questions. "That's not relevant," was his standard reply.

"Then you're goin' to spend time in jail, Judge," Heimer said.

"The charges being what, Chief Heimer?" Caplin replied in an exasperated tone.

"Kidnapping, well, attempted kidnapping anyway."

"The boy was with his parents, just not next to them. They were close by," Caplin said.

"And one of you coons had a knife and was ready to slice the boy up," Heimer replied. He pounded the desk and began to pace.

"Our intentions were merely a ritual," Caplin confessed repeatedly, "much like your Freemasons. I do believe you are a Mason, am I correct?" The chief didn't answer.

"Ritual my behind," Heimer said. He raised his arms and cracked his knuckles above his head before he reached for his coffee cup. He lifted it, took a sip, and put it back on the desk. "Fine. Ritual called what? Murder in the first degree or just plain sacrificial torture?"

"I'm not at liberty to tell you more than that but—"

"But what? You think I'll let you jigaboos walk on out of here just because this was a colored boy? I don't rightly care what you were going to do to that boy but I know it wasn't right and you ain't given me any explanation that seems to explain anything different."

Deprived of sleep, the colored lawyer's eyes drooped. Caplin reached through a slit in the camouflage suit he still wore and pulled out a small notebook. Very slowly, each word enunciated for clarity, he said, "Chief Heimer, dial this number." He yanked the page out of the notebook and tossed it on the desk. "When the person on the other end answers, just say this one word, 'Dazo,' and listen to the response. The person will not ask any questions. He will not answer any questions. What you will hear will clearly explain the circumstances behind this entire incident so even you will understand. I'm positive you will find there are no grounds to hold us any longer."

The chief was sick and tired of Caplin's voice; he thought anything would be better than hearing the lawyer say another word. He grabbed the note and dialed.

The number Robert Caplin provided was in Philadelphia. Heimer knew that because he had a cousin there whom he called once in a blue moon just to talk sports. The phone rang three times before a deep male voice answered. "Hello."

"Dazo," Heimer responded.

Three blocks away, Gene Skyles steeled himself as he walked through the gate and up the fifteen steps to the porch of the Castle. He glanced at the yard, which remained somewhat akin to an open-pit mining site. His hands were a bit shaky when he pressed the doorbell and shook more when he heard Hitchcock react the instant the bell rang. Skyles listened anxiously to the dog's threatening bark as it thundered down the main hall and plastered his paws just below eye level on the door. Ed Danson took his sweet time to get to the door and, when he did, he hesitated to open it.

"Stay, Hitchcock. Sit, boy!" he said to the dog as he turned the knob. "Well, if it isn't...what's your name again there, Mr. Virginia?"

"Gene Skyles, Mr. Danson."

"Of course. What may I do for you today, Mr. Skyles?"

"Sir, the Negro boy's grandpa died and—"

"Well, I'm so sorry to hear that. Please pass my condolences to the family."

"Yes, certainly. Because of the passing, the boys are unable to visit and dig at this point. I...well...the boys...well, we came by Saturday morning to dig as we had discussed...and agreed, but we saw this"—Skyles motioned toward the mess in the yard—"and we...or, well I was wondering—"

"Oh, that, well, you see, after we talked I got this hankering to see for myself, so I spent a little time digging. But those boys need to do a better job with that research of theirs 'cause there was nothing there. Now I need to put my entire yard back in order. Shoot, I ought to have them boys come by and fix this yard. They caused this mess."

"Really?" Skyles said, his head cocked by what he heard. "So you're saying you dug up your yard? And there was nothing there? No treasure? Nothing?"

"Oh, I hit some old wooden slats, probably from an old shed at some point but..." Danson looked out over the piles of dirt and then down to Skyles. "So that teacher, maybe she could give those boys an A for effort in their research and report, but that treasure? Nope, not there."

Skyles turned his head and shoulder back toward the yard for another hard look, then turned to Danson. Reluctantly, he said, "May I ask what your plans were if you had found treasure there as the boys described? I mean, they had that thing nailed down to within feet. They told you exactly where it would be. If you found it, then what?"

"Why, son"—Danson chuckled—"if...and I say if...if I dug it up, I guess it would be mine. Makes sense, don't it? My property. My effort. Those boys didn't do any digging." Though Danson continued to smile, Hitchcock sensed his owner was growing agitated. He popped up and stood on all fours with his hackles raised.

"But we had a deal."

"I do believe the deal was to allow the boys to dig. I'm telling you, I did that for them. I did the digging. There was no treasure and now I have a yard full of holes. That's about where it all stands." Hitchcock focused on a raven that flew close to the porch. He lunged forward a step and barked.

"Hush," Danson yelled. He grabbed the dog's collar and pulled him back inside the door. "I believe the boys had you going on that one, you and the teacher both. Ha, they got me as well. I had a sneaky suspicion they might do that." Danson wore a peculiar grin, not one that suggested his previous concern for his precious yard.

"Well...I thought the deal"—Skyles looked away and hesitated—"anyway at this point, I guess it doesn't make much difference. I thank you for your time. I'll pass along the news to the boys. Thanks." Skyles turned and headed down the steps.

"And don't forget to tell that colored boy how sorry I am to hear about his grandpa."

Blocks away, Jackie Robinson Eddings and his mother wrestled with the task of going through Gabe's possessions. Jackie was given a few days off from school to mourn Gabe's passing. Those days would run into his Christmas break, time enough for a reflective farewell and time to reconsider the Gullah treasure.

All the window shades in the house were pulled down. Inside the house the darkness was perfumed with witch hazel and wintergreen, lingering favorites of Gabe. Hestelle Eddings started in the bedroom. Every item of clothing she touched brought tears to her eyes. She held piece after piece against her cheek before she neatly folded each and placed them in an old steamer trunk that reeked of mothballs. Jackie had more interest in the stack of boxes in the corner where he had found the Poe letters weeks earlier.

With Sherman in his cage silently looking on, Jackie went through box after box. Each box had an assortment of items—taped photos of unrecognized people, missing corners on photos of a young Gabe (his face circled in pencil), pictures dated August 28, 1893, with the aftermath of the great hurricane in the city, a faded photo of the Pritchard Place Plantation House, where Gabe was born. There were letters from friends and newspaper clippings so fragile he dared not open them. Buttons and pins and a pipe. A smashed belt buckle with "CSA" on the front. Everything was old and interesting—somewhat—but Jackie was looking for letters, the ones he had once seen and maybe others Gabe may have stashed away, something more to determine where the Gullah treasure might be buried, since it appeared it was not at the Castle. From top to bottom he searched, but found no letters from either Poe or Lembath.

Otis Heimer placed the phone back in the cradle, leaned his elbows on his desk, and began to massage his temples with all his fingers, trying to force the train whistle in his head to pipe down. Caplin watched and waited to let the phone call sink in.

"Chief Heimer, do you have any questions I might answer for you?"

Heimer continued to look at his desk while he massaged deeper. Without looking at Caplin, he said, "So Poro, you call it? And it is a secret society from back in Africa? And it's here in Beaufort, in the Lowcountry?"

"Yes."

"And all this razzmatazz with the creatures the other night was a ritual, an induction ceremony? For the boy?"

"Yes."

"And the previous sightings of these...of you and your colored friends there, dressed like goons...those events were a part of this ritual?"

"Not exactly."

"What do you mean, 'not exactly,' Judge?" Heimer looked up, his eyebrows dipped deep in thought or pain or both.

"The previous events were traditional Poro education, a rite of passage to manhood for the boy."

"And you kidnapped him from his family? For a week?"

"His grandfather was aware. In Africa the boys are in the bush for many weeks, some up to a year."

"Not his parents. His parents weren't aware this was just some African Negro secret society hoopla?"

"His Grandpa Gabe—Gabe Pritchard—accepted full responsibility. He would tell the parents at the appropriate time. I have a statement, a letter, sir, Chief Heimer. I have a letter I prepared, signed by Mr. Pritchard, explaining all of this."

"Why haven't I heard of this Poro outfit before?"

Caplin was a bit coy with his response. "Chief Heimer, the Gullah community is a very private society. We handle our own issues. The praise house unites folks, enforces social norms, and acts as a governing body to adjudicate many issues you'll never hear about. It helps." Caplin eyed Heimer to detect his concern. "Poro activities like these happen all the time, but this boy is special."

"You're telling me. That boy has been in here, well...you know. You've been here with him, haven't you, Judge?"

"Yes, but he is special in other ways, primarily because he is in a white school. Again, there are many things happening among the Gullahs, many centered around that boy and around that school and the school board with its decision."

"Don't get me started," Heimer exclaimed. He leaned back in his chair, twiddled his thumbs on top of his belly, and looked around the room. "Okay, counselor, here's where we go from here." He pointed at Caplin with both index fingers. "You and your band of creatures can go. I'll have the sheriff go back out to that shed and retrieve your creature masks and—"

"No need to do that, Chief. The masks have been taken care of already."

Heimer rolled his eyes. "Tampering with evidence, counselor?"

"Any charges presented, your honor?" Caplin fired back.

"Okay, take your friends and go. I want you back in here tomorrow with that letter signed by the kid's grandpa. Understood? No letter and I'll have my posse round up all four of you."

"Charge being?"

"I'll think of something. You just have that letter here tomorrow."

"Yes, sir. I'll see you tomorrow."

"Go unlock the D-cell and let them three coons out," the chief hollered to the desk clerk in front.

Robert Caplin looked over his shoulder and simply shook his head before he followed the clerk to the back of the jail to meet the others.

CHAPTER 37

Ed Danson locked his basement door and climbed the Castle stairs to take Hitchcock out for his last stroll around The Green before turning in for the night. The ten minutes they spent walking was a welcomed nightcap for the both of them. Thunder and arcs of lightning in the distance threatened rain and quickened their pace, Hitchcock losing his leisurely sniff-n-poop protocol along the nonstop web of cracked, moss-laced concrete. The breeze ahead of the storm rattled palms and whipped the droopy Spanish moss in the oaks. On their return, a light rain danced off the marsh mud. Danson wondered how many of the glass bottles unveiled by the low tide might have notes inside.

His wife had left earlier in the evening to visit her sister in Columbia to do some last-minute Christmas shopping in the big city, leaving him with double-duty bedtime chores. He dried Hitchcock, fed him his usual late-night horse-sized ration of kibble and went upstairs to brush his teeth. By then the storm had arrived with a vengeance, a rare event for this time of year. The Castle—true to its name—absorbed the shock waves of thunder that echoed above the marsh. Torrents of horizontal rain exploded against the windows. His bedroom, nearly the size of a gymnasium, flickered like an old-time movie amid strobes of lightning. When he flipped on the bathroom light, there was a quick flash of light, then no light at all. The Castle, as old as it was, had been rewired numerous times and came with the standard electrical challenges of many of the antebellum homes in Beaufort. Light switches that worked sometimes but not always seemed to be a common issue. He tried the switch again and got nothing. Then he realized hitting the switch the second time had turned off power to the lights, so he tried the switch a third time and—*voila*—light.

Finished in the bathroom, he changed into his pajamas, turned to leave, and noticed something he had not seen before. Next to the faulty light switch was a rather small red handprint. It shocked him, initially. Then he stepped back and chuckled. He and his wife had long joked and teased each other about living with a ghost. The Castle was the notorious home of a local legendary Lowcountry ghost named Gauche. Though Ed Danson had never personally seen the ghost, on a few occasions, guests had mentioned hearing strange sounds and witnessed furniture moved in their rooms. Family members had mentioned their sightings. Some swore by the fact that there were red handprints left by the ghost, but in all the years Ed Danson had lived in the house, he had never seen anything, heard anything, or associated anything with a ghost. His wife, however, did believe and often tried to convince him otherwise. *Nice try, Grace. Always the joker. Turnaround is fair play, dear.* He doused the bathroom lights, hopped in bed, and despite the splashes of lightning on the walls, he drifted off as quickly as any other night.

It was nearly half past two when things changed for Ed Danson. He was awakened by the flash of light in his bedroom. By then the storm had passed and the light was not another blast of cloud-to-ground electricity. He cleared his eyes and noticed the bedroom lights were on. *Another wiring issue,* he thought. The longer he lay there, the more he wondered. The lights, all table lamps in different parts of the room, on different switches, were all on. He sat up and scanned the room. Everything seemed to be in order and in place with one exception, an addition that opened his eyes. Seated in the French chaise lounge on the far side of the room was a small body, a dwarf-sized male dressed in colorful finery to include a quirky hat with red-and-blue tassels.

"What the heck!" said Danson.

"Ah, *oui.* Monsieur Danson, *n'est pas?*" the colorful visitor asked.

"Who…what are you doing…" Danson stumbled over the words. "Hitchcock!"

"*Mon Dieu. C'est moi.* Gauche," the little man replied.

Danson didn't know what to think. His wife, as clever as she was, could never pull off a stunt as wild as this. "Gauche, as in our ghost. Our friendly, live-in, somewhat-foulmouthed guardian angel ghost?" Danson was not sure how to address whatever or whoever it was talking to him.

"*Mais oui,*" the spirit replied, then added, "*mais non!*" He extended his arm and waved his hand as if to say stop. "Oh, but why French? I can use your English or the Queen's. Which would you prefer, Monsieur Danson? May I call you Ed?"

"Yes and plain American English will do best," Danson said, wondering why he was responding to…a ghost. *Am I nuts?* he thought to himself, then pinched his forearm to ensure he was truly awake. When the jester hopped off of the chaise lounge, Danson sat up straighter.

"You know, I have always wondered why you people say I am French," Gauche said as he strolled across the room to approach the bed. "Ah, *oui*, of course…because one of your gabby guests thought I spoke an archaic form of the language, and then tried to communicate in that language by tapping out code. I must say, rather amusing, Ed. Rather amusing." Gauche did a brief tap dance to mimic the code tapping. He stopped then rolled in laugher.

"I am a jester. Pure and simple." He leaned against the bedpost and continued, "I am British, Ed, till the day I die…or…well, until I am asked to return." He laughed. "How I long for my British home." He hopped up on the foot of the bed where he sat cross-legged. "I proudly sailed with Sir John Hawkins out of Plymouth, England in County Devon in 1564. When he buried the treasure, he trusted me to guard it. He said he would return, but nay…I have not seen him. One does not live forever, now do they, Ed? And here I remain, guarding the treasure as directed by Sir John, as I call him. Quite fortuitous you built this house. Though I don't need such things, it is nice to be indoors now and then."

"So why are you here, I mean…now…tonight?" Danson asked, wondering how the little munchkin got into his house and up to his bedroom.

"Just doing what Sir John instructed me to do. Seems the treasure was moved."

"What do you mean?" Danson said with a serious, quizzical look on his face.

"Come, come, fellow. Surely I have sufficiently explained my purpose. And you, sir, know full well the whereabouts of that treasure."

"What? I—"

"Don't make me take you there, Ed." Gauche turned toward the lamp on the far side of the bed. He lifted his chin slightly and the lamp lifted off the stand. When Gauche jerked his head to the right, the lamp yanked the cord from the wall and flew across the room, but the bulb never dimmed. It hovered above a rug near the double-door entrance, then landed, unplugged, still lit. "Would you like to be my next trick, Ed? I mean, I can move you in a similar fashion. And I guess we would move to the basement, would we not, Ed?"

Danson tightened. He willed himself to stay outwardly calm and relaxed though the hair on his arms and dark brown stains in the armpits of his pajamas proved otherwise. His heart searched for a rhythm more waltz-like than the jitterbug beat that made his stomach dizzy.

"Or we can try this." Gauche waved his left arm and produced three juggling balls. With one hand he juggled, first with his left hand, then with his right, each time tossing the balls higher. In midmotion he tossed each of the balls, one at a time, to a spot near Danson's pillow where each burst into flame. Danson jumped out of the bed, his back against the wall and watched as the flames walked across the bed, leaving no marks behind, before they disappeared. "I'm saving their scorch marks for you, Ed. Your own special gift."

"What do you want? What's going on?"

"I live here, so we can share secrets, can't we, Ed?" Gauche said, crawling toward the pillows and rolling to his side. For the first time, the bells on his pointed slippers jingled as he moved.

"Yeah. Sure. Secrets," Danson echoed.

"Who should go first? Age before beauty. Why don't I go first? I'll tell you my little secret, then you can tell me yours. But these are secrets, so you can't tell anybody else."

Danson nodded and pressed himself tighter against the wall.

"My secret is…I have a friend named Ricky and he and the Negro boy and a third boy named Skeet visited your…well, our house. And, just like you told the police, you had a shirt to prove it. Actually, I met Ricky out on your lawn. Now what secret do you want to share, Ed? Let me suggest you tell me your little secret about the treasure."

"I told you I don't know anything about a treasure."

Before he could swallow his last word, the three flames reappeared around his feet. Danson uttered a pathetic mousy scream.

"What?" Gauche asked.

"I said—"

The flames grew to knee height.

"It's in the basement. Yeah, the treasure is in the basement."

"Is that all? Is that all there is to your secret? Seems like it's much bigger than that." The flames climbed higher, tall enough to lick the drawstring on his pajamas. "Didn't you plan to keep the treasure for yourself?"

"No, not at all. The kids. It's for the kids," Danson said, nervously, his hands raised to block the flames.

The flames climbed to his chin. Surrounded, Danson watched as tongues of fire lapped close to his face.

"And why did you tell your visitor you had not found the treasure? Oh, but if you had, did you plan to keep it for yourself?"

Danson hesitated. Long tongues of fire licked the sweat that dripped from his forehead to his chin.

"I...I...I was mistaken. I meant to give it to those boys," he declared.

"And I trust you will, Ed," Gauche replied. "I trust you will." Gauche stood on the bed, took a deep breath and blew to extinguish all three flames. Danson slumped.

"Oh, I trust you, Ed, but I want to share a wee more history. Would you mind?"

Danson shook his head nervously.

"The Gullahs call me a haint and, as such, I set hexes. You do know what hexes are, don't you, Ed?"

Danson watched Gauche hop off the bed and, faster than a blink of the eye, stand in front of the doors to the bedroom.

"Hexes aren't magic, not like the flames. Hexes are cast for a reason and can only be removed when certain conditions are met. So the hex be upon you, Ed." Gauche chuckled and pointed toward the lamp by his foot, the same lamp that he moved across the room earlier. He curled a finger to pull the door open. He flipped his palm upward; the lamp floated off the floor. As he pushed his arm forward, the lamp drifted through the doorway; the door closed behind it. When Gauche lifted his hand toward the ceiling, the lamp followed until it reached the transom above the bedroom door, where it stopped as a halo behind the silhouette of a large bird. "The raven now becomes my eyes and ears. You will never see me again. You will never escape the raven."

"What are you saying? What do you mean?" Danson needed to understand.

"I mean until you break this hex, until you give the boys the treasure, all of the treasure, the raven will make your life as sad as they were when they saw your yard after you dug it up." Gauche looked above and winked at the raven. It croaked before it heaved its body off the sill and landed on a lampshade next to Danson. "Do you understand, Ed? Just our little secret."

With his eyes on the bird, Danson nodded in agreement.

"Oh, and while I am here, there is one more thing. Consider it a part of the hex as well." Gauche walked back toward Danson and stopped just short of his bare feet, though three feet below. Danson looked down to see the ghost looking up. "You need to correct the folklore around here. I don't care how you go about it, but I'm not a bloody Frenchman. I am a proud subject of the King...er...I beg Your Majesty's pardon, the Queen. And I've lived on these grounds and in this house far longer than you or anyone else could imagine. I've befriended many before you. The Escamacu Indians who lived here. And the Gullahs who saved this monstrous pile of bricks. I'll behave"—he winked—"and continue to be friendly to you, your family, and your guests until I'm recalled to Britain as long as you don't violate this hex. Do those things. Be wary of the raven, Ed."

Danson did not respond. Gauche toddled to the center of the room. A rush of December air pushed the windows inward; the chill sucked out the warmth from floor to ceiling. A mist from the earlier rain formed a cloud that drifted around the pint-sized spirit. Next to Danson, the raven lifted from the lampshade, circled in flight overhead one time, and flew out the window. The cloud and Gauche did likewise.

When he felt it was clear, Danson quickly closed the windows, wiped his face with a wet washcloth, and returned to bed. Drifting off to sleep was not easy this time, but eventually he managed to chase the nightmare away.

CHAPTER 38

When Mary Alice Forten arrived at the school on Tuesday morning, she found a note in her office distribution box. *No idea how to find Mr. Skyles. Have him see me soonest. Mr. Edward Danson.*

The dispatch clerk in the front office of the Beaufort Police Department knocked on Chief Heimer's office door shortly after nine Tuesday morning.

"Yeah. What is it?"

"Chief, you have a Mr. Robert Caplin here. Says he needs to see you," the female clerk said through a door she opened wide enough for only her timid voice to enter.

"Send him in," he hollered back.

Bundled to battle the winds and the rain that continued to fall through the night, Robert Caplin stepped to the front of the chief's desk, where a puddle formed under the edges of his black woolen overcoat. He tapped his fedora with its wilted red feather against his leg to bounce the rain off, waiting for the chief to look up.

"What do you want this time, Judge? You must like it over here; ya keep coming in like this. Have to start charging you rent you spend so much time around here," the chief said, not bothering to look up from his desk.

"Mr. Heimer—"

"Chief! How many times do I need to remind you?" He looked Caplin square in the eyes.

"My apologies. Must be the rain fogged my memory," Caplin offered in a tone that questioned his sincerity. "You asked me to bring by the letter I referenced yesterday in our discussions."

"Yes, yes, so I did." Heimer took another sip of coffee and placed his cup to the side. He loosely stacked the papers smeared across his desk, then placed them atop a menacing Alex Karras on the cover of his *Sports Illustrated*.

The colored lawyer reached into a satchel he carried that looked like it had been used by the pony express, pulled out a white envelope marked "Private: Gabriel Sampson Pritchard," and handed it to Otis Heimer. The flap on the back was sealed and taped. At some point someone drew squiggly lines over the taped flap to ensure there were no undisclosed openings.

Using a penknife the chief pulled out of his pocket, he opened the envelope and studied the contents. It was one sheet packed to the gills with legalese; Heimer understood very little, but the letter proved the point Caplin had made the day prior. It appeared the whole Poro story was on the up-and-up.

"Question for you, counselor," Heimer said, placing the letter flat on the desk. "This letter was signed by a dead man, I mean the deceased Mr. Pritchard, so he's not one to vouch for its origin. And you signed this letter. But seeing how you are one of four potential perpetrators in this case, seems like I can't expect you to vouch for the authenticity of the thing." Heimer scanned the letter further while he scratched his nose with the eraser on a pencil. "And this third signature? Who's this character?"

"Sir, that is Ezekiel Tombee, Attorney at Law," Caplin replied.

Heimer scratched his head and squinted back toward the man standing in front of him.

"He was the voice you heard when you dialed the number I gave you yesterday."

"And this letter was signed on the ninth of October this year?" Heimer said, pointing to the date on the letter.

"Yes, sir. You might challenge the other two signatures, but that third signature can certainly verify that he visited Gabe, witnessed his signature. I signed as the legal counsel for Mr. Pritchard."

"This Tombee fella. You say he's a lawyer? How do I check on him?" Heimer asked in his attempt to disprove the letter.

"Mr. Tombee is in Philadelphia. He is the primary legal counsel to Mother Bethel A.M.E. Church and, by extension, to the business of Poro in the United States. I am sure you will find his credentials highly regarded in Philadelphia and elsewhere," Caplin answered with an air of confidence.

"Okay, Caplin. I'm not wasting any more of my time on this or you or your buddies. I have other gators to wrestle, like your boy Eddings's pal, Skeet Gundy." He wiped his face with both hands and dragged his bottom lip to his chin. "I had a meeting with his foster home caseworker yesterday. We agreed that pressing charges really would not do anyone any good. I mean there was strong evidence it was Gundy who stole the truck, but the kid would end up in the reform school either way, so we decided to just pull him out of that foster home and send him up to the juvenile detention home in Florence, that Industrial School for White Boys. I'll get the truck business all straight with Stanley Croft. The truck was a heap anyway." Heimer added one final comment. "And for your sake, I have half a mind to send that colored boy up to that Negro Reformatory, too."

Caplin closed his eyes to latch his tongue, surprised to hear such bigotry after Jackie had proved himself both in character and moral strength.

"My letter, sir," Caplin said, extending his hand toward the chief's desk. When he had the letter in hand, Caplin was quick to walk away from the chief and the puddle in front of his desk.

Heimer lifted his coffee in a farewell toast to the colored lawyer. "Here's to you, Judge...and all your kind." Taking a sip, he cringed when he found his hot coffee had turned bitter and ice cold.

Mary Alice Forten passed Danson's message to Gene Skyles during her lunch break. He told her that he had visited Danson the day before to confront him about the digging and the hole the boys saw on Saturday. She begged him to let her go along if he planned another visit to the Castle; she had a few choice words of her own for Ed Danson, all academic of course.

Danson was shocked but cordial when Skyles appeared with the teacher later that day. "What a pleasant surprise, Miss Forten. I didn't expect to see you here," Danson said, rolling his eyes.

"I thought I would accompany Mr. Skyles when he returned, because I wanted to say—"

Before she began, Danson noticed a shadow on the lawn, then looked skyward. Marsh birds were common sightings, wide-winged bodies with long stilts for legs, but the shadow that caught his eye was broad and black, circling above. "Excuse me for one moment, Miss

Forten," he said as he pushed between the two visitors to the top of the steps.

The shadow he tracked was the raven as it flew from the marsh side of the Castle and perched high in the leafy canopy of the singular live oak looming over the mounds of dirt and the pit in his lawn. He turned back toward Forten. "I'm sorry, Miss Forten. I don't mean to cut you off, but I'm kind of short on time today. My wife is due back from Columbia, the maid didn't show today, and I have a little straightening up to do upstairs. Mr. Skyles, yesterday when we spoke I must admit I was a little skeptical of your intentions and motives. The boys had presented such a wonderful case of research and all, I wanted to be sure their efforts were not in vain. Um...uh...I failed to show you something." Danson stumbled on his words. Despite the chill in the air, he glistened with sweat. "Would you follow me, please?"

Forten and Skyles would have cartwheeled the three blocks from the Castle to Jackie Eddings's house had it not been for the rain, their overcoats, the ridiculous nature of such jubilation, and of course, the fact that they were both adults over twenty-one. They skipped onto the porch, knocked on the door, and shared a few giggles while they waited. And waited. Nobody answered.

"Gabe's house," Skyles said. "They're probably at Gabe's house." Wind in their faces, Skyles led Mary Alice the block and a half to Gabe's house. When they knocked, Hestelle Eddings came to the door.

"Mrs. Eddings, it's so good to find you. Is Jackie here? Oh, sorry. You remember Miss Forten, Jackie's teacher?"

"Yes. Why sure. And yes, Jackie's here. Why?" she asked with a hint of concern.

"We have some great news for him. May we speak to him, please?"

She opened the door and looked toward the back of the living room where Jackie continued to go through boxes. He turned and stared with a sad and quizzical face.

The teacher and friend walked over to Jackie. Skyles turned toward Mary Alice and nodded.

"He found it. The treasure, Jackie. Mr. Danson found it. Just where you said it was. We saw it, Jackie. It's amazing. I...I...I can't even begin to describe it," Miss Forten said, finding it hard to talk and breathe.

Jackie turned ashen with the news.

"Knock, knock," a voice from the door joined the confusion. It was Robert Caplin. "Wow, quite a gathering, Hestelle. Glad to see you found help to go through Gabe's things."

"Oh no, Mr. Caplin. Jackie's teacher and friend just stopped by. Dey had some news. Dey say dey found de Gullah treasure."

Caplin didn't know what to say, uncertain there ever was a treasure and not convinced anyone had found it. "Well, that's very interesting. Actually, that's absolutely amazing." Caplin hesitated and approached Jackie. "I have a bit of a find for you, too, Jackie," he said, handing him a stack of five letters, old letters like the kind Jackie had seen once before. "Gabe asked us to keep these for him—for safekeeping—a few weeks back. I'm sure he would want you to have these now."

Jackie quickly looked at the first letter, careful not to tear it, then passed it and the others to Gene Skyles.

"Mr. Skyles, dey be de letters I saw before, but never could find again." While the others looked on, Skyles scanned the first letter, then the second. Four letters in all, each drawing his smile broader and his eyes wider.

"This is it. These letters…they…they are Lembath letters sent from William to his daughter. They were arguing over her health. Lembath wanted her to leave Charleston and come to Beaufort." Skyles stopped and read more of another letter. "Here he scolds her. He even calls her 'Anna Belcher,' using her middle name, just like my parents did to me when they were mad." He read the next letter and dropped both arms to his sides, closed his eyes, and tossed his head as far back as it would go. "He mentions Poe here." He slapped the letter, lightly. "He told her, Anna, he would make sure Poe never found her again if she insisted on staying in Charleston." He smiled and looked toward the floor and shook his head slowly. "So he buried her in that unmarked grave at the Circular Congregational Church."

Jackie had waited long enough. "Can we go to the Castle? Can we go see de treasure?" Jackie asked while Skyles read through the last letter Caplin had given him. This letter looked different from the others. The paper was parchment and crisp, but yellowed and fragile. The handwriting, especially the signature, looked different with broader strokes and more curlicue swirls. As he read Skyles's expressions grew more somber, more pensive, troubled and confused.

"Mr. Danson told us to share this news with you boys and come have a look," Mary Alice said, surprised Skyles had not mentioned that himself; Skyles continued to read the last letter.

"Mr. Caplin, have you looked over this letter?" Skyles asked, looking up at the lawyer.

Robert Caplin nodded.

"And your legal interpretation of the letter? Anything? This isn't from Poe or even about him."

Jackie waited with the others. Caplin extended his hand and Skyles gave him the letter.

"Well, without any reference materials or legal review, I would say this letter provides two key points." He turned to Hestelle, then nosed into the letter itself. "The first point in this letter was that it appears John E. Lembath relinquished ownership of his personal property to Benjamin Thomas Pritchard as retribution for his purchase as a slave from Oliver Pritchard, with the exception of and in consideration of the safekeeping of the Lembath House. So Lembath gave everything but the house to Benjamin if he would protect the house itself, which he apparently did." Caplin looked across to Skyles. "The date on the letter is November 7, 1861. That was about the time when all the whites left before the Union came in. We call it the 'Great Skedaddle.' "

Looking back to Hestelle and Jackie, he continued, "That means everything in the house on that date—the silver, china, art, and anything in the house to include letters and items identified in letters—was Benjamin's, and rightfully now yours," Caplin explained.

"De treasure?" Jackie asked.

"If you have a letter to Mr. Lembath that was in that house on that date, the letter belonged to Benjamin Pritchard. By extension, the clue and any treasure recovered as a result of that clue would also be considered property of Benjamin Pritchard, and though it might be located on Mr. Danson's property, ownership remains yours, but"—Jackie rolled his eyes as Caplin finished—"it may be difficult to defend in a court given circumstances."

Looking between Skyles and the colored attorney, Mary Alice quickly said, "I assure you, he told us no more than thirty minutes ago, he has absolutely no interest in keeping the treasure. He said the boys did the research, he just added a little muscle to the project."

Jackie was so excited he nearly left the house without his coat, but Hestelle caught him in time. They stopped at the Clemonds' house along the way. The rain had stopped. In the block to the Castle, Ricky moved faster than Jackie had ever seen him walk. With the boys in front, the group saw Danson at the foot of the stairs. Dressed in a heavy woolen sweater, puffing generously on a cigar and wearing a smile, he kept an eye on the raven evermore watchful high above. Hitchcock remained on the porch, poised like a sphinx ready to pounce on command. Both boys took note, but ignored the threat. The Castle owner led the group under the stairs, through a door that led to a semi-submerged, damp, and musty earthen basement, to a dark room toward the back of the house. The room held garden equipment—rakes, hoes, shovels—which all added to the dirt floor. The prize was in the middle of the room— three wooden chests with iron fixtures. Though not pristine in appearance, the wood showed little sign of decay. The Mediterranean or Spanish style iron work was etched with elaborate designs. Each chest was "bigger than a bread box." Caplin figured they were less than a foot wide, maybe a foot and a half long, and about a foot high with domed tops.

"Like in the book. In the library," Ricky screamed, holding the sides of his head with both hands. He forgot to swallow. Drool flowed across his lower lip and onto his jacket.

Not far from the boxes—along with a hacksaw, a small sledgehammer, and a chisel—were dented and broken locks.

"Since this was your project, why don't you open the chests and see what your research found?" Danson said. He had extinguished the cigar, but continued to chew on the slimy tobacco tip above the band.

The boys exchanged glances, then approached the boxes as if they were sleeping bears. The others in the room tiptoed closer behind them. Jackie and Ricky bent over and, together, tipped the lids back. The boxes were filled with silver disks, irregular-shaped coins. Ricky dropped to his knees and dipped his hands into one of the chests like he was splashing water on his face. Jackie inspected one of the coins that fell on the ground. He marveled at how old it must be and at the images on it— two pillars encircled by writing on one side, on the opposite side a shield, quartered with heraldic lions and castles. Ricky tried his best to dig through the chest filled with metal. As he dug coins fell from the chest by his knees. Eventually, he found what appeared to be a small brick of solid gold.

It was difficult for the boys—actually, all of them—to leave the storage room, but when they did, Ed Danson reassured them he would take good care of it. "You boys have done a great job. This is probably the biggest find in the history of the city. Miss Forten, I do believe these boys deserve an A-plus for their work and extra credit for actually finding it."

"I couldn't agree more, Mr. Danson. I'll be sure their story makes it into the *Beaufort Gazette*, and I will be sure to send a special note to the Clemson alumni office to tell them you've guarded it for centuries, well, your family has."

Thinking of his ghostly visitor of the previous night, Danson replied, "Can't argue with that. It certainly has been in good hands."

As they emerged from under the house, the sky was a palette of purple and black. The sun peeked below the clouds and lengthened their shadows as they passed through the gate. Danson watched them turn and head back up East Street, the boys consumed by antics of their youth. Ed Danson relit his cigar and heaved a sigh of relief while he watched the raven soar above the Castle and beyond the marsh. Danson waved for Hitchcock to join him. They passed through the gate and toward The Green, Hitchcock in the lead, as always.

CHAPTER 39

Amid the hustle and bustle the week before Christmas always brings, following the discovery of the Gullah treasure, Beaufort was a coastal town filled with more than "Silent Nights" and cordial seasonal spirit. The research paper article Mary Alice Forten submitted to the *Beaufort Gazette* aroused a completely different buzz up and down Bay Street and at the Piggly Wiggly a block over. The Bank of Beaufort worked together with Ed Danson to haul the chests out of his basement and moved them into the bank vault for safekeeping. The bank provided three sturdy new locks and, per Danson, gave the keys to Jackie Eddings with instructions that no one was to even view the chests without Jackie's knowledge and approval. Ricky and Jackie spent every day of the week in the vault. They spent one entire day on the floor counting their pieces of eight, which totaled eighteen thousand—plus or minus a few Ricky missed—in all. The president of the bank calculated the silver value of their find was worth almost $24,000; the boys didn't know what to think. But when the bank president asked Jackie for one of the coins to show to a friend who collected coins, they were even more astonished to learn their treasure could be worth as much as $2.5 million. The next day, with little prompting, Robert Caplin stepped in to help coordinate an option to sell the well-preserved coins, all in near mint condition, tarnished only by the centuries buried in the sandy soil of the Lowcountry.

Ricky posed the biggest obstacle to the effort. He wanted to keep the treasure—at least his portion—one chest of coins. Cybil and Elliott Clemonds struggled to convince him the treasure really belonged to the Pritchard family, to Jackie's mother. Ricky insisted the chest was his; it was his treasure. On the fifth day sitting together on the vault floor, Jackie made a deal with Ricky. He could keep all three chests if he allowed Jackie to have the coins. Ricky demanded more. He wanted all three chests with ten coins in each. "I want to give them to my parents. Christmas presents," he said. Jackie simply smiled and extended his hand.

"Shake on it?" Jackie asked. "A deal?"

Ricky shook his hand. "Deal."

Caplin worked with Hestelle Eddings on handling the newfound wealth. Though the temptation was ever-present, she heard Jackie each time he reminded her—as he did with Ricky—that this was the Gullah treasure and not hers. Based on the lawyer's recommendation, they decided to establish a trust. Working with Ezekiel Tombee, they initiated the paperwork necessary to place the entire value of the treasure—except for the few coins the boys shared for their own—into a trust with Penn Center designated as the beneficiary, which made it available for the entire Gullah community in the Lowcountry.

On Friday the week before Christmas, Jackie took a handful of coins to the hospital to prove to Skeet they had found the Gullah treasure. When Jackie entered the juvenile ward, Skeet was sitting up in bed, his free hand pointing at words on the page as he read the latest *Action Comics*. As Jackie approached, Skeet looked up, then back down, not interested in a second visitor, especially since it was Jackie. To Skeet their relationship remained what it had been all along despite Jackie's attempts to close the gap in a friendship.

Even Jackie's story about the chests and the sight of the silver coins did nothing to brighten Skeet's spirits. Skeet told Jackie that the hour before Chief Heimer had visited and told him that on the Monday after Christmas, he would come by to process Skeet's discharge and transfer to the South Carolina Industrial School for Boys in Florence. Skeet never lifted his eyes.

Lost for words, Jackie wished Skeet a Merry Christmas, dropped the coins on his blanket, and left.

On Christmas Eve, Robert Caplin paid a visit to the Eddings. He brought small Christmas gifts for Hestelle and Irvin. In addition to a gift for Jackie, he had an envelope.

"Grandpa Gabe dictated this letter to me a while ago, Jackie. I wrote it in his exact words, just like they came out of his mouth, straight from his heart. He wanted you to have it after he died. With all the excitement around the treasure, I thought I would wait. Tomorrow being Christmas, consider it a special gift from Gabe."

It was as if the exchange was in slow motion. Jackie followed Caplin's eyes as he extended the envelope. Jackie looked away, then at the lawyer's hand. The envelope wasn't like the others Jackie found in Gabe's house; this envelope was new, white, and crisp.

"Thank you," he said as he lifted it away.

Per Caplin's suggestion, Jackie placed the envelope under his pillow. The first thing Christmas morning, before getting dressed, he pulled it out and opened it. It was a letter, typed, easy to read. Jackie sat on the edge of bed and began.

The Secret of the Gullah Treasure

My Boy Jackie,

Don't be sad da' I be gone. Da' be life. Dey be things I ain't never told nobody. You need to know dis. De Poro saved my mamma from buckruh white men on de plantation. And de Poro saved my daddy when de buckruh come to take him land away. De Poro be here from on dem slave ships from Afficky. Been here since and be here to save you, too. I telled de masked Poro da' when I die and cross obuh de ribbuh, dey make you de new chief, de Dazo, after me. Dey be problems but hope be de future so keep de hardest fight for de lost causes. Don't be no marches or riots like dey do. Don't be afraid to speak for what be right. Don't use no fists. Before you judge dem people, walk in dey skin, no matters dey color. Teach dem white kids in you school what we Negroes been through…de whipping and beating on dem boats and how dey put we Gullah on dem box, naked, and dey sold we like animals, dey families teared apart for good. Find what in dey soul. De blind man sees wid more than he eyes. De deaf man hear wid more than he ears. Aks questions to sort right from wrong. Listen to you heart. Love will teach you to trust and da' changes hatred to love what makes friends out of enemies. Remember, forgiveness be forever. Don't be afraid to forgive. Dey be good and bad in all of us. Release dem spirits da' move in de soul and forgive even de worst ones. We all must live…together…an' do things for others. De Gullah treasure you be hunting be not buried. You might can find gold and silver, but de real Gullah treasure be in de heart of every Gullah, it be de love we Gullah peoples has for everyone. Da' be de treasure. I be gone soon but wid you always. (Signed by hand with an X) above his name, Gabriel Sampson Pritchard.

The anticipation of presents under the tree and the ambrosia-like aroma of Christmas already cooking in the kitchen were not enough to lure Jackie from his room. He stayed in his bed, brushed tears from his cheeks, forced a smile, and let visions of Gabe dance through his head. For Jackie, the letter from Grandpa Gabe was the best gift he could ever hope to get. The second best gift was in the box from Robert Caplin. It was an Eisenhower jacket adorned with worn ribbons and tarnished brass, the one from the window display.

On December 27, the Monday after Christmas, Otis Heimer didn't bother to read the summary of accidents and incidents from the holiday weekend duty log. He stopped by his office long enough to drain the pot for a thermos of coffee before he drove the squad car to the Beaufort Memorial Hospital. He went directly to the admissions office still decked with tinsel above the door. He exchanged holiday cheer and conned them into another mug of Christmas coffee to sip while he processed paperwork to release Robin "Skeet" Gundy to his care as the court-appointed transport from Beaufort to Florence and the sick bay at the South Carolina Industrial School for White Boys. He wore a spiteful grin as he entered the juvenile ward, an expression which melted away instantly when he found Skeet's bed empty. He questioned the floor nurse on Skeet's whereabouts; she had no idea. For the next three hours, Heimer and the hospital staff checked the halls, rooms, and wards, but on that day, Skeet Gundy was nowhere to be found.

EPILOGUE

Case 3:10-RSG-91029
Filed 02/24/93
Document 1   **Page 32 of 32**

Special Agent = SA
Interview: J.R. Eddings reference background
              investigation pertaining to ████████████

TRANSCRIPT (cont'd):

129. SA: A few more questions.
     JRE: Make it quick. I have work to do.

130. SA: So police-archived records verify what you
have told us. You were involved with or named Robin
Gundy a part of three separate incidents in 1964. Is that
correct?
     JRE: Yes.

131. SA: To what extent?
     JRE: Whatever the records say. Are we about
done?

132. SA: Were you aware Robin Gundy was
scheduled to be processed into South Carolina Industrial
School for White Boys in 1964 but was not apprehended
until 1965?
     JRE: Yes.

133. SA: Can you explain how he vanished from the
hospital in 1964?
     JRE: No.

403

134. SA: Rumors suggest otherwise.
     JRE: Believe what you want. My answer is no.

135. SA: So you have not seen Mr. Gundy since late
1964?
     JRE: I have.

136. SA: When was the last time you saw Robin
Gundy?
     JRE: 1971.

137. SA: Circumstances or purpose of that meeting?
     JRE: Nam. March. Operation Lam Son 719 to be
exact. He saved my life.

138. SA: Care to explain?
     JRE: No. Not important now.

[Pause.]

139. SA: And since?
     JRE: No.

140. SA : Have you heard from him?
     JRE: Not directly.

141. SA: Meaning?
     JRE: I have heard from others, namely Mr.
Ezekiel Tombee, that Rob Gundy is now a well-
respected part of his community and doing exceptional
things in Philadelphia.

142. SA: Yes. He is currently a lieutenant in the Philadelphia Police Department. (Pause) Do you know why we asked you to come in?

JRE: To provide background information on Skeet, uh, Rob Gundy.

143. SA: As Director of Penn Center, and the assumed voice of the Gullah community, simply stated, is Mr. Robin Gundy fully fit and qualified to be the next Chief of Police of Beaufort?

JRE: Yes, no question about it. Rob Gundy is a product of Beaufort. His roots are here. He learned many of life's lessons here and continued to grow under the demands of Philadelphia. We need to bring him home. He needs to work for us. He understands our people. He appreciates the struggles we face.

144. SA: Thank you. That's all. We appreciate your honesty and candor.

At the conclusion of the session, Jackie—now J.R. Eddings—walked out of City Hall and admired the indignant bright yellow-eye in the sky. He donned his scratched aviator glasses and said to himself, *Skeet, you taught me to lie and I did. I taught you to live and you did. Let's make this place right like we should've done many years ago. Gabe's watching us. Remember: Bird is the word, Skeet. Bird is the word!*

Carl E. Linke

The Poe letter:

Charleston
Dec. 9. 1828.

My Dear Sir,

By way of beginning this letter, for a month I have struggled with illness, dismal privation, and the plague of evils which consorts them. Even until today I remain dangerously so, and quite unable to write normal correspondence of any sorts, even an ordinary letter. Throughout my miserable existence I have thought how deeply and sincerely I deplore the attacks which you have addressed to myself so personally and individually. There are but a few things which could afford me more pleasure than the opportunity of holding you up to the ridicule of public scourging for your written lies about my character and person.

That said, it is with all due respect, nevertheless, I remain inwardly compelled to do you a very great favor. You need be under no uneasiness about your money. I believe there is due you your wager of 2100 B. Now, I do not intend to object to this insistence at present, for that would lead me into a virtually incessant dialogue, besides being out of place in me.

I am reminded that I am your debtor and my conscience rides me to address you due. Money, beyond doubt, can be wagered and won, but this is not the totality of the need you require. As I have no money myself, I have enclosed what is known by many in Charleston and from your fields on the island of St. Helena, to be of greater value.

Pray do not think me careless of my promise to see to the debt you so publicly demand albeit against my innerself after these eight months. For were it not for the tales of an old Negro by name of Jupiter, I scarcely doubt my words would offer such a generous prize. The public forum be my judge, but to you sir, my debt is paid locked by cipher for your safe keeping.

Yr. Ob. St.
Edgar A. Poe.

Mr. William Lembath

DISCUSSION QUESTIONS FOR READERS

1. How important is the setting in the story? Explain.

2. What is the dominant theme of the novel? Other themes?

3. Several plots unfold as the story progresses. What are they and how are they revealed?

4. In what respect was the teacher's pairing of Jackie with Skeet and Ricky significant?

5. How would you describe the relationship between Jackie and Ricky? Why was it so?

6. Many times during the story Jackie has an opportunity to expose Skeet for what he is. Should he or should he not do that? Was he right to lie?

7. In the end, did Jackie do the right thing for Skeet?

8. Why do you think nobody could find Skeet when Chief Heimer went to get him after Christmas? What happened to Skeet?

9. Jackie faces pressure throughout the story. Where does he experience the most pressure? From whom or what?

10. What do you think is the secret of the Gullah Treasure?

Author photo by Tina Lee

Carl E. Linke is the author of two previous novels based in the south, *Haint Blue* and *Flagrant Three*. He lives with his wife Penny on Lady's Island in the Lowcountry of South Carolina. They have two grown children.